POISON KISS

A DARK HIGH SCHOOL BULLY ROMANCE

STEFFANIE HOLMES

POISON KISS

I may be blind, but they won't see me coming.

Cassius. Victor. Torsten.
My monster. My strength. My heart.
Three cruel, broken kings who kissed me with poison
And woke me from my slumber.

I used to think that my future lay beyond ivy-covered walls,
College, a career, a white-picket fence…
But now I'm bathed in blood and fire.
Now I wear their thorny crown,
and sit upon a throne of skulls.

I fight for a different future – a brutal, beautiful new world.
I'll burn the world for them, for us, for our family,
even if it means paying the ultimate price.

Illis quos amo deserviam.
For those I love, I sacrifice.

Poison Kiss is a new adult, dark contemporary romance with three hot, dangerous guys and the blind girl who rules them. It is intended for 18+ readers.

Victor, Cas, and Torsten think they know everything that goes on in Emerald Beach, but do they? Find out when you sign up to Steffanie Holmes' newsletter and get a bonus scene in your free copy of *Cabinet of Curiosities* – a compendium of short stories and bonus scenes – when you sign up for updates with the Steffanie Holmes newsletter:

http://www.steffanieholmes.com/newsletter

JOIN THE NEWSLETTER FOR UPDATES

Victor, Cas, and Torsten think they know everything that goes on in Emerald Beach, but do they? Find out when you sign up to Steffanie Holmes' newsletter and get a bonus scene from *Poison Ivy* inside your free copy of *Cabinet of Curiosities* – a compendium of short stories and bonus scenes. Sign up for updates with the Steffanie Holmes newsletter.

https://www.steffanieholmes.com/newsletter

Every week in my newsletter I talk about the true-life hauntings, strange happenings, crumbling ruins, and creepy facts that inspire my stories. You'll also get newsletter-exclusive bonus scenes and updates. I love to talk to my readers, so come join us for some spooky fun :)

A NOTE ON DARK CONTENT

I'm writing this note because I want you a heads up about some of the content in this book. Reading should be fun, so I want to make sure you don't get any nasty surprises. If you're cool with anything and you don't want spoilers, then skip this note and dive in.

Keep reading if you like a bit of warning about what to expect in this series.

- There is some bullying in the first and second books, but our heroine holds her own. No heroes in this story threaten or are involved in sexual assault of the heroine.

- Cassius' language is violence, and twice in this book he exhibits violence toward Fergie - once in a fight between the two of them in the arena (which she wins), and once when he believes he has to kill her, but can't go through with it.

- Fergie experiences revenge porn - both in her past and present.

- Fergie is sexually assaulted by a teacher in the first book.

- The Poison Ivy guys are part of a dark criminal underworld in Emerald Beach. There is some murder, violence, torture, and other crimes in this book, including a crucifixion and a blood eagle.

- There is some discussion of suicide and child abuse, but nothing on-page.

I'd definitely call this book 'dark', and it's for readers who like their heroes a little psychotic and their heroines badass. If that's not your jam, that's totally cool. I suggest you pick up my Nevermore Bookshop Mysteries series – all of the mystery without the gore and violence.

Enjoy, you beautiful depraved human, you :) Steff

To James
For being my lighthouse

Illis quos amo deserviam

PROLOGUE

VICTOR (THREE YEARS AGO)

"Victor, Juliet, come down – it's dinner time."

Reluctantly, I toss down the book I'm reading for English Lit and head downstairs. I have an essay to finish by tomorrow, and I've been too busy with basketball practice and building a garden at the Emerald Beach Hospice to get to it until tonight. I want to keep studying, but it's Thursday night dinner in the August house, and no matter what's going on in our lives we don't miss Thursday dinner.

I enter the dining room to see Noah setting the table and Mom tapping away on the laptop that's set up in Gabriel's place. He's on tour in Australia, so it's noon on Friday for him, which means that he's only just rolled out of bed. My father stares forlornly out of the screen, his long, dark hair mussed on one side of his head, as Mom tries to get the audio to work.

"Gabe, can you hear me?" Mom fiddles with the volume switch.

"Every time we have one of these calls, it's like hosting a bloody seance." Gabe holds his hands up and wiggles his fingers as if he's summoning a ghost. "Can you heeeear me? Are you out theeeere?"

"Don't get me started on you and your seances," Mom grumbles as she collapses in her seat. "Vic, remind me to tell you about the time your father organized a seance for my nineteenth birthday that ended in a shootout and the discovery of a secret passage."

"I've heard that story before, Mom." I roll my eyes as I reach for the rolls. "About a hundred times."

"Right, of course you have. All I can say is, be grateful that your resourceful and beautiful mother fought that particular battle so you don't have to deal with a gang war and a psychopathic twin sister."

"That, and your dear old dad blocked off that secret passage with concrete before you were even born," Noah adds.

I roll my eyes. "That's so annoying. Juliet and I would have loved a secret passage to play in."

I peer across the table at my sister, hoping to catch her eye and share our private joke. Our parents don't know that we found another secret passage years ago – it leads from a sliding panel in the back of Juliet's closet to a trapdoor beneath a gnarled old tree in the woods behind our house. We used to play in it as kids, but now we use it mainly for sneaking out to parties.

But my sister isn't in her seat to share our private twin moment.

That's odd.

Juliet knows how Mom gets about Thursday night dinner.

She was hanging out with some friends after school. I know because I waited in the parking lot for her for twenty minutes but she never showed up. She often does that when she's distracted by some cute girl or new designer collection and forgets to tell me that she doesn't need a ride.

But all her friends know to get her home in time for Thursday dinner.

Why isn't she here?

I whip out my phone and fire off a quick text. Hopefully, Jules will see it and get here before Mom notices and kicks her ass. Luckily, Mom's still distracted by secret passages and tales from her misspent youth.

"—it was a bit of a shame to brick it up, but a secret passage in a house filled with teenagers is a bad idea – I'm not giving the two of you an easy way to sneak out. At least now, with that passage blocked and all the modifications we made to Howard Malloy's security system, this place is finally mildly more secure than a slice of Swiss cheese—" Mom drops her fork. "Hang on a second, where's your sister?"

Damn, foiled.

"She's probably still in the shower or something," I say, frantically pounding out another message to Jules.

GET HERE NOW. MOM'S ABOUT TO GO POSTAL.

"Not good enough. She knows what time we eat." Mom moves into the hallway and calls up the stairs. "Juliet? Dinner's on the table. Could you answer me, please?"

Nothing.

Mom meets my eyes with her icicle gaze, and my stomach twists. "Vic, where's your sister?"

C'mon sis, don't get us both in trouble. I will Juliet to appear, but she remains ominously absent. All three of my parents in the room exchange a look, and Gabriel leans forward on his chair, his dark eyes flecked with concern.

"Did she go somewhere after you picked her up?" Eli asks me, his expression quizzical.

"I don't know." Fear twists in my stomach. Even if Juliet was hanging out with her friends after school, she should be home by now. She'd never, ever miss Thursday night dinner. "She didn't show up to meet me."

"She *what?*" Noah slams his glass down. "You didn't think to mention this until now?"

"It's not a big deal. She often forgets to tell me that she doesn't need a ride. I saw a bunch of her girlfriends heading off in the direction of the mall. I figured she was with them."

"When we allowed the two of you to drive to school by yourselves, it was with the very explicit instructions that you know where each other is at all times." Noah's already dark eyes are storms of rage. "You don't know where your sister is."

"I'm sure she just lost track of time," I say quickly, but even I'm not so sure now.

Mom picks up her phone and calls Juliet. "It's gone straight to voicemail." She tosses the phone to Eli. "You put that tracker thing on their phones. Follow it. I want to know where she is *right now.*"

Eli fumbles the phone as he clicks through to the app he installed that tracks me and Juliet wherever we are. It's a bit annoying to think that our parents can find us no matter what we're up to, but it's a necessary part of life when you're the child of a crime boss.

"She's still at school." Eli shoves his chair back. "I'll go and get her."

"I'll drive." Noah's already shrugging on his coat. "And Victor is coming with us. I want to have a word with both twins about managing their safety."

I'm too nervous about my twin's absence to worry about how ominous he sounds. I don't care if Noah takes our car away. All I want now is to see my sister alive and okay. I jog after my dads and manage to hurl myself into the backseat before Noah stomps on the gas. I yank the door shut, and Noah careens off in the direction of Stonehurst Prep. Neither he nor Eli says a word, but Noah's knuckles gripping the wheel are bone-white.

We pull up at the front gates. I can see lights on in the library and the auditorium – the debating club is practicing and there are rehearsals for the school's production of *Heathers*. Noah grabs the phone from Eli and points toward a dark corner of the student lot, where a narrow path cuts through the new greenhouses toward the art suite. "She's in that direction."

I jump out of the car and follow Noah and Eli as they move through the lot, behind the trash cans, and start to search the path. The horticulture club – of which I'm the president – made our end-of-year project to plant this area with trees and shrubs native to California. It looks nice in the daytime, but at night it's shrouded in creepy shadows that move in the breeze. It's also... not somewhere that Juliet would hang out. My sister isn't at school a moment longer than required unless she's working on one of her fashion assignments in the art suite. And she doesn't like to get dirt under her nails.

So why is she in the bushes?

Why do I have such a bad feeling about this?

No, don't think that. Juliet's fine. She's probably hiding behind a tree, ready to leap out and yell, "boo!"

Noah skids to a stop in the middle of a clump of Californian lilacs. "Here," he frowns at the screen. "This is where it's telling me her phone is."

She's not here. No one is here. It's just a random spot in the middle of the garden.

A lump of fear rises into my throat. Eli moves away, calling Juliet's name. Noah and I exchange a look, and as one we drop to our knees and start hunting through the shrubs. We don't want to say aloud what we're looking for, what we don't hope to find...

My hand brushes something smooth hiding in the leaves. I pick it up, my heart pounding.

It's Juliet's phone, and it's been smashed to pieces.

Wordlessly, I hand it to Noah. He frowns at the phone, his

shoulders tense. The fear bubbles in my throat. I open my mouth to say something, but I don't have the words—

At that moment, Eli comes running up. "I've found a bunch of footprints," he says, making what my mom likes to jokingly call his Sherlock Holmes Orgasm Face. "At least three pairs in the soft dirt over there. There are signs of a struggle. They lead out to the loading zone behind the greenhouse. I think someone might've—"

His phone rings, cutting him off before he can say what he thinks these bastards did to my sister. I can see my mom's name on the screen. Eli grabs it from Noah and brings it to his ear, hitting the speaker button so we can all hear. "I think we have a problem, Claws. They—"

"They took my daughter," Mom says, her voice cold and slow and furious. "They called me just now. They have demands."

The kidnappers want Mom to resign as Imperator and hand control of the August family over to a guy named Frank Hermann, a second-rate soldier who's worked as a go-between for Mom with our European contacts. Hermann has delusions of grandeur and managed to convince a couple of low-level heavies to grab Juliet in support of his flaccid coup.

This guy seriously can't expect this to work. Mom's not just going to hand over one of the most powerful and lucrative criminal syndicates in the world to some random idiot. But if Hermann's this deluded, what's he going to do to my sister when he realizes this isn't happening?

I didn't think it was possible, but the drive back to our place from school is even more tense than the one on the way there. As we pull into our driveway, we nearly hit Cali's car coming back out. Seymour must've just dropped her off. Livvie's already parked in the driveway.

Cas opens the door and crushes me in his arms. I try to wriggle out of his hug, but my best friend isn't having it. Being loved by Cas hurts sometimes – tell that to Cas' favorite fighter. The first guy Cas trained for the ring won his first match, and Cas was so elated he threw the guy in the air... and broke his spine in two places.

The memory of the fighter's limp body crunching against the ground spurs me to struggle harder. "Cas, I... can't... breathe."

"We'll find her," he growls, ignoring my protests. "Torsten hacked into the security footage at school. He tells me it was easy. That place needs to get better security. Anyway, we've got the details of the car. Cali thinks she knows where the kidnappers are hiding out. She's gone to handle it."

I swallow. When Cassius' mother handles a job, the body count shoots through the roof. And I want my sister to come out of this alive. "We should go with her. She might need backup—"

"That's what I said," Cas spits out. "But she says we're too young. She took five of her best assassins, and she thinks that'll be enough."

Please let that be enough.

Torsten appears in the doorway behind Cas. "The kidnappers are not clever people. They didn't obscure their plates or use a stolen vehicle. They should have used the side entrance because the camera is obscured by an oleander bush, but they used the front entrance and I have a clear shot of the driver. He has dark hair and blue eyes and a blue cap with a Prada logo on it, but I think it's a knock-off because the P is the wrong shape—"

"Torsten, I love you, but I can't deal with this much detail right now." I stagger into the foyer, collapse in a designer chair, and stare up at Cas, who has his hands in his pockets and looks almost as helpless as I feel. "Whoever they are, it doesn't change the fact that they *took* her. Right under my nose."

Cas opens his mouth, but his brother Gaius comes in from the kitchen and clamps his hand over Cas' face. "What my little bro *means* to say is that you have every tool and resource we can gather looking for her." Gaius meets my eyes with his steady gaze, and I know he sees how close I am to losing my shit. "I've got every contact in the club working my networks, trying to find out who else is in on this little coup."

The Poison Ivy Club. Of course, Gaius and his little group of thugs have the inside track on every piece of gossip at Stonehurst Prep. If someone at school saw what happened or helped these guys in any way, Gaius will find it.

I run my fingers through my dark hair as I think of my sister, alone and frightened in some dirty, horrible place. "I hate this. I can't just sit here. I need to *do* something."

Gaius throws his arm around my shoulders. "I know, buddy, but you don't have the power here. I do, and our parents do. We'll find her, and we'll make sure this can never happen again."

Yes, I think as I ball my hands into fists. *We will.*

The waiting is agony.

I pace across the foyer until Mom yells at me to stop.

I go to the rage room and smash a Biedermeier hutch into splinters.

I cuddle Eli's kittens until they get bored of my angst and start batting my eyelashes.

I hear Eli and Noah fighting in the kitchen. Noah wants to punish me for leaving school without Juliet. "Don't," Eli says. "As angry as you are with him right now, he's even angrier at himself. He lost his sister. I know it's hard, but our job isn't to punish him, it's to reassure him that we're going to get her back."

"What if we don't?" Noah growls.

Exactly. What if we don't get her back and it's all my fault?

"We'll get her back," Eli says, and I've never heard him sound more sure of anything in his life.

I lie on the couch while Mom stands at the window of the ballroom, staring out into the garden and the pool area. I know she's thinking about her twin sister, Mackenzie Malloy, and how that bitch almost wiped out our entire family before we even began. And now Juliet's in danger and, not for the first time, Claudia August wonders if she did the right thing by assuming the role of Imperator.

She tells us all the time that she could have ridden off into the sunset with her three husbands and never had to look over her shoulder again. But she couldn't walk away from her father's legacy, or Livvie and Cali. Just like I'll never walk away from my sister, even though she's getting out of the family business.

Mom's phone rings. She grabs it off the table.

My heart stops beating. I jerk upright.

"Cali, did you—"

Please...

Mom sinks to her knees. The sob that escapes her lips is one of utter relief. I run to her and wrap my arms around her, laying my head on her shoulder as she talks to Cali.

"Oh, thank fuck. She's okay. She's okay."

Tears streak down Mom's cheeks. I taste salt on my tongue, and it takes me a moment to realize it's from my tears. I curl up around her, my shirt wet with her tears, and for the first time in my entire life, I know that it's possible to break the great Claudia August.

"She's okay. My baby is okay."

Juliet is safe. They didn't hurt her. Everything is okay.

But I know that things will never be okay again.

Twenty minutes later, Cali appears in the doorway with Juliet beside her. My twin's hair is a mess, her clothing creased and rumpled, and her sparkling eyes dull and frightened. She runs to me and buries her face into my shoulder.

"Oh, Vic, it was so horrible," she sobs. "They tied me up and I have rope burns and they wouldn't let me eat and they kept saying that if Mommy didn't listen to them things would be very bad for me."

"Things ended up quite bad for them," Cali says as she strides across the room and dumps a large document box on the floor in front of Mom. The bottom is damp and a little warped, and dark liquid seeps through the corner onto the Persian rug.

Mom lifts the lid and inspects the contents. She makes a face. "You brought me their heads?"

"I thought we could display them on pikes at Colosseum, so any other would-be conspirators will think twice before pulling this shit."

Mom wrinkles her nose. "For the last time, no heads on pikes."

"I can't believe you don't want your daughter's kidnappers' heads on a pike." Cali sounds utterly aghast. "What kind of a crime lord are you?"

"One who doesn't like oozing brains staining the carpet." Mom shoves the box away with her toe.

"Philistine," Cali mutters. "I think we should put it to a vote—"

"If you insist, darling," Livvie purrs as she glides into the room. "It's two against one. No heads on pikes."

"Everyone's a critic." Cali turns on her heel to leave, but

stops in front of me and Juliet. She peers down at my sister, those cold eyes stripping away skin and breaking bones. Juliet squirms uncomfortably. Cali's lips curl into a smile that's anything but warm. "I'm pleased that you're okay."

"Me too." Juliet's body shudders in my arms. "Thanks for saving me."

"My pleasure," Cali barks. With a final sweep of her dark, cold eyes, she turns and stalks out.

I peer at my sister in concern. What the fuck was that about? "Did you and Cali have some heart-to-heart on the way over here?"

"Nothing like that. She's just scary, is all." Juliet nuzzles into my shoulder. "I'm so glad you found me, brother."

Found you? I'm the one who lost *you. If I'd been a good brother, you never would have been kidnapped in the first place.*

After Cali leaves, Gaius whisks away the leaking document box, and the room returns to a more normal state of chaos. Mom and my dads swarm Juliet, hugging her tight and alternating between showering her with praise for her bravery and scolding her for skipping out on me so often. Juliet basks in their words, the color returning to her skin as she recounts the tale of her hours tied up in an old shipping container while Hermann and his cronies argued about their coup. Cas and Gaius pour drinks for everyone and order pizza. Torsten settles himself in the corner with one of the kittens and draws.

It's one of the best Thursday night dinners we've ever had.

My twin never once lets go of my arm. Not that I'd have let her if she tried.

Finally, Juliet extracts herself from all of us. "I'm taking a shower," she says, licking the oily cheese off her fingers. "I need to get the smell of the docks and Hermann's broken dreams off me, or I'm going to go insane."

Mom doesn't want to let her out of sight for a moment, but Jules is right – she looks nothing like her usual put-together self. Her hair's a mess, there's dirt and grease smeared on her skin, and her Stonehurst uniform is torn. She'll feel so much more normal after a shower, and my sister deserves to feel normal again, even if it's just a farce.

Nothing will ever be normal after this. Not now that I know how quickly everything I love can be torn away from me.

Mom looks like she's about to protest. She reaches out to pull Juliet into her body again.

"I'll guard her." I leap to my feet. Before Jules can protest, I drag her upstairs.

Juliet and I have rooms next to each other, each with a private bathroom. I follow her into her closet as she starts sifting through her piles of clothes, but she plants both hands on my chest and shoves me into the hallway.

"I know you're scared, twinny, but you're not watching me shower." She wrinkles a nose that's the mirror image of mine. "Gross."

"Fine." I reach past her into the top drawer of her bedside cabinet and pull out the pistol she keeps there. Everyone in this house sleeps with a loaded gun next to the bed, and we all know how to use them. It's just what you do when your mom's a crime lord. "I'll be outside, standing guard. Call me if you need me."

"Sure." Jules rolls her eyes. "I'll get you to rip off the wax strips on my bikini line."

It's my turn to wrinkle my nose. "Gross."

"I'll be *fine*, brother."

I fix her with what I hope is a big-brotherly look. "I'm here all the same."

She rolls her eyes again and slams the door in my face. A few minutes later I hear the water running and her singing Sam Smith lyrics at the top of her lungs. My sister seems to have bounced back from her ordeal just fine.

Me? I'm not so sure.

I pace the floor in front of her bedroom door. I assess the weak areas in my defense of the hallway – the blindspot right behind the suit of armor, the window that doesn't quite give me the right angle on the garden below. I consider asking Mom to move Juliet to the eastern wing – it would be easier to defend those rooms from intruders. But if they were to scale the wall and come in from the outside...

My mind whirs through a thousand different and horrible ways today could have turned out, each of them ending with me cradling my sister's limp, lifeless body in my arms.

I know I'm making myself crazy, but I can't help it.

I nearly *lost* her.

Who am I without Juliet? She's the other half of me.

Footsteps echo on the marble floor, startling me from my waking nightmares. I move down the hall to peer around the corner, my finger touching the trigger as I draw out the gun—

"Relax, buddy. It's me."

Gaius.

I hate when he calls me buddy, but Gaius Dio is not a guy you talk back to, especially not after he's given you a nickname. Cas' brother stands at the top of the staircase, his hands raised on either side in a gesture of surrender. Amusement dances across his face.

"What are you doing up here?" The words come out harsher than I intended. Gaius is the most influential person at our school, and judging by the way he handled that document box, he's at least a little involved in his mother's business. He may have invited me and Cas and Torsten to hang out with his group this year, but that doesn't mean we're his equals. He's fucking intimidating, and I normally wouldn't consider speaking to him the way I just did, but this is not an ordinary day. "Juliet's in the shower, and I'm busy."

"I can see that. You're doing important work, protecting your sister from the big bad wolf." Gaius stands on a squishy cat toy, and it squeaks loudly. I nearly jump out of my skin. I have to jerk my finger off the trigger so I don't accidentally fire.

"My sister almost *died* today, Gaius. Leave me alone."

"Relax, I didn't come up here to bust your ass, Vic. I admire you. If that had been Cas who they took, I wouldn't have let my mother cut their heads off. I'd have done it myself."

"If it had been Cas," I say, "he would've bitten off Hermann's dick and made him eat it."

"Yeah, he would," Gaius laughs, and the tension dissipates a little. "I learned long ago that I don't have to protect my brother. Which is just as well, because it's a tough enough job trying to protect the rest of the world from him. He's an asset to the club, but he needs managing or he'll go too far."

"I manage him," I say.

As much as anyone can manage Cas.

"Yes, I've been watching you with him. That's why I came to talk to you. We need to discuss the future of the Poison Ivy Club."

I'm surprised by the change of subject. "What about it?"

"It might've escaped your attention that I finish school next month. Cali wants me to go to college and get an *accounting degree*, can you believe it? She thinks I need to know how to balance the books as well as clobber people over the head with them. But that leaves the club in a precarious position – it must disband or carry on with new leadership."

"Okay." I don't understand why he's talking to me about this. Gaius has his inner circle of juniors – mostly guys on the football and wrestling teams with more muscles than brain cells.

Surely they should be the ones to help him make this decision since they'd be the ones running the club?

"At first, I thought I'd just shut it down – do some kind of final stunt before ducking out for good. Leave the Poison Ivy Club on a high." Gaius looks pensive. "But I realize I don't want the Poison Ivy Club to be over. I built my own little empire at Stonehurst. This isn't a family business I inherited from my mother – it's *my* legacy and I want it to continue, to become something that might change the future. But the guys I've got working for me right now... they're just thugs. They lack the imagination to see the club's future. They don't know how to use our network of contacts and favors as a precision weapon instead of a dull bludgeon. The person who takes it over needs to be someone with *vision*. I think that someone is you."

"Me?" I'd be less surprised if he told me he was giving up crime to join the traveling cast of *Cats*. "What about Cas?"

"Have you *met* my brother? He's no leader. Why do you think Cali wants the Dio empire to pass to me? Cas is all rage and no brains but you... you're more like me. Tonight, when you were waiting for my mother to deal with the kidnappers, I saw how much you wanted to do *something*. If Cali hadn't managed to retrieve Juliet, you would have gone after Hermann yourself, isn't that true?"

I nod. There doesn't seem sense in denying it. I wasn't about to leave my sister's fate in anyone else's hands, not even the most notorious assassin in the world.

"That's what I admire about you, Vic. You're always thinking, always scheming. If you had the club at your disposal, you could keep your sister and anyone else you cared about safe. You'd never feel helpless again." Gaius pats my knee. "Think about it."

My stomach churns as I recall the all-encompassing help-lessness that welled up inside me when we found out that Juliet had been kidnapped, and how I'd been relegated by my family to the role of the annoying kid who fucked everything up while the 'adults' fixed it.

I never, ever want to feel that way again.

"I don't have to think about it." I slide the gun back into my belt and offer Gaius my hand. "I'll do it."

That night, Juliet crawls into bed with me, something she hasn't done since we were eight years old. She pulls the sheets up tight around us so the baddies can't get in.

"I was so scared I'd never see you again," she whispers, her eyelashes fluttering against my shoulder.

"Well, here I am." I hold her tight. "I'll never let anything like that happen."

"But what about when you go away to college?"

"What about it?"

She draws back, propping herself up on one elbow as she stares at me. "You're going to that fancypants Ivy League school and I'm... not. How can you watch over me from your Harvard dorm, Vic?"

"We're going to college together. I'm not leaving you behind."

"Don't be silly. You're going to *Harvard*. I don't have the grades to go to a place like that."

"What about that fashion school? The one you always talk about? It's not far from Cambridge. You just need to pull your grades up and then you could go there. We'll live together and I'll make sure that we're safe." Ideas are already whirring in my mind. "Of course – the house!"

"What house?" She glares at me sleepily as I roll out from the blankets and walk into her room. She follows me, hissing as I flick on the light. Juliet keeps her 'vision board' over her desk – it's a mishmash of pictures cut from magazines and printed off the internet. It represents her ideal future. It's filled with beautiful gowns and runway shows and expensive hotels in exotic locations, and right in the center is a real estate image of a big white house with a gabled roof and a little shop on the ground floor. I pluck the picture off the board and bring it back to her.

"*This* house." I thrust the picture under her nose. "Remember when you first saw this – we went to Lucile's ninth birthday party and it was in a real estate prospectus on her coffee table? You want this house, and it's in Cambridge and I'm going to get it for you."

"Mom's never going to buy us a house." Juliet's lips pout. She's not wrong. Mom has strict rules about what she will and won't do for us. She doesn't want us to use her influence and money to get ahead in life. She's always going on about the merits of us working things out for ourselves.

"She doesn't need to. I promise you, I'll find a way to make this house yours." I don't know how, but I feel my promise stirring in my veins. This is what my sister needs. This is what she deserves after her ordeal, and I'll make it happen for her. So what if I'm too young to buy property or I don't have access to that kind of money. For Juliet, I'll find a way.

If people think they can hurt my family, they'll see we rise stronger than ever. The next generation of the Augusts is not to be trifled with.

"And you'll live there with me?"

"We'll all live there together. You, me, Cas, and Torsten. That attic room could be Torsten's art studio. Your shop will be on the ground floor, and Cas can open up a training school nearby and act as your bodyguard while you're at school. It'll be perfect, you'll see."

"It's a nice dream, brother. But it's not going to happen. You can't buy real estate, and I don't have the grades to get into fashion school." Her eyes light up. "But maybe you could use Gaius' club to help me?"

My blood freezes. "What makes you think I have any influence over Gaius?"

"Don't play dumb. I heard you." Jules wiggles her eyebrows at me. "Gaius wants you to take over his secret, exclusive club, that secret club that everyone knows about that does favors for Stonehurst students who can pay his price. I want a favor, brother, just like what Gaius is doing for Gemma. And I'm willing to pay whatever price you demand if you get me into that school and that house."

No.

I don't want that.

Not after...

My girlfriend Gemma hired Gaius to make sure she stayed top of the class. I was the one who suggested it. I introduced them both. She's under so much pressure from her parents to be perfect, I thought that if he could get a couple of her test scores changed, she could relax a little bit and she'd stop crying into my arms every night from exhaustion and misery.

But Gaius handed the job over to Cas, and Cas fell hard for Gemma because she's the exact opposite of him in every single way, and that makes her a nut he wants to crack between his huge, swinging knuckles. He's already put at least two of her biggest rivals into the hospital, and now I'm sharing my girlfriend with my oldest friend. That part is hot, but...

Gemma's not the same. Poison Ivy has changed her. Being around Gaius has changed her. She's top of our class list but she doesn't care about schoolwork anymore. All she wants to do is party and get drunk and high with the Dio brothers.

I tried to call her earlier to ask if she'd seen Juliet, but she was partying at Cas' house and was so out of it she didn't even know it was me on the phone.

I wanted to fix Gemma's problems for her. That's what I do – I'm the guy with the answers, the responsible one, the superhero who swoops in and saves the day. Only, I couldn't save my sister, and I'm terrified that I've fucked up Gemma's life by putting her in Gaius' hands.

I won't do the same thing to my sister.

"I can't use Poison Ivy for you, Jules. That's nepotism, and I don't want to throw my weight around and have people afraid of me. I want to be a different kind of leader. I want to leave my own legacy – one that's not as bloody as Gaius'."

Mom is always going on about how she has to make sure that she never forgets that her power can be used for good as well as evil, and I want to be the same. She taught me to filter her decisions by what will best serve her people. I won't allow my sister to go down the same path as Gemma. I *won't*.

And maybe, now that I have the power of the club behind me, I can find a way to save Gemma, too.

Juliet makes a face. "I *need* you to help me."

I shake my head. "You don't need the Poison Ivy Club. You're brilliant. You'll get in. You just need to work harder. You've got three years to catch up, to put the work in."

"You sound like Mom's clone." She sticks out her lip. "Hard work will only get you so far when everyone's out to get you. You may think I'm brilliant, Vic, but the teachers don't. Mrs. Vasco called my spring collection a Valencia copycat without the claws. The pattern-drafting teacher, Mr. Branch, says I have no sense of line. You don't understand what it's like because everyone thinks the sun shines out your ass."

We go back to bed. Juliet sighs and rests her head on my chest. She must be exhausted because in moments, she's breathing deeply, her body warm and heavy against mine. I stroke her hair and consider what she's asking of me.

Maybe I won't use Poison Ivy to get Juliet into fashion school, but I *will* use it to keep her safe. I'll make sure that she owns that house. It'll be a beautiful place to start our new lives, a place for my family – Juliet and the guys, where we can all be ourselves away from the pressure of our family obligations.

I'm drifting off to sleep, my sister cradled in my arms, when something niggles at me. It's the video Torsten pulled from school of my sister being dragged into their car. Juliet goes with them, her head hung, her body limp. But as they flip her around to shove her into the trunk of their car, I notice something gripped in her hand. A knife.

But why didn't she use it?

The men had concealed weapons, but they needed her alive. At the moment, they were completely vulnerable. Both Juliet and I have endured hundreds of hours of knife-fighting lessons from our overzealous mother. She knows what the fuck she can do with that weapon.

But she did nothing.

School might've been over, but there were lots of kids all over the parking lot. All my sister had to do was cry out or kick some shithead's Mercedes and the kidnappers would've been foiled.

So why didn't she?

And why am I too afraid to ask her?

PROLOGUE

"These are perfect," Livvie breathes. She steps back to admire the painting as her two soldiers hang it on the wall.

I disagree. It's *not* perfect. The brushstrokes on the bridge are all wrong. The lighting is too muted. Some of the blues are muddy.

I want to toss it out and start again, but Livvie says I'm too precious about the paintings. "No one cares what they look like," she snaps whenever I ask if I can start again. "As long as they can trick an expert for long enough for us to move them overseas."

I know I can do that. Over the years I've perfected my techniques, and now I'm good enough to fool most art authenticators. Forging art for trade isn't about the skill of the painter – any person with basic art skills can copy a Mondrian or a Matisse. The real skill is in mixing the exact pigments, choosing the correct canvas, and constructing the piece without using anachronistic materials. Most forgers are caught because they don't pay attention to these details.

But I like details.

And I like it when Livvie smiles at me.

So I don't say anything. I stare at the abomination with lips pinched shut and try not to think about the fact that the people who profess to be the greatest art dealers in the world cannot tell this isn't a real Monet. Livvie will be paid handsomely by the Italian businessman who commissioned the piece, which will be used as a mechanism for hiding his wealth. No one will know that the piece displayed on the wall in his palatial mansion isn't the real thing.

"Yes, this will do nicely. I have back-to-back appointments with potential clients coming to look at the collection. I hope you're hard at work on more, because I have a feeling this could be what finally elevates our family out of the muck my father wallowed in."

Livvie is obsessed with the idea that the Lucians can be so much more powerful. She thinks that other criminal enterprises don't take her seriously because she trades in entertainment – booze, drugs, gambling, high-end call girls (only those who offer their services of their own volition, since the Lucians gave up the skin trade when Livvie came to power). She's always talking about respect – how to command it, and the best way to punish those who don't give it to her. I presume that I'm useless in this department because she seems to punish me all the time, but then, I don't understand because everyone seems to obey her commands, and I thought that's what respect is.

Since I started painting for her, things between us have been better than ever. Livvie hasn't yelled at me or got exasperated with me in months. She's finally found a use for me. I make art that she can use to attract high-profile clients to the bank of Livvie Lucian. Yesterday, she told me that she can see I have a bright future in the Lucian family.

Now I'm going to destroy that future.

I don't want to do it. I don't want her to hate me. I've known hate before, and it makes me feel like a tiny ant being squashed under someone's boot. Livvie's terrifying, especially when she yells, and she's often yelling at me.

I used to think it meant she hated me, but Victor explained that she yells because she's frustrated. He says it's as if Livvie and I speak two different languages and we can't figure out how to make each other understand. She thinks that if she yells louder, I'll be able to figure out what she means.

That's ridiculous, but people always do things that make no sense to me, so why should Livvie be any different?

Vic and I have worked out a script for what I need to say to her. He thinks that this will help her to understand me. I memorized the script, and now all I have to do is say it. I open my mouth, but I can't get the words out. I stand there with my mouth open until she notices and says, "You look like you're trying to catch flies with that dopey expression. Stand up straight and shut your mouth. My clients will be here any second—"

"Mother," I say, wincing at the inaccuracy but pushing ahead regardless. Vic says that Livvie likes to think of herself as my mother. "I'd like to talk to you about something."

One eyebrow arches. I think she's surprised. I don't usually initiate conversations with her. "Yes, Torsten? We can go to my office for privacy—"

"I'd prefer to speak here." I'm more comfortable in the gallery. There's no one else in here now. We're alone. I have many directions I can run.

"As you wish." Livvie crosses the room to one of the low padded benches set up so clients can sit and study the paintings. She sits on the edge, crossing her legs. "What's this about?"

I begin my script. "As you know, I'm graduating high school next year. I would like to apply for art school. I feel that my work is of a standard that would justify a place—"

But the next words of my script are drowned out by Livvie

throwing back her head and laughing. I run back over the words I spoke, trying to figure out what's so funny. Have I inadvertently made a joke? I do that sometimes because I don't usually understand jokes. It must be a good one because Livvie's eyes are full of tears.

"Did I say something amusing?"

"Yes," she wipes her mouth. "Yes, son, you did. You can't go to art school, you know that."

"I can. I have a brochure."

"Oh, well, if you have a *brochure...*" her face collapses into laughter again. "Torsten, love, that's not what I meant. There are two reasons you can't go to art school. One is that I need you here. We're expanding this line of the business and you're the greatest commodity we have. The Lucian family has always been the underdogs of the Triumvirate. We've never been taken as seriously as Dio or August because we deal in pleasure. In entertainment. But if I can provide a new service to those who wish to safely secure their money away from the thieving hands of the tax collectors, well, that's big business. That puts me in a different *league*. This family is heading for great things, and it's because of you. You won't have time for school with all the work we have coming."

Vic prepared me for this argument. "If I went to art school, I would learn new techniques. I'll continue to work for you, and my work will be better. I'll help you provide better service to your clients."

But Livvie stands and moves away as if she hasn't heard me. Her heels clack as she walks along the edge of the gallery, gesturing to the large Raphael I'd done earlier this year when I was fascinated with the Renaissance masters.

"You taught yourself to paint like this," she sweeps her arm around the gallery. "And *this* is so close to the old masters that we're fooling the finest minds in the international art world. You don't need to learn other techniques. And even if I did allow you to attend an art school, none of them would accept you. This is the second reason you can't go. Art school is about developing your style and creating *new* art. It's about using your work to say something about the world. You have never created an original piece of art in your life, son. You copy the work of others. Your art doesn't speak, and you can't speak through it."

Tears of frustration well at the corners of my eyes. "Maybe I could if I went to school. If I learned—"

"Every report card you've had tells me that you don't want to learn. You yell at teachers when they say things you don't like—"

"—that's because they're *wrong*—"

"—you refuse to do assigned work. You won't answer questions or take tests. What do you think art school is? It's four more years of all the things you refuse to engage with at school. Why would I pay for that when you have all the art you could ever want right here?"

I can't answer. I'm afraid that if I open my mouth I'm going to scream, and Vic said I absolutely under no circumstances should do that. My hand flaps, and I shove it behind my back so Livvie can't see it. She hates when I do that.

"I'm sorry, love. I know I've upset you—"

"I'm not upset."

That's not a lie. I'm *not* upset.

I'm devastated.

"—but I have to speak the truth. I don't want you to go out there and make a fool of yourself. You're too precious and too important to me. Do you understand?"

I stare at her.

"Torsten, do you understand me?"

"Yes."

I spin on my heel and walk away.

Cas warned me that she'd say no. He said that Victor lives in the land of fluffy bunnies and unicorn farts. I pointed out that Victor lives in a mansion in Harrington Hills with several cats but no rabbits, and Cas laughed. And then he told me exactly what I should do if Livvie said no.

"I don't understand," I asked him after he'd laid it all out. "How will leaving home help me get to art school?"

"Trust me. You're going to art school, if Vic and I have to drag you there ourselves."

I trust Cas, so now I drag myself up to my room and pack my things. I made a list in my sketchbook already so I don't forget anything. I pack up my paints, brushes, charcoal pens, two pairs of underwear, three pairs of socks, two t-shirts, a sweater, my jacket, a pair of jeans, my Stonehurst Prep uniform, my razor and toothbrush and toothpaste, my phone and laptop and cables and hard drives. I shove two empty sketchbooks into the side pocket and zip my backpack closed.

Isabella watches me from the doorway as I move my finger down the list, checking that I have everything.

"Are you going to school?" she asks.

"No."

"You have your backpack. Why would you have your backpack if you're not going to school?"

I can't answer that question without telling a lie, so I don't answer. Isabella has never needed me to reply to keep talking, though. "It's a funny time to go to school. No one will be there."

"I'm not going to school," I say as I shove past her.

"Then where are you going?" she cries as she runs after me. Her legs are much shorter than mine, so she has to sprint to keep up. She grabs my shirt on the stairs and I stop so that I don't pull her over.

"I am going to stay with my friend Cassius," I say. "Can I have my shirt back now?"

She fists my shirt even tighter. "Why?"

"I don't know." It's true. I don't. And that's a little frightening. I don't like not knowing things. All I've ever known is this big house and my sisters and Livvie and the Triumvirate. Well, that, and the flashes of memory that come to me sometimes of before, of a woman with a strange accent, and of searing, unending pain. So much pain that it makes the scars on my body tingle. "Because I don't want to know my devil any longer."

Cas said something once, "better the devil you know." He explained that it was an old saying and it's not actually about a devil (which is good, because devils don't exist, so if Cas is seeing devils that might mean he has brain damage). It means that it's better to stay in a bad situation that's familiar instead of leaving and finding yourself in a new, unfamiliar situation that's even worse.

I think about that a lot. I'm not sure exactly what happiness is, but when I read about it in books, it doesn't sound like the way I feel.

What Livvie's given me is so much better than the life she took me from. But I'm not happy.

Maybe it's not possible for me to be happy, but I guess I don't know until I try.

I rub at the scars on my legs – my real parents gave them to me. Even though I got them as a baby, they're not tiny like baby scars. They grow with me. Livvie points to them every time she reminds me that she saved me from that life.

The scars I carry from her aren't visible, but they grow with me, too.

"Torsten, won't you even say goodbye?" Isabella asks as she clings to me. I need to go, now, or I will lose my nerve, so I keep walking down the stairs, dragging her along with me.

"No," I say as I peel her hands off my shirt.

I walk out the front door, down the drive, and out the gate, and I keep walking.

1

CASSIUS

"My... what?"

I glare at my brother in utter incomprehension. My brain struggles to connect the pieces. I know the grey mush between my ears doesn't work right anymore, but hallucinating my brother and some dude he says is my dad? That's messed-up even for *me*.

Maybe I'm even sicker in the head than I realize.

I do the only thing I can think of to test if I've gone cuckoo.

I punch my brother in the face.

"Ow. Fuck!"

Gaius staggers back, cupping his hands over his nose. Blood spurts between his fingers.

I shake my fist and stare at my knuckles. They sting from connecting with something solid – my brother's nose.

It's him. It's really Gaius.

My brother is back. Everything will be okay now.

Gaius is still trying to staunch the bleeding when I throw my arms around him. "Ow, watch it—"

"I missed you so much." I bury my head into his shoulder, the way I used to do when I was a tiny kid, before Cali told us both that hugging showed weakness. I don't care about looking weak now – my mother can hardly move, so she can't exactly tell me off, and I haven't touched or spoken to or even seen my brother since the night he took the rap for my crime.

"When you miss someone, you don't punch them in the face," Gaius grumbles, but he throws his arms around me in return.

My big brother has come back, and he smells the same and his arms feel so strong as they fold around me, and he'll make everything right again, just like he always does. Gaius will make my mother love me again. He'll fix the Triumvirate and prevent a war. He'll take over running things while Cali recovers because I don't know what the fuck I'm doing.

He's here. He's *here*. The joy bubbles inside me. I laugh and laugh and laugh as I hold him close, so close he'll never be able to leave me again.

I wish Fergie were back from training. I can't wait for her to meet Gaius. She's going to *adore* him.

"Little bro," Gaius chokes out. He beats his fists against my back. "I... can't... breathe..."

"Right." I drop him from my embrace. He falls into a pile on the floor and picks himself up, frowning as he rubs at the blood-stain from his nose on the collar of his immaculate suit.

"You haven't changed a bit," he says with a smirk. "Well, apart from the fact you're now bubblegum blue."

A memory flashes in my mind.

At least, I think it's a memory. The image is sharp in my mind, but it's not something I remember. Gaius is about fourteen, and he's on his way to high school in his Stonehurst uniform, when I run up to him with one of my toy swords, begging for him to play with me.

'Stay away from me, Cas," he said as he turned to glare at me, and the look in his eyes...

Maybe my brain damage has knocked something loose, because in this memory, Gaius does *not* look like my brother.

He looks like he hates me.

Like he's imagining wrapping his fingers around my neck and squeezing tight.

And then Cali steps into the room to pull me away from him, and the look is gone. He smiles down at me and ruffles my hair. "I'll be back tonight, little bro. I'll play with you then." And I follow Cali into the house as he leaves, and I'm shaking with fear...

But that didn't happen, did it?

I have absolutely no recollection of that day, but the vision is so clear that it makes my skull hurt.

I can't ask Gaius about it. Not after he's been to jail for me. Not when he's standing here, alive and *free*. I file it away as something to talk to Fergie about when she finally gets home.

"Get me a towel. I'm bleeding everywhere." Gaius pinches his nose. Seymour rushes off to find something to clean up my mess.

"Why are you here?" I demand.

"Isn't it obvious, little bro? You need my help," he says. "I get news in jail, you know. And all I've heard over the last few months is about how the Triumvirate is falling to pieces and Emerald Beach is up for grabs for any criminal bold enough to make their move. I'm here to make sure that doesn't happen."

"We're not falling to pieces," Cali says, even as she slumps into a chair, gripping her crutch so hard her knuckles turn white. She glares up at the man who Gaius called my father, and he's lucky looks can't kill because he'd be wearing his intestines for a necklace right now.

"And you just walked out of jail to come and help?" John says as he comes up behind Cali and rests his hands on her shoulders. He sounds more curious than angry.

Gaius snorts. "Who's this guy?"

"Answer the question," Cali snaps.

Gaius looks John up and down, his lips curling back into a sneer. His gaze flicks back to Cali as if John isn't even someone worth considering. "I don't know why you're surprised, *Mother*. I'm a *Dio*. I could have walked out of that jail any time in the last three years, and no one would have batted an eyelid. I stayed because I've been making contacts – I've got the kings of the East Coast eating out of the palm of my hand. I've got Cosa Nostra chomping at the bit to do deals with us. I've got the Triads lining up to employ our boys. I'd have landed the Romanian gangs, too, but when I heard what was going down, I decided I was needed here more. No need to reward me, your undying gratitude is all I desire."

"Why didn't you tell us you were getting out?" I demand.

"I tried to. You didn't answer my message."

"My phone broke. I got another one..." I lose my train of thought as my gaze falls on the other guy who's with Gaius, the one Cali's currently shooting daggers at with her eyes. Gaius said he's my father.

But that's ridiculous. My daddy is worm food.

But I can't deny that this guy looks like me – he has my sharp cheekbones and my broad shoulders and my square brick of a jaw. He's white as a vampire's ass, but I figured my darker skin is all Cali's genes anyway, and the rest of me could have come from this guy.

He's wearing a suit that looks even more expensive and tailored than Gaius', and his hair is shaved close to his head. The corners of his hard, cruel mouth pull back into a tentative smile.

"It's nice to meet you at last, son," he says.

I whirl around to look at Cali. I need her to confirm this.

One look at her stormy face and I know the truth.

This guy is my father, and she's *pissed as fuck* that he's alive.

Gaius grins that sly smile of his as he shoves the other man forward. "Meet your father, Cas. This is Ares Valerian, one of the finest assassins Cali ever trained, fresh out of jail and looking to meet his boy. You're welcome."

Ares *Valerian*? What the fuck kind of name is that? And yes, I know that I share my name with some grizzled old Roman historian. But still, why the fuck does everyone have weird names these days?

"Get him out of this house," Cali breathes.

I think actual steam is coming out of her ears.

"You shouldn't exert yourself." John tries to lead her back down the hallway. "Come back to bed and I'll make sure he's gone—"

"Cali, darling." Ares throws his arms wide. "How about a little sugar for your man?"

"You're not my man." She ducks under John's arm and lunges at Ares, but the movement makes her wince. She drops one of her crutches and it clatters on the floor. Instinctively, I bend to pick it up for her, but I'm too slow. Gaius has already swooped in and returned it to her.

"It's lovely to see you, son," Cali hisses through gritted teeth. "But that man needs to go, or we'll have another body to deal with."

"I'm not going anywhere," Ares Valerian says in a voice as smooth as satin. "We're all going to sit down and have a rational discussion as a family. Because if what I've been hearing in jail is even halfway true, this empire is in danger of collapsing."

"My empire is just fine," Cali snaps. "And you're not part of this family. You're a sperm donor, nothing more—"

"You cut me, Cali. Maybe your passion has faded, but you can't deny a man the right to get to know his only son." Ares turns back to me, and the smile he flashes is so unnervingly like my own that I'm lost in it. "Isn't that what you want, Cas?"

"Don't talk to him!" Cali screams, lunging again. John catches her and hauls her back just as Ares bursts out laughing. "Don't you speak to him like he's yours—"

"Okay, okay," Gaius holds up his hands. "Everyone, ceasefire!"

His voice booms in the high, sterile space, bouncing off the walls. I freeze, momentarily stunned by memories flicking past at lightning speed – my brother calling goodbye as he heads out the door, or yelling to one of his friends during a party, or dragging the latest Poison Ivy client up to the secret library and slamming the door in my face.

Cali slumps in John's arms. She stares daggers at Ares, but for now, she's silent. John peers between Ares and Gaius and me, trying to figure out what's going on. Milo mops Gaius' blood off the floor, his face bent down, focusing on his work, but I know that he's listening to every word.

Gaius makes sure all eyes are on him. He takes a deep breath. "Obviously, I went about this the wrong way. I thought you'd appreciate the surprise."

"Oh, dear boy, don't you know that Cali hates surprises?" Ares grins at my mother. "When the condom broke, that was a surprise."

With a howl, Cali grabs a vase from the hallway table and hurls it at Ares. She's still so weak that it lands a foot in front of him. He peers down at it, then back at Cali, an amused expression on his face.

"Okay," John says, dragging Cali away from the scattered shards. "You're leaving."

"No. Not while he's here—"

"Cas, can you take care of this?" John peers at me. I realize that he's asking me to be a leader, to take responsibility for sorting out this shitshow. No one's ever thought I could do that before, apart from Fergie. My chest swells a little to see it. "Gaius can stay, but Ares needs to be moved far away from here—"

"—into the middle of the ocean," Cali snaps.

"—and he needs a guard. Pick the most trustworthy soldiers."

"I got it," I say, puffing out my chest to show how serious I am.

"Who are you again?" Gaius seems to have only just noticed John standing with our mother.

"I'm John, Cali's husband."

There have been few times in my life when I've seen my brother surprised. He's a little like Victor in that way, always perfectly in control of everything. This is one of those rare times.

Gaius stares at John, taking in his pressed tennis outfit, receding hairline, and obvious lack of criminal empire. His mouth hangs open.

"*You?*"

"Yes, me." Fergie's dad puffs out his chest and tries to make himself appear big and confident and tough. He fails, so he extends a hand instead. "It's nice to meet you, Gaius. Cali has told me a lot about you."

"Has she?" My brother looks amused. He doesn't offer his hand to shake. "She's told me absolutely nothing about you."

"How could I?" Cali snaps. "You don't answer my letters."

For a moment, Gaius' face clouds over. "They didn't let me have your letters," he says. He moves across the foyer, and before I know what's happening, he pulls over a white chair from the wall and sets it down behind Cali, who collapses gratefully into it. "They wouldn't let me communicate with any of you. They thought you might've placed me in jail as a messenger, and didn't want to risk me carrying information for you."

"I'd much rather you have brought me information than that

piece of shit," Cali growls. "What sewer did you drag him up from, anyway?"

"Isn't it amazing? It was a complete fluke. I was exercising in the yard one day and this guy wanted to work in sets. We got to talking and figured out we both came from Emerald Beach. He mentioned the Triumvirate and I said I was Cali Dio's son, and... well, his whole face just lit up."

"I thought I found my long-lost boy." Ares claps Gaius on the shoulder before turning to me. "But then he tells me that he's not my son, but that my son is out there, dying to meet me. So we made a plan together to get out, to get back to our family—"

We're interrupted by the squeal of tires on the street. I notice the almost imperceptible tightening of Cali's eye muscles as she listens for her guards. She thinks it's someone coming to finish her off.

Ares whips a gun from his belt and points it at the door, just as it slams open and Vic staggers inside.

"Cas!" he yells, seemingly oblivious to all of us gathered in the foyer. "We need to go. Now!"

"How the fuck did you get past the guards?" Cali grumbles. "Are they all taking the fucking day off?"

Victor's eyes bug out as he notices the others in the foyer for the first time. His features pale as he moves from face to face, taking in my brother and Ares and the gun pointed straight at his head.

"Someone's killed all the guards," Victor gasps. "Twenty dead bodies are lying in a pile on the driveway."

Gaius steps out from behind a statue and picks his teeth. "That's my bad. They wouldn't let us inside. I thought someone must've been holding my mother prisoner in her own home, because how could she not have put her eldest son on her security list?"

"Her eldest son—" Victor stops dead in his tracks. "Gaius. You—you're back?"

Gaius takes a dramatic bow. "Little Victor August. It's nice to see you've grown a little hair on your chest."

Vic looks completely flummoxed, which is not a common state of affairs for Victor August. Then his eyes flick back to Ares, who's still holding up that gun, and his eyes grow wide and crazed. He sees the resemblance.

"And that guy with you is—"

"My dad, yeah." I grin. "He looks a lot like me, right?"

Victor wheezes. "Sure, Cas. He looks like you. I—I—"

He shakes his head. I go to him and grab him under the arms just as he sways on his feet. "This isn't a coincidence," he says. "It can't be."

"What isn't a coincidence?"

I notice that Vic is pale, even for a pretty boy white guy. He's pale as death.

"You have to come with me." He grabs my shirt, tearing the fabric. "Fergie and Gabriel have been kidnapped."

2

TORSTEN

I'm working on a series of drawings for my secret project in the library when I notice noise downstairs. There is always noise in this house, so I ignore it until I hear a knock on the door.

"Torsten! Open up! I know you're in there!"

It's Victor.

I open the library doors. Victor grabs my wrist, his grip so tight that it hurts.

"I'm drawing," I say as he drags me toward the stairs. "Let me finish—"

"Torsten, you can't finish. We need you. Everyone's going to Claudia's house. Fergie and Gabriel have been kidnapped."

Everything in my body goes cold.

Someone has taken Fergie.

I drop my sketchbook on the floor as Victor yanks me forward.

"What can I do?"

Vic doesn't answer. Maybe he doesn't know what I can do. This is concerning. Victor always has a plan. But right now he's yanking my arm so hard that it hurts and not answering me, and I'm worried that this means he doesn't have a plan.

I have to do something.

Fergie's in danger.

Anything.

And I'll burn the world to find her.

3

CASSIUS

W e drive in a convoy to the August house – me and Vic and Torsten in Vic's Jag, followed by Gaius and Ares in a hulking great bulletproof Cadillac in the middle, and Cali and John being driven by Seymour at the rear, practically bumper to bumper to prevent my brother from pulling any kind of stunt.

Cali wants to keep an eye on Ares, and no way was I waiting around for her to secure him in her chamber, so they'd both be coming with us.

The fizzle of excitement at my brother coming home is obliterated by the fear of what's happened to Fergie. Vic's thinking the same thing, because he tears erratically through the traffic, his knuckles white on the wheel. His words play in a loop over and over in my head.

This isn't a coincidence.

This isn't a coincidence.

I don't know what he means – that my brother had something to do with Fergie's kidnapping? That's insane. Gaius wouldn't do that. But I know that this has to be doing a number on Vic. He went a little... overboard... after his sister was kidnapped. That's when he took over the Poison Ivy Club and started maneuvering things to make sure he got into Harvard and Juliet got that house. That's when he got it into his head that it's his job to protect everyone.

And now Fergie... fuck.

Spartacus sits primly on my lap, his little whiskers twitching as he watches the road. It didn't seem right to leave him at home, not when his mama is in trouble. I'm too afraid to touch him because I'm so fucking pissed that I might crush his bones. But he seems perfectly content to claw my kneecap.

I can feel the red mist closing in around my eyes. I try to push it back because if I lose it in the car I'll knock us off the road. And Fergie needs me alive because some kidnappers need to be choked with their own entrails, and I'm not trusting Torsten to get the job done.

Vic must be thinking the same thing, because he finds a way to get the words out to stop me from giving in to my monster. "So, your brother and your dad... what are they doing here?"

"Gaius came back to help us." I can't keep the pride out of my voice. That's exactly the kind of thing my brother would do. "Word about all the crazy shit going on reached him in jail, so he's come to help Cali straighten everything out. And as for Ares... my dad... Gaius found him in jail. They lifted weights together. Can you believe it?"

"No." Vic's eyes narrow. "I can't, Cas."

In the backseat, Torsten flaps his hands around his face. He didn't bring his sketchbook – he dropped it upstairs and there's no time to grab it, and so he's doing the flapping hand thing to keep himself calm instead. It's one of those times when I want to grab his wrist and snap it. But it's not Torsten's fault he needs to do that, so I sit on my hands and focus on not losing my shit.

"What the fuck are you saying, Vic?"

Vic opens his mouth, then snaps it closed. We go another

block before he opens it again. "All I'm saying is that we shouldn't trust Ares yet, okay? We find Fergie, and then we can deal with him, okay?"

"Okay."

We pull up at the house just as Livvie arrives with three of her girls in tow. "We were at the hairdresser," she explains as a damp curl falls over her eyes. "We didn't even stop to finish our foils. Those bastards will pay for hurting Fergie."

Livvie sounds so sincere. I remember the conversation we had before the fight, when Livvie offered to align with our family if I took over as Imperator and supported Fergie and Torsten's marriage. Only last month she was determined to stab her so-called sisters in the back, and now she's here pretending to be on their side?

I move to grab her, but Vic inserts himself in front of me. "Don't touch her," he says. "She's not our enemy today."

"She wants to—"

"I know," he says. "You told me everything, remember? But I can't help but wonder if Livvie's schemes to maneuver Torsten and Fergie together are because she's just as enchanted with our girl as the rest of us."

I don't have time to tell him that's fucking insane, because Claudia flings open the door. Livvie barrels inside, throwing her arms around Vic's mother and drawing her in for a crushing hug like she didn't try to backstab her.

"Oh, honey, I'm so sorry. We'll find them. You know we will. That man of yours will move the fucking heavens to get home to you."

"See?" Vic nudges me as he picks up Spartacus from the footwell of the car and cradles the cat against his shoulder. "After everything that's been going down, all the sneaking around and the backroom deals to secure their legacies, all it takes is something like this and our mothers are a team again."

I'm not so sure, but right now it doesn't fucking matter if Livvie's growing a turnip out of her nose. We need to find Fergie and Gabriel, and we'll do it faster by working together.

For now.

"All right, enough with the waterworks." With John's help, my mother hobbles up the steps and fixes Claudia with a glare that could melt the ice caps. "We're going to slit the throat of every lowlife in this city until we get the bastard who did this."

I scratch Spartacus under his chin. *I can't fucking wait.*

"We already know who did it," Claudia says, her whole body shaking. "Zack Lionel Sommesnay. He's called with his demands. He wants me to give the Imperatorship of the August family over to him within twenty-four hours, or he'll kill them both."

4

FERGIE

I rub my cheek against my shoulder, trying to scratch the itch caused by the fabric of my blindfold rubbing under my eye. Some fucking idiot has blindfolded me, so that's hilarious.

These must be the world's most incompetent kidnappers.

Yup. So I got kidnapped.

I – Fergie Macintosh, martial arts champion, stepdaughter of the deadly Cali Dio, and Poison Ivy girl – have been kidnapped.

This would almost be embarrassing if it wasn't so terrifying.

I'm tied to a chair somewhere very cold that reeks of old fish, with a smelly rag in my mouth and a blindfold around my useless eyes. Opposite me, Gabriel is also tied up. I can't see him, obviously, so I don't know if he's injured or even what direction he's facing or if they used the same coarse rope as they have on me, but he greeted me brightly when they brought me in, so he's been there even longer than I have.

I don't know how long that is, but it's at least a few hours since I left Cali's gym. They gagged us after they made the call to Victor. I think they got sick of Gabriel singing "Always Look on the Bright Side of Life" over and over.

Which, honestly, I was getting sick of, too.

I mean, don't get me wrong, if I have to be kidnapped with anyone, I'd choose the hot AF lead singer of my favorite band, Broken Muse. Actually, no, I can think of a million other people who'd be more useful to be kidnapped with. Vic's dad is the type of guy who becomes rather chatty and silly when he's scared, and I'm not sure that's the best way to tackle this situation.

Plus, hearing him talk always makes me think of Vic.

Fuck, *Vic*.

He must be a mess right now. I heard his voice over the video call when our captor showed me and Gabriel tied up. He sounded so utterly broken. I know that after what happened to his sister three years ago, this is a particularly acute torture for him. Part of me wonders if Gabe and I were chosen as kidnapping victims for precisely this reason. The Augusts have already been through the pain of it before.

This is *personal*.

Which means that I'm pretty sure I know who's behind it.

But Sommesnay is the least of my problems right now. Something else is bothering me.

I'm getting cold.

Not just 'need a sweater' cold, but cold to my bones cold. My whole body aches, as if I have an ice cream headache all over. My brain hurts the most – a throbbing, blinding pain behind my eyes.

And I know it's going to get worse.

The door clicks. There's a brief rush of warm air, and then the biting chill takes over once more. I don't raise my head. I'm not giving the guy the satisfaction of seeing me react to him.

"Hello, Fergie, Gabriel." Zack Lionel Sommesnay's clipped German accent sends a chill down my spine that matches the temperature of the room. "I'm pleased to see you're both still with us."

"You bastard," I growl, but I've got the rag in my mouth, so what comes out is, "lew-arrrrse-ed."

Sommesnay chuckles. "Ah, that's the Fergie Munroe I've come to admire. You're a real little spitfire. Too bad you and I ended up on opposite sides of this war. I had such high hopes for you, but you tethered yourself to the Augusts, and so you must die alongside them."

Die?

Hang on a sec.

That's not how this is supposed to go.

I thrash in my chair. Beside me, Gabe makes a keening groan into his gag.

"Yes, I'm terribly sorry to reveal that part of my plan involves leaving the two of you as corpsicles for dear Claws to find." Sommesnay chuckles again. "It's just too delightfully poetic to force her to relive what she went through with her daughter with the girl she considers her adopted heir. I know what I told them in the video – Claudia August has twenty-four hours to sign over her family assets and the position of Imperator to me, or I put a bullet in your heads. But what she doesn't realize is that the cold in this room will kill you both in a few hours."

What? Fuck.

"Oh, yes, you have noticed the chill? You're inside a freezer, and I have turned it on high. You might think it will be hypothermia that kills you, but that's just going to make your death excruciating. It's actually the lack of oxygen that will do you in. I estimate this room to be about twenty feet by ten feet. Is that what you had on your plans, Fergie?" Sommesnay's tone is mocking. I'd love to smack him in his self-satisfied face. "This gives you approximately sixteen hundred cubic feet of breathable air. Now, this *technically* gives the two of you enough for maybe half a day in here. But the problem is that every time you exhale, you breathe out carbon dioxide, which is highly poisonous. You're going to keep breathing in that carbon dioxide, and once it accounts for over five percent of the air in this freezer, you'll both die. I estimate that will take around three hours."

Three hours.

And he's just hanging around, wasting our precious oxygen with his yammering.

Dick.

The pain in my head flares. I bite the rag to stop myself from crying out.

"...so, while dear old Claudia is running around, making her arrangements, signing over her empire in the vain hope that it will save you, you will already be dead. That death will be a sweet relief after you experience the effects of the freezing temperature," he says conversationally, as though he's discussing the weather. "It won't be long before you'll feel dizzy and confused. Your breath will slow, and every gasp for air will feel like stabbing a knife into your lungs. Too bad you didn't think to bring a sweater."

I hear a sound that might be Zack rubbing his hands together like a cartoon supervillain.

"Don't breathe a word about this, though," he says, as if we had a chance. "I want it to be a surprise. I've got a call scheduled with Claudia in twenty minutes to discuss the terms of her surrender, and you two are going to be the main attraction. I bet she'll have Cali and Livvie and all your boyfriends watching. Isn't that sweet? None of them will know it's the last time they'll ever see you both alive."

With a final gloating laugh, Sommesnay knocks on the door. Someone on the outside opens it, and he disappears into the warm, breathable air, leaving me and Gabe alone with our fate.

If what Dru suspects is right and this Zack Lionel Sommesnay is going after Claudia August, this is the way to do it. Take away one of her husbands and the girl her son is in love with – the girl who's become a lynchpin of the Triumvirate's future – and sit back and enjoy her suffering.

My dad... and the boys... I can't bear to think of what this will do to them...

It's clever. It's evil.

And it's going to be Sommesnay's undoing.

This dickstain should kill us both on camera, right now, in front of Claudia. That *would* mess her up. Nothing is more important to Claudia than family, and I think now she considers me an extension of that family. I'm not going to suggest it, but if I was the criminal mastermind, that's what I'd do.

Leaving us alive gives them time. Not as much as Claudia will think we have, but three hours is three hours. My boys are coming for me, with the full weight of the Triumvirate behind them. They will rain down the fires of hell on anyone who hurts us.

Vic, Cas, and Torsten are looking for me right now. I know it. They have no intention of paying the ransom Sommesnay demands. I have to trust that they'll put the pieces together and figure out how to get us out of this freezer in time.

I can help with that, but I need to focus.

Zack let one very important piece of information slip during his supervillain speech. He asked me if I had the freezer's dimensions correct. He's asking this because he knows I've been in this freezer before, and that I checked its dimensions.

It's the freezer for the old Chinese takeout shop in the building he gave me – the one Claudia is going to convert for artifact storage. I know *exactly* where he's hiding us. All I need to do is figure out how to communicate that to my boys during the next call.

I'm going to assume that Sommesnay hasn't made it obvious

on the video that we're in a freezer. When they saw us on the last call, it probably looked like we were in a plain, dark room. Only Torsten and Claudia know about my secret building, and Claudia doesn't know that Zack's the guy who gave it to me. Torsten doesn't know that the building has a freezer. No one will guess where we are.

But Sommesnay said that he's calling Claudia back with instructions. When he does, Vic will ask for proof of life, and Sommesnay will pan the camera to me, the way he did before. I'll need to do something to give them a clue.

I clasp my hands together, trying to see if I can squeeze my wrists through the ropes, but they're too tight. Next, I roll my shoulders and shuffle my arms along the back of the chair, grateful to my old jiujitsu master for all that shoulder mobility conditioning. It takes a lot of effort, but I'm able to shuffle my hands from one edge of the chair to the other.

My fingers stretch out, and they scrape the wall behind me.

I touch ice.

A layer of ice has formed on the wall.

I rock the chair back and try to punch my finger into the ice to feel how thick it is. All I succeed in doing is bending my finger. Tears spring in my eyes because it fucking hurts. I run my finger over the small indent I've made in the ice, feeling the perfectly round little hole...

I have an idea.

I grit my teeth as I curl my fingers along my hip, shifting my body so that I can slip my hand into my pocket. I can just get the tips of two fingers inside, but I angle my hips so that the object slides out, and I catch it before it calls on the ground.

It's a coin. A tiny little obol Claudia August gave me the day she picked me up in her car and asked me to work for her.

Claudia said these coins were used to pay the ferryman. I've been carrying it around ever since, in case it brought me good luck. It hasn't worked so far.

I grip the coin between my fingers and press it into the ice, punching a small, hopefully round, hole.

Hopefully, my luck is about to change...

5

TORSTEN

My stomach knots as we enter the ballroom at the August house and I see it's full of people. Cali, Cas, and John sit on the couch. John holds his head in his hands. Livvie is bent over the drinks cart, pouring glasses for everyone. At the window, Claudia August paces. Noah tries to grab her arm, but she shoves him away and resumes her march across the rug. Spartacus jumps from Victor's arms and bats playfully at her ankles.

There's a guy I've never seen before leaning against the piano, and he's looking at Cas and smiling. His toothy grin seems weird for such a serious situation, but I know that people don't always smile when they're happy. Behind him is Gaius Dio, Cassius' brother. I thought he was in jail.

Cali lays her gun on the table in front of her and nods to Gaius and the stranger. They nod back. There's some sort of understanding between them that eludes me. I don't know what's going on there but I don't care. Not when Fergie is in danger.

At the thought of her trapped and afraid, somewhere where I cannot reach her, my stomach contracts. The room spins.

We have to find her. We *have* to.

Vic nudges me forward and points at his phone on the table. "Zack Lionel Sommesnay is going to call us back on that phone in exactly twenty minutes for our answer. Well, more like seventeen minutes now. It will be a video call because he knows we'll expect proof of life. Can you set it to record the call and put the video on the TV? We want to be able to see the room in as much detail as possible, in case there's any clue as to where he's holding them."

My breath rushes out in a hiss of relief. Victor has given me something to do, a way I can help. I kneel down and start tapping away on the phone. I locate the correct cable and set up the feed. As I finish the sync to the TV, I become aware of the conversation around me. No one else has a task to do. Everyone is yelling and talking over each other.

"How did this happen?" Livvie snaps at Cali. "I thought you increased security at that gym of yours. I thought the boys were watching her every minute."

"I did increase security, but Sommesnay has someone on the inside," Cali says. "They knew our schedule for the day and waited until Cas left Fergie alone at the gym before taking out my guards."

"Then you should have a better screening process for your security!" Livvie yells. "We all trust you to keep our heads on our shoulders, and you've gone and got two of our own kidnapped—"

"The information about our meeting place came from *your* schedule," Cali shoots back. "The only people who could have known it were your family and household staff. The leak is on the Lucian side."

Livvie's face scrunches up.

"So whoever did this is working across the different families," Victor says, voicing the thought I'd just had myself.

"We think so," Cali says. "We've suspected that he was targeting Claudia specifically, but if he has people amongst my soldiers and Livvie's household..."

They fall silent.

"This is why you need me," Gaius pops his head up. "This whole situation is a shambles. Let me sort it out for you. Ares and I met kidnappers in jail. We know how they think. We can—"

"No," Cali says. "We're the Triumvirate and we will deal with this. Give me five minutes with Livvie's staff and I'll put down the leak. We can clear house and regain control. We're not giving into stupid demands from upstart little crows."

I open my mouth to point out that Zack Lionel Sommesnay isn't a crow, but Victor squeezes my knee to silence me.

"I agree that we need another purge, but this guy is clearly unhinged," Livvie says. "And I say this knowing I'm standing in a room filled with sociopaths. If we refuse, he'll make good on his threat, and those two are toast. I know none of us want that."

"Must you be so crass?" Cali shouts.

"Always, darling. It's the only way to get your attention. I'm simply suggesting that waving our proverbial dicks around isn't the way to get Fergie and Gabriel back alive. We tell this Sommesnay that we accept his demands – congratulations, he's the head of August, order a cake, blah blah blah. We pretend to make the arrangements, and then when he shows up to accept the crown, we take him out as a united front."

"That would rely on us being a united front," Cali shoots back. "You're the one who's been trying to force Torsten and Fergie to marry as a way to crowd out Claudia—"

"Don't sound so righteous. I'm simply looking out for my family's best interests," Livvie says. "Exactly as Cali Dio would do. *You're* the one who's been playing Fergie's fame for your own interests, and all the while Claudia is trying to poach your step-daughter for her own—"

"Enough."

They all turn toward Claudia. Her face has gone all red. "This is what he wants," she says. "This is what all his crusade against me is about. Sommesnay wants the Triumvirate weak. He wants us fighting and backstabbing each other. That's why he blew up the museum. He knew it would destabilize every-thing we've worked so hard to build. That's why he shot Cali – he knows that her entire family's fortune rests on her immortal, bloodthirsty reputation. And that's why he sent that bomb to Victor. He doesn't want me dead. If he wanted me dead, he'd have shot me months ago. He wants me to fall and bring the entire Triumvirate crumbling down around me. I'm not going to let that happen."

She turns to Cali and Livvie. "We've done exactly what we swore we'd never do – we each let our individual desires and personal issues trump the common good. That stops now – either we're in this together, or we're out for ourselves. It's your choice, and I won't hold that choice against you. If you choose to stick with me, to back the empire we've built, then we'll face Sommesnay together. But that means choosing to put the insanity of the last year aside. We go back to being the three musketeers – all for one and all that shit. If you can't do that, then you can leave now and bet on swooping in to pick the bones of the August empire after Sommesnay ruins it."

"You're going to give it up?" Livvie's eyes grow wide.

"What choice do I have?"

"He's got to give you time. We find them before the time is up and then—"

"How are we going to find them? Did you see the wall behind them in the last video? It looked like it was made of metal. They're on a truck and probably halfway to Mexico by now. We have to face reality. Sommesnay has been planning this for a long time, and he's not going to like us messing with his plan. If we go after them, he'll kill them both."

No. No no no. I don't like what Claudia is saying. I don't give a shit about the Triumvirate, but Fergie… we have to save Fergie…

Vic looks like he's going to throw up. "We can't give Sommesnay what he wants. He's unhinged, and I say that as a friend of the most unhinged guy in this room. Who knows what he'll use the August empire for? I want Fergie and Dad back as much as anyone, but we have to consider the big picture."

"We don't," I say. No one listens to me.

"We have no guarantee that if you hand over August, he'll actually let them go," Victor points out. This is true. Sommesnay seems like the kind of person who lies.

"We're wasting time." Claudia stands. She brushes her hands over her thighs. "He's calling back any minute for my answer."

The phone rings. It's exactly seventeen minutes, and I appreciate Sommesnay's punctuality. Claudia hits the button, and the TV screen fills with an image. It's Zack Lionel Sommesnay, and he's standing in the room where he's holding Fergie. I assume it's the same room that Claudia saw, but the walls aren't metal as she said. They're more… white. Sommesnay leans his hand on the back of a chair.

Slumped in that chair is Fergie.

She's bound to the chair. Her head hangs limply, her red hair curtaining her face. The tips of it are spiky and matted together in clumps, and her clothes are bloody and torn. I can't see her face from this angle, and it's all my heart craves. Just to see her blink or her cute nose twitch…

She's pale, so pale that for a moment I believe she's dead already and my heart caves in, but then she lifts her head a little. Her eyes reach through the TV screen and punch me in the gut, demanding I pay attention. I know Fergie can't see me, that she has no idea I'm on the other side of the TV, but something in her expression commands me to *notice*.

So I notice.

"Hello, Victor," Sommesnay says. "I see that you're no longer alone."

"Leave my son alone," Claudia speaks up. Her voice is cold. It doesn't tremble. "I'm who you really want to speak to."

I notice the tips of Fergie's hair – they're not actually matted but *frozen*. I notice her pale skin and the rigid way she's sitting.

"Hello, Claudia." He smiles at her, but from the way Victor shifts beside me, I'm guessing it's not a friendly smile. "I know you don't know who I am, but I know you."

I notice the thick red coat Sommesnay wears, and how his hands are in his pockets.

"I'd remember your face if I met you before," Claudia says.

I notice Fergie's eyes flicker – they stare out at me, then dart to the left, then stare out again.

"Yes, I daresay that you would."

I notice the wall behind Fergie, white with ice like the inside of a freezer. Even though Fergie can't see, because she's light-sensitive, her eyes often follow movement or light sources. But they don't randomly flicker around. I glance to the right, but there's no light in that direction. The shadows in the room indicate a light source from above.

"Torsten. It's nice to see the Little Artist again." Sommesnay uses that nickname the press gave me as a child. He says it with a smile, but it doesn't feel friendly. I think he is mocking me.

"It's not nice," I say. "Let Fergie go."

Sommesnay chuckles. My mother whirls around. "You met him?"

Zack Lionel Sommesnay holds his belly as he laughs. Beside him, Fergie's eyes draw me in. She blinks, and I notice that tiny icicles cling to her eyelashes. Her pupils shift, looking down and to the right, and then back again. Down and right, and back, again and again.

"Oh, dear. I hope I haven't caused trouble," Zack gasps through his laughter. "Why, if the good people of the world's criminal underground knew that the three mighty families of the Triumvirate were on the outs, I don't know what they would do."

I wish he'd stop talking. I need to concentrate. Sommesnay gives a meeting place for the final handover in twenty-four hours and hangs up. I replay the video. Fergie keeps rolling her eyes to the left, again and again and again.

I lean forward, and then I notice it. The wall behind Fergie isn't smooth like the rest of the walls – it's covered in little pockmarks. It takes me a few moments to realize that the walls are white because they're iced over. That explains why Fergie looks wrong. She's cold.

Fergie's eyes flicker left, left, left. I squint at those pockmarks. And suddenly, I *see*.

It's Braille.

I don't know how she's done it, since she's still tied to the chair, but she's made a message in Braille on the wall. Instead of raised dots, she's punched little holes in the ice. If she'd written words, Sommesnay might've noticed it, but this just looks like chipping ice... unless your girlfriend is blind and she taught you how to read Braille.

"I know where Fergie is," I say.

No one listens to me. They never do. They keep on arguing.

"I know where Fergie is," I yell.

This time they fall silent. One by one, everyone in the room turns to look at me.

"Why didn't you say?" Claudia demands.

"I did."

"Where are they?"

I rattle off the address in Fergie's message. Claudia pales. "That's... that's the storage facility we're using for the artifacts. Why would he bring her there when it's crawling with my guys? Fergie found that building for me. It has an old industrial freezer on the first floor, which we were kitting out to use for storing the scrolls. She's right here in Emerald Beach!"

"Torsten, you're amazing." Vic slams into me, hugging me so tight that Spartacus has to wriggle out from between us to avoid being squashed.

"Fergie's the one who's amazing," I say. "She wrote a message in Braille on the wall. But we need to hurry. If she's in a freezer and the ice is already that thick on the walls... how large is the freezer?" I blurt out. I wouldn't normally speak to Claudia, much less ask her such a direct question, but Fergie's in trouble.

"About twenty by ten feet. Fergie measured it for the artifact storage—"

I do a little calculation on the back of a music magazine. "Fergie and Gabriel have a couple of hours at most left before they die of carbon dioxide poisoning, more if Zack goes into the freezer again and introduced fresh air."

"But he said we have twenty-four hours." Vic's face pales. "How do you know that?"

I shrug. "It's not important. We need to go and get Fergie."

"We shouldn't rush in," Gaius adds.

"If Torsten says it's true, then we believe him." Cas grabs the magazine from my hands and waves it above his head. "We need to get over there."

"You can't just drive up to the door and demand her back," Gaius scoffs. "We need a plan."

"Fine. You plan." Cas tosses the magazine at Gaius. "We're going to get our girl."

Cas runs for the door, and since his hand's still clamped

around my wrist, I'm dragged along with him. We pile into Vic's car and tear away from the house. We don't even stick around to wait for Cas' brother.

Victor drives faster than the allowed speed limit in a residential area. Cas tosses a handgun over the backseat. "Don't shoot your foot off," he tells me.

"Why would I shoot at my foot?" I check the magazine is loaded and rest the gun on my knee, safety off. My brain might work differently, but I'm the stolen child of a crime queen – I know how to shoot.

"Did you know Sommesnay gave her this building?" Vic asks me.

"No. I know he gave her *a* building, but I didn't know what she was using it for or that it had a freezer in it."

"Why did he give her a building?" Vic pounds the wheel with his fist. "Damnit."

"Because he wanted her to—"

"That doesn't need an answer," Cas says. "It's okay, Torsten. We're going to find her."

Cas and Victor exchange one of their looks that I can't decipher.

"This isn't a coincidence," Vic says through gritted teeth. "Your brother—"

"We're not talking about Gaius now. We're getting our Queen back. Torsten, find me a floor plan of that building. We need—" Cas' phone rings. It's the ringtone he uses for his mother. They talk in low voices, their training kicking in as they plan the best way to approach the building.

I scour the city planning online archives and locate a floor plan, showing the different floors of the building and the freezer on the ground floor, at the back of the commercial kitchen. I hand my phone to Cas and slump back in my seat.

I don't know what I'm supposed to do now, so I stare at the

gun in my hands. I've practiced on a range hundreds of times, but I've never killed a person before.

I stroke the barrel.

I'll do whatever I need to do to keep Fergie safe.

We park a couple of blocks away from the building. Cas pulls a bunch of knives from the trunk and hides them in various places on his body, then he tucks a second gun into the pocket of his leather jacket. "Here's what's going to happen – I'll go in through the front. I'll provide a distraction and draw Sommesnay's men outside. Meanwhile, you get in the back and get Fergie and Gabriel out. The alley behind the kitchen has an entrance. There will be guards, but hopefully I'll be able to force Sommesnay to pull his troops to the front. You shouldn't encounter more than two or three."

I flick my gaze from Cas to Vic, confused by this new situation. Cas is the one barking orders and Vic is the one who is jittery and erratic.

"We'll take care of them." Victor pulls one of Cas' hoodies out of the trunk and pulls it over his head. "I don't want them to recognize us until we're right on top of them," he says, tossing me another hoodie, which I pull on. It's too big for me and hangs almost to my knees.

Cas jogs off in an easterly direction, and we get back in the car and loop around the block to get as close to the rear of the building as we can. The minutes pass in agony. A clock ticks down in my head – every second Fergie has left to live flitters away.

I jump as gunshots bark through the street. Cas has created his distraction. Pedestrians scatter and shopkeepers slam the doors on their shops. In this neighborhood, gunshots are a regular part of the soundscape. They know to get out of the street when the Triumvirate needs to settle a score.

Using the chaos around us to hide, we pull into an empty

parking space and crawl out of the car. Victor uses his hands to indicate that I should cover him while he makes a run for the kitchen door. This makes logical sense because he's the better runner, and I'm a better shooter. Around the front of the building, we hear Cas engaging in a firefight, and I see a man leave the rear of the building to circle around the street to try and get behind them. One less guy we have to kill.

I kneel down behind the wheel well of Cas' car. Victor moves down the street, creeping behind cars as he approaches the rear entrance – a thick wooden door with a faded sign above advertising Chinese takeout. Vic's going to have to cross the street soon.

A single guard stands inside the kitchen, his head visible through the window. Any moment now, he'll see Vic.

I steady the gun against the wheel well of the car and take my shot just as Vic makes a run for the entrance. The gun kicks in my hand. Glass shatters and blood paints the wall behind the guy as he drops to the ground.

I smile. I may not understand team sports, but I've always been good at shooting. It's precise, with simple rules. Hold the gun like this. Hit the target.

That guy hurt Fergie. I don't mind killing him.

Vic flattens himself against the wall, gun raised. He scans the area. A moment later, he sticks his arm out and makes a motion that we've agreed means I follow him. I race across the street, nervous that another guard might be hidden nearby, but no one takes a shot at me. I flatten myself beside him as we crouch beneath the broken window.

Vic whistles his approval. "That was a beautiful shot, Torsten. If you ever decide to give up art, Cali has a sniper job with your name on it."

"I don't need a job right now," I say. "My allowance is sufficient—"

Vic laughs. "Sure, Torsten. Come on."

We listen hard for signs of anyone else inside the kitchen. There's nothing, but if the dead guard has a friend, then he's probably hiding and listening, too. I crouch lower while Victor moves inside. His head remains on his shoulders so I assume everything is fine.

I follow behind Vic, careful to step around the dead guard so I don't get any bits of him on me. Vic runs through the puddle of blood and tracks crimson bootprints across the kitchen as he shoves past a dusty stove and sink filled with spiderwebs. "Where is it?" he growls.

I glance all around and...

There it is. The steel door to an industrial freezer. There's a keypad beside it that looks like it's been installed recently – Zack Lionel Sommesnay must've hacked into the security system Fergie was installing for the museum artifacts. Either that, or one of Claudia's soldiers gave him the code.

My heart leaps. The clock in my head tells me that we have fourteen minutes and twenty-two seconds before Fergie and Gabriel run out of oxygen. I dig my tools out of my pocket.

"I'll stand guard," Vic says, nudging me toward the panel. "You do your thing."

"Of course I will. You don't know how to crack a code."

Vic moves back through the kitchen. I can hear more shooting out the front of the building, but that's not important. I kneel down and study the lock – it's a pretty standard piece of kit. I've cracked hundreds of them. I connect my phone, run the program I wrote, and within seconds I hear a click as the door unlocks. Vic comes running over and kicks it in.

I duck inside after him and skid to a stop as I take in the sight before me.

Fergie stands with her arms folded over the body of another guard. A circle of red extends from the body, fast turning to crimson ice in the cold temperature. An arc of bloody ice fans across the wall behind her.

"T-t-took you long enough," she manages to get out through chattering teeth. "That guard came in to check on us, and I took him out, but the door had already swung shut behind him."

My body surges with happiness.

Fergie is alive.

Victor slams into her, holding her upright just as she collapses into his arms. She reaches her hand under Vic's forearm and grips my fingers. She doesn't let go.

Fergie's alive. We got here in time.

Fergie's alive.

I'm aware that I'm shaking. And not because of the cold.

I never knew it was possible to feel this way about another person, that if you lost them, you'd be lost yourself, that all you want to do is wrap them in bubble wrap so that nothing can ever hurt them again. I'm frozen in place – not by the temperature, but by the sight of her, powerful and defiant and so very, very alive.

"I'm okay," she whispers. "They didn't hurt me. But Gabriel's passed out."

He's slumped in his chair, his head resting on his shoulder. He looks like he's asleep.

Vic pushes Fergie into my arms. "Can you get her to the car?" he asks.

I nod, raising my gun.

"Thank you, friend." He bends over his dad and slaps his cheeks. I don't like the sound of it – Vic's skin slapping Gabriel's frozen cheek – but I think he's doing it to try and wake Gabriel up, and I suppose that's an acceptable reason to slap your father.

Fergie sinks into my arms. The sensation of her is so overwhelming that I stagger backward. But I don't let her go. Even if it hurts, I won't ever let her go again.

"I'm going to have to carry Gabriel, so I might not be able to shoot," Vic says.

"That would not be wise," I agree. "You might hurt yourself."

Vic laughs as he flings Gabriel's arm over his shoulder. "Yes, I might hurt myself. Go, you fool. I'll be right behind you. Go!"

Fergie loops her arm over my shoulders, and I help her out of the freezer. She's a little wobbly, but she can walk. I take her back through the kitchen, around the dead guard and the puddle – I know she'd hate to get blood on her favorite boots – and out into the street.

We get two steps toward Vic's car before someone starts shooting. I shove Fergie to the ground, dragging us both behind the wheel well of a large SUV. Fergie gasps and presses her body against me. She's so cold to touch. Almost as if she is a corpse.

But she's not a corpse. Because we got to her with eleven minutes and thirty-eight seconds to spare.

I raise the gun. I try to pull my arm from Fergie's grip so I can steady the gun, but she squeezes me harder.

"Please," she whimpers, her voice hoarse. "Don't leave me."

"I'll never leave you," I say.

It's awkward to twist in this position and get a good shot, but I won't let go of Fergie. The guy shooting at us is behind a blue Nissan on the other end of the street. We'd have to get past him to get to the car. He has planned it this way, set himself up in a good position to prevent our escape. But he's spraying bullets around in the way people do when they don't know how to shoot. I will wait here forever to get in a good shot, but he won't. He moves around. He twists to try and see what we're doing. He sticks his head out an inch too far.

I take my shot.

The man cries out as the bullet goes through his shoulder. He's not dead, but he's in a lot of pain. And he won't be able to aim properly unless he's ambidextrous (which is possible, as approximately one percent of the population are ambidextrous, but unlikely enough that I think we can take a chance).

I pull Fergie to her feet. "We're running," I say.

"Don't let go of me, Torsten."

Fergie's whole body tenses. I think she must be afraid to run blindly through a hail of bullets, not knowing what's in front of her. I am afraid, too. I am afraid that the injured man will get lucky, and she might get hit and I'll lose her.

But even if she's afraid, she runs. Her legs pump alongside mine as we charge across the road. I hold her close. I don't let her crash into anything.

We make it to the car. I yank open the door and shove Fergie into the backseat. "Lie down," I say, but I don't have to tell her because she's already crawling into the footwell. "Be as small as possible."

I climb into the front. A bullet hits the windshield, cracking the bulletproof glass. Bulletproof glass isn't actually bullet-proof. If you hit it a few times in the same spot, it will crack. But this glass just stopped my head from exploding, and I'm grateful.

I shuffle low behind the wheel and wind down my window. I watch the kitchen door, but Vic hasn't come out yet. A figure sprints around the corner of the building, heading straight for us. I aim my gun, but I don't pull the trigger because it's Cas. He's followed shortly afterward by his brother, Gaius. I was so concerned about Fergie that it didn't occur to me back at Claudia's house to ask why Gaius is here.

It occurs to me now.

Gaius is supposed to be in jail.

Before Vic took over, Gaius was the person you went to at Stonehurst Prep if you wanted to make things turn out a certain way. Maybe it's good that he's here, because we want this situation to turn out a certain way – Fergie and Gabriel and everyone else alive, Zack Lionel Sommesnay bleeding out in a puddle of blood.

The gunman rolls over, turning toward Cas. He lets off a couple of poorly-aimed shots – his shoulder must be giving him a lot of trouble. Either that, or he's a terrible ambidextrous marksman. Possibly both.

Vic chooses that moment to run from the building. He has his dad in his arms. Cas yells at him, beckoning him to follow him. Instead of running at us, Vic ducks into the alley with Cas.

The gunman points his weapon at Cas, but when he pulls the trigger, it's out of bullets. That's why you should never take a shot unless you're certain you'll hit your target. Cas yanks the weapon from his hand and tosses it away, then grabs the guy's head between his beefy hands and twists.

The snap of a neck breaking echoes in the empty street.

Cas drops the guy in a heap at his feet. He signals to the others, and they fan out to sweep the street and the surrounding buildings, making sure they've got rid of all Sommesnay's people. When he gets the signal that everything is clear, Cas jogs over to me.

"What are you doing in here?" he yells, leaning in the window. He glances over my shoulder and his whole face lights up. "Hello, Sunflower."

"Hello, Cas," her voice rasps.

"Victor said to wait in the car," I tell him. "I should get out of your seat so you can drive—"

"Torsten, they shot out the tires. The car can't go anywhere." Cas is smiling as he pulls open the door. I think that means he's not annoyed with me. "You did an amazing job in there. You got our Queen out. Come on, we'll go around the front and Gaius will drive us back. Everyone's arrived now that the fun is over. We have a lot of cleanup to do."

6

FERGIE

Seymour breaks every road rule in the book to get me and Gabriel to Galen's clinic in record time. The nurse checks me over. Apart from a few bumps and scratches and the burning in my throat, I'm fine. They give me some oxygen and pain medicine and tell me to take it easy.

It's Gabriel they're worried about. I strain my ears to listen in to the hushed conversations between Galen and his team as they rush around the clinic. They're worried about oxygen starvation in his brain and damage to the tissue in his throat.

Will Vic's dad be okay?

Will he be able to sing again?

It's not long before my corner of the clinic is crowded with people. Milo drove Dad here, and he won't stop hugging me and kissing my forehead the way he's always done when I got upset or had a nightmare as a kid. Torsten and Vic show up minutes later with Eli. Torsten holds my hand and squeezes my fingers again and again, constantly checking I'm okay. I am okay, thanks to him.

"I knew you'd figure out the Braille," I whisper to him. "Thank you."

"Thank you for teaching me," he whispers back. "Thank you for still being alive."

He drops my hand, and I'm swept into Vic's arms. His body trembles as he holds me tight, crushing our bodies together. He tips my head back and kisses me deeply, desperately, sucking all the oxygen from my lungs.

"I thought..." he breathes through his kiss.

"I know." I pull back and lay my head on his chest, listening to his heart pound against his ribs. "I'm so sorry to put you through that again."

His chest heaves. "You're not the one who has to be sorry."

My heart breaks for him. Being trapped in that freezer sucked, but I know it must've been a hundred times worse for Vic, not knowing where I was, remembering how helpless he felt when his sister was taken.

"You weren't helpless this time," I tell him. "You found us. You saved us both."

"Torsten figured out the code," Vic says. The words are difficult for him to get out. "My mother gave you that coin. Cas and Cali created the distraction. They came up with the whole plan. I... I fell to pieces..."

"You were the first one to burst through that freezer door." I breathe in his dark chocolate, hazelnut, and whisky scent – a scent that always makes me feel like I've come home. "As soon as I heard your voice, I knew everything would be okay."

Victor squeezes me even tighter. "I feel like everything's falling apart. Just when we thought we had everything under control..."

"That's exactly what Sommesnay wants. He knows about Juliet's kidnapping." I remember him telling me during his arch-villain speech. "He designed the kidnapping specifically to torture your mother."

"I don't know *how* he knows," Vic shudders. "We kept it quiet

– we didn't want to risk sparking a rebellion within our ranks. Only a handful of our most trusted people know about the kidnapping, although I suppose it's possible that someone *betrayed* us and told Sommesnay."

He bites out the word *betrayed*, choking on his scorn. Loyalty is more of a Cas thing – Victor, I know, would betray someone he loved if he thought it was the right thing to do – but this is too personal for him. He approaches this with one foot in the past. He still remembers being that helpless boy hoping his twin sister comes home alive.

But he's not helpless anymore.

Vic buries his face in my hair. Someone lays a hand on his shoulder, and I sense Vic's dad, Eli, drawing us both into an embrace. I relax against the man – like Vic, he gives excellent hugs.

"Claudia is with Cali – they're dealing with the August men who were working for Sommesnay," Eli says. "But she wants me to tell you how sorry she is that you got messed up in this—"

"It's fine," I croak out. "I chose to throw my lot in with you guys. I knew the risks."

"It's not fine," Eli's voice cracks, and I know he's thinking about his old friend breathing through a machine in the bed next to mine. "We didn't see this coming, and we should have. Sommesnay had so many people on the inside... including Torsten's sister, Trudi."

"*What?*" Vic cries.

That makes sense, actually. It explains how Sommesnay knew so much about Torsten's... unique heritage. I think he'd been teasing us all along, dangling the story of the Little Artist over our heads and delighting as we grasped for its meaning.

"According to our sources, she's been feeding Sommesnay information for months." Eli's voice is grave. "This is a huge blow. Three of Cali's top assassins were also working for him.

One of them is responsible for Cali's injury. He cracked and told us that his assignment was only to hurt her, not to kill her. Sommesnay refuses to let them go after the Imperators or our families. Apparently, he wants that honor all to himself."

Shit.

Cali was shot by one of her own assassins?

I think back to that room in the gym where she was training the neighborhood kids to fight, and the fierce dedication she brought to her work and her training. She may have the smallest arm of the Triumvirate, but her people are the most fiercely loyal.

How could they turn on her?

And Livvie's own daughter was working for Sommesnay? I met Trudi. I liked her. Torsten told me she was at the meeting he went to at Tombs where Livvie first proposed that he and I marry. She must've been the one who told Sommesnay about Juliet's kidnapping and made him see that I was important to all the families.

Cold creeps into my chest as I realize that we can no longer trust anyone. Except for the people in this room.

"What's happened to these traitors?" I ask. No one else has asked. Maybe it's rude to speak about it, but I'm still new at this whole organized crime thing. I need details.

"Cali's taking care of them," Eli says, his voice sharp. I know he's worried about how Torsten might react to the news about his sister. "She'll be busy with them for a while. She and Claudia and Livvie need to bleed them for as much information as they can, as many names as it will take to purge the Triumvirate of this sickness. We need to know how deep this conspiracy goes and why some of our most loyal people were ready to betray us to Sommesnay."

I have a few ideas, but I keep them to myself for now. My head hurts too much to be thinking about Triumvirate business at the moment. I lie back on my pillows and listen to Torsten's pen scraping over a page in his sketchbook. Livvie had thoughtfully reunited him with it. He doesn't waver as he sketches. It's as if he hasn't heard about his sister's betrayal, but I know he has. Torsten may not say much, but he's always listening.

He didn't like Trudi. She called him a freak and treated him like an annoyance. But like his mother, he longed for Trudi's approval and love, and to know that she went out of her way to hurt me would cut him up inside. He'll grieve when he's ready and in his own Torsten-y way, and I'll be here for him when he needs me.

I lie in bed, my hands wrapped around endless warm mugs of Milo's chili hot chocolate, while Torsten holds my hand or draws in his sketchbook. Vic paces between my bed and Gabriel's and occasionally talks on the phone, getting updates as his mother watches Cali at work on the traitors. Cas is with them, doing the work he's born to do, being the monster who keeps death away, but I worry—

"Where is she? Where's my Sunflower?"

Cas' voice breaks me out of my slumber. His heavy boots clang on the tiles as he rushes to my side.

"I brought you a friend," he says, dumping something small on my lap.

"Mew?" Spartacus demands to know where I disappeared to.

"Hey, boy. I'm okay. Your uncle Cas helped to save me." I wrap my arms around my kitty and hold him tight, hoping like hell Galen won't hear his plaintive cries for dinner and kick him out of the clinic.

"I brought flowers, too." Cas thrusts an enormous bouquet into my arms. "Sunflowers, because obviously, and these ones are a rose called 'Madame Isaac Pereire,' and they're bright red and smell like raspberries."

I bury my nose in the flowers. They do smell heavenly, but

there's only one scent for me. I toss them aside and pull Cas close, wrapping my arms around him and breathing in his unique perfume – plum and musk and carnations, dark and dangerous and born of hell itself. I don't smell blood on him. I am disappointed.

Cas must know exactly what I'm doing because he pulls back and chuckles. "Ah, my little monster. You're as hungry for vengeance as I am. I had to shower before I came here because I was drenched in the blood of those traitors."

I can't help the smile that spreads across my face as I stroke Spartacus. "Good. And Sommesnay?"

He pauses. "We swept the entire area, and we picked up several soldiers from all three families who've been working for the kraut-sucking bastard, but Sommesnay himself was long gone."

"No!"

"Don't make that face at me, my bloodthirsty little minx. You'll get to hammer those nails through his wrists soon enough. We still have a few cards left to play."

"Such as?"

"I've sent a team to collect her," Cas growls. "I'll make her tell us everything she knows."

"Her? Who do you mean by 'her'?"

"I mean, the one person who might know where the fuck Sommesnay is hiding."

7

FERGIE

I beg Galen to release me, and a few hours later he relents. Vic stays at the clinic with Gabriel, who is awake but still struggling to speak, and Cas drives me and Torsten and Spartacus back to his house in Cali's car, since Vic's is shot to hell.

Torsten disappears upstairs as soon as we get home. I know that he needs time on his own to decompress and deal with everything that went down today. I put down the kitty and move toward the kitchen, my stomach rumbling. But Cas' arm snakes around my waist and yanks me to him.

His lips brush my ear, and a delicious shiver rolls down my spine. "I have work to do, Sunflower. She's in the basement. Do you want to wait up here?"

"Fuck no."

"Good girl." Cas says those magic words that make my pussy flare with heat. He's already hard, his cock lengthening against my ass. Nothing like the promise of blood to make my step-brother wild.

In one motion, he spins me around and captures my mouth with his. The world recedes and it's just the two of us, violence pulsing in our veins as the rush of today's fight drives us together.

My nails dig into his biceps as his tongue slides against mine. I thrust one hand beneath his shirt, running my fingers over the death lily scarification on his heart, feeling the ridges of his devotion to me.

I tip my head up to meet him, demanding that he own me in every way...

With a groan, Cas pulls back, but his hand cups my throat, his fingers trembling as they press into my skin. "Torsten says you killed a guard."

"Yeah. I realized that bending my wrist around to make the Braille message gave me enough space to slip a hand through. I got myself free and untied Gabriel, but the door was locked on the outside, so I had to wait until someone came back to check on us. Luckily for me, someone did. As soon as I heard the door click, I jumped on the guy. Under normal circumstances, I'd never have got the drop on him, but the dickweasel didn't expect me. I got the rope around his neck and then it was all over for him."

"You are so fucking hot," he growls, pushing me against the wall. His teeth nip at my bottom lip. I'm still wearing a hospital gown from Galen's clinic, and he slides his hand up inside it, cupping my ass to angle my hips closer to him.

"What about the prisoner—"

"They'll keep." He pulls my panties to the side and shoves two fingers inside me.

I gasp as my eyes roll in my head. After the adrenaline rush of our rescue, and the heady anticipation of the grisly work waiting for us in the basement, I'm so fucking wet and wanting for him.

My stepbrother finger fucks me into oblivion. The orgasm starts to hum in my toes, but as it climbs through me, he removes his fingers.

"The fuck?" I growl, trying to grab him and pull him back.

"Patience, little Sunflower," he says with a smirk as he drags me upstairs.

We pass the hallway with our bedrooms – I wonder if my bedroom still belongs to me, now that Gaius is back. It's the place where we first fucked, when Cas tricked me into believing he was Cali's pool boy. It seems like so long ago now and yet... I'm soaked and trembling just remembering the way he came inside me that day, how his cock and his cruelty had opened something inside me, made me feel again.

Now, I feel *everything*.

And I want more.

I try to drag Cas toward my room, but he has other ideas.

"Nice try, sis, but you're coming with me."

I let him drag me down the next corridor to a set of familiar carved doors. Cas punches in the code and they open for him, and he pulls me inside the secret library. Another room that hums with memories – the day I sat on the couch and became a client of Poison Ivy, the night Cas, Torsten, and Vic placed me in that swing and changed my life forever.

I used to think of my life as a great fissure that formed New Fergie from the ashes of her predecessor. I thought The Incident was what broke Old Fergie so I could be made anew, but I know now that it was the three of them that finally cracked open the coal surrounding my heart and showed me what it meant to *live*.

Before Poison Ivy, I lived for tests and competitions and gathering accomplishments around me like a Viking hoarding his gold. But the three of them got under my skin, and now I see that those things were just my way of distracting myself and hiding from who I truly am.

Since I signed my name in their ledger, I've been tortured and fucked and kidnapped and used as a pawn. I've broken the law a hundred times over. I've fought in the ring and meted out my own brand of justice to those who've wronged me. I dyed my stepbrother bright blue and destroyed a priceless whisky collection. I've *bathed* in the blood I spilled.

Never, ever, has life sung in my veins the way it does now.

And it all began in this room, with this unhinged monster who understands me like no one else. Who saw the real me hidden beneath all the bullshit and wasn't afraid to get his hands dirty to drag her into the light.

Like recognizes like, and right now my Cassius pulls me inside, and I remember just as the doors slam shut behind me that Cas' brother had this room stocked with all kinds of dirty little secrets. I have a suspicion Cas is about to show me one now.

He kicks aside books and other debris as he moves me around the chairs and toward the back of the room. My thighs hit the edge of something hard – a desk. I thought Euri and I had broken all the furniture in here, but apparently we hadn't made a dent in this antique.

"I know smart chicks like you always have a thing about doing it in libraries."

There's a crash as Cas sweeps something off the desk and it smashes on the floor. I don't even care as his large hand splays across my back, pushing me down until I lay over the surface. My arms flop over the edge of the desk. My heart hammers in my chest.

I hear something metallic crunch and know that a secret compartment is opening somewhere below me. Cas keeps that hand firmly on my back while he leans down and slips my wrists into cuffs attached to the corners of the desk.

Oooh, secret handcuffs.

The metal is cold against my skin as he clips the cuffs shut. I tug on them, noticing how heavy and secure they are. These aren't some fluffy sex shop starter pack – these are the real deal. I'd expect nothing less from my depraved stepbrother.

Only once I'm secured does Cas lift his hand from my back. He kneels behind me and secures my ankles into two other cuffs. I'm immobile, splayed across this ancient desk with my arms and legs over the edge. I couldn't move even if I wanted to.

Cas takes great delight in tearing away my hospital gown. I'm naked and shivering, but not from the cold. My ass is in the air, my pussy aching with need of him.

Cas' hips shove between my thighs, stretching me even wider across the desk. A delicious ache shoots down my legs. He grabs my hips and yanks me closer. The cuffs bite as my arms stretch.

Playing this game with him is like being back in the arena. I'm completely in the moment, my mind blissfully blank as I return to the most base instincts.

I don't have to see my stepbrother to feel him above me, looking down at me completely at his mercy and fantasizing about what he's going to do to me.

I understand that for Cas, these moments of domination during sex are the way he controls his monster. He might have terrified other girls, but I'm not like other girls. I'm his mirror, and I know that without the rules of his little games, he might not be able to tell where the sex stops and the violence begins.

And the rule is that I'm at his mercy, and he gets to decide whether I've been good or very, very bad.

Cas' hand trails up my thigh, and I quiver with anticipation. "You spent all those months trying to resist me," he purrs. "Trying to put me in my place. And all this time, you were a little psycho yourself. My good girl, Harvard-bound stepsister loves the sound of a neck snapping and the feeling of fresh blood trickling through her fingers."

And even though back in the freezer killing that guy was

scary as fuck, I am so fucking wet that I find myself agreeing with him. I did love it. I loved the surge of adrenaline in my veins as he collapsed in my hands. I loved reaching the very edge of what my training allowed me to do, and pushing over the edge, into the darkness.

I buzz between my legs, so ready for him to take me. But he's going to tease me because it's all part of the game. He's the cat playing with his prize. He plunges a finger inside me, pumping it slowly as he groans.

"Tell me all about it. I love it when you talk blood and sunshine."

I rock back what little I can against the restraints. "I killed someone today, Cas. I garroted that man with the rope he used to restrain me because he stood in the way of me getting back to you. He jerked and gasped and then he just... stopped. And I wished you were there to have seen it – you'd be so proud of me. I *need* you to tell me exactly how proud you are of me."

Cas' other hand comes down on my ass. The bite of his slap is so familiar and so needed that I'm afraid I might orgasm just from that. He curls his finger inside me, rubbing that rough spot on my walls that sends me into the stratosphere.

"You're amazing," he breathes, timing his words with each thrust of his fingers. The pad of his thumb finds my clit and rubs it in time with his strokes. "You're a miracle. You're the girl of my dreams. Next time, we'll kill one together. We'll cut them up and smear ourselves in their blood and fuck until their life is gone, the way we did with your lowlife ex. You're the only woman for me, my heart, my Queen, and I will lay the corpse of every person who wronged you at your feet in supplication—what are you doing here?"

He keeps stroking me, but he moves, his attention focused on someone else in the room. I tense. I was so out of it because of Cas' magical fingers that I hadn't even heard the heavy doors swing open.

"I was in Fergie's room and I saw you walk past the hallway," Torsten says. He's standing near the doors, and he doesn't acknowledge what he can see us doing. "Can I watch?"

"It's up to Fergie," Cas says. I can tell from the hard slap of his hand on my ass that he relishes an audience.

"Yes," I moan as Cas' fingers pound me harder.

I'm going to be sore tomorrow.

But I'm going to be in blissful heaven tonight.

Torsten's footsteps thud across the rug, and I hear him breathing as he comes to stand in front of the desk. He doesn't touch me, doesn't sit down. He simply stands still and *watches*. I shudder on the table, reveling in the thrill of his eyes raking over my body, seeing exactly what Cas is doing to me and how much I love it.

Even blind girls like to be watched.

In front of me, Torsten's breathing grows heavy. Just knowing he's there watching what Cas does to me... fuck.

Just when I'm on the very edge, Cas jerks his fingers out of me. I cry out, desperate for him to finish me, but he simply tsks and makes featherlight strokes with his fingers down my ass.

"Please don't stop."

"But you come to me to learn about torture," Cas says, his voice thick with his desire. "I'm simply teaching you my tricks."

"No tricks," I growl. "Make me come. *Now*."

"You're hardly in a position to make demands, my Queen." Cas slides down my cunt, the pads of his fingers barely grazing my flesh. It's not enough and he knows it. I groan in frustration and try to push my hips closer, but I'm trapped.

"Patience, Sunflower. Good things come to good girls who wait their turn."

He moves his fingers away, dancing them over the backs of

my knees, along my thighs. I know he's doing it just to piss me off. My pussy tingles just anticipating his touch and feeling Torsten's eyes drinking in every moment.

Cas kneels behind me, his breath caressing my most sensitive places. He's taking a good long look at me, and I can hear Torsten's breathing hitch with a gasp. They're both watching, and it's so intimate...

"You're soaked already." Cas' lips are so close, so close. "I want to drink you up."

He licks slowly around my cunt, his tongue darting inside me, savoring me like an ice cream on the hottest day in summer. I try to squirm because his tongue isn't as much pressure as his finger, and I need to come like five minutes ago. He chuckles against me. His hand comes down hard on my ass, and I cry out.

"Such an impatient girl. She's so hungry for cock, Torsten. You should do something about that."

The chair creaks as Torsten stands up. I hear his zipper opening. I lick my lips with anticipation.

"Open up, Sunflower. Open wide for Torsten."

I part my lips. Torsten makes a choking sound as he approaches the table. He still struggles with sex sometimes – all the textures and sounds and scents and feelings are too intense. But I'm tied to the table so I can't touch him at all, save for my warm mouth that's practically watering in anticipation of swallowing him.

"Look at her, friend. Our sweet Queen is hungry for cock," Cas goads him. "She's about to get as much as she can handle."

Torsten kicks off his jeans. A moment later he touches the tip of his cock to my lips. I swipe my tongue over him, enjoying the sweetness of his pre-cum.

Cas flicks his tongue over my clit. He hooks his hands around my thighs, spreading me wider as his tongue dips and circles, painting lines of pleasure.

I open wider, and Torsten pushes himself inside my mouth. He doesn't grab the back of my head the way Cas or Vic would, but he doesn't need to. He's so big that I have to stretch my mouth wide to fit him in. He groans as he hits the back of my throat.

"Don't go easy on her," Cas instructs from behind me, circling a finger around my asshole. "Remember, our Queen likes it rough."

Torsten tastes so good. He fucks my mouth in that slow, careful rhythm of his. I can tell that despite Cas' instructions, he's trying not to give me too much or too fast. Unlike Cas, I don't think Torsten likes to see me choke and gasp and gag on his cock.

Instead, I circle my tongue around his swollen head, dancing it over the veins until he murmurs my name.

"Fergie..."

"Tell me what she feels like," Cas demands. "How does that tight little mouth feel around your dick?"

"It feels..." Torsten struggles for a word. "Amazing."

"Damn right, amazing. That's what she is. Our Queen. And we are never, ever going to let some filthy little upstart get his hands on her again. She's ours, isn't she?"

"She's ours."

Cas' tongue devours me. I buck against the table as he grows more brutal, more frenzied. The pleasure builds inside me. I'm on fire. I'm ready to burst.

I strain against the cuffs as my body tenses.

Cas thumps his tongue cruelly against my swollen clit, and I fall over the edge and keep on tumbling.

I moan around Torsten's cock as the pleasure crashes over me.

Cas doesn't even let me recover from the orgasm before he shoves himself roughly inside me. I cry out again as my body stretches to accommodate him. Why couldn't any of my guys have a normal-sized cock? Why'd they have to be such monsters?

Drool dribbles down my chin, and I can tell from the sounds Torsten's making as he thrusts harder that he's let go of his sense of chivalry.

Cas' fingers dig into my ass as he pounds into me. He gets in sync with Torsten, the pair of them slamming into me at the same time before drawing back together, stretching and contracting my body.

A feral sound escapes Cas' lips, and that does it – I come undone again, spilling my orgasm over his cock, milking him until he's so close that he has to pull out and steady himself.

"I will never get tired of watching you come, Sunflower," he says as he slaps my ass. "Do you have another one in there for us before I come inside you?"

"I don't know," I try to say, but my words are muffled by Torsten's cock, so what comes out is, "Mfffontow."

"There's one way to find out..." I hear Cas rummaging around in a drawer. "I know it's in here somewhere... a-ha."

I don't know what 'it' is, but he turns something on and it makes a vibrating sound. A moment later, something presses against my clit and it's vibrating, and because I'm stuck in this position, I can feel the vibrations through my whole body.

Fuck me dead.

Cas holds the vibrator right *there* as he slams into me again. Torsten continues his steady rhythm. My lips are so stretched, and with no way to close my mouth and swallow for even a moment, saliva trickles down my chin and drips on the floor. I must look a complete mess, but they love me like that.

"Do you like Torsten fucking your face?" Cas drawls as his cock touches dark, hidden places inside me. "Do you like taking two cocks at once, like a Queen? Do you like having a harem of devoted men you can use whenever you need?"

And just like that, I come *again*.

I come so hard that I black out.

You thought a blind girl couldn't black out? Think again – all you need is one cock in your pussy, one in your mouth, a finger in your ass and a vibrator held against your clit.

When I come back to earth again, the cocks are gone. I can taste Torsten's saltiness on my tongue and feel Cas' cum trickling down my thighs. Cas unlocks the cuffs and helps me to my feet, rubbing my wrists.

"You have welts there," he says. "They look like they hurt."

"Good," I say. "When I touch them I'll remember this moment, and I'll be happy."

In a rare show of affection, Cas wraps me in his arms and kisses the top of my head. "How did I ever get so lucky to have you in my life?"

"Somewhere in your stabbing and torture, you must've done something good. Okay." I stand up, crack my back, and roll out my wrists. "I'm ready to get some answers now."

8

FERGIE

The three of us clean up quickly in our bathroom. I pull on jeans and my favorite Blood Lust t-shirt, and then Cas leads us down to the basement and performs some kind of magic on a hidden keypad in the wall that makes the gym mirror slide open.

"Won't you come into my lab," Cas intones, imitating Frank-N-Furter. "And see what's on my slab..."

Oh, fuck.

Realization hits me as I feel the draft between the mirrors expand. I can't believe that I didn't put that together. Zack told me that Cali has a secret room in the house where she conducted her gruesome 'business,' and Vic and Juliet were even punished with cleaning out its drains. But I never put it together that the strange draft I felt between the mirrors in the gym was Cali's secret torture chamber bunker.

The gap between the mirrors is too narrow for Cas to lead me with his elbow, so I grip the back of his shoulder as he takes me inside. The walls have a weight to them – it's a kind of sense I have of underground spaces – not something you can explain to sighties, but I can tell the room is underground from the weight in the air.

We emerge into a larger space – some kind of underground cavern, judging by the echoes from the heavy domed ceiling. "We have everything we could possibly need for our work right here," Cas explains proudly as he leads me around the perimeter of the room. "Every weapon you could possibly imagine – and even a few you can't – hang from the walls in this room. And in the center, we have our pièce de résistance—"

"Fergie, get your roid-rage ape to let me go. Now," a familiar voice snaps.

It's Dru.

Of course it is. I should have realized who Cas meant when he said he had the one person who'd know where Sommesnay is hiding – his girlfriend.

Fuck, will the betrayals never end?

"I can't do that, sorry." I toss my hair over my shoulder. Cas shows me a chair. I turn it around and straddle it, leaning over the back as I face her. I don't know what she's tied to, but I hear metallic creaks and scrapes when she moves, the sound of heavy chains dragging across the concrete floor. "Your boyfriend kidnapped me and Vic's dad."

"Yes, and I called to warn you, remember!"

"Is that what you were doing?" I tilt my head to the side. I remember her call, but I don't know what to think now. Finding out about Trudi has made me unsure of what to think. "Or were you distracting me so his thugs could get a jump on me?"

"Fuck, no," Dru splutters out. Her chains rattle again. "Listen, you've got this all wrong. I was into Zack when he first came to Emerald Beach. I wanted revenge on Poison Ivy for ruining my life. So yeah, your boyfriends and I don't exactly get along. But *you* got that revenge for me, not him. And all his other stuff was starting to get a bit much for me – all he talked about was

Claudia August this, revenge that. Then I found some other girl's panties in his pocket. After everything I did for him, and all the laws my mother broke to help him make things difficult for the Triumvirate, that bastard was cheating on me. I kicked him out a few days ago, I don't know where he's gone, but a bunch of his bomb-making shit is still at my house. I was clearing it out when I found a burner phone, and I listened to the messages. It was Torsten's sister giving Zack details about this meeting between your parents, and suggesting it would be the perfect time to grab you. I called you straight away."

"So Sommesnay was responsible for the bombs, too?"

"Bombs?" Dru sounds surprised, and not the kind of surprise that's easy to fake. "There's been more than one?"

"Someone sent Vic a parcel bomb, but Claudia's security team found it before it went off."

"Then that's probably him, too." Her voice sounds resigned. "Zack did the museum. That's a fact. I didn't know about it until I locked him out and started going through his stuff. He's got all this scary shit at my place – equipment and chemicals and stuff. I'll give it all to you if it will help you find him. I think he needs to be put down, Cassius Dio-style."

"Where's he hiding out now?"

"I don't know."

"Sure you don't," Cas coos from the other side of the room. I can't see what he's doing, but there's a metallic sliding sound, and Dru screams. The sound bounces off the walls, high and grating.

"Cas, stop. She doesn't know where he is."

The words fly out of my mouth before I can stop them, but I realize they're true. I believe Dru.

"That's what she says now," he growls. "But when I'm finished with her, she'll tell the truth."

"She's telling the truth now!"

If she's double-crossing me, I'll find her later and gut her myself. But all I hear is my friend's voice. She's afraid and in pain, and I need to make it stop.

I suck in a deep breath and speak loud enough to be heard over Dru's screams. "Dru's always told the truth, Cas. Even when it wasn't the smart thing to do. She went to the police about you, remember? She knew that she was putting herself in danger, knew that she'd bring the wrath of Poison Ivy down on her own head, but she did it because she cared about Gemma. Because she wanted Gemma to be safe, and she didn't know that you were trying to protect Gemma, too."

Cas moves toward me. "That's not true."

"Isn't it? Dru was Gemma's best friend. She's..." A lump forms in my throat as I think about the two girls who've had my back ever since I started at Stonehurst Prep. "She's like Euri – she stands with her girl even at the risk of her own life. She put Gemma first, exactly as you did, and you punished her for her loyalty. Poison Ivy destroyed her because Victor felt that she attacked you by going to the police, and you blame her for Gaius being sent away because that's easier than blaming yourself. Am I right?"

Cas stops whatever he's doing. The room falls silent except for Dru's sobs.

'You're right," he whispers, the words so quiet that even with my sensitive hearing I can barely pick them up. "I guess she did help Gemma. And I repaid her by..."

He trails off, not repeating all the awful things they did to Dru. And that's when I knew I had him.

"Something I'm learning from your mother is to know when to spare a life as well as when to take one," I say. "Dru's given us everything she knows, I'm sure of it. Is this really what you want Dio to be known for – leaders who fly off the handle and torment teenage girls into making false confessions? If you go through the world burning every person who crosses you, Cassius, then eventually you'll have no one left. Both you and Dru cared for Gemma—"

"Cas never cared about her," Dru spits out. "He just couldn't stand that Victor had something he didn't—"

I held up a hand. "Maybe you don't want to make this worse for yourself."

Dru doesn't continue. But I do. "I don't know what happens to us after we die. But I'd like to think that if Gemma was looking down on the people she left behind, it would be pretty amazing for her to see her best friend and her boyfriend working *together* to bring down an unhinged bitcoin billionaire with a hard-on for revenge."

"Can't I just torture her a little?" Cas pouts.

"No. Dru called to warn me. She's not our enemy. If I'm wrong, you can take it out on my ass later, but I'm not wrong."

"Can I still bend you over and fuck you senseless again?" His whole voice lights up. He's got bloodlust stirring in his veins, and he's going to need to fuck again soon, or things will get ugly.

"I'm counting on it. Now get her down and let's talk like allies instead of enemies."

He sulks. "Fine."

Torsten helps Dru out through the gym and places her on one of the sofas. I can hear Vic's voice as footsteps echo down the stairs. They must've come back from the clinic. I reach out to him, and he runs to me immediately and throws his arms around me.

"Is Gabe okay?"

"He'll live," Vic's voice is grim. "Galen's worried about his voice. There's some damage to his throat and we don't know yet if it will affect his voice chords permanently…"

His voice trails off as a shudder wracks his body.

"Vic, are you okay?" I get a sense this is about more than his dad's voice.

He shakes his head vigorously, forgetting I can't see it. But I can sense his shoulders moving. "I've been calling Juliet all day, but she won't pick up. Do you have any idea where she could be? I haven't seen her for a few days."

"You haven't seen her?" I thought they were still talking, which is why I think to wonder where she'd got to. I had my revenge on her, and as far as I'm concerned, Juliet is done.

But she's not done to Vic. He shudders in my arms. "Fergie, I nearly lost you, and she... and she..."

His whole body shakes. Vic August is not in control. Far from it – what little he had is slipping away with every moment.

"Little Victor August," Dru croaks. "Fergie, look what your cat dragged in. As far as I'm concerned, he can toss you back."

Vic moves away and I hear him at the bar, mixing a drink for her. He brings it and places it in her hands. Dru cries out as he spills a little in her lap.

"You still remember that a gin sour is my favorite?" Dru's voice sounds a little weirded out.

"Of course I do." There's a hint of nostalgia in Vic's voice. "Remember all those parties we had down here in the basement, watching Cas challenge everyone to arm wrestling contents? He broke Travis Durant's arm. And that time he smashed Clive Hawkins' head through the television—"

"I remember your sister forcing her tongue down every girl's throat," she quips back. "Including mine, after one drunken game of truth or dare."

"She's tenacious when it comes to pussy." Victor's voice cracks. He collapses on the couch beside me, and I can feel the tension coiling in his body. "Dru, I'm sorry that we came after you. We were all devastated when Gemma... when she... we should have been there for you instead of attacking you for calling the police on Cas. I was heartbroken and I didn't handle things well. If I could take it all back..."

"I got into *Yale*, August. On my own merit, even. Your little club didn't break me, and Fergie's crusade against you and Papa Smurf here has provided more joy than I could've possibly imagined. So let's call it even, shall we? And get on with the business of stopping Zack."

"You *want* to stop him?"

I still can't believe she wants to help us after Cas strung her up...

"Do I want my ex-boyfriend to stop trying to hurt you and blow up random bits of our city? Fuck yes. I'll tell you everything I know about him," Dru says. "But it's not much. I don't know if it will help. He *is* German. The way he talks about the country, I think he's not lying about spending at least some of his life there. His name is fake, but I don't know what his real name is. He has a lot of money, but I don't think he got it from bitcoin or his real estate investments. He's been planning this for months, this move of his on Claudia August."

"If he's an expert on bombs, he can make one from anything," Torsten says.

"Right." Vic swallows. "Hooray."

"What does he want?" I ask. "That's what I don't understand. Okay, he hates Claudia August because of something she did. Fine. All the Imperators have enemies. But what does he actually want to achieve out of all this? When he kidnapped me, he wanted Claudia to make him Imperator, but it didn't actually seem like he cared about the job."

"See, I'm a little fuzzy on that, too," she says. "I tried to ask him, but he'd turn it into this tirade about what Claudia did to his parents, and after a while I just tuned him out. I can tell you that he believes everything wrong in the universe comes from Claudia August. If I had to guess, I think he wants to torture her, to take from her everything that he believes she's taken from him. And he won't stop until he does it."

Her chilling words hang in the air.

"You have to find him," Dru begs me, pressing my hand between hers. "There's no telling what he'll do next."

9

VICTOR

We sit in the basement with Dru, having a few drinks and chatting. I'd forgotten how cool she was – we used to hang out a bit back in the early days of the Poison Ivy Club, before everything got messed up.

The banter, the drinks, Fergie's hand resting protectively on my hip – it makes me forget that Zack Lionel Sommesnay kidnapped Fergie, and that he's still out there. Cali and Claudia may have cut most of the rot from inside our organization, but that doesn't change the fact that the guy who masterminded this is still out there.

I sense a shift in the air and look up. Gaius is standing on the stairs, watching us with an unreadable expression. Cas follows my gaze, and his whole face lights up when he sees his brother. Cas is so simple sometimes – he loves his brother with a fierceness that only Cas is capable of. Gaius went to jail to save Cas. Now he's back. Simple.

Things are so simple to Cas.

Gaius = family.

Family = life.

I used to think like that, too. But I'm not so sure anymore.

Juliet and I haven't really been talking since the night of the fashion show. We do our punishment work for Cali in stony silence, and at school, she goes out of her way to avoid me.

But today of all days I need to know where she is, and I can't reach her.

And *he's* here.

Gaius fucking Dio.

A cold shiver goes up my spine as I watch Gaius thump his younger brother casually on the back like he hasn't been gone for three years. Everything about him seems completely normal. He hasn't changed one bit from the fun-loving slightly unhinged guy I used to hang out with.

But I know better than most exactly what Gaius is capable of. He is Cali's son, after all.

And he just *happens* to show up in the middle of all this, with Cas' biological father in tow? That can't be a coincidence.

Gaius groomed me to take over the Poison Ivy Club. He taught me everything I know about deception, about making people trust you so you can take what you need from them. I've seen him at work, and I know what he's capable of.

And I think he's up to something. But what?

Gaius is just about to slap my shoulder when he sees Dru. He stops, watching her with narrowed eyes. "Hargreaves."

"Gaius," Dru says with a smirk. Even after everything she's endured, she won't give Gaius the satisfaction of watching her sweat.

This woman survived *everything* the Poison Ivy Club did to her, and she came back to Stonehurst Prep knowing that she'd have to face us at our strongest. She helped Fergie when it would have been better for her to keep her head down and do nothing. She gave us as much information as she knew about Sommesnay while Cas had her trussed up, and now she's sitting here with us, having a drink like we're all friends.

Gaius nods to her, and with a quick glance at me, he goes to the bar and pours himself an enormous vodka.

When he returns, he sits down next to Fergie and offers his hand. "We haven't been formally introduced. I'm Gaius Dio, founder of the Poison Ivy Club. I understand you're sleeping in my room."

"It's my room now," she says, but she shakes his hand. I watch her features, but she's not giving anything away. My stomach twists. For most of my life, I've been in awe of Gaius – the way he can walk into a room and command attention, and turn every situation into something that advantages himself. I wanted to have his strength, his resourcefulness, and his power, and that was partly why I jumped at the chance to take over his club. But looking at him now, I see what Cali has seen for some time – Gaius may have the brains to run the Dio operation, but he doesn't have the heart.

Cas may be a monster, but he does what he does because of how fiercely he loves his family. Gaius doesn't love anything except power. And from the way Fergie angles her body and curls her lip ever so slightly as he talks, she can see it, too.

"Did you at least save my drum kit before you turned my room into Barbie's goth dreamhouse?" Gaius asks with a cocky grin. Fergie raises an eyebrow, and I know exactly what she's thinking.

He's been upstairs, snooping around her room.

"Milo put them in the garden shed," Cas says. He's practically jumping in his seat, he's so happy to have Gaius here. "I wouldn't let Cali throw them out."

"You've always got my back, little bro."

Cas glows under his brother's praise. It's been so long without Gaius around that I'd forgotten he could be like this. One word from his brother and Cas is under his spell.

"Where's my—where's Ares?"

"I've just dropped him off at a hotel. The Elysium. I figured he'd be better on neutral territory," Gaius says. The Elysium is the only decent hotel in Emerald Beach not owned by the Lucian family. That's the reason we set Torsten up there, too. "He really does want to get to know you, but Cali's going to be a bitch about it, so be careful."

"I can handle her." Cas closes his bloody knuckles into a fist. "Did I tell you that she's training me and Fergie to take over as Imperators?"

Dru's eyes widen as they study Fergie, but my Queen sips her drink in contented silence, that half-smile playing across her lips.

"I figured as much," Gaius says. "I heard whispers that Cali was injured, but she looks even worse than I expected. I think it's good that she has an exit strategy."

"We'll talk to her," Cas flashes his brother the biggest, most unhinged smile. "I'm sure she'll want you to take over now that you're back."

"That's big of you, Little bro." Gaius leans back in his chair and sips his drink. "I know how much you wanted the job, and knowing Cali had you at her side has helped me stay sane inside. I'm honestly not sure if I want to be an Imperator anymore, so we'll see."

Gaius starts to regale us with tales from the yard. In so many ways, it's as if he never left. He falls into the conversation easily, remembering places and events and people from Stonehurst as if his reign was over yesterday. Gaius always did have a way of making people feel at ease around him.

That's what made him so dangerous.

I smile at him as he takes over the group, pouring drinks for everyone and even making Dru laugh. I even remind him of some of the crazy shit we did together, and he enthusiastically launches into the stories for the others.

No one can see that I'm studying every move he makes.

I'll play happy families for Cas because he's so ecstatic that his brother is back. But inside, I'm wary. Gaius didn't just wander out of jail scot-free with Cas' father in tow. He's sold his soul for his freedom, and I know the price will be high.

None of this is a coincidence – if only I could figure out what it was all about.

MOM PHONES TO say they're bringing Gabriel home from the clinic. I grab my coat and shoot Cas a look that I hope conveys how much I need him to be careful around his brother, especially since his brain damage impacts his ability to make judgments.

"I'm coming with you." Fergie grabs her leather jacket.

"You don't have to. Stay here and get to know your stepbrother."

Gaius is at the bar, pouring more drinks as he delights Dru with some story about prison shower etiquette. Torsten's in the corner working in his sketchbook, oblivious as usual. I'd feel better if someone were here to keep an eye on Cas and make sure he doesn't get dragged into any of Gaius' bullshit, but I can't say that to her in front of them.

Fergie squeezes my hand, and I can tell from the way she tilts her head to the side that she understands what I'm worried about.

"Vic, stop worrying about everyone else for five seconds. Your dad's just been involved in a life-threatening kidnapping. You *need* me. Let me be the one to look after you for once. Besides," she smiles, "I want to see how my new best friend, the lead singer of Broken Muse, is getting on."

I pull Fergie close, and my chest swells with love. I can't

believe that this woman is mine. This impossibly strong, brave woman is thinking of me even after everything she's been through.

I cup her cheek, tracing the line of her cheekbone with my thumb. I stare into those fathomless emerald eyes that might not see the world but still hold her soul. A chill runs down my spine when I think about how close I came to losing her, but it's quickly replaced by the hot tug of her love.

I didn't lose her. She's mine.

She's *ours*.

I lean down and brush my lips over hers. She responds by cupping the back of my neck with her hand and bringing my head down for a deep kiss. As her body melts into mine, I realize how much she needs this kiss.

Almost as much as I need her right now.

Fergie's been operating on adrenaline since she got captured. She's like Cas – she does what she needs to do to survive, and only *after* the blood is wiped away does she process what happened and how she needs to deal with the trauma of our world.

And what she needs right now is me.

I'm here for whatever my Queen requires.

My own hand shifts behind her neck, cleaving her against me. Those hours where she was kidnapped were the worst in my whole life. It brought back all the memories of losing Juliet, but a hundred times worse because while my twin is a part of me, Fergie is my whole heart.

I need to hold her and touch her and make sure she's still real.

"Let's get you back to my place," I growl as I lead her up the stairs and outside. Noah lent me his car since mine is shot to shit, and I help Fergie to the passenger seat and then practically leap into the driver's side.

I tear down the road while Fergie leans across and rubs my swollen dick through my pants. My house is just around the corner, it's only *minutes* away, but I can barely even wait that long. I want to be inside her right fucking now.

"We'll say a quick hello to Gabriel, and then I want you in my room," I gasp. I'm so hard thinking about laying her down on my bed, spreading those beautiful legs of hers, and tasting my favorite treat. My dick pushes painfully against my waistband.

"I can't wait that long," she growls.

"My house is only around the corner—"

"No. I need to taste you now," she commands, her hand sliding between my legs.

I stiffen as her fingers make quick work of my zipper. She draws my cock out from the waistband of my silk boxers. I'm hard as steel already, and when her hot little mouth closes over the tip, I nearly yank the car into a streetlight.

"Fergie—" But my protests die as she slides me deeper, until I can feel her lips at the base and my tip at the back of her throat. It's so good, so fucking hot and wet and right. I slow down a little. I can barely focus on the road with those lips sucking me deep. I glance down to see that curtain of fiery hair draped across my lap, and I'm ready to come undone for her.

The entrance to the secret tunnel into our underground garage is just up ahead. I hit the button to activate the doors and plow inside just as Fergie sucks me deep again. I park up behind Eli's Porsche, hit the button to make my chair go back, and lie back to enjoy this gift from my Queen.

Fergie's tongue is like nothing else. She knows exactly how to lick and suck, exactly how much pressure to use to drive me crazy. She plays with my piercing, giving it light little tugs with her tongue every time she reaches the top of my shaft, which make my eyes roll back in my head.

"Fuck yes," I growl out, my fingers lacing through her hair as her head bobs up and down. "Fuck, Duchess, I'm about to..."

I'm right fucking there, right on the edge, but I don't want to fall over. Not until I've given her what she needs.

I summon every atom of self-control I possess and push Fergie off me. She makes a pouting face and huffs as she flips her hair over her shoulder. I throw open the door and drag her outside.

"I could feel you were so close..." she moans, but her protest turns into a shriek of delight as I spin her around and plant her hands on the hood of the car.

"I've always wanted to see a girl sprawled out over the hood of my car," I growl as I slide my hand down her ass. I kneel behind her, pushing her legs apart to give myself easy access, and bury my face between her legs. "Sadly, my car is all busted up, but this one is just as good."

"Vic..."

The first taste of her is all I need to die a happy man. Cas is right, our Queen really does taste like raspberries. I swirl my tongue around her clit. Fergie's back arches against the hood. I hold her down with my free hand, squeezing the globe of her ass cheek a little, reminding her that in this moment, she's mine and I'm going to make her scream my name.

Because right now, I need to feel like I matter to someone.

That's one of the many, many, wondrous things about being with Fergie. When I'm with her, whether it's worshipping her pussy or just hanging out, she's always completely in the moment. She isn't in her head or thinking about something else. She's with me, mind and body and heart, and seeing her like that makes me believe that I could one day let go, too.

Fergie's so wet that she's glistening. I plunge my tongue inside her, needing the sound of her panting my name.

I lick and swirl and suck until she's a gibbering mess. "V... V... Vic, please..."

"That's it, Duchess," I moan as I plunge a finger inside her ass. "Tell me who makes you feel so good."

"Vic, you doooooo—"

Her words dissolve into moans. Her legs squeeze my face, then convulse as she gives herself over to the pleasure. Her body slumps, and I stand up and wrap one arm around her waist to hold her against me as her legs stop working.

She murmurs, "That was..."

"World-shaking? Earth-shattering? Cunt-destroying?" I smile as I nibble her earlobe. "Don't hold back, Duchess. Tell me what you really think."

"Mmmm." She turns her head to face me. Her pretty face glows with a light sheen of sweat. Her pink, swollen lips curl back into a smile. "I think... you can do better."

"Oh, yeah? Is that a challenge?" I push her back down against the hood and bury myself inside her in one hard stroke. She cries out as her body opens for me, and I push myself right up to the hilt. She's so hot and wet and needy, wiggling her hips to drive me even deeper.

Because I came only a few minutes ago, I know I'll go for a long time. That's a good thing. I want to make Fergie come so many times that she forgets all about that horrible experience in the freezer.

I want this, right now, to be what she remembers about today.

She squeals and squirms, and I know that my piercing is hitting all the right places.

My pulse hammers in my veins, and something inside me unlocks as I feel her clench around me. I let out all of the grief and the worry and the need for control. I pour all of my insecurities and fears into her, and she picks them up and carries them for me.

And when I finally come inside her, a weight I didn't even know I was carrying lifts from my body, and I have to hold her tight to keep from floating away.

I feel lighter than I felt in a long, long time.

"We should probably go upstairs and see your dad," she breathes.

"Yes, we should." I kiss her shoulder.

Neither of us moves for a long time. Something about the cavernous stillness of the garage makes this moment feel bigger than either of us. I go soft inside her, and then hard again, but I don't fuck her. I just lie on top of her, holding her against my chest and enjoying the feel of my whole body being cocooned by this woman.

Eventually, though, the cold reality settles over us. She starts to fidget, and I know it's time to face what's waiting for me upstairs. I slide off her, wipe us both off with a clean towel from the bag beside the workbench, and help Fergie back into her clothes. We link arms and walk into the house.

"Mom?" I call out. "Gabe?"

"Ballroom," Mom calls back.

I lead Fergie into the house's ballroom. We don't throw balls because we don't live in a fucking fairy tale, so our family uses it as a kind of living room. Eli often has rescue cats in there – we have four now who dart around the cat castle that takes up one whole third of the immense space. The other half of the room is taken up with a big lounge suite and my mother's knife-throwing target. (She usually practices at Cali's gym, but she set up the target when she was my age and it's sentimental.)

My family sits around Gabriel on the comfy couches, takeout containers spread out in front of them.

At least, *most* of my family.

Juliet is absent. I plunge my hand into my pocket and grip my phone. No calls. No messages.

Our dad nearly died and she doesn't care.

"Hey, son," Gabriel smiles as he sees us. His voice is hoarse, the words a struggle. "Hello, fellow survivor. You were quite something to behold in there. I wasn't so out of it that I didn't see you choke that guy."

"It was nothing." Fergie lets me lead her over to the nearest chair. She sits, crossing her legs and looking every bit the warrior queen. "*You* were incredible."

"Please, I did nothing."

"You kept my morale up with all your silly songs. I never would have been able to do what I did without you."

They smile at each other. The love in Fergie's voice for my dad makes a warm feeling spread through my chest. She no longer sees him as a famous musician whose music sings the stars for her.

After their ordeal together, they're bonded for life.

They're family.

"Hey, Dad," I lean over and give him an awkward side hug. "How are you feeling?"

"Like someone put me in an industrial mincer and cranked the handle," Gabriel answers.

"Don't suggest that to Cali, or she'll add one to her dungeon," I say. After watching my mother clean house with Cali today, I've had more than enough blood to last a lifetime.

"Did you get anything out of the Hargreaves girl?" Mom asks.

She has one hand on Gabriel's lap, her fingers knitted in his. Her other hand fiddles with a loose thread on the edge of her sweater. She lifts her chin, and her icicle eyes lock with me. I choke back a gasp.

All my life, my mother has been this invincible force. Juliet calls her The Iceberg because she might look benign on the surface but underneath she can cause carnage and mayhem. But right now, she looks nothing like the invincible Claudia August.

She looks tiny. And afraid.

"Not really," I answer. "Dru doesn't know where Sommesnay's hiding or what he plans to do next. She doubts he's really a real estate guy." I can't bear it any longer. I have to ask. "Mom, have you heard from Juliet?"

Mom shrugs. "Milo said he saw her get dropped off a couple of days ago and let herself in, and the security system says that she hasn't left, so she must still be in her room. She hasn't come down or answered my calls."

"Nor mine."

She's been here all this time?

"I know she's still pissed because I punished her over that business at the fashion show, but this silence is a bit ridiculous. Her father nearly..." she snaps her mouth shut. She can't say the words.

"I'll talk to her." I stand. I hate how hope spreads across my chest. If Juliet *is* here, in the house, that's a sign of something.

Fergie stands, too, but I push her down.

"This is a twin thing. I need to talk to her alone."

Fergie nods. She's an only child, so she doesn't understand the twin bond. And sure, she and Cas call each other brother and sister, but that's... kind of fucked up. It's not the same as the bond Jules and I share.

I take the stairs two at a time. Juliet's room is right next to mine. I peer into the open door, expecting to see my sister's usual mess of clothes on the floor and makeup scattered everywhere, hoping to find her flopped across the bed painting her nails or scrolling through her phone.

But instead...

My heart drops to my knees.

The room has been stripped. The top of the vanity is empty

of makeup and sticky notes. The walk-in closet door hangs open, revealing dozens of empty hangers, shoes scattered over the floor, and drawers and baskets flung everywhere. Even the silk duvet is gone from the bed.

The panel hiding the secret passage in her closet is slightly askew.

Juliet's gone.

10

VICTOR

I step into the room, turning in a slow circle, trying to understand what I'm seeing. How can she just be gone? When did this happen? When was the last time I stepped foot in this room?

Too long, a cruel voice in my head whispers.

You did this, Vic. You've been punishing her for your crimes.

She's my sister. She's done some evil things, no question. But so have I. I think about some of the things Poison Ivy has arranged, and shame burns my skin. Juliet may have used our connections for her own personal gain, but I don't have the moral high ground...

I sit down on the edge of the bare mattress and stare at my phone. I type out a message.

Vic: I'm sitting in your room. I guess it's not your room anymore.

My phone vibrates. My sister's name flashes across the screen. My heart clenches as I raise the phone to my ear.

"I left three days ago," she snaps. "Some twin you are. You're too busy with your blind bitch girlfriend and your little plots that you didn't even notice I'd gone."

"I—"

"No, Vic, it's over. As far as I'm concerned, you're not my brother anymore."

"Don't say that." I choke on the words. She can't mean it. "We can sort this out, Jules. I'm so sorry. I think I understand why you did all of it, and I promise I won't let you take any more punishment for it. I should have stuck up for you—"

"Yes," she sniffs. "You should have."

"And you and Fergie were friends once. Surely, you can—"

"No."

Tears well in my eyes. "Didn't you see all my messages? All of Mom's? Gabe was *kidnapped* today. Gabe and Fergie. I nearly lost them both. Can you understand that I'm... I'm not in a good place. I need to see you. I need to know you're okay. Please..."

"I don't follow your orders anymore, Vic. I'm not going to hang around just to bolster this idea that you have of yourself as the great protector. You failed me. Again. I need to protect myself now."

I hate how much her words sting, how much they feel like the truth. "When will I see you again?"

"Sooner than you think," she snaps before hanging up.

11

FERGIE

I spend the night curled up in Victor's arms. Cas called to tell me that Torsten tried to locate Juliet via the tracker on her phone, but she'd disabled it. He said they'd come over if we need them, but I know if they were here, Vic would fall into his usual role as the leader, the protector, the one holding everyone together. Tonight, he needed to drop that facade.

He needed to fall apart.

I hold him as he rests his head against my chest, listening to my heart. We don't talk about Juliet or what happened today. He talks about plants, and climate change, and his parents. He talks about the first time he saw Gabriel sing with his band, and the time Noah took him out for ice cream after he lost a basketball game, and how one of Eli's cats ate the first flowers he ever grew.

He cries a little – silent, fat tears that drip onto my shoulder. He doesn't wipe them away. When he stops crying, he sounds brighter than I've heard him for a long time. He kisses my belly button and asks, "Where are you going?"

"Nowhere." I stroke his head. His shoulders shake. "I'm staying right here with you."

"No, Fergie. I mean, where are you going to college?"

"Fuck, Vic, I don't know." It all comes back to me. "Shit, in all the chaos of getting kidnapped, I forgot to tell you. Euri called me at Cali's gym. See, when I was pissed at all of you, she and I wrote an article about the Poison Ivy Club and all the things you'd done, and I told her not to print it but she did and—"

"I know. I've seen it. We all have."

"Vic, I'm so sorry."

"You have nothing to be sorry for. No one forced me to take over the Poison Ivy Club from Gaius. No one made us turn it into this business trading favors for elite college admissions. We did that. *I* did that. I don't regret all of it – some of the people we helped really deserved their places. Like you, but you weren't the only one. Some of the favors we used were for the greater good. But the rest… we were stupid and selfish and high on our own power. Now all those people we helped are going to get their spots rescinded, and that's my fault. I never should have messed with things—"

I kiss his knuckles. "If you hadn't, we might never have met."

He chuckles. "Even without the Poison Ivy Club, hell itself would've conspired to put you in my path, Fergie Macintosh. But all of this is on me, not you. If I hadn't been so full of my own self-importance, none of this would have happened. Juliet would have never co-opted our influence for her own greed. Cas would have never believed he was so invincible. And I would be going to Harvard next year instead of possible prison time."

"You know your mother won't let you go to prison."

"She might, just to teach me a lesson." Vic sighs.

"She won't, not in the middle of all of this." The cogs turn in my head as I start to put together all the things I've learned from the three Imperators. "They'll find a way to cover this up. The article complicates things, but they'll find a way to spin this in your favor. They always do, and then you can still go to Harvard with me—"

Victor laughs as he kisses my cheek. "I admire your optimism, but I think it's too late. Harvard will rescind my spot. It's okay, I accept it. But I'll fight them if they try to kick you out."

"I don't want to go without you."

As I speak the words, I realize to my surprise how true they are. Harvard has been my dream for... ever since I saw my mother in her Harvard sweatshirt in one of Dad's old pictures. They met at college and fell madly in love and had the most amazing adventures, and I wanted the same thing. I wanted to have a life, and a love, like theirs.

I worked so damn hard to make that dream real, and then Dawson ripped it away from me, all because I wanted to fit in. I was so lost when I came to Emerald Beach that I couldn't see that I'd given up too soon. I didn't want to fight Dawson because that meant exposing myself to the world as the blind girl who was tricked by her boyfriend because I was so desperate to fit in. Instead, I followed Dad to Emerald Beach with my tail between my legs.

And then I met Victor August, and he showed me that anything is possible if you're clever and cunning. He taught me to believe in myself again, and along the way, my Harvard dream lost its glittery shine.

I don't need a fancy Ivy League school to show me what I'm made of. I don't need to show the world that I'm smart and special and that I can achieve things even though I'm blind. I fought Cassius Dio in the ring... and won. I'm being groomed for leadership by two of the biggest mob queens in the world.

I have the family I've always craved.

I don't need Harvard.

But I do need...

I push Victor's head off me. "I hate to do this, but are you okay if I leave you for a bit?"

"I'm fine, Duchess. I'm sad, but I'm not going to fall to pieces."

"Good." I smile as I slide my feet into my boots. "There's something I have to do."

SEYMOUR WALKS me up the path, then retreats to the car while I hammer my fist on the door. A moment later, it swings open with a creak.

"Fergie?" Euri says in a small voice. "What are you—"

I throw my arms around her and pull her into me. She resists for several moments before relaxing into the embrace. It's another few heartbeats before she raises her arms and hugs me back.

"What happened?" she chokes out. "I kept trying to call you, but you wouldn't pick up, and then I tried to go to your house and your dad told me that you'd been kidnapped—"

"Yup. That happened. But I'm fine now. The kidnappers, not so much."

"Fuck, Fergie. I'm so sorry. I can't believe I let them publish that article, and all this time you were tied to a chair in a warehouse somewhere—"

"An industrial freezer, actually. But you got the chair part right." I squeeze her so tight that she gasps for breath. "And you have no reason to be sorry. I came to apologize to you. I had a lot of time to think while being trapped in that freezer. I've put you through hell this year, and I never should have asked you to pull that article in the first place. No matter how I feel about Victor and Cassius and Torsten, this was supposed to be your revenge, too. I didn't mean to try and take that away from you."

"You were trying to protect me," she says. "I knew it was dangerous to put my name in the spotlight against the Triumvirate, but I was so angry. I didn't want them to get away with it again."

"It really is okay. And don't worry, they won't get away with what they did to your sister, or to you. I spoke to Victor about it. He's not going to fight whatever punishment they deem acceptable."

"That's... surprising." Euri ushers me inside and down the hall to her room. She shuts the door and helps me sit on the bed before flopping down beside me. A moment later, I hear her knitting needles clacking nervously. "I've already had several calls from different newspapers and CNN. You probably have too, but they just haven't been able to reach you. I'm not going to give another interview. I told my truth in my piece, and that's all I wanted."

"You should do those interviews. It'll be good for your career."

"No." Her needles clack faster. "Not like this. It doesn't feel right after what happened to you and to Victor's family. If someone kidnapped my dad, I'd be devastated. And Torsten must've been in a state to lose you. Your boyfriends may not be my favorite people in the world, but I'm not going to profit off their pain any more than I already have."

"You're too good for this world, Euri Jones."

"I know." She lowers her voice. "The school called my parents. Apparently, they hired security and a big PR firm to keep the press away from the school for the moment. Principal Garcia is bringing all of us in for a meeting to discuss what's to be done. It was supposed to be today, but they couldn't get ahold of any of your families. I guess you've been busy."

Her voice wavers. It must be scary to think that someone you know was kidnapped.

I reach across and hug her again.

"We were busy, but it's all sorted now."

"I bet Cas sorted it." There's a hint of a smile in her voice.

"I'm just glad to finally have that psychopath on my side," I grin back at her.

"He was always on your side, girl." Euri reaches under her bed and comes up with a handful of candy bars. "He just had an unhinged way of showing it."

"I'll make sure everyone is at that meeting. I didn't lie to you when I said it's okay if I don't go to Harvard."

"Fergie, you can't say that. It's *Harvard*. You'll never get another opportunity like that. Oh—" She presses something into my hands. Her phone. "Read it," she says.

I have her phone read out the screen to me. It's an email from the admissions office at Blackfriars University, this fancy institution in England. And it says...

I drop the phone before the voiceover is even finished, and wrap Euri in my arms. "You got in."

"I did!" She's whispering. "I haven't told my parents yet."

"You'll have to tell them soon. They're probably going to notice if you go to college in another country."

"Yes, you're right." I hear the bed creak as she flops down on it. "Although I don't even know if I'll accept the offer."

"Of course you're accepting. Blackfriars is where you want to go, right?"

"I don't know. My parents do have a point. I've been so excited to get out of Emerald Beach that I didn't really think about... getting out of Emerald Beach. But now that I've got the letter, it's hitting me, you know? I'd be completely on my own. What if I can't find things? What if no one wants to be my friend? What if I'm not as smart as I think I am, and I fail and I waste all that money?"

Euri's knitting needles clack-clack-clack away.

"Are you kidding? You're amazing. You have taken on one of the largest crime organizations in the world and lived to tell the tale. If you can survive senior year with Fergie Munroe as your best friend, you can survive anything."

"Fuck, I hope so."

Euri and I hang out for the rest of the day, gossiping about anything and everything. We order pizza and I update her on what it's like to be kidnapped. When she hears about Dru, she grabs my arm. "Should we invite her over? We've got heaps of pizza. The girl just found out her boyfriend is a terrorist. She probably needs a little girl time."

"Sure. I love that idea."

Euri messages Dru and then decides she's going to paint my nails. She's halfway through painting my toenails sparkly crimson (at least, that's what she tells me she's doing) when the doorbell rings. Euri jumps up. "That'll the pizza. I'll go get it."

Euri returns a few minutes later with a stack of pizzas... and Dru.

"Hey, Fergie." Dru flops on the bed. "Love the toenails. I've been hanging out on the front steps with the pizza guy and your driver. They're talking about England winning the soccer—"

"Seymour's still out there? And he likes soccer?" That was something I never knew about the kindly man.

"Apparently, it's his job to watch over us," Dru says with a laugh. "I must admit, it's nice that someone in your circle isn't a giant dildo."

"I know. I'm sorry for what Cas did in the basement—"

"Don't sweat it. I already have enough Cas trauma to last a lifetime, so it just rolls off me like water off a duck's ass. *I'm* sorry my douchebag ex kidnapped you and Vic's dad. I feel awful. I mean, I hated those guys for what they did to Gemma, and to me. But I didn't want people to *die*. If I'd known what he planned, I would have told you—"

"I know. It's okay. And the guys know they can trust you now.

You don't have to hang out with us or anything, but if you're in trouble, they'll have your back."

"Thanks. And yeah, they'd better. I think they owe me." Dru flips open the pizza box, and the scent of hot cheese and pepperoni fills the room. "So Gaius is back?"

"Yeah. I don't know how he swung it."

"He's exactly the same. I hate the guy and yet, as soon as he starts talking to you, he makes you feel like his best friend in the world." Dru sighs. "So, what are our plans for the evening? Because I think you should go somewhere fancy and show off that sexy-ass pedicure."

"What do you have in mind?" Euri asks nervously.

Dru grins. "I'm dying to hit the dance floor. We're going to a club."

12

FERGIE

I text the guys and tell them where we're going, because I know they'll hate me if we go out clubbing and they don't come, too. Vic responds immediately that he'll be there in ten minutes, and Cas tells me he's dragging Torsten out, too.

"I want to go to Tombs," Dru says as she leans across the seat to sync her playlist with the car's stereo. I swear I hear Seymour sigh as loud drum and bass blast through the speakers. "I've never been and I've heard wild things, like that some psychopath killed a guy on the dance floor for looking at his girl."

"You'd better be careful, because you're looking at that girl right now," I say as I flip my hair over my shoulder.

"Fuck me," Dru whistles through her teeth as she sways her hips on the seat. "Papa Smurf is a walking red flag."

Don't I know it?

But he's mine.

It's still early when we arrive, but the place is packed. We get in line, but the bouncer waves us through. It turns out that Livvie's put me on her permanent guest list. The perks of dating gangsters, right?

Inside, the place is pumping. My vision swims with dancing lights – I can even make out the shapes of some of the neon hieroglyphs on the walls – a half-circle, a squiggly line, a bird. It probably spells 'fuck' in Ancient Egyptian or something. I bet Claudia knows. I should ask her.

Dru drags us over to the bar. "I've been dying to use my fake ID. What'll it be?"

"Something fruity," I say.

"But not too much alcohol," Euri pipes up.

"Sure, grandma." I can hear the smirk in Dru's voice.

Euri is in trouble tonight.

The two of us stand around, attempting to half-ass dance to the music while the crowd jostles us. Euri gives off nervous energy. This isn't exactly her scene – I don't think she's done much clubbing apart from that crazy night after Sean's birthday – and she's aware that her name's on the article that's put the Poison Ivy Club in the limelight. But she's here, trying something different, and I think she's braver than anyone else I know.

I'm about to suggest we see what's taking Dru so long when Euri stiffens beside me.

"F-F-Fergie, Gaius Dio is here."

Shit. I'd completely forgotten to mention him to her. "Yeah. He appeared on Cas' doorstep the day I was kidnapped."

"He shouldn't just appear *anywhere*," Dru snaps. A cocktail glass is shoved rather forcibly into my hand. "He's supposed to be in jail for killing Konrad. Someone should be punished for taking that poor kid's life."

I don't answer, because she's not wrong. Konrad's death is a tragedy, and he deserves justice. And although I know that Cas is the real culprit behind that incident, I don't want him to go to jail, so I won't say a thing. Being part of the Triumvirate and loving three men with blood on their hands changes your sense of right and wrong. Cas was wrong to do what he did, and he hasn't truly paid the price yet, but the world has a way of righting the scales of justice.

I'm intrigued to get to know Gaius. I know that Vic doesn't trust him, but Cas is so happy to have him back. I need to figure out where I stand on the Gaius-o-meter because it appears he's determined to insert himself back into the fold.

"Can you guys keep an eye on Gaius for me?" I ask. "Cas is so happy he's back, but I don't know. The timing is strange and..." I trail off, deciding not to tell them about Ares Valerian's arrival just yet.

"Don't you worry – I'm not letting Mr. Older Dio out of my fucking sight," Dru growls. "Fergie, your stepbrother is heading this way, which means I'm out of here. Euri? You coming with?"

"No, I'll stay." Euri steps in closer to me as Dru slips away. A moment later, a thick arm slides around my stomach and pulls me close, and I'm enveloped in the scent of plum and musk and carnation.

"You're the hottest fucking girl in this place." Cas drops a kiss on my forehead.

"I'm surprised they let you back in here." I raise an eyebrow.

"Sunflower, they know what happens if they refuse me." His hand snakes around my waist, pulling me close. "Besides, I haven't had a chance to show you my moves."

"You have one move, Cas," I tease him. "Bashing in the heads of anyone who laughs at your pathetic dancing."

"Oh yeah? You're about to find out." He grinds his hips into my ass, and I can't help the thrill pulsing through me as I feel his cock stiffen against my leg. "You ready to make everyone in this place jealous?"

I'm about to reply, but another voice interrupts.

"Hey new stepsister," Gaius leans in, his breath hot on my cheek. He smells like expensive vodka and bad news. "Who's your hot friend?"

I open my mouth to introduce Euri, but she cuts in. "You know me, Gaius. I'm Eurydice Jones, Artemis' younger sister. She's the girl you pushed down the stairs."

"I remember Artie," Gaius says. He turns away from me. I can't see their faces, obviously, but I can *feel* their conversation – Euri's tense, her body stiff beside me. Gaius' voice is soft, a little contrite. "Listen, Yoni—"

"*Euri*," she snaps.

"—Euri, sorry." He does sound sorry, but I'm almost positive that Gaius has read the article and he knows *exactly* who she is. "I've done a lot of shit in my life, and trust me when I say that you get a lot of time in jail to think about that shit. Your sister is one of my deepest regrets. She didn't deserve what happened to her. Sometimes the best people get caught in the middle of our club, right? I don't know if you can accept this apology, but I want to make it because—"

I don't hear the rest of the conversation because Cas drags me into the crowd. People press in on me from all sides, their movements unpredictable as they gyrate with the music. I don't usually like this part about being at concerts or clubs – I tend to stick toward the back of the room, where I have more personal space. But with Cas' arm tight around me and his huge presence plowing through the dancers like the bow of a ship, I feel safe.

"Where are Vic and Torsten?" I yell over the pounding music.

"In the VIP suite," Cas says. "We can head there after, but I wanted to dance with my girl."

And he does. I'm surprised because Cas does not strike me as the dancing type – we both share a love of loud, angry, head-banging music and maiming people. But he holds my hips and grinds up against me, moving effortlessly in time to the beat and driving me so close to the edge as it's possible to get with all your clothes still on.

"What do you say we take this upstairs, little sis?" he whispers roughly in my ear as the beat drops. "We can go to one of the private suites and—"

But Cas doesn't get to finish his thought. I don't know what happened, but one second his hands are planted firmly and possessively on my hips and his hard-on is pressed into my ass, and the next, there's a stranger's hand pulling me into another body.

No, not a stranger.

"Mind if I cut in, little bro?" Gaius' voice lands in my ear, his vodka scent sending up all kinds of danger flags.

I remember the first time I spun around on this dance floor, dressed as Queen Cleopatra, and Cas maimed the male models I'd hired to escort me just for looking at me. I expect Cas to tell his brother to fuck off, but instead, he laughs.

"Look after my girl, big bro." Cas yells that he'll see me in the VIP suite after the song. And then he *leaves*.

Fucker.

I want to run after him, but I won't find him in the crowd, and I'm not going to let Gaius see that I'm nervous. Just because Cas trusts him doesn't mean I've decided to welcome him into our fold. This is an opportunity for me to feel out Gaius and see if I can get some clue as to what he's doing out of jail. So I plaster on my best bimbo smile and get busy – my hands over my head, my hips flowing, my ass grinding against my other stepbrother.

Gaius doesn't hold back. His hands roam over my sides and hold me as he spins and dips me. His touch is arrogantly confident. No one should be able to touch Cas' Queen the way he is, and he wants the world to know it. But he doesn't push things too far, either. His hands stay where they should.

"I've heard so much about you," he whispers in my ear as he steers us toward a less-crowded area of the dance floor. Here, the music is muffled by a screen, and we can hear each other.

"Everyone in prison is talking about Fergie Munroe, the girl who gave my brother blue balls. And blue everything else."

"I've heard a lot about you, too." I think of Euri, and Vic, and the stories they've told me about Gaius' rule over the Poison Ivy Club.

"It's all lies," he says casually as he spins me so my chest presses against his. "Whatever they told you, I'm so much worse."

I believe it.

Everything about this man sets off warning bells inside me. Of the brothers, Gaius is by far the more dangerous one, because he knows how to manipulate people. Cas has a sadistically simple view of the world – black and white, wrong and right, friend and enemy. But Gaius... I know there's a lot more going on inside his head than what he's revealed, and I don't have the luxury of believing it's for the good of me and my boys.

Gaius wanted to be Imperator. Now, Cas and I are being trained in that role. He will want it back, and Cas will bend over backward to give it to him. But I don't know if that's a good idea.

Gaius' arms wrap around me, hemming me in so I can't escape him. At least, that's what he thinks. My jiujitsu training kicks in and I mentally plan at least three ways I can break his hold on me and smash his head through the glass screen, but for now...

For now, I want to hear what Cas' brother has to say.

"Why did you come back?" I ask.

"Straight to the point, I admire that," he says. "I came because of the rumors I've been hearing. That my mother was shot on a job, that she's weak and losing her grip on the Dio empire, and that she's passing on the family business to my unhinged brother and his blind girlfriend. I came because the Triumvirate is crumbling and there are wolves at the door ready to fight over the scraps. You saw the truth of that yourself."

"Zack Lionel Sommesnay kidnapped me because of a personal vendetta against Claudia August. He has no desire to rule the Triumvirate."

"Maybe not, but the people who follow him do. They're tired of sharing the spoils between three greedy Imperators who are too busy with their own personal squabbles and family lives to care about the rest of the organization."

"That's not true at all," I shoot back. "Cali and Claudia and Livvie care about their people. They make sure everyone is looked after—"

He chuckles. "You're so naive. You might know that and I might know that, but we're not talking about the *truth*. We're talking about ruthless, ambitious criminals here – those who see money to be made and power to be gained, and they will never be satisfied with their slice of the pie. They want more, more, more, and they'll trample over the graves of the Imperators to get it."

"How do you know all this?"

Gaius laughs. "Because I've been in a position to listen all these years. Why do you think I volunteered to go to jail in Cas' place? Because a coup has been brewing for some time. I needed to find a way to get amongst our people and root it out. But I couldn't do that as the son of Cali Dio. That's why I took the fall for him and refused to talk to my family. I had to fall, and I had to make them believe I was ousted, so they would trust me."

Okay, that's interesting. If it's true, that's... quite clever.

"Why didn't you let Cas do it, instead?"

Gaius scoffs. "My dear brother is so loyal, the moment some bastard said something about Cali in the yard, he'd have staved the guy's head in and his cover would be blown."

"You have so little faith in Cas. He's not the same lost little boy you left behind."

"No? Tell me, honestly, do you think Cas is capable of

ruling Dio on his own?" I don't appreciate the smirk in Gaius' voice. "Do you think that he'll be able to negotiate contracts with our overseas partners or raise the profile of Dio? So much of the dissatisfaction in our family comes from us giving too much ground to Lucian and August. Our soldiers want to be more than guns for hire. Is Cassius the man to forge a new path?"

"Give him more credit," I hiss. "He's doing so well, and he's still learning—"

"A few months ago, he nearly killed a guy in this club because he was dancing with you. And then he blinded a class-mate because he went behind his back. There's a difference between being ruthless and unhinged. Tell me I'm wrong."

I open my mouth, but I can't get the words out. Because Gaius isn't wrong. I haven't heard anything about Dio soldiers wanting the business to expand, but then, I'm still a new face, and I was the one who publicly humiliated Cas. Even though Cali and Cas both endorse me, I don't have their level of trust. And I can't imagine anyone feeling comfortable going to any of the Dios with their grievances or ideas.

"I thought so," Gaius pats the top of my head like I'm a puppy. It takes all my self-control not to snap his wrist in half.

"And what's up with Cas' father?" I whisper, changing the subject.

"A surprise, but one we can use to our advantage. Ares wanted to marry Cali. He thought he would rule by her side, and others thought so, too. You have to remember that when Cali came to power, the idea of a woman ruling as Imperator – espe-cially a woman without any Dio blood – was new. It was a hard pill to swallow. Ares had a lot of supporters. Cali marrying him would have solidified her reign, and he would have helped the family to expand and move into other lines of business. Dio could have been more powerful than Lucian and August combined. Instead, we're the smallest family. We do the dirty work while the others take the glory."

"That's not true!" I'm incensed. "There's an art to Dio's work."

"You're right," he says quickly. "Of course you're right. But what is true and what people believe are rarely in concert. Ares wants to help. He wants Dio to be powerful again, and he wants to do it at Cali's side."

"She's married to my father," I hiss. "She loves my father."

"Exactly. And how do you think that looks to the assassins? It looks like Cali Dio – the most terrifying assassin in the world – is losing her touch. If we use Ares, he can help her to rebuild the trust between her and her people. And so can I. But if we want to stabilize the Dio empire, you and Cas need to step aside."

"That's not happening. Cali wants us to succeed her. Together."

Gaius sighs. "I've come to help my family, Fergie. But the only way I can do that is if I take over. Mom doesn't have the power any longer, you're a fucking novelty to them, and you know my brother isn't capable of ruling. It has to be me – or Dio will fall. Livvie is already circling like a vulture, waiting for her chance to strike."

"I'm not so sure that she is any longer," I say. "And the answer is no. Cali is Imperator, not you. I'll step aside on her orders only."

"You're making a mistake." He says this easily, casually, and the words carry more malice than if he had hissed them. "We look after family, and you are too fucking talented to be wasted. But this family needs me in charge, and soon you'll see that."

He releases me then, and I stagger back, reeling. I think of the pile of bodies Cali and Claudia drove out to Everlasting Hart ranch to feed to Clarence. They believe they've purged enough of the malcontents to keep their soldiers in line, but what if it isn't? What if Gaius is right and they've only scratched the surface of the soldiers' dissatisfaction? What if—

"Fergie, there you are." Dru catches my arm, yanking me from Gaius' grasp. "You're needed in the VIP suite."

"But—"

"No buts." Dru drags me away. Her pull on my arm is so hard that she nearly trips me as she drags me up the stairs.

At the top, Euri falls into my arms, just as something crashes behind her.

"Make him stop." Euri buries her face in my shoulder.

"Who? Cas? What the fuck is going on now?" I hear glass shatter. Did he see me with Gaius? After all this time, I thought he trusted me—

"Not Cas. *Vic.*"

Shit. *Okay.*

Vic yells something, and I hear more glass smashing. I turn to Euri. "What's caused this?"

"It's Juliet August," Euri whispers. "And she's dancing with some guy."

"Not some guy," Torsten says. "Zack Lionel Sommesnay."

13

CASSIUS

Watching Vic lose his shit and smash up the VIP area is wild.

Part of me is proud of him.

Part of me is afraid of him, because whatever's got Vic so twisted up that he's resorting to this public display must be pretty bad.

And a *tiny* sliver of me looks at his twisted face and the way people shy away from him, and I feel a hit of shame. That's what people do when the red mist descends on me. This is what they see.

Fergie loops her arm around mine. "Can you stop him? He won't want people to see him like this, and I can't walk over there alone without risking getting hit by debris."

"Sorry, Sunflower, but he needs this. Whatever's inside him has to come out somehow, or that stick in his ass will end up so far inside him it'll poke his organs."

"This isn't funny, Cas." She frowns, an adorable crease appearing between her eyebrows. "He's been on edge ever since he found out that Juliet left. Since before that, actually. He can't seem to let go of the person he believes she is, and I don't know if I can—"

"Oh, for fuck's sake. I'll do it." Dru grabs me again. "I'm not afraid of an August tantrum."

Dru marches across the room. She grabs Vic by the collar just as he throws a chair over the balcony, and slaps him across the face.

The sound barks like a gunshot in the crowded club. It reverberates down my spine, reminding me how much things have changed. Six months ago, no one – *especially not* Drusilla Hargreaves – would dare raise a hand to Vic. But now she's slapping him around like she owns this club, and it's so fucking weird and hilarious that I burst out laughing and can't stop.

Fergie shoots me a dirty look, but it takes me a bit to gain control over my giggles. It's the brain damage – I've lost what little ability I had to control my emotions. If I want to laugh, I laugh. If I want to smash things, you'd better get the fuck away from me.

Vic launches himself at Dru. He swings wildly, and I recognize the feral look in his eyes. He doesn't see her. He doesn't see what he's doing. The red mist has him in its thrall.

I surge forward and grab Vic around the waist. I hoist him up, trapping his arms with my knees as I slam him face-first onto the couch, planting my weight on him so he can't get up.

"Let me at him." Vic tries to swing at me, but the angle's all wrong and the blow glances off my elbow. "I'll break his stupid neck."

"Who?"

"Zack Lionel Sommesnay. He's here and he has his hands all over my sister."

Fuck.

Sommesnay's here.

He dares to show his face in Livvie's club?

He's dancing like he doesn't have a care in the world after kidnapping our girl.

The red mist doesn't creep up on me like it usually does. It slams into me, the force of my rage so powerful that it knocks me sideways. I drop Vic's body on the floor. He cries out in pain, but I don't hear him over the blood pounding in my ears.

He hurt my Fergie.

He dies tonight.

"Where?" I growl.

"Don't do anything, Cas," Fergie cries. "We're in the middle of a crowded club. Just let him go. No one else is getting hurt tonight."

Normally, one word from those crimson lips and I'm tamed. But not tonight, not when Sommesnay's bones aren't yet in liquid form.

"I saw them beside the stage," Vic brushes himself off. "He's dancing with my sister."

I storm down the steps, shoving people out of the way. I'm vaguely aware that behind me, girls are screaming and that stupid glass screen near the bar is now in pieces on the floor, but I don't stop. I don't turn around. My vision pulses with the red fog.

Sommesnay must die.

I don't give a fuck about Vic's fucking sister. She was all too happy to help me destroy Fergie. It was her idea to release the video, and she stole from the Poison Ivy Club and went behind our backs.

But Sommesnay *hurt* Fergie.

I'm going to enjoy this. I've been looking for a subject to practice my Viking blood eagle.

I reach the edge of the stage. The DJ throws down his headphones and flees, and the speakers scream with feedback. I tear men from their cowering partners and study their faces, searching for the man who hurt my girl. I throw a guy into the lighting rig and another one through a table. Where is he? Where—

"Cas! Over there."

I whirl at the sound of Vic's voice and follow his finger toward the stage door. Of course. The coward has fled. I shove more people aside and throw open the door. Vic pants at my heels.

"Hello, Cas." Juliet blocks the hallway with her body. "You can't—"

I crash into her, sending her flying backward. She screams as I pin her to the wall with one hand. The other reaches into my boot for my knife.

"Where is he?" I press the blade to her throat.

"Cas, that's Juliet." Vic grabs my arm and tries to pull me off his sister, but I won't let the witch get away this time.

"WHERE IS HE?" I thunder.

"Gone," she manages to smirk, even though I've got that knife against her throat. "He's already in his car, speeding far away from you."

"Where's the coward slinking away to hide?"

"I don't fucking know where he's holed up." Her big eyes, eyes that are so much like my best friend's, and yet so much more sinister. "Vic, make him get this knife away from my throat."

"Cas, can you chill the fuck out?" Vic tries to grab for the knife, but I growl at him, and it must be fucking terrifying because he backs off, hands raised. I press the knife deeper into Juliet's skin. She whimpers as I draw a line of blood.

My veins pulse with life. I missed Sommesnay, but Juliet's right here. She's under my power and she's hurt Fergie so, so many times, for reasons that still aren't clear to me. She said that she was protecting Victor, but she's hurting him now by leaving him and showing up at the club on Sommesnay's arm.

It would be so easy. It would feel so orgasmic to cut her stomach open like a piñata and pull out all the treasures...

"You were out there grinding your ass against the guy who kidnapped our girl," I snarl, bending her head back so far I can hear something click in her spine. "I never liked you hanging around with us, and now... now I'm going to enjoy ripping your ribs out one by one and making a necklace out of your knuckles before I go after your little boyfriend—"

"Don't touch him," she chokes out. "I'm... so close..."

The haze makes it difficult to focus, but something in her words jolts me. Juliet isn't begging for her life.

She's asking me to spare Sommesnay, and that's not like her.

Something slams into me from the side, and although I'm not able to be thrown around, the weight loosens my grip on Juliet, and she manages to slip under me... straight into her brother's arms.

Vic winces as he rolls the shoulder that he used on me, and glares up at me. "Listen to what she has to say."

"She's lying—"

"Cas, let me spell this out in plain English. Even this should get through that thick skull of yours – if you kill my sister, we are no longer friends. Now," Vic peers down at his sister. "Why were you here with Sommesnay?"

"Because I've spent the last few weeks trying to convince him to fall for me, *obviously*." Even though she's trembling, Juliet can't resist a flick of her hair.

Vic opens his mouth, but no sound comes out.

The great Victor August is speechless.

Not me. I'm ready for action. I whirl around and advance on them both, ready to tear her away from him if I don't like her answer. "Why?"

"*Why?*" She puffs out her lip. "Because everyone hates me! Because I want to show Mom that I can be valuable, too. Because Vic's been talking about responsibility and loyalty for our whole fucking lives, and some of it has stuck, okay?"

Vic finds his voice. "Jules, you can't do that. No way will Sommesnay believe you. You'll get yourself killed—"

"So? If I stuck around the house, your trained dancing bear would have killed me, anyway." Her eyes flash at me. "True?"

"True," I growl.

Juliet shoves her brother away. "See? And Sommesnay believes me. He thinks Mom disowned me, which is practically true—"

"It's not true! Mom wants—"

"—but if I bring her back the information she needs, then she'll have to welcome me back. That is, if you two stooges don't ruin my plan. Now, let me go so I can find Sommesnay and give him my 'woe is me, Cas tried to kill me' act so he'll trust me enough to reveal his next move." She rubs the cut on her neck, where the blood is already drying. "Thanks for the wound, by the way. It helps to sell the story."

I grab her and slam her back against the wall. "How about I separate your head from your body? That should give your story the credibility it desperately needs."

"Juliet," Vic yells. "You're not safe with him. He tried to kill Dad."

"Don't you think I know that?" she whispers. "But he thinks I hate your fucking guts, and right now I'm closer to him than anyone. Who the fuck do you think I am, Vic? Do you think that I'd betray our family just because I was forced to do a little yard work for Cali Dio? Give me some fucking credit and tell the bear to let me go."

"Drop her, Cas."

"She's lying," I growl. My fingers tighten around her throat.

Juliet's eyes widen, and she kicks and thrashes, but she's a pathetic little stick and I can break her like a twig.

"No. She's not. I know my twin. She's telling the truth. Let her go."

"No."

"Cas," Fergie comes up beside me. I didn't even know she'd followed us down here. Her voice is the only thing that can reach me. She grabs my wrist, and her touch burns through me until it's so hot and so certain that I unclench my fingers and drop the knife. Juliet ducks under his arm and puts a stack of chairs between us.

"Keep him away from me," she growls at her brother.

"Juliet, please," Vic begs. "You don't have to do this. Come back and I'll make Mom see reason. You won't have to do any more work for Cali, I promise you. Just please, don't gamble your life with Sommesnay."

"Unlike you, Sommesnay won't dare hurt me," she says with a defiant flick of her hair. "He needs the information that only I can give him."

The red mist closes tight as the full impact of those words sinks in. I turn to Vic, and I can tell from the way his face crumples that he understands what Juliet isn't saying.

"You told Sommesnay how to get to Gabriel," Vic whispers.

"I swear I had no idea what he'd do with him," Juliet says. "He was never going to kill either of them."

"That's not what he told me," Fergie said. "He set up the freezer so that both Gabriel and I would be dead within a few hours."

"Bitch, please," Juliet scoffs. "What would be the point in that? As you said, only a stupid kidnapper kills the only leverage he has. And Sommesnay's not stupid. That freezer had plenty of air. He showed me the venting system he had installed. You could have survived in there for weeks. He wanted to scare you into shutting up because you're so fucking annoying."

"If that were true, Gabe wouldn't be in rehab right now, trying to get his voice back." Vic's voice cracks. "He's our dad, and you let Sommesnay take him. He might not ever be able to sing again. How *could* you?"

Juliet pales, but she stands firm. "He'll be okay. You got to them in time."

"Jesus, Jules. Livvie's daughter was giving Sommesnay information, too. Do you know what Cali just did to her?"

"I can give you a demonstration," I growl.

Juliet raises her chin. "She bought into Sommesnay's bull-shit. I don't. Sometimes the work we do is dangerous, and we all accept that, even Gabe. That's what you tell Mom."

"How long has this been going on?" Vic demands. "Sommesnay only went after Fergie and Gabriel this week. That's not enough time for you to... what? Prostitute yourself for his trust?"

"Oh, nothing so crass as that, Vicky darling. I'm not a *Lucian*. Our love has been burgeoning for a while," Juliet stands defiant, her hands on her hips, "as soon as my own family made it clear that I'm not wanted. I knew it would be the right move to befriend him, to make him trust me. If I bring you Sommesnay's head on a platter, will that be enough to bring me back in?"

"You were never out, Juliet. We just want you to—"

Juliet holds her finger to her lips. "Don't talk to me, Vic. You'll ruin everything."

She shoves her brother in the chest. He staggers back, his eyes wild, but before he can pick herself up, Juliet has streaked away, out of the club and into the fathomless night.

14

CASSIUS

M y eyes fly open at the sudden chill in my body. I splutter as freezing cold water slams into my face.

"What the fuck?"

I shake my head as water drips down my nose and onto the sheets. I bolt upright and immediately wish I hadn't. The room spins wildly, and bits and pieces of the night before dance in my blurry vision. Dancing with Fergie at the club, watching Vic throw a tantrum, slicing his sister, finding out that dear old Juliet is trying to wheedle her way back into the August good books by pretending to be with Sommesnay, deciding that the best way to deal with mopey Vic was to help him get shitfaced... which apparently involved me punching a bartender and drinking vodka through a funnel, and Fergie and I crashed in her bed in a tangle of limbs and Spartacus' fur...

My brother's features leer down at me from the haze of my hangover.

"Get up," Gaius commands.

"Why the fuck would I do something stupid like that?" I try to roll over, but he catches and flips me onto the floor. I don't have the reflexes to break my fall, and land hard on my shoulder.

"Your father's here. He's going to take you to breakfast."

That's such a wonderfully ordinary sentence, and it's so completely foreign that I stare blankly at my brother, trying to make it sink in.

"Mew?" Spartacus pops his head up from between the covers. He doesn't believe it, either.

"The fuck?" I blink again. "My girlfriend beat me to a pulp and damaged my brain, so I think I heard you say that my father is taking me out for breakfast."

"He's downstairs, so hurry the fuck up and put a shirt on before Cali discovers he's here and gets stabby."

He's serious. My father is downstairs.

My father.

What the fuck am I supposed to do with that? Things have been such a whirlwind with the kidnapping and getting Fergie back that I haven't had a chance to think about the implications of Ares' appearance. Cali and Claudia needed my help to tease out the information about Sommesnay's informants, and I jumped to attention like a good little soldier because I needed to bathe in blood after what happened to Fergie.

Good old Cas, the deadly weapon, the blunt instrument of the Triumvirate. Point him at a problem and he'll annihilate it. He may be a monster, but at least he's a loyal monster.

But what happens when they take my loyalty for granted?

Death and maiming I can do, but this? This subterfuge, reading people, feelings stuff... I don't understand it. I need someone to tell me how I'm supposed to feel about the guy who fathered me appearing in my life.

"Can Fergie come too?" I ask my brother.

Gaius looks over at her. She's still sound asleep, her mouth open and adorable little breathy snores coming from her. A line of drool hangs off the corner of her mouth. She's so perfect. "If she can claw herself out of bed and be ready to go in five minutes, then sure."

He leaves, and I shake Fergie awake and tell her what's happening.

"I hate you," she grumbles, but she staggers into the bathroom and I hear the water running while I frantically try to find a shirt that doesn't have bloodstains on it.

Four-and-a-half minutes later, we emerge downstairs looking vaguely like human beings. Fergie's wearing her favorite skintight leather pants with a floaty lace shirt over top, belted at the waist with a cincher. She looks like some kind of sexy fucking pirate. I long to drag her back to bed...

But it's not to be. Gaius leads us outside. We pass through the guards at the front gates. Ares waits for us across the street, although still in range of the sniper rifle my mother keeps at the window of her bedroom. He either has a death wish or he underestimates just how much Cali wants to hang his balls from the ceiling with piano wire. He leans on the hood of his Cadillac, his arms folded, and his smile far too fucking chipper for this early in the morning.

"My son. Even dyed blue, you look dashing. I'm so happy you agreed to join us." He moves around the car and holds the door open for us. "And Fergie, such a delight."

She lets him seat her behind the driver's side, and then climbs in beside her, which I do not fucking appreciate. I manage to hold in my shit as Gaius drives us all to Guido's, a little Italian restaurant in Tartarus Oaks that we all love.

We're seated immediately at our usual private table in a tiny garden courtyard.

Fergie and I order coffee and a giant buffalo chicken pizza. Ares takes his time perusing the food section before ordering a chocolate croissant and a pot of tea.

Tea?

My father drinks tea?

What the fuck am I supposed to do with that?

Gaius and Ares keep up a steady stream of conversation – about prison, about Sommesnay's intentions, about the current state of the Triumvirate. They keep asking for my opinion, but all I can do is grunt. Beside me, Fergie squirms in her seat. She's uncomfortable, too, and I don't have to be a mind reader to know it's for the same reasons.

The two of them are talking about our family, and about all the ways they think it's gone wrong. And maybe they have a point, but they weren't here. They didn't have to live this shit, but they've decided they could do so much better.

Fergie and I are the ones Cali's training to become Imperators. And Gaius knows this, because I've told him and Cali's told him. But my older brother has slipped back into his role as the oldest son, the one who was destined to rule.

And despite Fergie telling me over and over that I am the future of the Dio family, I can't help the niggling feeling in the back of my mind that Gaius is the one who should be in charge. After all, he's the clever one and I'm just the blunt instrument.

Our food arrives. I take one whiff of the buffalo sauce and my stomach turns. I slam my fist on the table.

Gaius yelps as hot coffee splashes on his shirt. "Ow. Why'd you do that?"

"Why are we here?" I growl.

"We're here because I want to get to know you," Ares says, sipping his tea with his pinkie out like he didn't just spray croissant crumbs into his lap. "We've missed out on so much time. All these years, I've lapped up every scrap of information I can find about you. Any time a new inmate came in with a story about you, I'd make them repeat it over and over until I had the details memorized. Gaius has told me so much since we become friends. But their stories are no substitute for *you*, Cassius. You're my son and you are flesh and bone, sitting across from me, looking like you want to murder me. You're a wonder to me, Cas, and we've had so many years stolen from us. I want to start fresh."

I don't want to engage. I don't want to like him, because Cali hates him, and even being here feels like I'm betraying her, but he's smiling at me across the table and it's like looking into a wonky mirror, and Gaius is there, smiling too, and I just want... I just want...

"Why didn't you write to me?" I blurt out.

Fergie's hand squeezes my knee. I tear my eyes from my father to look over at her. She turns her head to me and even though she can't see me, she *sees* me. She senses in that way that only my shadow can sense the twisted knots in my gut, the way I'm tugged in two directions – between my brother and my mother, between my dream of being Imperator and the overwhelming desire to throw off the responsibility of this mess and go back to being the monster that everyone expects.

"You know that's not how prison works," Ares says. "I didn't have your address, and Gaius wouldn't give it to me."

Fergie's jaw tightens. I turn to my brother. "Why not?"

"Because the prison authorities read all the incoming and outgoing mail," Gaius says. "And I mean this in the nicest way, brother, but you aren't exactly good at understanding which words are in your best interests to leave out."

"What were you in jail for?" Fergie asks. She keeps her voice light and even, and I admire her control because I can tell that she's furious.

"Oh, murder. It doesn't matter. What matters is that Cali Dio put me there. I was out on assignment and she arranged for me to get caught. She thought it was for the best." Ares' eyes cloud over. "She's probably right. At the time, I hated her, but I can see now that she was only trying to protect our boy. I was a mess back then. I wouldn't have been a good father. But prison changed me, Cas, and I want the chance to be a father, if you'll have me."

We talk for hours. I ask him every question I can think of – I ask him about his life growing up in New York City (a place I've still yet to visit). I ask him how he got into crime (he was a thief for hire before Constantine Dio introduced him to the path of bloodshed and honor). I ask him about falling in love with my mom, and about the jobs he used to run for Cali.

Fergie listens intently to every word of our conversation. She says little and pushes her food around her plate. When we're done, I'm more confused than ever.

Gaius offers to drop us back at the house, but Fergie suggests we take a walk around the neighborhood. Tartarus Oaks isn't exactly the safest place for the two of us right now, but I have a gun in my belt and at least three concealed knives. My girl is pretty deadly, too. I know without her needing to tell me that Fergie wants to talk away from Cali's house. So Gaius and Ares drive off and Fergie loops her arm in mine.

We walk past Mom's gym, around the block, and past the building where Sommesnay held Fergie prisoner. We find a concrete retaining wall overlooking an empty lot and sit, our legs swinging, our fingers entwined.

"My father seems like a great guy," I say.

"Is that what you truly believe?"

"He says all the right things. Cali hates him."

"Do you hate him, Cas?" Fergie says. "It's okay if you do. He hasn't been there for you, ever. If he wanted to get to know you, he would have found a way."

"So you agree with Vic?" The tension rises inside me, but I can't be angry with her. "You think this is too big a coincidence?"

"Your brother spoke with me last night," she says.

"Yeah? He's the best, isn't he?"

"I don't know, Cas. He's..." she pauses. "He wants to take over as Imperator."

"He should take over."

As soon as I speak the words, I know it's true. A weight lifts from my shoulders.

Fergie blinks. "I thought you wanted this. I thought it was your dream."

It's strange, because she's right. All I've wanted my whole life is to be Cali's heir. Her favorite son. The one she trusts above all others.

"It was, but..." I shrug. "All these things Cali's been showing us – the accounts and payroll and the millions of pieces that have to fit into place to make a job go off perfectly... I don't know how to do any of this stuff."

"But I do." She holds my arm. "Cas, you shouldn't put yourself down so much. You're a great leader. Dio is lucky to have you."

"I'm a soldier. I love killing people. I thought that meant I'd be good at Mom's job, but..." I shrug again. "I don't want to fuck up everything she's built, especially at such a crucial time. Maybe Gaius would be better at it. He can do the thinking and I can do the killing."

"And what about me?" She lifts an eyebrow.

"Can you do both?" I ask. "You can work with my brother. I want to see the two of you leading this family to its greatest heights. But only if you promise to come on jobs with me sometimes. I want to see you in action, Death Lily. I want you at my side."

She leans into me and squeezes me tight, her tiny body so fragile and precious. But my Queen isn't so easily broken. "I'd like that very much."

15

FERGIE

After breakfast with Gaius and Ares, who I do not trust as far as I can throw them (which isn't far – I *am* blind, after all), we head over to Vic's house to see how Gabriel is doing.

We find the whole family in the ballroom. Gabriel stands in the corner, his chest puffed out as he runs through some vocal exercises with a new coach. He sounds hoarse and wheezy and – quite frankly – a bit shit.

I feel awful.

If I'd found a way to get us out of that freezer, instead of having to wait for the boys to rescue us, then my favorite musician in the world wouldn't be struggling to sing a scale.

"He's in good spirits, but I can tell he's frustrated," Claudia whispers as she settles in next to me on the couch. I hear her sip on a coffee. "At this rate, his next tour will be postponed. But they think that with time and rehabilitation, he'll get back most of his former range. I'd rather him take the time to heal properly than push himself and do more permanent damage."

"I'm so sorry."

"You have nothing to be sorry for. You brought my husband

back to me alive. I can never do enough to repay you for that." She pats my knee. "You're quite something, Fergie."

Gaius and Livvie's voices reach my ears, and I strain to listen to their conversation. What the fuck is he doing here?

Everyone seems to have accepted Cas' brother back into the fold. But is it too easy?

Gaius is telling them the same story he told me – that there's a faction within the Triumvirate who wants to overthrow them, and that Sommesnay's scheme only scratched its surface.

Livvie scoffs. "They can get in fucking line."

But Claudia seems to take what Gaius is saying more seriously. "Vic tells us that Juliet is undercover with Sommesnay. Can you find a way to keep an eye on her? I need someone to make sure that she's safe and pull her out the minute it turns to shit."

"I'll look after her personally," Gaius says gallantly.

"I'll do it," Cas pipes up.

"Not a chance, little bro. Sommesnay will see you a mile away, whereas he doesn't know who I am. I can get close and protect Juliet without attracting attention, but you and your little lady are magnets for drama. Did you see the headlines?"

A phone lands in my lap. I pick it up and turn on the screen reader so that it reads out the headlines on the news site. I expect to hear some nonsense about the British royal family, but instead, there's a clip from the video of Cas running around the house after I dyed him blue, and the headline reads, BAD BLUE BLOODS: HOW POISON IVY INFILTRATED THE IVY LEAGUES.

Oh. That's right.

Euri's article.

It feels like a million years ago when I agreed to bring down the Poison Ivy Club. I may have forgotten, but the world has not. And we still haven't fully grasped the fallout of that piece.

"Cali says that the school wants you all in a meeting on Monday," Gaius continues. "They're going to figure out what to do with you."

"We'll all be there," Claudia says in a voice that implies that Vic might arrive to the meeting in a body bag. "We've been concerned for some time that this little club might become a liability. I thought it had been shut down, but according to this excellent piece of journalism by our Fergie, you boys have made a mess worthy of a Shakespearean tragedy."

I toss the phone back to Gaius. "I'm sorry for this."

"It doesn't matter," Cas scoffs. "They won't send a Dio to prison for this."

"Are you sure about that, little bro?" Gaius smirks. "After all, *I* got sent to prison. And what about your girl here? Despite what she says, I've heard that Harvard was your dream, right, Fergie?"

I grit my teeth. "Dreams change."

"Fergie's going to Harvard," Vic says firmly. "She worked so hard, and the article implicates us, not her. We'll find a way to—"

"Leave it to me." Gaius pokes his head between me and Cas, and it takes everything I have not to slap the self-satisfied smirk from his voice. "Go to your meeting. Trust that everything will work out."

16

VICTOR

"I think you all know why we're here." Principal Garcia clasps her hands on her lap and glares at our assembled party.

Beside me, Juliet slumps in her chair with her arms folded. I'm surprised she showed up at all, but she was named in the article and I guess she still cares enough about graduating high school.

I long to reach out to my sister, to offer her some kind of comfort. But we haven't talked again since I found her at Tombs.

I'm dying to ask her about Sommesnay, about her role in all this, about how Gabriel is doing, but I don't dare. All I can do is meet her gaze with my own and try to send her a message through our twin bond. But this isn't a fantasy story and I'm not telepathic, so she turns her nose away and slumps even further in her chair.

Our mother kicks her in the shin, and Juliet sits up straight. Mom's here with Eli, who's usually the one who comes to school things – although they're used to awards ceremonies, not disciplinary hearings. I'm glad Eli's here instead of Noah, who would blow up and make this worse than it's going to be.

And it's going to be *bad*.

All of us are gathered in the 'conversation room,' which is a room filled with chairs and beanbags where Principal Garcia brings students and parents to have difficult conversations, because Stonehurst Prep loves kooky, new agey ideas like that. Fergie sits next to Eli, her dad beside her. Both their backs are ramrod straight, and her dad keeps swallowing. I'm pretty sure that he's remembering having to deal with Fergie's school after Dawson released the video.

I reach across and squeeze Fergie's hand. She squeezes back.

Cas and Cali stand behind us, refusing to take a seat. They lean against the wall with their arms folded and their best 'disgree-with-me-and-I'll-gut-you' expressions. Torsten sits in pile of beanbags in the corner, a sketchbook propped up on his knees while Livvie frantically texts on her mobile. Euri sits in a chair under the window, trying to make herself as small as possible between her two stony-faced parents. They don't look like they've spent much time in principal's offices, either.

Principal Garcia leans back in her chair and gestures to all of us. "Thank you all for taking the time to come in for this meeting. We would have liked to have dealt with this sooner, but you've been difficult to pin down."

"Family business," Cali barks.

"Yes, well, I hope that your business is concluded, because we need your full attention on the future of your children. This matter is deeply serious and will take time to resolve, and I need your cooperation. For Fergie's benefit, I'm here with the vice principal, Dave Levine, one of our college counselors, Kamilla Renaldo, and Helen Peabody, an admissions officer for Harvard, who happens to be a golfing buddy of mine. Now, let us begin."

Kamilla has also chosen not to take a seat. She peers down at us with those hawklike eyes of hers.

She smiles.

Garcia shuffles a stack of papers on her lap, making a show of it. She knows exactly how to make any student forced to sit in the conversation room break out in a cold sweat.

I'm sweating.

Despite my role as Poison Ivy leader, I kept an impeccable record at school. If Principal Garcia knew what we were really up to, she's always done a good show of looking the other way. The staff know the rumors about us, about our parents, and they keep their distance. But they can't ignore the article – it's too big, too public. I have to hand it to Euri and Fergie – they knew exactly how to hit us where it hurt.

So much has changed since Fergie embarked on her revenge mission, but the past always has a way of biting you in the ass.

"I assume all the parents are aware that an inflammatory article was published in the school newspaper, *The Stonehurst Sentinel*, last week," Garcia says. "This article was reprinted in the *New York Times*, something that has never before happened in the history of our school journalism. The contents of the article detail a long-running scheme of Victor August, Cassius Dio, and Torsten Lucian – with some help from Juliet – to manipulate admissions of students at Stonehurst Prep to Ivy League and top 20 colleges."

"Jesus fucking Christ," Livvie glowers over at Torsten, who's painting away obliviously.

Sometimes I wish I could have that kind of freedom – to just follow whatever niggling desire tugs at my mind, without consequences, without worrying what people thought of it.

"As you can imagine, this school has long prided itself on impeccable moral character, and this article has caused a mountain of headaches. We must take swift, decisive actions. I will outline my proposed plan here. Firstly, any students found to have employed the help of the Poison Ivy Club will have their college admissions reviewed and, in many cases, possibly revoked. I've thought long and hard about appropriate punishments for the instigators of this club, but quite frankly, I'm at a loss to come up with a punishment that will fit the scale of this crime. Luckily for me, since you're all over eighteen, this will be a police matter."

Police matter?

I didn't know the police would be involved. Fuck. We have people on the inside, but they'll only be able to help us so much. The authorities are dying for an excuse to poke around in our families. They'll be digging around our homes, searching for clues. They'll overhear something they shouldn't, and Cali will have to silence them all and things will get so much worse—

I glance at Mom. She looks oddly unconcerned.

"As for the school's response," Garcia continues. "Vic, Cas, Juliet, and Torsten are expelled, effective immediately."

"You can't do that," I leap up. My mother grabs me around the upper arm and yanks me back down again. I think about Torsten, who only ever followed our lead and deserves to get his diploma and go to art school. And my sister – she may have burned several bridges thanks to Fergie's fashion showcase stunt, but she's now infamous enough that some fashion institute will snap her up. And Fergie... she may have written the piece, but anyone at school will tell the cops that she was our girl. Will this be bad for Fergie? She *has* to go to Harvard...

I'm the leader. I made Poison Ivy into what it is. None of them should fall because of what I did.

"I *can* do that, Mr. Lucian," Garcia snaps. "It's my job when students break the law, as you have done. You should have thought of that before you took illegal photographs of students, teachers, and university admissions officers in compromising situations and used them as blackmail. We have enough proof to do much, much worse, but it will all be handed over to the police."

Behind her, Ms. Renaldo nods vigorously.

She sold us out.

"Victor!" My mother glares at me, and I sink down in my chair as her respect ebbs away.

"We never used the pictures," I say.

"That's not what Meredith Forsythe says." Garcia leans back in her chair, and I know she's got me. Because Juliet stole my phone and sent those pictures, the trail leads back to me.

"Vic," Eli hisses. "Shut the fuck up."

I zip it. Because they're right. It doesn't matter if we did use the pictures or not. Our parents warned us that the Poison Ivy Club would get us in trouble, and it's brought a mountain of hurt down on my family at the worst possible time.

Garcia continues. "They will not be allowed to graduate with the rest of their class. And—"

"We can make it go away," Livvie says.

"Excuse me?"

I whirl around and glance at Torsten's mother. Livvie's eyes glow with thrill. She *loves* this. I glance back at Mom, and I see a hint of a smile on the edges of her icicle eyes.

They have a plan.

Of course, they have a plan.

I wish they'd fucking filled me in.

Livvie stands. Today she's wearing a knee-length wrap dress that accentuates her tiny waist, a fur stole over her shoulders, and a pair of large, dark sunglasses she hasn't taken off even though we're inside and it's the middle of fucking winter. She lowers the glasses down her nose and peers at the principal. "This article is causing you all kinds of stress, Ms. Garcia. I can see it written all over your face. The angry parents, the dwindling enrollment, the rescinding of promised donations, the press clamoring for blood. It's all rather distasteful – a stain tarnishing Stonehurst Preparatory's fine reputation. Well, the three women in this room have a reputation, too, and I think that if you heard what I have to say, you might be rather interested."

Livvie's gaze turns meaningfully to the college admissions officer and others sitting beside the principal.

"Oh, yes, um… right." Garcia stands. "Dave, Kamilla, Helen… could you excuse us for a moment?"

Kamilla shoots daggers at Livvie, but there's nothing she can do. Dave looks ready to protest, but Helen clearly knows the reputation of the people in this room because she nods firmly and stomps her stiletto heel down on Dave's foot. He winces, but says nothing as the principal stands and holds open the door to her private office. Livvie glides inside, but not before she shoots Cali and Claudia a triumphant look.

We all stare at the closed door. I can hear muffled voices but I can't make out the words.

They emerge several minutes later, Livvie looking smug and Principal Garcia looking as if she'd been run over by a bus.

"Right." The principal collapses into her seat. "Okay."

"Yes?" my mother asks, all light and innocence.

Garcia gulps down a glass of water. From the expression on her face, she wishes it were something much stronger. "Here's what's going to happen. Victor, Cas, Torsten, and Juliet are suspended for two weeks. Victor, your place at Harvard has been rescinded."

"Crimsons aren't cheaters," Helen says primly.

I expected nothing less, but the reality of it weighs heavily on me. I've been so caught up in my mother's world and in letting Gaius talk me into running the Poison Ivy Club that I forgot to be a normal high school kid.

I made it into Harvard on my own merit, without having to call on any of my favors owed. If I wasn't Victor August, if I wasn't part of something so much bigger than myself, then I'd get to actually enjoy what my hard work has earned me.

But that is not the life for me. I'm more sure of that now than ever before.

"And as for Fergie and Euri—"

There's a knock at the door. The secretary pokes her head in. "Principal Garcia, a police detective is here to see you."

"Oh?" Garcia's face pales. She must've made certain agreements to Livvie, and now she has to get rid of this cop. "Um, yes, send him in."

I cannot hide my grin as Gaius stalks into the room, his broad shoulders stuffed into an immaculate Armani suit and a shiny black briefcase slamming into his leg.

Principal Garcia's eyebrows shoot way up. "G-G-Gaius Dio?"

"Never heard of him," Gaius says smoothly, extending a hand. "Howdy, Principal Garcia, I'm Bruce Dickinson, the officer in charge of the Poison Ivy investigation. I'll need access to your files."

Beside me, Fergie cracks up laughing. "Bruce Dickinson is the lead singer of Iron Maiden," she whispers to me.

Of course. Fergie and the Dio brothers share a love of loud, obnoxious music.

I glance back at Cali, but of course her expression is unreadable. They arranged this. They've somehow got Cas' brother, a convicted felon, to be the detective in charge of investigating the accusations Euri and Fergie made in that article.

The power of the Triumvirate at work.

Suddenly, it's all so ridiculous that I can't hold in my laughter any longer. I clamp my hands over my mouth, but a giggle bursts out.

Torsten looks up from his sketchbook. "What's funny?"

This just makes us laugh harder.

A slap around my ears. I clutch my head and glance up at

Gaius, who's glaring at me with a serious. "The law is no laughing matter, young man," he growls.

No, it's not. And even though I'm suspicious of Gaius, especially now that he seems to have wormed his way back into Cali's good graces, I can't help but be grateful that he's here. I'm the luckiest guy in the world to have the only law that matters in this town – the law of the Triumvirate – on my side.

17

FERGIE

After Gaius leaves with a stack of Poison Ivy school records and promises that these "delinquent youths would be severely punished," everyone gets their laughter under control and Principal Garcia gives Helen a chance to speak.

"Fergie and Euri, we would like to offer you both a position at Harvard. Euri, I understand that there was some misunderstanding with the school around your early application. I'd like to assure you that this has been sorted now, and we would happily accept you both as students if that's what you wish." She beams. "In addition to this, you've both been selected for a Young Writer Award, which will give you a full-ride scholarship for the entirety of your four-year degree."

Um, holy shit.

A full-ride scholarship? To Harvard?

In my wildest dreams, I couldn't have imagined this. Beside me, Dad squeals. Actually squeals like an excited puppy.

"Fergie, that's amazing." He wraps his arms around me and kisses my head. "I always knew you'd do it. Even after everything you've been through, even after we told you to give up on your dream, you never did. I'm so, so proud of you, and your mom would be proud, too."

Tears cluster in my eyes at the mention of my mom. I swallow hard. *I hope she'll be proud of what I'm about to do.*

Across the room, I hear Euri's parents making excited noises. Her mother snaps, "Hurry up, Eurydice. Tell the woman that you accept her generous offer."

Euri clears her throat. "Th-th-thank you very much for the kind offer. But I'm afraid I have to decline."

Yes, go Euri!

I want to fist-bump her, but that's a complicated maneuver when both of you are blindies.

"We apologize for our daughter," Euri's father says hurriedly. "She doesn't know what she's saying. This whole thing has come as quite a shock. Of course, she'll be delighted to accept—"

"No." Euri's voice is firmer now, and I beam at her in encouragement. "I won't be studying at Harvard. I've already accepted a place at Blackfriars University in England."

"Oh, my good friend George went there!" Claudia says. "It's an excellent school."

"I'm sure you'll love it," I say.

"She will not love it because she's not going," her father growls. "Euri, we already discussed this. England is too far away for you to study, and we can't afford to send you there. You've wanted to go to Harvard ever since you were a little girl—"

"No, *you* wanted me to go to Harvard since I was a little girl," Euri shoots back. "Actually, you wanted Artie to go there, but because of the Poison Ivy Club, she didn't go at all, so now you've pinned all your hopes on me. Well, I have an offer of a full-ride scholarship to Blackfriars, too. And that was before the article came out. Unlike you, they think I'm good enough."

"But what about your eyesight?" Her mother sounds on the verge of tears. "You won't be able to navigate that huge campus by yourself. And a plane ride over on your own! At least here we can watch out for you—"

"All those things are challenges I can overcome. I have to do this for myself. I'm doing it with or without your blessing, but I'd like it to be with." Euri's voice shakes. "I don't want to upset you but I... I need to be my own person. I need to find out what I'm made of. And if that means you're not proud of me anymore, then..."

"Oh, Euri..." her mother sobs. "Of course we're proud of you. You cannot imagine how much. We had no idea how you felt about Harvard. We didn't mean to push you. If you want to go to Blackfriars, we'll support you, but we're your parents, so it's also our job to worry about you. We'll do that until the day we die, no matter where in the world you are or what amazing adventure you have."

"Thanks, Mom." Euri sniffs.

"Well, I guess that's settled. Fergie?" Helen's voice turns to me. "What do you say? Are you going to be a Crimson?"

That's a very good question.

Harvard.

I allow the dream to wash over me – the life I've imagined for myself since I was a kid. I picture myself walking around that old campus, browsing the tiny bookshops, sipping coffee in a quad, freezing my ass off at stupid football games while yelling fight songs, spending hours hunched over my notes in a dusty library, and stuffing my head with ideas and arguments that obliterate everything I thought I knew about myself and remake me into someone new. Someone *normal.*

"I'm sorry," I say. "But I'm going to decline, too. I'm not attending Harvard next year."

Beside me, Dad stiffens. "Are you sure, Fergalish? This was your dream."

He's right. It *was* my dream. Dad's always supported me no

matter what I wanted to do, and ever since I found my mom's old crimson scarf in the back of a closet, I've dreamed of Harvard.

But I don't anymore.

Now, when I close my eyes to sleep at night, my dreams are filled with three impossible boys and a future forged in blood.

Harvard is the last piece of Old Fergie that has to die so that New Fergie can rise from her ashes.

"I'm certain," I say.

"Is there another school? Are you going to Blackfriars with Euri?"

I shake my head, not believing the words coming out of my mouth. "I won't be going to college. I have other things to do."

Vic gasps.

Dad squeezes my leg. "This isn't the life I wanted for you, and you don't have to choose it just to make me happy. You can be anything you want to be, Fergalish. Don't throw your lot in with the Dio clan unless you truly mean it. I am proud of you, no matter what you achieve."

"Thank you, Dad." His words turn my veins into liquid sunshine. "And I truly mean it. I want to be part of protecting what Cali's built."

"Good." Cali's strong, tiny hand falls on my shoulder and squeezes hard. "Because we've got work to do."

18

CASSIUS

As silent as death, I slip through the gate at the side of the Tartarus Oaks house. Moving in the shadows, I creep around to the back door, careful to avoid stepping on any of the children's toys scattered on the path.

I have my toolkit strapped to my leg, but Mom always taught me to try the door first, because there's no sense wasting effort if you don't have to. Sure enough, when I twist the handle, the door swings inward.

The guy doesn't even lock his fucking back door. What an idiot. He deserves what's coming to him for so many fucking reasons.

I move inside. The TV is on in the living room, blaring a porn channel at top volume. Takeout containers litter the table, and there's a half-eaten slice of pizza facedown on the floor, congealed cheese glued between the carpet fibers.

I take the stairs the silent way Cali taught me – not everything you learn at her gym is about how to pummel a guy's face in. I've had to perfect the art of moving my huge bulk stealthily through all manner of terrain. There's no sense in knowing how to kill a mark if you can't get close enough to take your shot.

And today, I'm getting up close and personal with Kaleb Walker.

I reach the landing without incident. Upstairs there are four rooms off the landing. I see that one is a bathroom, one is a child's bedroom, and the one at the end of the hall is the master suite. The door is open a crack and I can see the faint, flickering glow of a computer screen. The sounds of monsters being slain cover my footsteps as I move closer.

A baseball bat and mitt lean against the wall. I reach down and grab the bat.

I watch Kaleb through the crack in the door. He's eating microwave popcorn and slaying swamp demons like everything in his life is peaches and fucking cream.

Eat up, Kaleb, because the real demon is standing right outside your door.

I kick the door and it slams against the wall. The guy jumps nearly the fuck out of his skin, but that's the least of his problems now.

"Hello, Kaleb," I growl.

"W-w-who are you?"

"Your nurst wightmare... I mean, your blurst... I mean, don't talk back to me." I slam his face into his desk. "You run a site where people post naked pictures of their exes without their permission. You traffic in revenge porn, and I'm here to shut you down."

"It's not me!" he blubbers.

"Don't lie to me." I lift his head long enough to slide a printout onto the desk, then slam his face down on top of it. "That's your name on the domain registration, is it not?"

"Owwww, fuck, my nose!"

When I lift him again, blood is splattered across the printout. "Answer the question."

"Yes. Okay, yes! It's my site!"

"You exploit these women for clicks. You get all these jealous, pathetic incels riled up in the comments, and they go into the real world and ruin girls' lives."

"Hey, man, I just provide the server space. What people do with it is their problem. And if these girls didn't want naked pictures of themselves on the internet, they shouldn't take naked pics—argh!"

He cries out as I slam his head again. Blood splatters over his computer screen. I drop him on the floor and attack the computer with the baseball bat.

"You've got servers?" I demand. He's weeping like a little bitch. "Servers! Where are they? Tell me or I bash your head in."

"I-i-in the next room!"

He points to the wall. I leave the room and find the servers in the spare bedroom beside his. I smash them, too. I should have brought Vic along. He would have loved this part.

"You're officially out of business," I growl. "If I hear that your people are operating another site or have restarted this one, I will be very angry, and you do not want to see me angry. You're going to make sure that all your friends in your little network of online douches obey this rule, too, or I'll hold you personally accountable."

"I–I–I'll tell them."

"No, you won't." I drag him into the center of the room. "But when I'm done with you, they'll get the message."

I set about my grisly work. Kaleb's screams are so loud that I'm surprised no one in the neighborhood calls the police. I did leave my bear claw marks in the guy's front door, so anyone who stops by knows that I'm at work.

When I'm done, the sun has long since fallen below the horizon. I call Fergie. "I have a surprise for you. Can you get Seymour to give you a ride if I give you a Tartarus Oaks address?"

"Cas, I'm at Vic's." She sounds grumpy. "And it's the middle of the fucking night."

"Even better. Come play with me, naughty girl."

Fergie arrives a few minutes later, driven by Vic. I go outside to greet her and walk her upstairs to the bedroom. Vic slinks up the stairs after us, a disgusted expression on his face as he takes in the pigsty of a house and the obvious signs of a kid.

"This is no place to bring up a child," he murmurs.

"Well, it won't be a problem for little Jimmy any longer. Surprise." I fling the bedroom door open to showcase my achievement.

Vic takes one look in the room and sprints down the hallway. I can hear him retching. He's so chicken shit.

Fergie grins at me as she tightens her grip on my arm.

"What's the surprise?"

Oh, right. I feel so stupid. Of course, she can't see what I made for her. Fergie's so capable that sometimes I make flubs like this. Blame the brain damage.

"You're looking at Kaleb Walker, owner of the site where Dawson posted your video. Or rather, you're looking at the blood eagle I made of him."

"Blood eagle?"

"Yes. It's a Viking punishment, they wrote about it in poems and shit. I've separated his ribs from his spine..." I take her wrist and place her hand on Kaleb's body, showing her the finer elements of the grisly execution. "...and then I swung them outward, and pulled his lungs through the opening to create the 'wings' of the eagle. I was hoping he'd still be alive when you got here so we could watch him die together, but he carked it. I think it's difficult to live through the blood eagle. It's quite beautiful. Don't you think it's beautiful?"

"It is beautiful," she breathes. Fergie spends a bit of time touching the corpse, seeing my present with her fingers. She stands and attempts to wipe the dried blood from her hands. "Cas, I adore you, and this is very sweet, but I've already forgiven you. You don't need to atone."

"But I want to," I growl. "I want to claw the eyes out of every single human who watched those tapes without your consent."

I want to undo what happened to you, but I can't.

Ever since Fergie said that she's not going to Harvard, I've renewed my mission to make the people who wronged her pay. Vic won't let me take on Juliet, so I've made a list of every person associated with the revenge porn website, and put Torsten to work cracking the identities of the people behind the awful comments on Fergie's video. Kaleb is the fourth person I've made into a blood eagle this week. I'm getting better.

Each one makes the wretched guilt that churns in my heart hurt a little less.

Because I know the truth.

If she'd never met me, Fergie would be Harvard-bound right now.

Even without the Poison Ivy Club, she would have found a way. She's so resourceful and clever. But I snuck into her room and tore apart her defenses and got her addicted to my world of bloodshed and depravity, and now she's given up on that dream.

But why be a brainy lawyer when you can be queen of a crime empire?

"Brother, you're the sweetest psychopath I know." Fergie leans in and plants a kiss on my bloodstained forehead. "I wanted to hurt them all, too – once upon a time. But I don't anymore. I need to put that chapter of my life behind me. The Fergie who wanted that life is dead and buried, and New Fergie – she wants you. And you don't have to prove yourself to her."

"But..." I search for the words. My brain takes so long to process everything she says to me. "I don't want you to hate me for taking Harvard away from you. We were supposed to get you in—"

"A wise blue man taught me that hate is only another side of love." Fergie's smile lights up the whole room. "My future is with you, and Vic and Torsten, and the Triumvirate. You heard the admissions officer – I could have gone to Harvard on a full-ride scholarship if I wanted to. I could have turned my back on Emerald Beach and never looked back. But I chose *you*, Cas. I chose you because I think we have a chance to create something truly remarkable, to build on what your parents have started. And being part of that excites me – I'm alive in a way I've never known before, and that's not just because of the filthy things you do to my body. But when you gift me with these men from my past, I have to look back at the person I was before. And I don't want to be Old Fergie anymore. Do you understand?"

I do. Because when I think about the video, I look back at the monster I was to her, and I'm overcome with waves of shame that threaten to pull me under. Galen might say that I have brain damage from the fight, but what actually happened is that Fergie knocked sense into me.

I don't know if I'll ever forgive Old Cassius for what he did to her, but I'm a new man now, and I'll step forward into the sun with my Queen at my side.

"What does looking forward mean for you?" Fergie asks, looping her arm in mine and nudging me to leave the room.

"It means now that you're not going away to college," I say. "So you and Gaius can learn the ropes from Mom and take over when she retires, and I will be our top assassin. I'll run the gym and the school so you can focus on our most important work. Oh," I rub her smooth stomach. "And I'll put a baby inside you. We'll make an heir worthy of the kingdom we'll build."

"And where are Vic and Torsten in this future of ours?"

"I don't give a fuck about them."

Fergie folds her arms and fixes me with that sightless glare of hers.

"Fine," I huff. "If they want to put babies inside you, then that's cool. But I get to go first."

She kisses my nose. "You were my first in all the ways that counted, Cas. You were my first taste of freedom and my first glimpse of destiny. Now, how about we go tell Kaleb's Mom that she doesn't have to fight for full-custody any longer, and then you and I go and get some ice cream? New Fergie loves ice cream."

I'm in the art gallery, listening to Nick Cave at top volume and sawing planks of wood for my secret art project. Sawdust swirls around me, coating the paintings on the wall with a fine layer of grey snow. For once, my mind, which always balances precariously on the edge of overwhelm, is calm and happy—

"Torsten."

I jump as a voice disturbs my calm.

I drop the saw and glance up, and my mind starts to race as Livvie's face emerges through the dust.

"What are you doing to my art gallery?" She glances around at the piles of lumber and the half-filled garden pond.

"It's art," I say.

"I gathered."

"You always said I could use this room for my work." I pick up the saw. "If that changed because I'm not living here, then—"

"No, no, it's fine, but..." She touches her toe to the edge of a planter box I've filled with tulips. "This is... quite a departure from your other work. Can you explain it to me?"

"It's a surprise. For Fergie."

She watches me, and I think she expects me to say more, but I can't. I don't know if I'll even be able to explain it to Fergie when the time comes.

Livvie's heels clack as she crosses the room. She sits down on one of the leather benches, crossing her legs and clasping her hands over her knees. For a long time, she says nothing, her eyes flickering over the displays I've started and the ruined surfaces of my copied paintings. Her eyes widen.

I wish I knew what she was thinking. If Vic were here he'd be able to tell me based on the way her mouth is set in that thin line, and if Fergie were here she'd tell me that it doesn't matter what Livvie thinks. All that matters is what I think.

But that's not true. Livvie is powerful. She can give me the things I want or take them away. And I don't know what she's doing in here or why she's *staring* at me.

Livvie puffs out her cheeks. "This past year, a lot of things in my life that I thought were permanent have been stripped away. When Sommesnay blew up the museum, I got scared. And don't you dare tell anyone that, but I know you won't. I was so afraid, Torsten, so afraid that if he could collapse a whole building down around me, nothing in my life is as secure as I believe. Ever since, I've been fighting to ensure that Sommesnay can't destroy me, or destroy us."

I say nothing. Livvie doesn't seem to expect me to respond. Her eyelids flicker shut as she continues, "I remember growing up in my father's house as the afterthought, the daughter he never wanted or respected. I remember how precarious my life felt. When I found Claudia and Cali and we built the Triumvirate, I thought that my life would never feel precarious again. But that changed when I rescued you, and then the girls. Suddenly, I saw that these beautiful children who I love with everything I am are my biggest weakness, and that evil people will try to use them against me.

"What I'm saying is that I've let my own insecurities get in the way of being a good mother. Especially to you, my first, my special boy. I was so worried that your... *uniqueness* would make you a target that I've been extra hard on you. The more you tried to forge your own path, the more I fought to hold you close—"

"Forging a path would be very difficult," I say. "You would need a lot of metal and a very large forge. It would be more sensible to make a path out of concrete."

Livvie laughs, and while the sound of her laughter usually makes my stomach twist, today it feels good. "Yes, Torsten. I agree. That would be difficult. I'm saying that I know I've made your life difficult, especially recently. I've tried to push your relationship with Fergie, and undermine your friendships with Cassius and Victor. I've created a rift with my two closest friends because I was so afraid of losing them, or losing my children to Sommesnay, and all the while my own daughter was working with my enemy. Trudi's gone – Cali got rid of her and I know it was the right decision, the only decision, but I am so, so, sad..." Livvie draws a shuddering breath, her shoulders trembling. "I should have learned from you that in our cruel world, friendship, and love, and loyalty are more important than anything."

"Cassius says that hate is another side of love," I say, trying to be helpful.

"That monster is wiser than anyone gives him credit for." Livvie smiles. "I think you have hated me sometimes, yes?"

I keep my mouth closed. I can't lie to her, and I don't want to say yes because that's not very nice.

"That's okay, Torsten, I would have hated me, too." Livvie turns her face away from me. "But I want you to know that I've never hated you. I love you so, so much. And I admire you greatly. You're such a steady force, Torsten. We have had to deal with some horrific things this year – the bombs, Fergie's kidnapping, losing Trudi, and all of Sommesnay's antics. Through it all, you've been so strong. You put those you love first, you listen more than you speak, and when you do speak, you say what you mean. I think you're a fine human, and to think that you are this way in spite of me..."

"Because of you," I correct her. "I am who I am *because* of you."

Livvie turns to face me again, and I jolt with surprise at the tears streaming down her cheeks. I have never, ever known my mother to cry. She didn't even cry when Cali told her what Trudi had done, or when Cassius brought back what was left of her body.

"My son... my beautiful, misunderstood son. I came to tell you that if you still want to go to art school, I will make it happen. And if anyone has a problem with what you paint, they can take it up with me."

My heart feels like it's going to float away. All my life I've wanted to hear my mother say these things. I wished she could see me as who I am and not as the son she wished me to be. And all along, she *has* seen me. Loved me. Feared for me. What felt to me like her cruelty and her rejection were really her own fears keeping us apart.

And Fergie would tell me that it doesn't make the way she treated me okay, but after everything we've been through, it's a beautiful thing to hear.

I always assumed that I'm too strange to be loved, but Fergie taught me that we're all a little strange, that I deserve kindness and respect, and that I can ask for what I need.

I look at my mother and nod. I can't find the words I need to say what I'm feeling, but for once, she doesn't seem to need them. She holds her arms open. "Torsten, son, will you...?"

I shake my head. I can't do it. My hand flaps at my side.

Her mouth wobbles, but instead of yelling at me the way she might have in the past, she lowers her arms. "Son, I would like to work on our relationship. I would like us to be closer. I would like one day for you to be able to forgive me. Would you like that?"

"Yes."

"Okay." Her shoulders tremble as she stands and offers her right hand to me. "You can't do a hug, but could we maybe shake on it?"

I reach across my workbench and take her hand. Her fingers feel surprisingly small and frail and warm. The sudden touch courses through me, threatening to unravel me. I can smell Livvie's zesty perfume, mixed with the crab on her breath from lunch and the tang of the sawdust clinging to her designer dress. "Fergie and I do something to check that we're okay. I squeeze, and she squeezes back."

I squeeze her hand lightly.

Her eyes fill with tears again as she squeezes back. "I'm better than okay, son."

20

VICTOR

Days go by, tense and dripping with secrets.

My mother spends all day, every day, in her office, hunched over her shipping reports. There have been more attacks on her supply lines, and other criminal organizations encroaching on her territories. Livvie and Cali report similar incursions.

The word is out that the Triumvirate is weakened, and the vultures circle.

We scour the city but find no trace of Sommesnay. Juliet won't pick up her phone, although she does occasionally text to let me know she's still alive. I tell her that we are ready to move on Sommesnay the moment she tells us where he is, but she tells me to be patient, she's working on something.

I've stopped talking to the others about Jules. No one believes her, not even Mom. Fergie tries to listen, but I can tell that she doesn't trust Juliet. I can't say that I blame her, but my sister needs a friend right now. And I'm it.

I stalk Juliet's social media like a psycho, but my sister the socialite and up-and-coming designer is surprisingly absent. I resort to checking the society blogs for sightings of her at the parties and charity balls around the city. Nothing. Wherever Sommesnay has her holed up, he's being careful not to reveal himself.

It makes me nervous. No, that's not right. It makes me fucking insane.

Every few minutes I have to get up and check on Fergie and Mom.

I text Juliet constantly, demanding she reply so I know she's okay.

Every time the house creaks or a door slams, I'm certain it's Sommesnay come to kill everyone I love.

The one bright spark is that Fergie's been living here with me. I know she's worried about me – my blind girlfriend can't exactly hide the concerned way her mouth twists whenever my body clenches with nerves. But I can't say I'm sad to have her curled up in the crook of my arm at night or shoveling food across from me at Thursday night dinner. When Fergie's not at school, she's in the studio, helping Gabriel with his throat exercises, cleaning out cat cages with Eli, having long, shouty political debates with Noah, and helping me water the plants in the greenhouse.

Fergie fits in so well that she's practically family. My chest swells with pride to hear her and Claudia talking shop, but that pride is twinged with an inescapable sense of loss.

I think about my own shattered dreams of Harvard surprisingly little, although I hate seeing Fergie go off to school when I can't go with her. I don't like sitting at home doing nothing, especially when Sommesnay's still out there and he's made it perfectly clear that he doesn't care about collateral damage.

Juliet. Fergie. The two women I love most in the world – holding onto them feels like trying to catch sand in my fingers.

ON THURSDAY, I'm outside trimming leaves off my belladonna when my phone rings.

"It's me," Fergie says. I can hear the sounds of lockers slamming around her, and feel an uncharacteristic twist in my gut. I used to rule that school, and now I'm barely going to graduate, my girlfriend isn't going to college and my sister is shacked up with a madman in some gallant attempt to get back in our mother's good graces. Nothing about this year is turning out the way I thought.

"Hello, me." I cradle the phone to my ear. "Busy day?"

"Yeah, I had a history test, but I think I aced it." Fergie lowers her voice. "Vic, you need to relax, because I'm about to tell you something that you won't like."

"What's that?" My mind immediately whirs with horrific things that might've happened.

"I'm not going to be home for dinner tonight."

I'm momentarily stunned by her choice of the word 'home.' But then her words sink in. "You're going to miss Thursday night dinner. Why?"

"You know how Torsten's been working on this secret art project of his? Well, it's finally finished and he wants to show it to me. He says that his mother talked to him the other day, and he wants to tell me what she said, so that's... interesting. I'm going to go around to his place. I could just do it tomorrow but you should see how excited he is."

"He won't mind if you go tomorrow." Fergie's presence at the table for Thursday night dinner has helped everyone in the absence of my sister, whose ghost hangs heavy in the house. I don't want to face my parents alone.

"I'll mind," she says. "Besides, it might be good for you and your parents to talk without me. I know I've been a distraction for all of you, but that's not always a good thing."

"Fine," I sigh. "And you'll get Seymour to drop you off, and you won't go anywhere without a guard and you'll—"

"I promise I'll be careful, Vic. Livvie's got her whole place locked down like a Swiss bank. Sommesnay can't touch us there."

AT DINNERTIME, I drag myself downstairs. The dining table is set for six, just as it always is. Eli's already sitting in his place, staring at Juliet's setting with an unreadable expression on his face. I hope the information she's gathering will be useful, because knowing she's with him is tearing our family apart.

Mom sets the food in the middle of the table. We didn't have a Milo because Eli usually cooks, but on Thursday nights Mom likes to order in food from her favorite restaurants. She likes doing something special for her family. Lately, it all tastes like cardboard, but that's not the fault of the chefs.

I'm sliding into my chair when my phone rings. Mom frowns at me. "Phones off at the table. You know the rules."

I pull it out and see my sister's name on the call screen. "It's Juliet."

Mom's face transforms. She waves me into the hall. She knows Juliet won't talk if she thinks they're all listening.

"Where are you, sis?"

I can't believe it. She called. She called me.

"Quiet, Vic, I don't have much time." There's noise around her – glasses tinkling, forks scraping, the murmur of voices, jazz music. She's at a restaurant. "Zack's in the bathroom."

"You're out with *him*."

"Of course I am," she snaps. "This is what you have to do if you want information. And I've got something for you."

"What?"

"I can't say over the phone. You need to meet me. Now. I've got a plan to get out of here as soon as he returns. Meet me in the parking lot of the Elysium hotel. Come alone. I'm not talking to Mom. Or *her*."

I gather by *her*, she means Fergie. "But Jules—"

She's already hung up.

Mom glares at me as I return to the dining room. She clasps her hands at her waist in an attempt to hide how much they're shaking. "Well? What did she have to say?"

"She wants me to meet her. I have to go."

"You can't go alone, Vic." She grabs my wrist. "What if you're walking into a trap?"

"That's exactly why I have to go." I shake her off. "It's not a trap. Jules and I have a code for if something like this happens – a word that we say on the phone if one of us is in trouble. She didn't say the word. She really does have information. And she specifically said she'd only speak to me, since I'm the only one who trusts her."

"It's not that we don't trust her," Mom starts. "But she needs to—"

"I can't keep her waiting," I yell as I run off. I leap into the car and speed over to the hotel, remembering the last time I'd been there, when I'd come to pick up Torsten so we could find Fergie and he'd run outside, buck naked.

When I arrive at the Elysium, the parking lot is half-full of cars, and the hotel's restaurant buzzes with people. That must've been where Juliet was having dinner. My stomach growls as the scent of garlic and cream waft across my nostrils, and I think longingly of the food Mom and my dads are tucking into back home.

I scan the parking lot several times, but Jules isn't here yet. I pull the car into a spot in the darkest corner and wait. She's obviously sneaking out behind Sommesnay's back, so it might take her some time to get away.

I crane my neck to scan the hotel's facade. Thirteen stories of balconies, many with lights as couples share a drink on this brisk winter evening. Is Sommesnay here? Does he have my sister holed up in one of those rooms?

I wait.

I wait until I'm so agitated that I'm biting my nails and jabbing all the buttons on the dashboard.

I wait as the moon journeys across the heavens.

I wait until the truth bears down on me.

Juliet's not here.

She isn't coming.

I pick up my phone to call her, and then, behind me, from the direction of Harrington Hills, I hear a boom that shakes the ground beneath me...

21

FERGIE

The moment I step through the front doors of the Lucian mansion, I'm ambushed by my number-one fan.

"Fergie, Fergie, will you play Monotoly with me?" Isabella tugs on my hand.

"I don't know if I can. Your brother wants to show me something—"

"He said we had time." Isabella drags me into the living room and commands me to sit on the other side of the card table. She's already set up the Braille Monopoly set I gave her. Isabella loves me because Monopoly is her favorite game but everyone is too busy to play it with her. She calls it Monotoly, and it's adorable. "I'll be the horse."

"Okay, I'll be the top hat."

While Isabella rolls her second set of doubles and buys up Park Place, I send a quick text to Torsten, letting him know I've been waylaid by his sister. He replies, "Yes," which is very on-brand for Torsten.

I'm handing over the last of my hundred-dollar notes for

rent when Torsten enters the room. He doesn't say a word but I can smell solvents and paint on him. He's been putting the finishing touches on his project.

"I'm going to go with Torsten now," I say as I stand up. "But it's been fun getting my ass kicked by you again. We can start our game where we left off when I get back, if you like?"

"That would be awesome!" Isabella bounces around the room. Torsten hurries me away before Isabella ropes us both into a competitive Connect 4 tournament.

"Torsten, where are we going?" I laugh as he hurries me through the winding corridors of his mother's vast home.

"To the art gallery," he says. "It's supposed to be a surprise."

"Okay, then I won't ask any more questions about it. Tell me what your mother said."

"She said that she's sorry for the way she treated me because she's been afraid. She said that she wants me to go to art school."

"Torsten, that's amazing!" I can't believe that Livvie had the self-reflection to admit all that. I burst with happiness for Torsten. It's all he ever wanted. "Did she say that—"

"We're here," he says, as he throws open the doors to the gallery. Obviously, I can't see anything, but I can already feel that the space is different.

The Lucian gallery is a long, high-ceilinged room with a distinctive hollow echo. It smells of floor polish and plaster, with a slight metallic taste on the tip of my tongue that always makes me think of the desperate, longing kiss Torsten and I shared here.

But not anymore.

Now, the space feels *alive*. The echo has become full and rich and complex, and I can already tell that the room is filled with objects that fill the space. I'm assaulted by different smells – a heady floral scent mingles with wood and paint and plaster and all kinds of other things I'm not yet able to determine. There's the tang of sawdust from recent constructions, and the salt of the ocean. I hear water running and leaves rustling in an invisible breeze.

"Torsten, what is this?" I breathe.

"It's an art gallery for you."

"I don't understand."

He squeezes my hand and drags me into the room. "I wanted you to see what I see when I look at paintings. So I made the paintings into objects and smells and sounds. This is Monet's garden at Giverny, where he painted the water lilies and trees and flowers."

He pulls me into a display, and the floral smell practically overpowers me. I stand in the garden and breathe in that heady, impossible scent. We walk through a cobbled path and Torsten shows me where I can run my fingers through the water, touch lily pads, and listen to the plants moving on a breeze blown in from cleverly concealed fans. "Monet was fascinated by capturing movement," he says. "Ripples in water, trees swaying, the passage of time. I've tried to create a living, breathing garden."

How has he done this? It's amazing.

Next, we tour Mondrian's squares, stepping through huge spaces where Torsten uses different temperatures and textures to represent the thick black lines and primary colors the Dutch artist was known for. Torsten has music playing in this exhibit – the jazz music that inspired Mondrian to create his abstract pieces in a search for the visual rhythms of modern life.

With his hand still in mine, Torsten leads me into his exhibit for *The Scream* – that terrifying work that enraptured us both when we first came to the gallery together. He helps me to stand on a wooden bridge and encourages me to grip the railing. The salt tang of the ocean plunges into my nostrils. Unsettling, discordant music plays, and a yawning, gaping presence from below threatens to suck me in. A cloying scream rises in the back of my throat.

Torsten places his hand over mine as he stands beside me. He lets out a wild scream that echoes through the space, only to be swallowed by the void beneath us. And I remember that I don't have to hold back for him, that he made this for me so that I can understand what he feels when he sees these paintings, and so I toss my head back, and I scream.

We scream and scream, and it's terrifying but so, so cathartic. It's a release of everything that's been weighing on me. I scream until my throat is hoarse, and when I turn to speak to Torsten, I'm surprised to feel tears streaming down my cheeks.

"This is amazing," I breathe.

"I wanted you to see what I see," he says.

"It's so... Torsten, this is perfect."

"I also made tactile versions of the paintings." He drags me off the bridge and brings me to the wall of the gallery, pushing my fingers into the artwork. Instead of being flat, the planes and shapes of the image are rendered in relief. "Remember when you felt the sweep of the brushstrokes? I used this 3D printing method to exaggerate the textures and make these relief models."

My skin tingles beneath his touch as he moves my hand over the tactile paintings, describing the way each artist used texture and layers of paint. I've never heard him this animated before, and with every word I fall a little more in love with him.

I can't believe he did all this for me.

With the tactile paintings, I can understand the dimensions and skill of the artist. But in the living displays, Torsten has captured something so much more profound. He's captured the *feeling* of art, the *essence* of it, and that's something I've always believed was lost to me.

He's given me something I thought I could never have.

Torsten cuts off his talk about the Fauvists abruptly to ask, "Do you like it?"

"Torsten, I… I think this is one of the most brilliant things I've ever experienced," I say. "I think you need to exhibit these displays. The whole world should experience this."

"I can't do that." He recoils a little.

"Why not?"

"Because… because I made it for you. Because it's in my mother's gallery and we can't put the gallery on wheels and take it around the country."

I laugh a little. "No, silly. You could turn this whole house into a big crazy art gallery where people can walk through paintings and touch art in a way they never could before. Or you can pack down the displays and take them on a tour, the way Gabriel tours with his band. You set this up in gallery spaces all over the country, and other blind people like me can come and experience it."

"No one would want to do that."

"Yes," I say firmly. "They will. I know you've been told a lot of bullshit about what you are and aren't good at, but I'm telling you the truth now when I tell you that this is *brilliant*. What you've created here has allowed me to see art without eyes, and that's such a special gift. I don't want to hog it all for myself. I can put you in touch with the head of the blindness institute where I learned to echolocate. I know they'd be interested in helping you to get this up and running, and I bet we can convince Livvie to give you some money to cover costs."

Torsten squeezes my hand. "You would have to run it. I can't—"

"Why not?"

"Because…" he struggles for words. "Because no one will like it if I run it."

"That's not true. I think you're the perfect person to take this exhibition to the people who need it most. Everything you've created here comes from your big, beautiful heart. You told me once that you copy famous paintings because you want to understand them. From what I've felt and smelled and touched today, I think you understand these paintings better than anyone else. You don't have to go to art school to make this happen. You have the money and the skill to do it right now."

"But I can't," Torsten sounds firm. "The Triumvirate. You need me here. I have to—"

"You don't have to be part of it." I think about Claudia and her three husbands and how they each have their role in her life. Gabriel has his music career and isn't involved in the family business at all, and Eli's only involved on the administration side. "You don't really want to be the head of a criminal empire, do you?"

"No."

He doesn't have to think about it.

I've known for a long, long time that Torsten's heart isn't in the family business. It feels good that he's finally acknowledged it. He has so much that he can give the world, I see no reason to force him to accept responsibility for something that he wouldn't willingly embrace.

"So, it's settled. Don't be a crime lord. Make this exhibit instead. I'll talk to Livvie. I'll make it okay with her, although it sounds as if she already knows."

Livvie may have plans for Torsten to have some role, but I think I can bring her around, even if it costs me a pound of flesh.

"Okay." He squeezes my hand again. "Do you want to see my ideas for another display? I wanted to do Picasso's *Weeping Woman*, and I thought I'd use—"

His words are muffled by a low rumble. It begins beneath my feet and rises through my body, a tsunami of dark sound and shaking that overwhelms me. My legs fly out from beneath me, and I throw out my arms as I hit the floor.

A warm body covers mine. And then the world caves in...

22

TORSTEN

I cover Fergie's body with my own as dust and debris rain down on us.

I remember the day the museum blew up. Even though I was a couple of blocks away by the time it happened, the shock wave from it knocked me to the ground. I've been in many earthquakes before, and that's what I thought it was at first, but then the sound came – like the universe tearing through the middle.

That's the sound in my ears now – a rending, a tearing, a great, silent scream from the Earth itself.

It's a bomb.

Someone has bombed our house.

I don't know what to do except lie still and shield Fergie. Hard things hit my back. I wonder if I am dead. I don't feel dead. I feel exactly the same, except that a piece of plaster hit the side of my skull and it hurts.

After some time, the rumbling stops. The bone-rattling tremor ceases, and the sound inside the gallery is changed – the silence is so loud it hurts my ears.

"Fergie?" I lift myself onto my hands. Every muscle screams

with agony. Beneath me, Fergie groans and rolls onto her side. Her face is scratched and red from the dust, and her eyes are screwed shut, but she's moving. She's okay. I saved her.

I crawl onto my knees and force myself to stand up. I have to duck beneath a steel pillar. My exhibits are ruined. The bridge from *The Scream* is broken in half and Monet's garden is strewn across the room. The stone pillars that supported the roof have toppled over. One of them has crushed my Mondrian squares.

The roof itself... it's gone. I don't know where it is.

I hope Livvie won't be angry that I lost her roof.

Fergie is okay, and that's all that matters. I hold out my hands to her and help her to her feet. I place my hand on the back of her neck and make sure she doesn't hit her head on the steel beam or the fallen pillars.

Now that she's upright, I don't know what to do next.

"Something has happened," I say. It's as accurate a statement as I can make now.

"Yup. If I had to guess," Fergie groans, "I'd say Zack Lionel Sommesnay bombed your house."

I look around. Fergie's guess seems accurate.

Sommesnay has bombed Livvie's house.

Livvie said that he'd never be able to get past her guards, but evidence suggests he found a way.

I'm frozen. I don't know what to do. If Vic were here, he'd already be issuing instructions and making plans. Cas would be punching stuff, or people. But I'm frozen by the magnitude of this. There's too much to process. My nostrils are filled with dust. It's all coming at me at once. I feel my heart give chase, my...

"Torsten," Fergie's voice helps to anchor me, to drag me back. "I think that we need to get out of the gallery. More of the roof could come down on us."

"Yes." But I'm still frozen. I don't know where to go. There's no rulebook for what to do when your house is bombed.

"Okay, then. Let's get out of here. Your mother and sisters were in the dining room. We should see if they're hurt. You're going to need to lead the way, okay? And if it looks dangerous, like there are live wires or a fire or something, we go outside."

I help Fergie twist around the steel pillar. She groans and dusts off her clothing, but there's so much dust still in the air that we both break into coughing fits. She hooks her hand into my elbow, and I lead her in the direction of the main house. We have to duck under another steel beam and climb over the ruined frame of my bridge to make it.

Inside the house, I take my time leading Fergie around the worst of the rubble. It's slow going because I have to keep making decisions about what is dangerous and what isn't, and I'm not good at that.

The bomb hasn't completely flattened the house – the second floor no longer has a roof or any windows, and many of the rooms below have bits of the floor above inside them. I have to test every step to make sure it will hold my weight, and then turn around and guide Fergie so she puts her feet down in exactly the right spots.

As we move toward the front of the house, the damage is worse – walls torn into charred skeletons, parts of the flooring blasted away. My lungs burn by the time we reach the dining room... or what's left of it.

I can hear someone crying.

They're still inside.

The hand that isn't guiding Fergie flaps frantically at my side, but it doesn't bring any relief. I feel so completely over-whelmed. I want to curl up in a ball and stick my fingers in my ears.

The only thing tethering me to the here and now is Fergie.

She turns her head to me and gives me a gentle push toward the dining room.

"Leave me here," she whispers. "I'll stay right here until you get back. You need to help them."

I want to say that I can't help them, that I can't help anybody. I don't want to leave her side, but I need to reach my sister. I make sure Fergie's holding on to the doorframe, and I move across the room, picking a path around the large table. In places, I have to balance on the supports as the floor has been blasted away. Part of Isabella's dollhouse sits in the middle of the table from where it had fallen through the ceiling from her bedroom above.

The first I come across is Shera. Her arm is crushed by a piece of stone from one of the pillars that lined the edge of the room. Livvie loves pillars; she says they make the building look like it's an ancient temple, and she's the goddess housed within.

"Torsten," my sister moans. I push the stone off her arm, and she whimpers in pain but manages to get to her feet and follow me. Around the edge of the table, I find Isabella, crouched under the edge. She peers up at me with wide eyes.

"Torsten? You found me."

"Come with me." I hold out my hand. She doesn't take it.

"I'm scared."

"Honey, it's okay," Shera reaches for her. "We're here now. Everything's going to be okay."

"No," I correct her. "Everything is not okay. The house has been bombed, and if you don't come with me right now, Isabella, you'll be crushed when the ceiling falls in, and you'll die."

Shera shoots me a look. "You can't say that. Can't you see she's too terrified to move—"

But Isabella is crawling toward me. She grabs my wrist and uses it to haul herself out of the tiny hole.

"I don't want to be crushed," she sobs.

"I don't want you to be crushed, either."

She clamps on around my waist, which makes moving slower, but I'm not going to tell her to let go. We inch around the corner of the table. I hear Fergie's voice.

"Torsten, give me an update."

"I've found Shera and Isabella. I'm looking for Livvie," I call out to Fergie.

My foot slips into something wet. I grab Isabella to stop myself from sliding over. And then I look down to see what I've stepped in.

It's blood.

A *lot* of blood.

23

FERGIE

Isabella screams. The sound tears through me, and it feels like my body is screaming along with her.

"Torsten," I yell. "Are you okay? Please answer me."

"I'm okay," he says, still inside the dining room. "Livvie is not."

"What's happened?"

"She's dead."

He doesn't say any more than that. Isabella's screams say it all – the screams of a child who has seen something so traumatic they'll never be a child again.

A few moments later, Torsten's familiar vanilla and orange zest scent reaches my nostrils, and his warm, steady hand closes around my upper arm. "We're leaving now."

Our battered group moves through the house. Shera goes ahead and says we can't get out the front door because of live wires, so we go into the living room where I played Monopoly with Isabella only a few hours ago, and climb through the gaping hole where a huge picture window had once been.

Outside, we collapse on the grass. I can hear two of Torsten's other sisters there, clinging to each other and crying. "Where's Grace?" he asks. Through sobs, they tell him that she's dead, too.

This is...

I don't know what to feel. I'm too numb with shock to digest it all.

Livvie is dead. Torsten's sister Grace is dead.

Sommesnay got to them, even through the layers of security we put in place, and he managed to place a bomb inside Livvie's house. The only people who could have gotten inside were Livvie, her family, and her most trusted soldiers.

Cas' father is right. A coup is brewing.

My phone rings. It's 'Monster' by All Time Low, the ringtone I have reserved for Cas. I pick it up.

"I'm okay," I say as soon as I raise the phone to my ear. "We're both okay."

His breath rasps against my ear, ragged and distressed. "So the bastard hit Livvie's house, too."

"What do you mean, too?"

"Cali's mansion is toast." Cas laughs, but it's that unhinged laugh that shows he's on the verge of losing his shit.

My throat tightens. "My dad—"

"Relax, Sunflower. He's okay. He and Cali were in the garden when it happened. Milo's hurt, but nothing Galen can't fix. And I've got little Spartacus in my arms. Although he doesn't like the car very much."

"The car? You were just in a bomb blast. You can't drive anywhere." My legs feel like they've been put through a blender. No way should Cas be behind the wheel.

"You're probably right. But I'm willing to bet that bastard is at Vic's house right now. Want me to pick you up?"

"Fuck yes."

I click off the call. Torsten squeezes my hand, our universal signal to each other to check we're okay. I squeeze back a little.

"That was Cas. His house got hit, too. He's coming here to get me and then we'll check on Vic."

"I'm coming, too."

"Are you sure you don't want to stay here? Your mom and sister—"

I expect him to say his usual, "she's not my mother," but instead what comes out is a kind of choked gasp. It's just hitting him now, I think, what all of this means. Torsten is so easily overwhelmed, and I know from experience that grief can be the most overwhelming sensation of all.

"Torsten?" I squeeze his hand, but he doesn't squeeze back. His body goes stiff as he struggles with the wave of emotion hitting him at once. I know that we need to leave, but I remain still, holding his hand as he works through it.

"They're gone," he manages finally. "We can't do anything about that. But maybe we can..."

"Maybe." I don't want to make a promise to him, not after everything he's already lost. All I can think about is the last phone call I had with Vic, when I told him that I wouldn't be there for Thursday night dinner.

Sommesnay knew the whole August family would be home on Thursday night.

Torsten has to extract Isabella from around his legs and hand her off to Shera. Wheels spin on the drive, and I know it's Cas pulling up. He must've got here quick to beat emergency services. I can hear the sirens tearing toward us now. We need to leave before they delay us with their useless questions.

We know exactly what happened, and exactly who is responsible, and they can do jack shit to help us.

"Let's go. Now," Cas barks from the driver's side window. Torsten helps me to the car, and we slide into the backseat. Cas tears away before I even get the door closed.

Spartacus crawls out from under the driver's seat and curls

up on my lap, his presence momentarily calming. I pull out my phone and try to call Vic, but it won't do anything. I think it's been broken in the blast. Cas careens around the sharp corners of Harrington Hills, and it's not until a few minutes later that he breathes a deep sigh of relief.

"His house is still there."

"No bomb?" I ask.

"No bomb."

We're not too late.

"It's completely dark," Torsten says. "It's Thursday night. Shouldn't the lights be on?"

Yes, the famous August family dinner that's never to be missed. The lights should be on, the table set, the music turned up loud, and miscellaneous animals curling around feet as the Augusts dig into delicious food. My chest aches thinking about all the Thursday night dinners I've been part of in the last month, and how this loud, loving family welcomed me as one of their own.

Please let them be okay.

Cas tries to punch a key into the gate, but the buttons don't make their familiar beep. "Shit. The power's out. The gate locks when the power cuts."

Cas backs the car up and revs the engine. It takes me a moment to realize what he's planning to do.

"Stop!" I yell. "Don't do that."

"Mew!" Spartacus leaps on the back of Cas' seat, egging him on. Traitorous, violent cat.

"Why not? Vic's inside, and if that bastard Sommesnay is after his mother, then he's probably inside, too."

"I know that," I say. "And if we bust down this gate, he'll know we're here and he'll slip away from us again. He's already killed enough people today. We need to surprise him. How do we get inside without raising any alarms? Can we scale the fence? Claudia told me that Eli used to climb a tree to watch her when he thought she was her sister—"

"No such luck. After her sister tried to kill her, they had the wall raised several feet and the nearby trees cut down. It's impossible to scale."

"There's got to be some way inside. How did Sommesnay get in?" I remember something else. "What about the secret passages beneath the house?"

"They closed them up," Cas says. "Claudia wouldn't allow her home to have a security breach like that."

"No," a voice says. "Not all of them."

24

FERGIE

"Vic!" I cry out.

I throw my arms out toward him, but I'm not quite sure where he is in space, so I end up kind of half-falling into him.

"I heard the bombs," he whispers. "You're okay. I'm so happy that you're okay."

"I'm fine, thanks to Torsten. He led me and Isabella and Shera out safely. But I can't say the same for Livvie. She's gone, and Grace, too."

"Shit." Vic sounds stricken. "Is Torsten okay?"

"He's here and he's upright, and that's all we have time to care about now. We've already had an explosive evening, so let's not waste any time. How are *you* fine?" Cas demands. "*And* you're outside the house. How the fuck did you convince your mother to let you miss Thursday night dinner?"

"I *was* home," Vic explains. "I'd just sat down at the table when Juliet called. She said she had something to tell me, some information from Sommesnay. She begged me to meet her in the Elysium parking lot. I waited there for twenty minutes, but she didn't show. Then I heard the explosions, and I came back here to check on the house and found it like this – the lights out and the gates locked."

"We need to get inside the house," Cas growls. "I bet my favorite sword that those bombs were a distraction, a way to play this off as a crusade against the Imperators, when really it's about Sommesnay's personal revenge. You said there was a way inside?"

"Juliet and I found one when we were kids. There's a trapdoor in the woods, camouflaged beneath the roots of a gnarled old oak. It leads through the walls to a hidden panel at the back of her closet."

"Why have you never told us about this before?" Cas demands.

"It's a twin thing. It was our secret." Vic sounds uncomfortable. "We used to sneak into the forest at night because Juliet liked to make pretend fairy circles with her toys. I had to play Oberon. We haven't used it for a long time."

Vic slides my hand into his elbow and leads me into the narrow wooded area that surrounds his house.

"Now, until the break of day, through this house each fairy stray." I tease Vic by quoting Oberon's lines from *A Midsummer Night's Dream*. "To the best bride-bed will we. Which by us shall blessed be."

"I'll get you for this later," he whispers back. "But we should be quiet. If this is how Zack got inside, then he might have someone guarding the entrance."

"Trip away, make no stay. Meet me all by break of day..."

"You're a menace, Duchess." Vic helps me over a gnarly root. "Stop. It's here. The ground is disturbed."

He leaves my side to scrabble around in the dirt. Torsten comes up beside me, his fingers finding mine and giving them a squeeze. I don't know if I'm really okay, but I squeeze back because I need to be strong for him.

I know that many people might see Torsten standing here, not saying anything, not howling with grief, not displaying any emotion, and they'd assume that he was cold, indifferent. That he didn't care about his mother or sister. But I know that Torsten cares too much, and that he needs to process their deaths and fall apart in his own time, and I'll do whatever he needs to help him get through it.

My own grief hasn't even hit me yet.

I can't believe Livvie's gone.

I didn't always like her, but I admired her greatly. She was ruthless and clever and bold and ambitious. She loved her family and her friends with a fierceness that burns bright even though she's gone. And the guy squeezing my hand right now... she loved him most of all. She didn't always understand him, and she didn't have the tools to help him, but she *adored* him.

And now she's gone.

What will happen to the Lucian family now?

"Cas, help me with this," Vic calls out, jolting me away from the edge of my grief.

I hear Vic and Cas straining as they lift something heavy. It bangs against the tree roots, sending up a small cloud of loose dirt that makes me cough. Vic returns and takes my hand. "It's a steep staircase, gorgeous. It's probably easier if you climb down backward, like a ladder."

There's no question that I'm coming too. They know me better than to try and leave me behind. Vic moves down a few steps and helps to guide my feet, while Cas holds onto me and helps me find the sides of the hole. The air grows damp and thick, and a few moments later I'm standing on the floor of the tunnel beside Vic.

We shuffle down so Cas and Torsten can fit. "I'll go first," Cas says. "In case there are guards at the other end."

More shuffling as we flatten ourselves against the stone walls to allow Cas to squeeze his bulk past. When he reaches me, he pauses, his chest pressing against mine.

"It's a pleasure to go into battle with my Queen by my side," he whispers, his breath ragged as it brushes my lips.

Mmmm, yes. I tilt my head back, and he devours me. His body hums with the rage of the hunt, the pulsing heart of a warrior going into battle. We drink the bloodlust from each other, and when Cas breaks the kiss, I'm no longer afraid of what we'll find inside the house.

Bring it on, Zack Lionel Sommesnay.

I follow behind Cas, my hand on his shoulder. I find a scabbard there with a curved katana nestled inside. Cas has trained for years under the best of Cali's tutors, and I know that for all his brutality he can wield that weapon with the precision of a surgeon.

As we get closer to the house, Cas makes us slow down and shows me how to place my feet so I don't make a sound. The bare stone floor is replaced by a narrow staircase that reminds me of the secret entry into Galen's clinic from the maintenance shed. Just as my foot slides over the top stair, I hear a commotion behind me, and someone swears.

A loud SQUEEEAK blasts through the tunnel.

Cas whirls around, a growl escaping his throat. His hand jerks up, going for his sword, but in the narrow space, he can't draw it.

"Sorry," Vic says sheepishly. "I stood on a fluffy rabbit. I guess Juliet left one of her plushies down here and its stomach squeaks."

"Don't scare us like that," Cas mumbles. "I thought you'd been jumped—"

His words catch in his throat as the tunnel is flooded with light. An unfamiliar voice cries out, and something hard and cold scrapes across my face. I jerk back, but I feel something hot and sticky roll down my cheek, and the metallic taste of blood fills my mouth.

A stinging pain arcs across my face where the guy touched me. He cut me. The bastard cut me.

Cas roars and barrels forward, taking our attackers by surprise. I fumble my way out of the tiny hole after him, falling over shoes and dresses as I struggle to get my bearings. I can hear thumps and cries as the two men fight it out. Another guy is in the doorway, yelling at his friend to give him a clear shot. He must have a gun.

Shit.

I try to slip back into the rack of clothing, but one of them rolls on my leg, pinning me in place. I grab the guy's head and try to twist his neck the way Konstantin showed me, but it's much harder to do when your target has a thick neck and is thrashing about and trying to claw your face off—

"Ow," Cas moans as we slam into him.

"Sorry." I shove the guy away and flatten myself against the wall, deciding that it's better to let Cas handle this one. I hear Vic and Torsten fly out of the passage, and they spring on the other guy before he can get a shot off, which is good.

We don't want Zack Sommesnay to know we're here just yet.

Cas finds me inside the coats and hauls me out. "You're okay? The bastard didn't hurt you?"

"I'm fine."

"Your face." He touches my cheek. "He cut you."

I run my fingers along the cut. It stings, but it's not deep. I can feel the blood drying on my skin. It will probably need stitches, but I'm not going to die from it.

"It's cool. It makes me look more badass," I grin.

"You're so beautiful when you're bloody." Cas leans in close, his plum and carnation scent mingling with the tang of freshly-drawn blood and Juliet's spilled perfumes. His lips brush mine before he tilts my face up and licks the length of the cut. My body shivers with desire as his tongue scrapes across my cheek.

He growls low in his throat as he tastes my blood. "You're delicious." His hand palms my breast, his fingers scraping over the nipple, and I'm surprised to find it hard as a pebble. Cas growls again, and pushes my back against the wall and—

"Are you two going to throw down and fuck right here?" Vic snaps. "Or can we get on with this?"

"I vote for the fucking." Cas' finger pinches my nipple.

"No." I manage to find the self-restraint to push his hand away. "Vic's right. We need to focus. We don't know what's going on downstairs."

"We'll find out. Just let me take care of this guy." Cas tears himself away from me. I hear the remaining guard squeal as my stepbrother picks him up. His sword sings as Cas draws it again.

"Cas, we should keep him alive," Vic says. "We need—"

"No, please!" the guy wails.

The sword makes a graceful *whoosh* as it slices the air, followed by a *thwunk* as it slices through the guy's neck and bites into the floor. Blood splatters across my face. I can't help myself – I reach out my tongue and lick a droplet from my lips.

"—to find out what we can expect when we go downstairs," Vic finishes with a sigh.

"Sorry, Vic." Cas doesn't sound sorry at all.

"He cut Fergie," Torsten says. "He had to go."

I wipe the blood off my face with one of Juliet's remaining designer dresses while the guys strip the two guards of their weapons.

"I recognize this guy," Vic says. "He's one of Mom's soldiers. He works at the docks."

"And this bastard is at Mom's school," Cas says. I hear a thud as he tosses the second corpse into the closet and shuts the door. "Sommesnay still has help from the inside."

The guys fall silent as we all allow this to sink in. We thought that we'd gotten rid of all the traitors inside the Triumvirate, but these two guys played an active role in hitting all three of our houses.

How many more traitors are out there?

And what are they planning next?

What did Sommesnay promise them to go along with his plan?

That's not the important question right now. We need to find Vic's parents.

We creep out of Juliet's room and into the hallway. Similar to Cali's house, the August home has a large, double-height foyer in the center with two staircases sweeping around on either side. Vic and Cas go ahead of us and declare the foyer clear. Before they can stop me, I crawl to the edge of the staircase, still my body and my thundering heart, and listen.

In the silent house, I can hear everything – the animals scratching at their cages in the ballroom, the faint rustle of leaves brushing against the windows, and deeper in the house, muffled sounds of shouts and screams.

"They're locked in the dining room," I say.

"How do you know?" Vic demands.

"I can hear them."

"Our girlfriend *is* Daredevil," Cas declares.

"I'm not Daredevil. It's not a superpower. I just know how to listen." I *hate* when people say shit like that, and don't even get me *started* on blind superheroes with disabilities that don't actually disable them. Anyone can learn to listen the way I do, but sighties don't have to rely on sound because they've got their eyes.

"I don't know, I think you're pretty powerful." Cas' fingers search for my nipple again. "Especially when those lips wrap around my dick."

"Can we *focus?*" Vic snaps. "If Sommesnay is near the dining room, we need to figure out how to get to him."

"What's the problem? We know where the dining room is. We sneak up on him and BANG." Cas snaps his fingers. "I rearrange Sommesnay's limbs in the manner of Picasso."

"The problem is that Sommesnay's cut the power." I can tell Vic's struggling to stay calm. "The house is pitch black and it's filled to the brim with Claudia's antiques. We have no idea how many more men Sommesnay has inside, and we can't turn on a light or use the flashlights on our phones. One wrong move and we knock over a bust of Julius Caesar and it's all over."

"Ah, but have you forgotten your secret weapon?" I grin. "The blind girl. I can get to the dining hall without alerting anyone to our presence."

"Not happening," Cassius growls.

I stick my tongue out at him. "You should know by now that you can't tell me what to do. I'm the best chance we've got. I have this house mapped in my head. Sommesnay won't hear me coming."

"You're not going alone."

"I have to go alone. The three of you are useless. You don't pay attention to what's around you." Even Cas, who has had training by Livvie, isn't as silent and stealthy as I can be.

But no matter how much I protest, none of them will budge on that fact.

"Fine, Vic can come with me."

"Why not me?" Cas growls. "Unlike the rest of you, I completed my assassin training."

"No offense, Papa Smurf, but your blue skin glows like a beacon shouting, 'shoot me!' You're also bulky and harder to lead. And it's Vic's family down there, so he gets to be first unto the breach. You and Torsten stay behind here. We need to keep our exit clear in case shit hits the fan. Kill anyone who isn't us."

"Oooh, goody. A game." Cas carves his sword through the air in front of him. The blade sings as it slices the air.

I step out from our hiding place, taking a moment to steady my breath and catch my bearings. I don't want to risk clicking my tongue, but shouldn't need to. I *know* this house. I've spent hours here, hanging out with Vic. I even remember Juliet's room from the basketball party. I have mental maps of this house in my head, and all I need to do is focus.

First up is the easy part – the staircase. Vic places his hand on my shoulder. For the first time, I'm the one leading. I guide him over to the railing and we descend slowly, placing our feet the way Cas showed us so we don't make a sound.

Vic's breath rasps against the back of my neck, making my hairs stand on end. Every atom in my body buzzes – alert to any sound, smell, or change in the air. My feet hit the bottom stair. I remember in the center of the foyer is a round table, filled with busts of Roman emperors and fresh flowers that Eli brings home for Claudia. There are chairs on either side, often heaped high with Victor's basketball gear and Noah's books. I steer Vic close to the wall so we avoid hitting them. I stop and motion to Victor for him to scan the space for movement. Vic taps my shoulder. We're safe so far.

Down the hall, a slight turn to the left where the rugs meet to avoid the side table with the Egyptian statue on it, around the corner to the right and...

My fingers brush wood. It's the door to the dining room, and it's shut. Vic moves away from me, and I hear his footsteps recede as he checks the rest of the rooms in the hallway. He returns and whispers to me that they're clear.

I don't try the lock and risk alerting anyone inside. Instead, I press my ear against the door and listen.

I hear a voice that turns my blood to ice.

"Well, well, Claudia August," Sommesnay chuckles from inside. "We finally meet."

25

FERGIE

"Zack Sommesnay, I presume," Claudia sounds defiant, smug, even though her voice is clearly strained.

"Zack *Lionel* Sommesnay," he corrects. "Names are very important. Aren't they, Claudia Malloy?"

There's that name again – Malloy. I heard it when Claudia dragged me into her vehicle. It's the name of the man who used to own this house, the man who is Claudia's real, biological father – Howard Malloy.

From the way Sommesnay says the word, as if he expects some horrified reaction from Claudia, I know we've hit upon the heart of his issue. Sommesnay is connected to the Malloy family in some way.

"If you're trying to frighten me with that name, you've failed," Claudia says. "I have no affinity for it, and it holds no standing around here. Family isn't just about blood. I was raised by Julian August. To anyone who matters, I am his daughter."

But I can hear in her voice that she's nervous. Hearing that name on Sommesnay's lips has thrown her. I know enough of her story to know that Mackenzie Malloy still haunts her nightmares.

"I'm not trying to frighten you," Sommesnay says. His voice sounds odd – too loud, a little tinny. "I needed to get you alone in a room with me. I needed you to understand."

"Then come in the room and face me like a man," Claudia shouts.

It's then that I realize what I'm hearing isn't Zack's real voice – he has a booming quality that can only come from a speaker. He's not in the room – he's talking over the house's intercom.

Coward.

"I won't be doing that, I'm afraid," he says. "I prefer to watch from afar, way out of the blast radius."

"Aren't we just the little firestarter," she snaps. "Out with it, Sommesnay. At this stage, I'll die of old age before you get to the point."

"My point is that names are important," he says. "My name, for example. It's not the name I was born with, but it is a name that, when puzzled out, spells your doom. I assume you've figured it out by now."

"I honestly haven't spared a thought for you," Claudia snaps.

"Too bad. The clever Imperator of the August family should have figured out my little game by now and saved herself the hassle of wondering what I want. I thought you liked puzzles, Claudia August. I gave you a puzzle that you can really sink your teeth into. I'll even give you a clue. Rearrange the letters of my name and you get…"

He pauses dramatically, and I know he's enjoying Claudia trying to figure it out. I bet he has a camera watching the room, too. I must admit, I'm surprised we didn't think of it before. Zack Lionel Sommesnay is such a random name, but if it's an anagram, that makes sense. But what is it an anagram for…

"Shit," Vic whispers, his body stiffening beside me. "If you rearrange the letters of Zack Lionel Sommesnay, you get 'Mackenzie Malloy's son.'"

26

FERGIE

I reel as I put the pieces together. I rearrange the letters in my head, the same as Victor's just done, and I come to the same conclusion.

Zack Lionel Sommesnay – Mackenzie Malloy's son.

Claudia gasps. She's figured it out, too.

My head spins. It all fits.

Sommesnay's attacks have been deeply personal because he has a grudge against Claudia for killing his mother. Claudia told me that Mackenzie hid in Germany for a while – they even went to a small village on the Tauber River to search for evidence of her. Mackenzie must have had the baby in Germany, and then what? Given it up for adoption? Dumped it on some unsuspecting do-gooders? Whatever happened, it explains Sommesnay's German heritage.

From all accounts, Mackenzie Malloy was utterly ruthless and unhinged. She wasn't strategic. She didn't have a plan, and she kept messing up the plans her lover, Antony August, made. She simply lashed out and waited to see how the pieces fell.

Like mother, like son.

I press my ear even harder against the door. I need to hear *everything*.

"That's impossible," Claudia says, fishing for information. I assume she's trying to keep Sommesnay talking so she can figure out what he's trying to do. "My sister never had a son."

"Are you certain about that?" Zack asks. "Because here I am, a baby born on the dirt floor of an abandoned castle in Germany and dumped on the steps of a nearby convent. I've done the DNA tests. I found out who she was. I followed her trail, and it led me to Emerald Beach, to you. I thought I might finally have my true family at last, only to discover that you don't know the meaning of the word *family*. You killed her."

"Of course I killed her!" Claudia spits. "She was trying to kill me. She wanted to replace me in my own life, and she used my own cousin to do it."

"She would have been so much better at your job than you are," he scoffs. "You're so blinded by your precious husbands and your silly museum that you can't even see your empire crumbling around you. The Triumvirate is over, and I'm the one to bring it to its knees."

"This is absurd," Claudia says. "I'm not talking to a speaker in the ceiling. Either kill me now or come down in person and discuss terms. But don't—"

He laughs. "You're not exactly in a position to make demands, are you? And you have me all wrong, Claudia August. I don't want to kill you. You stole my mother's life from her. *She* should be Imperator, living in this fancy house with her beautiful children and three husbands waiting on her every whim. She had more talent in her pinkie finger than you have in your swollen, self-important head. So I'm going to steal your life from you. I already took your museum, and now I'm going to destroy your friends, Cali Dio and Livvie Lucian, and your precious Triumvirate. Then I'll destroy your husbands, and your soldiers, and your precious twins. Only then will I finally put you out of your misery."

So that's his plan. It explains why he's rooted out people within the organization who are dissatisfied with the Imperators, and why he's made such efforts to drive a wedge between the three families. Sommesnay is stoking the fires of a coup so he can swoop in and take everything Claudia holds dear.

And Cas and Vic and Torsten and I... all our antics have played right into his hands. No wonder he was so happy to meet me after I declared war on Poison Ivy. I *helped* this scumbag get this far.

Nausea rolls through me at the thought of my own role in what's gone down tonight.

"How do you know what your mother was like?" Claudia asks, changing tactics. She tries to speak, but breaks down into a coughing fit before managing to get the words out. "You never met her."

"I have her diaries. She kept diaries the whole time she lived in Germany, and she put them in my basket when she left me with the nuns—"

I tune out Sommesnay's yammering and focus on what else I can hear in the room. Claudia whimpering, someone gasping for breath. The dull thud of something hitting the floor. And...

...an acrid, chemically smell curls in my nostrils. Just a tiny whiff of it makes my head spin, and...

...and it's coming from beneath the door.

I grab the handle and turn it slowly, but it's locked.

"They're locked inside," I whisper to Victor. "Sommesnay's doing this remotely, sending his voice through the house speakers. He's pumping some kind of gas into the room. I can smell it."

Vic lunges for the door, but I hold him back. "We go in there now and we lose our shot to get Sommesnay."

"But my family—"

"I know. I can still hear them in there. They're alive, but we have to move fast. I wish we knew if Sommesnay was even in the house."

"He's here," Vic whispers. "The security system can't be reached from outside. Torsten helped Mom upgrade it. Sommesnay has to be in the house somewhere."

"Where?"

"Probably Mom's office. There's a master panel in there that accesses all the security features."

I tug him down the hallway toward the office. I'm not as familiar with this part of the house as I am with others, but I trail my hand along the wall to keep my bearings. Behind me, I can hear the echo of Sommesnay's voice booming through the speakers.

No, not through the speakers.

He's close.

He's right here.

Vic stiffens, and I know he's figured it out, too. Sommesnay is inside Claudia's office. He's walking around the room, taking great delight in describing to Claudia *exactly* how he infiltrated the Dio and Lucian houses and planted the bombs, and how he has people within every layer of their organization, people who want to topple the three Imperators from their thrones.

He has no idea we're right outside.

Vic and I move as if we're one person. I flatten myself against the door and wait for our chance, while he grabs the handle and prepares to throw it open. He waits for my signal, though this is not a perfect science – it's next to impossible to exactly pinpoint a body's position in space when you're blind, especially when you're listening through a wall. But all I need is for him to be close enough for me to take Sommesnay by surprise.

"I'll be the voice you hear as you watch your family die

around you," Sommesnay purrs into the headset. He's moved closer, and I hear the wheels of the desk chair slide across the floor.

A little closer. A little...

"Aren't you impressed, Claudia? Isn't this exactly what my mother would do?"

Now.

Vic shoves the door open, and I leap into the room. Sommesnay's cry indicates that we've startled him. That cry helps me to narrow in on his location. I barrel toward him and slam into him. I'm not large enough to bring him down, but I do send him staggering backward. There's a bang as he hits the side of the desk, and I'm able to use his surprise to feel my way up his body and get my hand in position behind his neck. I slam his head into the corner of the desk, and he collapses on the floor.

He's stunned, but not out, and he reaches up as he tries to crawl on top of me, his fingers fighting to close around my throat.

This is exactly what I've trained for. I feel his weight shift and I use it against him, curling my arms around his torso and trapping his arms. I press my elbow into his neck, cutting off his air. He makes this horrible wheezing sound, and then his body goes limp.

He's unconscious.

I don't stop. I squeeze tighter as the anger wells up inside me.

Livvie is dead because of him.

Gabriel's voice is broken because of him.

All this hurt, all this tragedy, because of him.

I keep squeezing and squeezing. I have to be sure. I have to know that he's gone.

I have to protect them all.

"Duchess, stop."

"I can't," I grit out as I twist my arm to dig it deeper. I have to make sure Sommesnay never hurts anyone I love ever again.

"You can." Vic picks me up under the shoulders and hauls me off. "He's dead."

"Shoot him in the head, just in case."

I expect Vic to protest, but a moment later, I jump as the silenced shot punches through Sommesnay's skull.

He's gone.

He's really fucking gone.

The shot loosens something inside me. I start to tremble, my whole body convulsing as the truth of what I've done becomes a physical trauma.

I killed a man in cold blood. I held his life in my hands and I decided he didn't deserve it.

Since meeting the guys, I've been involved in some pretty brutal killings – listening to the crunch of Clarence's jaws as they broke Coach Franklin's bones, helping Cas hammer in the nails on Dawson's wrists, and listening to his anguished cries as Cas' tongue brought me to ecstasy again and again. And then in the ring with Cas, when all my rage and hate and love took over my body and made me someone else. Some kind of monster who craved the blood of someone I love.

But this is the first time that I've taken a life *with my own hands*, that I've felt the breath leave someone's body and that final, weighty sigh as Sommesnay becomes a corpse.

I slump against Vic, and he wraps his arms around me. His lips brush my hair, and I realize that he's shaking, too.

"Thank you," he murmurs. And I know he's thanking me for so much more than choking Sommesnay to death.

I pull myself back, because we can't do this now. Not when Vic's family is still trapped in that room and poison gas is leaking inside. "We have to get that door open."

"Call Torsten's phone," Vic commands as he runs to the

desk. I don't know how he manages to pull himself together, to take charge, but that's why he was born to become an Imperator, not a botanist. I hear him punching buttons on a keypad. "Tell him that it's safe to run down, there are no guards or they'd have come running when we got in here. Tell him that I need him now. I don't know how to turn off that gas."

I don't remember making the call or speaking to Torsten, but I must have because moments later, Cas and Torsten burst into the office. Cas kicks Sommesnay's body, and it thumps against the wall, sending a painting crashing from its hook.

"Nice job, Sunflower. I would have liked to torture him a bit first – pull his nipples off with hot pliers, that kind of thing. But I bet staring into your eyes as you took the life from him was torture enough."

"I—" I turn to face Cas, but my legs will no longer hold up my body. I kneel on the floor. Big mistake. My hand brushes Sommesnay's arm. He's still warm, but something about him feels off.

He's dead. That's what's 'off' about him. He is now our *former* enemy.

Thanks to me.

Torsten runs for the desk. "This is going to take a few minutes to crack—"

"We don't have minutes," Victor yells. "Sommesnay's pumping the room full of poisonous gas—"

I hear Cas turn on his heel and run back into the hallway. Vic grabs my arm and we tear after him. We're halfway to the dining room when I hear a mighty crunch, which can only be my unhinged stepbrother throwing his monstrous bulk at the door.

"No, Cas, don't—" Vic yells, but Cas can't hear him through his red haze. Not even a solid oak door can withstand Cas' rage, and after a few more tries, something cracks and splinters, and thick, noxious gas floods the hallway.

"Get back!" Vic drags me away.

"Cas!" I try to scream, but the smell slams into me – this harsh chemical burn that brings tears to my eyes and fills my mouth with poison. I drop to the ground to try and get beneath it, and Vic goes down beside me, his arm falling over my shoulders as if he can somehow shield me from the poison with his body.

My eyes are on fire. I squeeze them shut. I don't need them anyway. I crawl forward, and Vic clings to me as he crawls beside me. I realize that he's not holding me because he's trying to protect me – without his vision, he's disoriented. He needs me to lead him out of here.

The knowledge spurs me on, and even though it hurts so so much, even though my body convulses as I'm racked by horrific coughing, even though my lungs are flooded with fire, I crawl as fast as I can, my elbows dragging over the rug as I fight to get us around the corner and through the nearest door.

I pull Victor into the ballroom – the enormous, cavernous space that Vic's family uses as part living room, part cat sanctuary, and part crimelord playground. The cats in the run along the edge of the room yowl and hiss as they claw at the netting. They can smell the gas, too.

And I think of Spartacus in the car, and what this chemical would do to his tiny body. Right now, I can smell the chemical leaking into the room behind us, but the space is so big that the air close to the ground is still clean, relatively speaking.

Vic's coughing violently, and he's moving so slowly that I'm basically dragging him. I need to get him outside like right the fuck now, but instead, I drop him in the middle of the floor and change directions, crawling toward where I can hear the cats screaming.

I navigate around the large couch, but forget about a small end table and crash into that, sending it flying. I hear something shatter, but I don't have time to stop and check it out. My hands brush the edge of the cat run, and I feel along it until I come to the door. I have to get up on my knees to reach the latch. As I sit up, my head spins so wildly that I nearly black out. I cling to the cage, fighting for air and strength.

In the end, it's the plaintive meows that bring me back from the brink. My head stops spinning for a moment, and I have enough dexterity that I can slide the latch and pop the door open.

Cats explode out of the run. They knock me backward as paws pound into my chest and claws scratch my arms. They leap over me and – judging by the almighty racket they make – head for the French doors, where I know there's a cat door that leads into a larger outdoor cat run. The door *thwuck-thwuck-thwucks* at felines fly through it.

I saved them. I—

"Feeergieeee—"

Vic's strained gasp reaches my ears just as the pounding headache explodes inside my skull, and the world goes white with pain, and I lose myself.

I come to, lying on a bed of soft grass, with a pair of hot lips closed around mine, pushing air into my ravaged lungs. My stomach lurches, and I throw my savior off me as my body doubles up, and I cough and puke and spit.

Charming.

I'll go back to sleep now, thanks.

"Fergie." Vic's arms go around me, crushing me to him even. "You're okay."

"Of course... I'm okay..." I wheeze. "I eat poison gas for breakfast..."

"There's my favorite little psychopath." Vic kisses the top of my head. He doesn't loosen his grip on me, not for a second. "When you collapsed, I thought—"

"Give her some room," a stern voice chastises him.

Claudia?

I whip my head in the direction of her voice. It's her, all right. She's admonishing Galen to take better care of me.

She's alive, so we got her out of the room in time, but what about—

"C-C-Cas?" I manage to choke out.

Speaking of psychopaths, what happened to my insane step-brother who broke down a door using only his shoulder and got a face full of poisonous gas for his trouble?

"He's here, and so is Torsten," Vic says. "They're my heroes. Torsten got the gas turned off, and Cas... I don't know how he did it, but he dragged Mom, Noah, Eli, and Gabriel out of that room before the gas got too much for him."

The pieces start to come together. "Juliet?"

"She wasn't with us," Claudia's voice wobbles. "She refuses to come to Thursday dinners now. But she called Victor before dinner, and—"

"I went to see her at the Elysium, except she wasn't there," Vic tells his mother. He speaks slowly, his voice breathy as the same realization hits him. "I think that she might have done that to save me. If she knew about the attack, she got me out of the house so I wasn't there when Sommesnay turned on the gas."

"She saved you?" Claudia's voice is high, incredulous. "But it was perfectly okay for Sommesnay to use that gas on me and your fathers?"

"I-I-I don't know what she's thinking." Vic's voice trembles. He's wrestling with his belief that his sister is somehow trying to help them, against the overwhelming evidence that she wanted her family to die. "Maybe she thought I would be able to save you all, which we did. On the phone, she sounded distraught. I don't think she had any other options—"

I know he's defending Juliet because he's not ready to face the truth of her part in this, but I won't indulge that fantasy. No matter how many times Juliet proves that she has nothing but contempt for her family, Vic always insists on believing the best in her.

But she did save him. Why only him? Is it out of twin-ly loyalty?

"We have to find her," Claudia says, and there's a grim determination in her voice that makes my stomach twist with fear. "Sommesnay threatened her, too, and he's no longer alive to tell us what he plans to do to her. What if he's hurt her? What if the reason she didn't show up to meet you is because he's already hurt her? She may have had no idea about the gas or the explosions."

Personally, I think that's giving Juliet way too much credit, but Claudia's right about one thing – we have to find her, because with Sommesnay gone, Juliet has answers.

"We can't do anything tonight," I say. "We don't know if Sommesnay is targeting other high-ranking members of the Triumvirate, or what his supporters might do once they hear that I killed him. There might be more bombs out there. We need to go somewhere safe and rest and regroup and come up with a plan."

A hand reaches through mine and squeezes.

"I know where we can go," Torsten says.

28

TORSTEN

We gather quite a group by the time we start moving toward my safe house. The news of the bombs would have spread quickly amongst the soldiers of the Triumvirate who live in the city. Those high-ranking soldiers loyal to the three Imperators are concerned for their safety. No one knows if there will be more attacks.

After we pull Vic's family out of their home, and Fergie and Cas are up and walking again, we find a crowd of August soldiers gathered on the street – smugglers and blackmailers who pulled their kids out of bed and want Claudia to keep them safe.

In a voice hoarse from the poison, Claudia tells them all that Sommesnay is dead, that he can't hurt them any longer, and that she has a place where they can stay while their homes are checked for explosives. They applaud her and tell her that she is brave and strong.

I study their faces, searching for some sign or slip that will alert us to the traitors in our midst. I know that some of them are faking it, and I wish there is some clue that can give them away.

There probably is, but not one I can see. I can't even read the emotions of the people I love, let alone this sea of strangers.

Sommesnay wasn't working alone. The Imperators thought they'd cleaned out the traitors from our ranks, but now Livvie's dead and some people in this crowd are lying.

I can't stand liars.

They are the worst kind of people.

Because of them, my mother is *dead*.

The Russian artist Maxim Vorobiev painted 'Oak Fractured by Lightning' after his wife's death – a stark, twisted tree sliced by the bright, white bolt of destruction. He said it captured the shock and pain of losing someone you love.

It is one painting that I never wanted to experience or understand, and yet now I am that tree, my insides sliced open by the fire of the heavens, my life cloven into two states – when Livvie was alive, and now that she is gone.

I think back to her visit to me in the gallery, to her tears and her apology and her promise to send me to art school. I think of all her schemes over the last few months, and I wonder if perhaps the tree stretched its branches toward the stormy skies and welcomed its own destruction.

We move on to Cas' house and unite Fergie with her father. Another crowd waits there for us. Cas wants to send them into Cali's basement to sort out their true loyalties, but he can't do that because the basement is filled with rubble. And because Claudia and Cali have forbidden it.

So instead, we visit my house and collect more people.

My sisters wave at us when we pull up. The mood is different here, the crowd is smaller, but they carry torches and they are singing – the words are in no language I recognize, but they make me feel the way Nick Cave songs make me feel – gloomy and exalted and lonely and not alone.

Soldiers hold up an object wrapped in white linen. Livvie's

body. They pulled her from the debris and insist on taking her with us. Claudia looks revolted by this, but Cali allows Livvie to be placed on the backseat of her car. My sisters sob. Fergie squeezes my hand.

"Am I supposed to cry?" I ask her. I don't know what to do. Fergie knows. She lost her mother. She can tell me what I'm expected to do.

"Grief is different for everyone." She squeezes my hand even tighter. "You're supposed to feel your feelings however they come out. I didn't cry about my mother for a long time. I was so young when she died, I didn't really understand what 'gone forever' meant, so each time I missed her it was like losing her all over again. But our relationship was very different from you and Livvie—"

"I loved her," I say.

"I know."

"I didn't realize it until just now. I wish I'd been able to tell her."

Fergie leans her head against my shoulder. "She already knew."

More vehicles arrive, filled with Cali's assassins and fighters who've come from her gym – a smaller group than both my mother and Claudia command, but they make so much more noise. Everyone piles into their vehicles behind us. I get into the backseat of Cas' car with Fergie, and everyone looks at me.

"Where are we going, Torsten?" Fergie asks.

I swallow. I feel the weight of all those cars and motorcycles behind me, all those people who think that I have an answer for them. I tell Fergie my idea, and she smiles and squeezes my hand.

"You did good," she says. "It's perfect."

We drive in silence. Fergie gets on the phone with Euri and asks if she can bring blankets and food and toys for the children.

She gives Euri Claudia's credit card number – she's memorized it by heart, which is something I like to do.

I wish I had my sketchbook with me. I flap the hand that Fergie isn't holding and tap my foot until Cas turns into a parking lot and announces that we've arrived.

Tombs is locked up for the night, but I remember all of Livvie's security codes by heart. I unlock the doors and turn on the blinding, pulsing club lights, and let them all inside.

When my mother built this club, she wanted it to double as her headquarters. Cali had the gym and Claudia had the museum, but my mother wanted a place that encapsulated everything that Lucian was about. It may be filled with sumptuous textures and fabrics, the finest selection of top-shelf liquor, and the hottest bands and DJs, but it's also a safe house. The few windows in the place are bulletproof, the doors are so thick that it would take more than a blast of C4 to blow them open, and it's a rabbit warren of hiding places and escape tunnels.

"As tired as I am, I'm not sure I'm going to be able to get any sleep here," Claudia says, peering around the dance floor as it fills up with our people. Cas stands beside me, cradling Spartacus in his huge hands. The tiny kitten has fallen asleep, his cheek resting on Cas' thumb.

"We're not sleeping down here." I tighten my grip on Fergie's arm as I lead her up the stairs. All around the VIP level are private lounges and bedrooms behind secret panels. Fergie's seen a couple of them, but there are more – enough for our families to have a safe bed for the night.

I show Claudia and her husbands to the throne room and demonstrate how to use the hidden keypad to open secret panels that reveal stacks of cozy blankets, towels, and toiletries, as well as how to operate the security feed that monitors the hall outside. My mother always thinks of everything.

No, not everything.

Not a bomb in our house.

I think of her now, or what was left of her after the debris from the blast tore through her body. I saw Cali's men bringing her inside – they're lying her body on a table on the stage so that everyone can pay their respects. They won't lift off the white sheet, because it's hard to respect a nightmare.

I think of Isabella's face, twisted and broken like the face in *The Scream*. Haunted, that's how the critics described Munch's figure.

My little sister is haunted by what she saw.

And I'm so grateful that Fergie is blind, that she didn't have to see it, that she won't have to wear that haunted face.

I show Cali and John to another room. Cas gets his brother on the phone, but Gaius says he'll meet us later. He says that he's going to try and get to Juliet. He says that he needs Vic to trust him, and pulling his sister out will be a way to do that. Cas yells at him to get to Tombs, but Gaius hangs up.

Vic is still calling his sister. Again and again, he hits the button to dial her number, and as soon as it goes to voicemail, he hangs up and calls again.

Euri arrives with a carload of supplies. "I got everything I could fit into the car," she says. "You know it's actually really fun to go to Target at midnight? It's so empty that it's like being in a zombie film."

We hand out blankets and sleeping bags, and as everyone is finding a space in the empty club, a truck arrives with two dozen pizzas and fries and gallons of soft drinks. I'm not hungry but I fight my way to the front of the ravenous horde to grab a couple of slices for Fergie.

"Thank you." She accepts two huge slices of buffalo chicken. "You're always thinking of me, but you have to think about yourself, tonight of all nights. What do you need?"

No one ever asks me that.

I have to think for a second, but then it comes to me – how tense my limbs are, how my wrist hurts from flapping my hand since I got us out of the house.

"I need to get away from all these people."

"Okay. Then let's do that." Fergie loops her arm in mine. "We've fed them and given them blankets, and Cas is working with Cali's soldiers to create a secure perimeter and check the club for any explosives. We've done all we can."

I lead her upstairs to the room I reserved for us. Vic follows us. Eleven minutes later, Cas joins us. He's dragging his feet and he has a sleeping Spartacus curled up on his shoulder. Vic's even stopped calling his sister. I think they must both be tired, too.

While Victor showers and Cas sets Spartacus up with a bed of towels and cushions, Fergie sits cross-legged on the bed. She holds out one hand, and I take it.

She squeezes, but I can't bring myself to squeeze back. It feels too much like a lie.

"I'm so sorry about Livvie," she says.

"You have nothing to be sorry about. You didn't kill her."

"No, I didn't. It's just what you say. I'm sad for you because you lost her. I know Livvie wasn't always perfect, she didn't always understand you, but she did love you."

"How do you know that?"

"Because she told me. And your mother was like you in so many ways, Torsten, so I don't think she'd lie about that." Fergie's eyelashes flutter. "And I also know because of the things she did for you. She told me about her life, about how her father cast her aside because she was a woman, and he didn't think a woman had any place running a criminal empire. She wasn't given the Imperatorship – she had to take it by force. She wanted you to have your chance to shine, the way she was denied hers. I know you want to hide away. But she was proud of you. She wanted you to be proud of yourself."

I think about this. When I lived with Livvie, I always felt like... like Fergie might feel if she was standing in the middle of a minefield. One false step and the whole world explodes, but with no way to determine what a false step might be.

Actually, I don't think that's accurate at all. If Fergie were trapped in the middle of a minefield, she'd find some way out of it. She's amazing like that, and I'm just... just...

I squeeze my eyes shut. "She was disappointed in me."

"She never, ever was, Torsten. I think she was disappointed in herself. From the moment she saw you, Livvie's been fighting for you. She fought to save you from your shit birth parents, and she's been fighting to find you a place in her world so you'd have the respect she knew you deserved. And yeah, sometimes she got it so fucking wrong, and I think if she'd stopped to talk to you, *really* talk to you, instead of barreling ahead with what she thought was best, things would have been better between you two. But I think her employing you to copy paintings for her was her way of trying to understand you. She wanted to find a way for you to fit in her world in a way that made you happy, because she didn't want to lose you."

Fergie's words stir up memories of Livvie, of the art supplies she brought me from her trips abroad, and the tutors she hired that I usually ended up screaming at because they tried to touch me or said something wrong about Degas. I think about her insistence that I sit at the table with the family, even when I hated it, even when I felt like everyone was looking at me, and I think about all the times she begged me to just be normal, even though I don't know what normal is.

I think about the tears she cried in the gallery.

Some of it still hurts. Some of it gives me a squirming feeling in my gut that I don't like. But some of it... I think I understand what Fergie's trying to say. When Livvie looked at me, she saw what I see when I look at other people. A blank. A puzzle that can't be solved. And all my efforts to fit in, to understand, often end up causing more problems or making me feel bad.

It's only because Livvie loved me that she fought so hard to solve me.

Fergie's hand squeezes mine again, and the memory of my mother becomes like a painting in my mind – a picture of colors and lines and strokes that I can break down and study. Not alive, but still and perfect and able to be studied.

"Tell me," Fergie whispers. "What do you need?"

I open my mouth, but I can't think of the words to explain. I want to say that I need Livvie to be alive again, because if she's alive then this hollow pain in my chest won't be there. I need to say that I finally, *truly* understand what Monet wanted to achieve when he said that he wanted to paint as a bird sings. I have a picture in my head of my mother, and I want to break her down into squares and circles and dabs of light, but it is not her and never will be. A moment with her cannot be captured, for they changed always and now live only in my head.

I want to say that in those dabs are something more precious – my impression of her. And I think it will change over time, and maybe one day I will paint her, and I won't paint her as Monet might but as Torsten Lucian, her son, her *son*, might paint, and that will be the greatest gift I can ever give her.

I want to say I'm sorry.

I want to say that I love her.

But what comes out is, "I need you. But..."

I need to tell her that tonight it's worse than ever – the feeling like a thousand little beetles crawling over my skin, the sound of Fergie's voice mingling with the murmurs from the nightclub, and the glug of the pipes and the savage rumble in my stomach.

I'm riddled with feeling and thought and sensation. I've been pummeled by a thousand raw nerve endings. She's the only one that makes it all go away. She turns all the smells into raspberries and all the beetles into soft flowers. I need to say something. I need to...

But Fergie is smiling at me. "Torsten, I understand what you need."

Fergie shifts her body away from me, angling herself so that only her head is close to me. She leans in and kisses me again. She's being so so careful to only touch me with her lips, but still the sensation of it is overwhelming. I'm filled with her, with her Fergieness, and I can touch her strength and make it my own.

She presses her lips to mine, letting them linger, waiting for me to be ready. I suck in a few breaths, and I try to focus on my body, on the feel of her lips so soft against mine. When I'm ready, I part my lips a little, pulling hers apart, and touch her lightly with my tongue.

The taste of her explodes in my mouth. She is everything sweet and good and wonderful.

We kiss until I lose myself, until I forget to be in my body that so often betrays me, my body that carries the scars of a past that Livvie Lucian saved me from. We kiss, and all the big feelings inside me can live inside the kiss.

Slowly, Fergie moves her fingers down my chest, popping the buttons on my shirt. The fabric moving against my skin, the soft skim of her fingers where she accidentally touches me, all of these sensations flood together, and normally it would be so overwhelming, but with her strength inside me now, it's addictive.

She finishes unbuttoning my shirt, and I lift my torso a little so she can slide it off my shoulders.

"If you want to, you can undress me," she says, sliding down one of the straps of her black tank top. Blood is sprayed in a graceful arc across her tits – Sommesnay's blood, from when Cas shot him. I can smell the metallic tang of it against the salt and raspberries of her skin, and normally that would make me want to vomit, but right now it's intoxicating.

I touch the hem, tugging the fabric between my fingers for a moment, just getting used to the feel of it.

I lift it a little, and my fingers grace her flat, soft stomach, the muscles hard and toned from all her training, the skin speckled here and there with dried blood and plaster dust from our house. I see the Death Lily tattoo she has – my drawing adorning her perfect skin.

I think of what she said to me in the art gallery before it exploded, that I did not have to be part of the Triumvirate. That I could make more of my sensory displays and take them on tour and make other people's faces light up the way hers did. I think about Livvie telling me that she will help me through art school, and that these two remarkable women have given me freedom.

My breath catches.

I press my fingers against Fergie's skin, focusing on controlling my breath as I move my hand up, pushing the top up until it's above her crimson lace bra – the same color as the blood she spilled to protect us all tonight.

She smiles – a genuine, glowing smile that's just for me.

For *me*.

I'm so in awe of how this woman could have chosen me.

Fergie shuffles forward and kneels over my body. She asks if this is okay, and I say, "No," because it's not okay, it's perfect. And she goes to move away, and I realize that I've confused her, and I pull her back and say, "Yes. I need you."

She sinks down on my cock, a beautiful little sigh escaping from her lips. I want to hold her hips, to thrust up even deeper into her the way Cas and Vic do. But I'm frozen with wonder of her, with the surety that if I touch her too much right now, I'll get overwhelmed and fuck everything up.

With Cas and Vic, Fergie can be vulnerable. In their arms, she puts aside her strength and lets them take care of her. That's what they do for her. But she and I are different. With me, she can revel in her power. She can be the one who has control.

I give that to her because in her arms, I am free.

She does this now as she rides me, bucking her hips and throwing her head and arms back. Only our hips touch, and my cock is wrapped in the warmth inside her.

It's the most intimate thing in the world.

Fergie angles her hips and slides a finger between her legs to stroke her own clit. It only takes a few strokes before her legs tremble and her lip curls back and she lets out a scream that sends Vic running from the bathroom, his hair still lathered in shampoo. But it's not our enemies closing in – it's our Queen taking what is rightfully hers.

Her walls clamp around me as she comes, and that sensation breaks through my defenses, and I come, too.

My mother is dead and my exhibition is destroyed and I'm living in a nightclub and my head isn't normal, but in that moment, I learn that it's possible to be free.

29

FERGIE

I flop down beside Torsten, not even caring that his cum is dripping on the club's expensive sheets.

Well, that was...

Amazing.

Earth-shattering.

Mind-blowing.

No, maybe no bomb metaphors. Not after today.

Torsten rolls off the bed and heads toward the bathroom to clean up. I'm so used to his abrupt departures that it doesn't offend me that he wants to shower the moment we're done. I just want him to be as happy as he makes me.

Besides, I couldn't move even if I wanted to – my legs are jelly and my head is made of cotton and I just want to bask in the post-orgasm glow for a moment and forget that...

A strong arm goes around my chest. My body reacts instantly, tensing and clenching even as a hot pool of liquid collects between my legs.

Cas' teeth dig into my shoulder.

"Torsten's mother keeps all kinds of toys in here," he whispers.

"Yes. I want—"

I don't even get to finish my sentence because Cas throws me over his shoulder. I scream and pound his back with my fists. He chuckles as he carries me across the room. My foot flails and brushes the edge of his rigid cock, and suddenly I'm not so spent that I can't get excited about what my stepbrother has planned.

Cas sets me down, angling me so I face away from him.

"Feet apart, gorgeous." He kicks my ankles, and I spread my legs for my stepbrother like the sick girl I am.

Something snakes around my wrist – a rope. It feels soft. Cas loops it a few times, then stretches my arm out and ties it somewhere to my left. Then he starts on the other wrist.

The rope pulls me forward, and I bend at the waist, noticing my stomach and hips leaning against something velvety. I'm at the foot of the bed, I realize. Cas has tied me so that my ass is hanging in the air over the end of the bed, and I'm leaning over so my stomach rests on the duvet.

"It's times like this when I wish you could see yourself," Cas says. "Not because I don't think you're perfect as you are, but because I want you to bask in your own perfection. Look at you, all trussed up and laid out for me. When your father first brought you to our house, I thought you were a gift. I thought my mother had given you to me as a toy to break because she wanted to teach me a lesson about ruling her empire."

That's so fucked up that I can't help but laugh. "That's really what you thought?"

"There's precedent," Cas says, and I decide not to ask because I've heard a rumor that Cali gave him a traitor to torture every year for Christmas, and I'm happy for that to just remain a rumor right now. "I was right about one thing. You *are* a gift. Today, we all learned that we can fucking die at any time, and that every moment where we're not dead is a moment to treasure. This is who I am; I'm the monster, and you are mine. This is who you are. You're a pretty package all wrapped up for me, and I'm going to enjoy my gift in every possible way tonight. But first, I kneel for my Queen."

A moment later, his hands grip my ass, pulling my thighs open wider as he buries his face in my pussy and laps greedily at my cunt.

In moments, I'm a blubbering mess under his skilled tongue. But Cas doesn't stop, because my stepbrother isn't nice like that.

He doesn't want to just give you an orgasm, he likes to tear them out of your body in a torturous battle of wills.

He keeps licking and sucking, increasing his pace and pressure even though my clit is fucking decimated. I wriggle against the ropes, trying to get a little bit of distance, but he won't allow it.

"Don't fight it, Sunflower," he murmurs. "Come for me again."

"Fucking hell, Cas. I didn't know we were having a party."

It's Vic. He's finally done with his shower, and I can hear him move around the room. The bed creaks as he climbs on, and his hand tangles in my hair.

A moment later, Vic pushes himself inside my mouth. I take him in eagerly. He tastes fresh from the shower, and his skin is still cool and damp.

I tug on Vic's piercing with my tongue, enjoying his gasp of pleasure.

Behind me, Cas draws back and pushes in deeper. I can feel every bump and ridge of him, stretching me, claiming me as his.

The two of them build up a rhythm, slamming into me at the same time, so my body feels like an accordion, stretching and compressing to take them both. Only this is a terrible metaphor, because accordion music isn't hot, and what they're doing to me with their cocks is burning me up in the best possible way.

They go slow at first, but as the pleasure builds they speed up, and I can do nothing but hang on and try to keep my jaw from seizing up and revel in the dirty, delicious pleasures they stir up inside me.

"Does that feel good, Sunflower?" Cassius asks as I moan and jerk beneath him. "Do you like sucking on Vic's cock while I pound into you? Do you like taking both of us at once?"

"Yes," I say, although it's muffled by Vic's cock so it comes out as, "Yrrrrff."

"Good." Cas pushes a finger into my back hole, making me squirm. "Then show us just what a good girl you are and come again for us. Come apart around us, baby."

Vic's fingers tighten in my hair as he slams his cock into my mouth. His piercing hits the back of my throat. I'm gagging on it and I love it.

Cas pumps his finger inside me and curls another around his cock to touch my clit. I'm so, so sensitive from my previous orgasms that just the ghost of his touch is enough to send sparks through my limbs.

Heat pools in my cheeks. I taste salt on the end of my tongue. Vic gasps. He's close. So fucking close.

So am I.

Vic spills his load into my throat, and I suck every last salty bit of it down for him. He sinks back against the bed.

Cas' fingers dig into my hips, so hard that he'll leave bruises there later. My clit buzzes, ready for another release. My stomach flutters with winged creatures – and I revel in the wild freedom of what we're doing.

Never in a million years did I ever think I'd see being tied to a bed and fucked in two holes as being free, but as my limbs collapse and every hollow part of me fills with them, I know that New Fergie has at long last come home.

30

CASSIUS

I wake with a warm body nestled in my arms. For a moment, I'm disoriented. My grip tightens around the flesh. Did I fall asleep with one of my victims?

But no, this body is warm, and it yields to my touch.

It's my stepsister.

My Queen.

She's asleep, and I stare down at her in wonder, remembering all those nights when I tore the locks from her door so I could watch her sleeping. She's so vulnerable in this moment, and that used to give me such a feeling of power over her. I used to rub my cock over her lips sometimes, just to enjoy the way she murmured against it in her sleep.

But now I know that power came from a place of loathing. I didn't believe I deserved someone like her. I still don't. I still pinch myself that she's lying in my arms, her face pillowed in my shoulder, so peaceful and innocent in sleep.

She trusts me enough to go to sleep in my arms. And that is a gift I will never, ever squander.

As I watch Fergie's eyelids flutter and the little bead of drool appear on her perfect lips, the events of yesterday come flooding back to me – the bomb tearing through Cali's house, getting my family and the little kitten to safety, finding out that Livvie is dead, sneaking into Vic's place, watching Fergie disappear into the darkness, her brow knitted and jaw tight with determination, breaking down that dining room door and running into the poison gas to bring out Vic's family, thinking that if only I could strangle the poison with my bare hands I would, I *would*.

I'd do anything to protect this woman, and these people.

My family.

My family... *shit*.

I sit up, rolling Fergie off me so I can clamber out of bed.

Gaius.

I haven't heard from him since he said he was going to go after Juliet for Vic, and that he'd call us back. He's out there, and Sommesnay had fuck knows how many men from our organization on his side. We don't know who to trust.

Vic's sprawled on the other side of Fergie, his arm tossed casually over her sleeping body. As my eyes adjust to the dim light, I see Torsten on the other side of the room, curled up in a chair, drawing frantically on the wall with a marker.

"Torsten."

He keeps drawing. I say his name twice more, in increasing volume, but he doesn't turn from his drawing. I can see that he's drawing fast, furiously, the lines almost abstract, but a face is emerging from the center of the image.

It's his mother.

Interesting.

The only time I've ever seen Torsten draw something that wasn't a copy of a famous painting was when he drew that mural of Fergie at his hotel. And even that was different – it was still done in the style of his favorite artists. I recognized Monet, and Dali, and the one who liked all the weird shapes. Fuck, whatever, all I know about art is from listening to Torsten yammer on about it for years.

The picture he's drawing right now... it's none of them. It's something completely new.

I clamp a hand on Torsten's shoulder. His body jerks from the chair, his fist swinging up at my face. I stop him easily, closing my hand around his wrist.

"I'm not your enemy," I say.

"I know."

His body sags. I let go of his wrist, and he sinks back into the chair and stares at his drawing like he can't understand what it's doing there.

"What do we do now?" he asks. And even though he speaks, I've known him long enough that I can hear the fear beneath his words.

It's a fair question. One of the Triumvirate is dead, and both Claudia and Cali have been attacked. Even though Sommesnay is dead now, the blow he struck to their leadership will echo through our three families. We have to do something to restore our power. And I'm at a loss to think of what that could be.

It's as it always is – put me in front of an enemy and I know what to do. But when it comes to being a leader...

"Gaius will fix this," I say.

He will. That's what he told me as I ran to the car. "Go to the others, little bro. I'll fix this."

Torsten peers up at me with huge, round, hopeful eyes. He believes me. Gaius will fix everything. Gaius came here with a plan, he said as much. All I have to do is find him and everything will be okay.

I walk Torsten down to the kitchen and demand Milo feed him. Torsten looks so haunted that he'll forget to do normal human things unless we force him. I sit on his vacated seat, watching Vic and Fergie sleeping. I long to wake them up and discuss our next move, but they're both dealing with their own shit from last night, and I want to let them live in the world of dreams for a little while longer.

I head into the now-empty VIP suite. I lean over the railing and look below. Crooks and criminals snore in every corner, their families huddled together under blankets. Empty pizza boxes and top-shelf liquor from the bar are strewn everywhere. It looks more like the aftermath of a raucous party than a gang war.

Livvie's white-shrouded body lies on the stage, watching over the slumbering hordes like a Viking goddess.

I move to the back of the room, plop my ass down in a velvet wingback chair, and dial my brother's number.

He picks up on the first ring. "Little bro," he says. He sounds tired. "You're awake?"

"Do you think I'm having a Sunday lie-in while the Dio empire goes up in flames?" I try not to think of Fergie curled up in bed.

Let her sleep. Let her dreams be so sweet – I want to protect her from this waking nightmare for as long as I can.

I hear him opening a door, and a can popping open. He takes a sip of his drink. "Everyone okay on your end?"

"As okay as they can be. We got Sommesnay – Fergie choked him, and I blasted his head off – but Livvie Lucian is still dead. What the fuck do we do? Who's her heir?"

Gaius whistles. "I almost didn't believe it when you told me last night. If anyone could cheat death, it would be Livvie Lucian. How's Mom?"

"I haven't spoken to her since last night. She's still sleeping, and I don't want to wake her unless the place is on fire." I don't say it, but I know what we're both thinking. Gaius has seen Mom walking around our house with her cane. He's seen the way she wheezes when she walks up steps. She's not recovering from the gunshot wound, and at some point, she's not going to be able to hide that. "We have this place locked down tighter than a nun's cunt. Milo's complaining about the inadequate kitchen facilities, but he still manages to cook a crazy breakfast and leave me to do to dishes."

At my mention of Milo, my chest tightens. As often as I like to think that I have no emotions, that I'm untouchable, there are a few people in this world who turn me into a ball of mush. And that cheery old chef is one of them.

"Where are you?"

"At the gym," Gaius says. "Ares and I are rounding up everyone who's left. You know that Sommesnay must have more people on the inside, right? I'm talking so deep inside they're probably part of our families. Trudi can't be the only one."

"Milo and Seymour are clean," I snap.

"Mmmm," Gaius sips again. "We'll check everyone as many times as it takes. A reckoning is upon us, brother. Just because Sommesnay's dead doesn't mean this is over. You may be safe inside that club for the moment with your blind Queen and the August harem, but the barbarian hordes are at the gates, and they're baying for your blood."

"If they want a reckoning…" My fingers tighten into a fist.

"That's the Cas I love," Gaius laughs. "I promise, I'll give you the bloodshed you crave. Tell Vic that I'm getting his sister out tonight. She's arranged it all. Get Claudia and Cali to Colosseum at eight p.m. sharp, and Juliet will hand over everything she knows. We'll finish this."

31

FERGIE

"I don't like this," I say as we pull up in the reserved Imperator parking at Colosseum. Cas is driving and Vic and Torsten are in the backseat. Wheels crunch on the gravel as Seymour pulls up behind us with Claudia and Cali.

"What's not to like?" Cas taps his fingers on the wheel with excitement. "Gaius said he'll fix things, and that's exactly what he's done."

"But *how* do we know that?" My hands clench into fists. Cas' loyalty can be really fucking annoying sometimes. "Why can't he just tell us what he's arranged? Is Juliet going to be there? Why can't he just tell us what she has? Why this cloak-and-dagger bullshit?"

"Because he doesn't want to reveal plans in case our phone calls are being recorded," Vic says, his voice betraying his concern for his sister. "We know this other faction has agents close to our families, but none of us know how close."

"It sounds an awful lot like you don't trust my brother, Sunflower," Cas says. His tone is light and joking, but behind it is a hint of hurt. He wants me to get along with Gaius so that the two of us will take over Cali's empire and he can go back to being a monster for hire.

"I don't, Cas. I have no reason to."

"He got us out of that mess with the school after your article."

I have to concede that's true. "Just because he can charm a school principal with a fake police badge doesn't mean he can pull something that will root out these traitors. Gaius just got out of jail. He doesn't have the contacts or clout that you have with your soldiers."

"Gaius also isn't bright blue."

I can't help but smirk. "Sorry, Papa Smurf. I don't understand why we're relying on him to fix things instead of fixing them ourselves."

No one says anything, so I know I've struck a chord.

"Shall we get inside and see what he's offering?" Vic says from the backseat. "If Gaius' plan isn't going to work, we can walk away."

He's right. Walking away is still an option. Something niggles at me, a buzz in the air that doesn't fit. But I can tell that Vic and Cas need to go inside and find out what Juliet has planned. "Okay."

I throw open the door and step into the moonlight. That buzz in the air grows worse, more urgent, warning me to run away. But I can't leave their side because I have a bad feeling. It's precisely because of that bad feeling that I move closer to Cas and squeeze Torsten's hand.

Dad and Seymour help Cali out of her car, and Claudia, Eli, and Noah huddle nearby. Torsten's sister Shera is here, too. Cas and Seymour hand around weapons from the arsenal in the back of their vehicles. Guns, knives, and swords are strapped to bodies. I get two daggers and a cool spiked medieval mace.

"Don't hit yourself with it," Cas growls as he pushes it into my hands.

"Don't sass me or you'll get a spiky ball around the ears," I shoot back, trying to lighten the mood. But my joke falls flat and cold, heavy dread settles in my stomach. I hope I don't need to use this thing, because a blind girl with a mace sounds like a recipe for a Darwin Award.

We walk toward Colosseum as a group, huddled together like gazelles seeking protection. That oppressive unease weighs on my chest.

We reach the gates, and I'm just about to tell them to turn back when that buzz in the air congeals into something solid. Palpable. Unmistakable.

The hum of a crowd.

Colosseum isn't empty. This isn't some secret meeting with Juliet.

"Can you hear that?" I nudge Cas. "She's assembled a crowd."

"That's not right. Why would she—" Cas stops in his tracks, his body tensing. He hears the noise, too. It ripples out to the others. Their footsteps change as they sense it. "What's going on?"

"We'd better find out what my daughter wants." Claudia shoves ahead of us, her voice grim.

No, no, no, I want to scream. *We don't have to find out. We can go back to Tombs. We can return with more of our people. We can regroup, reassess, and make our plans so we're not going in blind as fucking bats.*

Yeah, yeah, I know. It's an expression.

But I say nothing. It's not my empire to burn. At least, not yet.

Noah barks orders at the soldiers acting as our guard, getting them to fan out around us and stay alert for trouble. I expect them to lead us into the tunnel that goes through the cages and the preparation area for the fighters and comes out in the arena, but instead we head for the old workshops, passing through the narrow gates between the two halves of the roundhouse. I realize why Cas has chosen this – if a fight breaks out, in the narrow space we can make the most of our smaller numbers without the risk of being split up or cornered in a dead end the way we would underground.

We enter Colosseum on the platform that rises above the crowd. I can tell the moment they spot us because the mood changes. The noise becomes quieter, more menacing. A few people clap, but they're quickly drowned out by a roar of defiance – an angry sound without words or accusation. These aren't people here to air their grievances.

They're here for one reason – blood.

"We have to leave. Now." The words fly out of my mouth before I can stop them. But the howling crowd whips them away.

"Ah, they have arrived," Juliet calls from the direction of the arena. "Let us have silence for our illustrious leaders."

As one, the crowd falls silent. But it's not the awed silence commanded at the previous Triumvirate events whenever one of the Imperators took the stage. It's a menacing silence. The silence of a lion poised to pounce on his unsuspecting prey.

Why do I have the feeling that we are the prey?

"We need to get down there," Claudia says, loud enough that I can hear. I suspect she's talking to Cali. The air shifts as the adults surge forward, but there's a scuffle and some harsh words, and they fall back to stand beside us.

Warm fingers seek mine and squeeze. It's Torsten. "They won't let us come closer," he says. "There are armed soldiers, in front of and behind us, and they're... they're pointing their weapons at us."

"Whose men are they?" I know that all soldiers wear visible symbols of their loyalty to the families. The eagle for Dio, the lion for Lucian, and the sword and laurel wreath for August.

"They're..." Torsten leans forward. "I don't know. I recognize some from my mother's guard, and two of them were definitely Cali's assassins, but they're all wearing a new symbol. It's a snake."

This is bad. I know this is bad.

I squeeze Torsten's hand, and he doesn't squeeze back.

"Juliet August is standing in the arena," says Torsten. "She's wearing a purple cloak with that same snake embroidered on it. And she's with Cas' father."

What the actual fuck?

Okay. This is definitely bad.

"Where's Gaius?"

"He's tied to a chair. There's blood running down his face."

"We have to get out of here," I whisper to Torsten. "Now."

Cas must've seen his brother, because he has the exact opposite idea. He grabs my other arm and starts to drag me toward the arena, but we don't get far. I've barely gone five steps when something hard and cold jabs into my chest. "Don't go any further," a harsh voice says. "I've got orders to shoot."

"What are you doing, Thomas?" Cas shouts at the guy. "We've knocked off French diplomats and German radicals together. Why are you pointing that gun at me?"

"I don't work for your family anymore," he rasps back. "I have a new Imperator now."

"A new Imperator? This is ridiculous." Cali's voice snaps. "Stop being so stupid and tell us what is going on."

"It's simple, darling." Ares is speaking into the microphone. What the fuck is he doing? "We are the Gorgons, and we own Emerald Beach now."

Um, what?

I must be going deaf from Cas' heavy music, because I swear I just heard fucking Ares declare that he was taking over the city, and what the fuck is a Gorgon?

Lucky for me, Ares the traitorous bastard is here to explain. "The Triumvirate is a failed institution. It was a good idea, sure – three families working together to rule the criminal world. But over time, our Imperators have become soft. Worse, we're becoming a laughingstock – in jail, I heard that Cali and Claudia and Livvie care more about pillow fights and braiding each other's hair and the antics of their spoiled children than they do about the people who put their lives on the line for them every single day—"

"What the fuck are you talking about, you simpering old fool?" Cali screams. "You know nothing. You've been in jail for eighteen years, so why the fuck—"

"That's right," Ares says, "I've been in jail, listening to the stories of the men and women who take the fall for you and your fellow Imperators. Which is more than you have done. Do you three care about anything other than safeguarding your pointless legacies? You built a fucking *museum* to yourselves right in the middle of the city, and filled it with old crap using the money that should have gone to your soldiers."

How is this possible? How has Ares, who hasn't even been on the scene for eighteen years, become leader of this coup so quickly? He must've been one of the pieces in Sommesnay's toolbox, thrown in to disarm Cali and Cassius. It worked, because beside me, Cas is grinding his teeth with rage.

And Gaius... they have him as a hostage? What do they intend to do with him?

"That museum has been a lucrative business," Claudia says. "It's legitimized our antiquities trading and allowed us to welcome foreign investors into the city who wish to store their valuables in her vaults. Because of that, our profits have more than doubled year on year since it opened, and that's money that goes back to the people who support the initiative."

Her argument, although true, doesn't have the power I hoped. The people in the crowd take all the risks and see only what Livvie and Cali and Claudia have – the fancy houses, the fancy cars, the untouchableness that comes with being criminal royalty. They think it should be theirs, too. They wonder why they're paying a portion of their earnings so three women already wealthy beyond belief can continue to fill their coffers.

After over twenty years of peaceful reign, the people are hungry for change.

"Everything we do is for our people," Cali snaps. She won't win any supporters with her sunny personality, either. "We built that stupid museum so we could compete internationally, and—"

"Look how easy it was for someone to destroy it," Juliet says with a smirk in her voice. "And what have you done since then? Nothing. Your people *died* in that attack. And yet you've been acting as if nothing is wrong. All you care about is the love life of your blue son, and the rumor is that you're training up that bubblegum monster and his blind girlfriend to take over as Imperators, meanwhile Gaius, who is far more talented, languished in prison."

"Leave me out of this," Gaius cries. Beside me, Cas growls, the sound so menacing that it rattles my bones.

"We're not going to stand here and justify our decisions and defend ourselves against this nonsense," Claudia says. "Juliet, I understand you're upset with me, but taking out your personal frustrations like this isn't just unprofessional, it's dangerous. Without leadership, there is chaos. Do you all want to return to the days of Brutus?"

"Gaius, what's going on?" Cas calls down.

"What's going on is that Vic's sister and your dad tricked me, brother," Gaius says. "I was only trying to save our family. They tell me that if you come down here and join them, if you put the might of Dio behind the new regime, we'll have no bloodshed today."

"We worked together once before, Cas," Juliet purrs. "Remember when we destroyed that girl you're now clinging to? That was fun, but now you look at her like she's a blow-up doll you don't want to pop. You know that if you're Imperator alongside her that she'd push you out and take everything for herself, the way she always does. All you have to do is come down here and take my hand, and I'll give you everything that dark heart of yours desires – the power, the bloodshed, the pussy. I'll make you a god."

"I have two words for you, Juliet," Cas barks. "Blood eagle. It's how I'm going to end you, by pulling your organs out through your ribcage. And I'll enjoy every moment—"

"Jules, *please,*" Vic calls down, his voice tight with anguish. "What are you doing? This has gone too far—"

"No, Vic, what's gone too far is all of you. You've forgotten who we are and what we were born to do. Do you think I give a shit about fashion school? Do you think I'm some damsel in distress who needs to be rescued like your little Queen? No, brother. I was *born* to be Imperator, but Mother Dearest refused to see it because for all her talk of building a new kind of empire, she's blinded by the golden boy. And that's bad enough, but then you decided to plan my life out for me. The great and virtuous Victor August swoops in to rescue his sister from a life of crime and sets her up as a fashion designer, never mind that I didn't ask to be rescued.

"I'm used to being underestimated by the world," she snarls. "But when it comes from my own twin, it makes me want to burn everything down, Vic. So here I am, taking what should always have been rightfully mine. Come join me, brother, and

I'll find a place for your earnest Panglossianism in my new empire. Or stay with Fergie Munroe and your friends and my so-called parents, and I'll burn you all."

"Juliet, this is ridiculous," her mother snaps. "I've always groomed you and Victor to take over, but you never showed a shred of interest in—"

"In becoming a sentimental, out-of-touch hack like you?" Juliet says. "No, I have not. I am the Queen of the Gorgons, and I won't live in your or my brother's shadow any longer."

Vic sounds tearful. "Jules, you can't—"

"I can, and I am."

"Enough of this," Ares says. "Everyone in this room has an option. You may remain here with us, as new soldiers of the Gorgons. Or you may leave with your fallen leaders and make your fortunes elsewhere. But the Gorgons have this city now, and August and Lucian and Dio are no longer welcome."

"Mother, you and Cali have twenty-four hours to make your decision," Juliet cries. "You will leave this city peacefully and relinquish your contracts to the Gorgons."

"And what if we don't, daughter?" Noah calls out.

"If you choose to fight, then we'll execute Gaius. And that will only be the beginning."

"Fuck you!" Gaius growls.

Beside me, Cas howls like a wounded animal.

"Choose now, brother," Juliet says. "And choose wisely. I will welcome you and Cas and Torsten to our ranks if you agree to serve me, but this offer does not extend to your parents or Fergie. Think carefully. You do not want us as your enemy."

"Choose!" Ares barks.

There's a great tidal wave of movement. I don't have to see to know what's happening. The crowd is on their feet and moving, either toward the arena or in our direction. Cas grabs my arm and yanks me backward – I guess the guards have opened up to allow us to exit.

"They're letting us leave?" I ask.

"That's the honorable thing to do," Vic says. "The crowd is dividing, each soldier choosing their sides. For all of Juliet's talk, she knows this will only end one way – in a bloody war for possession of this city. We'll go back to Tombs and regroup and—"

He's cut off by a bloodcurdling scream, and there's a roar that's more guttural, more horrible, than any sound the crowd has made.

"Fuck, it's Clarence." Cas' grip on my arm tightens. "The bastards have set him free. Run!"

My blood freezes in my veins.

Clarence? Here?

But we're out in the open. How can—

A growl sounds to my left, jolting me out of my thoughts. Vic grabs me and sweeps me into his arms. This isn't the time to tell him that I'm blind, not an invalid, and I'm perfectly capable of running away from a lion by myself.

Because, seriously, fuck that.

Vic's breath huffs against my cheek as he runs. All around me I hear feet crunching on gravel, Clarence snarling, people crying, bones breaking beneath the trampling crowd.

Clarence has been trained by the people who used to own him to fear and mistrust humans, and to lash out violently if provoked. He's not killing to eat, but to escape, but the crowd fleeing from him will cause more death than his vicious teeth.

Vic drops me on my feet and helps me climb up onto the roof of an old workshop to escape the trampling crowd. Torsten is already there, and he gets everyone up onto a higher roof. Cali and my dad and the Augusts climb up afterward. We huddle together, listening, waiting.

Cas remains down below. I hear him rallying men as they fight for control of the arena. I don't have to see to hear the metallic shimmer of his sword slashing, to smell the blood he spills to keep us safe, to feel the weight of the full force of his brutality bearing down on Juliet's soldiers. Even though Cas is no longer a man, but a monster, I know he is not enough to stop this.

The sounds are terrible. People scatter in all directions. Gunshots ricochet from the old tin buildings. The screams chill my blood. Clarence is overwhelmed by the chaos and lashes out in the only way he knows how – by trampling bodies, tearing limbs, crunching bones.

And above it all, above the carnage and the bloodshed, Juliet's voice peals across Colosseum as she laughs. And laughs. And laughs until she can hardly breathe.

"Why are they doing this?" I sob.

Vic holds me close, and his voice is hoarse from yelling for his sister. "Because she can't leave any doubt who's in charge of Emerald Beach."

CAS IS the one to put down Clarence in the end.

He won't tell me how he did it, but as he climbs onto the roof to join us, I can feel him shaking. He hated to do it – to Cas, Clarence isn't simply an animal acting on instinct – the two of them are brothers. I lick the splattered blood from his cheek and kiss him deep until the shaking subsides, but I get the sense that even my monster has seen things tonight that he'll never unsee.

Poor Clarence. He didn't deserve any of this. I hope he's gone to kitty heaven where he never has to eat a foul-tasting rapist ever again.

It's a long time before Cas and Vic declare it safe to climb down from the roof of the workshop. We can hear noise from inside Colosseum – cheers and shouts from the crowd as Juliet and Ares hold some kind of wild victory party. I want to see what's going on in there, but I know we need to get out of here before we're seen, or worse... before they drag out another lion.

We head back to Tombs, and extend the invitation to the gaggle of people who still cling to us. We need to stick together. We are no longer Dio and Lucian and August. We are those who did not choose to become Gorgons.

Cas and Vic work the doors, interrogating each person as they show up, doing everything they can to make sure only truly loyal people join us. Torsten and I hand out supplies to those who didn't spend last night with us. People have brought their families – I guess after your Imperator's house blows up, you don't feel safe in yours.

Euri, bless her heart, goes out for more cots and blankets and pizza with Cas as her guard, and they promise to pick up Dru on the way home. I don't want any of my friends to sleep alone tonight, not now I know what Juliet's capable of.

When we're done, the dance floor of Tombs is more like a field hospital. Families huddle together in frightened groups. Galen has a first aid station under the stage where he patches up those who met the business end of Clarence's teeth. Above them all, Livvie's body is lying in state, and even though Galen told us he's done some work on her, I catch the faintest whiff of rot in the air that tells me we need to do something about her soon. But having a public funeral at her plot in Beaumont Hills cemetery is out of the question with the Gorgons out there.

As if we need something else to worry about.

"Fergie, you look starving," Milo calls out. Torsten helps me navigate my way to the club's tiny kitchen, where Milo is busy whipping up platters of food to feed people. The place smells amazing. He pushes a bowl of piping-hot stew into my hands. "Eat up. You're going to need your strength."

I learned long ago that it's no use arguing with Milo, so Torsten and I accept bowls and sit down to eat. As we do, there's a commotion from the stage, and a microphone crackles. The room falls silent. Torsten's fingers slide into mine and squeeze.

"Claudia and Cali are on the stage," he says.

Good. They need to say something. They can't let Juliet's haunting laugh be the last word.

"Thank you, everyone, for your loyalty," Claudia's voice booms through the club, quieting every conversation. "When I look around the room, I see many faces who've been with me since the day I took this family back from the traitor Brutus. And not just that, but those who have found their own family under the August and Lucian and Dio crests. Our dear Livvie is no longer with us, but Cali and I have been with her so long that we know her mind, and we know that she would have been proud to see all these faces here with us."

A cheer rises from the crowd, and I feel the roar rise in my own throat. Livvie *would* be proud of the three families standing together. But I'm also glad she didn't have to live to see what the Triumvirate has been reduced to.

Claudia continues. "We have dealt with many challenges to our power over the years. This is no different. I know you've heard and seen things in the media recently that make you believe that our three families are divided and that our contracts with the wider community are weakened. These are lies spread by our enemies. We are stronger than ever. We are not divided."

Another cheer. Cas and Vic drop down beside us. Torsten's fingers find mine and squeeze.

"We know you're worried about your families and livelihoods. Many of you will remember the last time there was a war for power in this city, when the streets ran red with our blood.

We don't want to repeat history. I'm going to hand you over to Cali, who's going to explain what we're going to do to take back Emerald Beach."

A cheer goes up as Cali takes the microphone. Her husky voice sounds strange being boomed from the club's speakers.

"Thank you. Thank you for your loyalty over the years, and thank you for standing with us today."

She sounds powerful and strong, but I can hear the strain in her voice. With her injuries, she's not supposed to be running for her life from lions. But very few people in this room know how badly she's broken, and Cali's pride won't allow her to show weakness in front of them.

"I'm not going to stand here and speak pretty words and make allusions to what's going on. A man I once trusted who has the audacity to call himself Cassius' father has conspired with Claudia's daughter to build a new family from within our ranks, and they are now holding my eldest son hostage. It has been a long time since another gang dared to establish itself in Emerald Beach, and I must admit to being a little proud that the only person who's been able to challenge us is a guy I once beat in the ring."

The crowd roars with applause at that. I bet some of them still remember Cali and Ares from those early days.

Cali continues. "Now, Claudia will tell you that we're all about choices. It's a free world, and if you're no longer interested in being part of the Triumvirate, despite everything we've done for you over the years, then she says that's fine. You're free to go. And of course, Claudia is free to run the August clan however she likes. But I have no such scruples. You fuck me over, you'd better sleep with one eye open, because I am coming for every last one of you who walks out that door."

You tell them, Cali.

"These 'Gorgons' promise nothing new." I can hear the air

quotes in Cali's voice. "It's all bullshit. You're deluding yourself if you think Ares and Juliet are looking out for anyone but themselves. But they do make an attractive proposal and a nice new logo. They have fooled a significant number of you into following them. Some of you are even here against the wishes of your families. I'm not going to pretend they don't have numbers on us.

"However, looking around this room I see that we have something more important. We have *expertise*. Assassins and scoundrels and criminals with decades of experience. Giving a kid a weapon and telling him that your club has no rules isn't the same as showing him how to use it. They may think we're weak now, and that's good. They get cocky, and we'll strike when they least suspect us.

"This is what my stepdaughter, Fergie, taught us all when she fought Cassius in the ring. We saw a blind girl face a monster, and how fierce strength and belief in oneself can triumph over sheer brute force."

I wonder how Cas feels about his mother talking about him like this, but he leans over and whispers, "You love that brute force when it's slamming my cock inside you, sis."

"Damn right." I smile back.

This new Cas is... he's incredible. His brother is in trouble, but he's holding it together for his people, for *me*. Knowing that such a beast of a man is on my side, now and forever, and that I don't have to waste a single ounce of energy on being afraid of him, makes all the difference.

He's *my* monster.

"Claudia and I have decided that we're going back to Colosseum tomorrow to give the Gorgons our answer. We're going back because they're not taking the empire we built without a fight. We need every man, woman, and child who's able to stand ready to be there with us. We must display strong numbers. I won't lie to you – things could get ugly. I promise that I have a plan, although you may not like it, and that my fighters will do everything they can to protect you. Or, you can leave town now and hope like hell that I can't find you. This is your choice. Who's with me?"

From the roar of defiance that rocks the foundations of Tombs, I know that every single person in that room thrusts their fist in the air. I yell my assent.

When I first met Cali, I thought she was a cold bitch and I wanted nothing to do with her.

But to hear her rally her fear for her first son, and her shock at Ares' betrayal, into a valiant last stand... I know I'd follow her into the pits of hell itself.

33

VICTOR

I slip away from the main floor of the club halfway through Mom and Cali's speech. It's not that I don't feel the loss of Livvie, but I can't stand hearing them talk about uniting our families against our enemy.

Not when our enemy is my own sister.

They all see it as black and white. We are good and righteous, and Juliet is on the other side, the side of the usurpers. To save the Triumvirate, she must be destroyed. Even our parents seem to have accepted this. Mom is downstairs right now calling for her daughter's head on a pike.

But to me, Jules is still the kid sister who gave my action figures makeovers and refused to put her head underwater in the swimming pool until she was twelve. She's the girl who made me sneak out into the woods to play fairy circles, and who came out to my parents by inviting a biker chick named Shay to Thursday night dinner and gleefully watching the hilarity. She could make me laugh with just a look, and she always had my back.

Always.

Just like she did the other night. I don't care what anyone

says, Juliet got me out of the house. She made sure I was safe.

She's not beyond saving.

I just have to find a way to reach her.

On the way to our bedroom, I pass Eli in the hall. He's standing in front of a statue of the cat goddess Bast, staring off into space, his eyes glazed and unfocused. He jumps as he notices me.

"Vic, hey." He wipes a hand through his golden hair, and I notice the bags under his eyes. "How are you holding up?"

I shake my head. "Tell Mom that I'm sorry, but I can't listen to another minute of that speech. She's not our enemy, she's my sister, and she's in trouble and Mom doesn't seem to care. How can she just switch off loving Jules like this?"

"I know." Eli opens his arms. "I know."

I fall into my father's embrace. As he closes his arms around me and I'm enveloped in his familiar scent, all the stress and horror of the last few days hits me full force. My body convulses with sobs. The hole in my heart where my sister belongs yawns open, the edges raw and burning.

Juliet, what happened to you? Why did you have to do this? Why did you have to leave me here alone?

"Listen to me," Eli says as he strokes my hair. "You're such a beautiful soul, Vic. You have always been such a good brother to her, and I know how much this must hurt you. I promise you that no matter what your mother says to appease her soldiers, behind closed doors, it's a different story. She's a mess; she's barely holding it together. But she can't let the people downstairs see that."

"But they need to see! They need to know Jules isn't our enemy. Ares has her trapped and—"

"Vic, you have to be careful that you're not speaking for her. Juliet told us what she wanted in her own words. She wasn't a prisoner. She didn't appear to be coerced. Part of loving her means letting her make her own decisions, even if they hurt us greatly."

"But *why*? What can Ares give her that I can't? I would have given her the job of Imperator if it made her happy."

Why does she not love me? Why does she hate our family so much?

"I know you would, son, and I think she knows that, too, which is why she's chosen this path." Eli pauses. "I think that your sister has been unhappy for a long time, perhaps longer than any of us can fathom. She's a lot like your mother in so many ways, so strong-willed and ambitious, and she feels as though she's been living in your shadow, in Claudia's shadow. Jules doesn't want to be handed power out of pity. She wants to be *worshipped*, like this cat goddess here. And the only way she can get what she wants is to cut us off. She's made it clear that she's turned her back on us, and she's counting on our senti-ment for her to make us weak. So we cannot be weak. We must call on our strength even when it demands that we do the unthinkable to stop her. But we can still love her, and we can still mourn the loss of her. Some people can't be saved, no matter how much we wish for it. Some people don't want to be saved. Okay?"

No, not okay. None of this is okay.

I nod.

Eli pulls back and studies me. His eyes glisten with tears as he places his hand to his chest, over his breaking heart.

"I'm so sorry for what you're going through, son. No one—" Eli's voice catches, "—should have to see their twin betray them."

But Juliet hasn't betrayed me. She wouldn't. She has a plan, but it's not clear yet because she had to scramble after we killed Sommesnay—

My phone rings. UNKNOWN flashes across the screen.

"Thanks, Dad." I nod toward my bedroom door. "I need to—"

"Yes, of course." He flashes me that sad smile. "I'll come and find you later and we'll talk more, okay?"

"Okay."

I sprint to our room and slam the door shut behind me as I press the button to accept the call. "Juliet?" I whisper.

A throaty laugh on the other end sets my heart thudding. "How'd you know, brother?"

I move to the door and check that it's locked. I lean against it and press the phone even tighter against my ear, as if I can crawl through it and reach her.

"Listen, I don't have much time. I know you must be pretty broken up about what you saw at Colosseum. You probably hate me."

Her voice catches.

"I could never hate you." Tears well in the corners of my eyes.

"You're the only one, Vic. The only one who gets me, who still believes in me. I was only trying to help, but it's all completely messed up. I knew that if I got you out of the house, you'd be able to save them, and you did! You did! But because Sommesnay died, Ares has taken over and he's out of control—"

"I know, it's okay, Jules. I know you were just trying to help."

"Oh, Vic," she sobs. "I was so childish. I wanted to piss Mom off so I thought it would be fun to join the rebellion. But then it all got out of control. I don't want this... I don't want them to hurt you..."

She hiccups.

"Shhh, Jules. It's going to be okay. I'll get you out. I promise."

"Mom will never take me back."

"She will." I would make her. "I'll protect you, just the way I always have. I'll make sure you're safe. But it would help if you could bring us something – something we can use against the Gorgons. We desperately need a win here."

"What if…" she blows her nose. "What if I give you Ares?"

"How?"

"He's put us both up in the penthouse suite at the Elysium. After we leave Colosseum tomorrow night, I can dismiss the guards and make sure the door is open for you. I have a stash of sleeping pills – I'll make sure he's knocked out. Kill him and get me out of there. Without Ares, the Gorgons will fall into disarray. They're too inexperienced to hold it together under the full weight of the Triumvirate."

"Jules, we have to act now. We can't wait for tomorrow. We don't know what's going to happen. You know Mom and Cali aren't going to hand over the city. We have to—"

"I can't do anything now. Only tomorrow night, when he's asleep. Please, Vic. It will be okay. Ares is going to let you walk away tomorrow. I've talked him into it. There are too many people with split loyalties – the Gorgons have left husbands and wives and parents and children behind in our ranks. They won't accept a massacre, no matter how much Ares wants one."

She has a point. "Are you sure you can get him to keep his word on that? He's not exactly truthful."

"I'm certain," she laughs bitterly. "I have my own ways of ensuring loyalty, brother."

I *so* don't want to know. My heart clenches. I don't like to think of how frightened and alone she must feel right now, how wrong it is for Mom to be downstairs calling for her doom when she's still trying to help us. "Jules, I wish you'd talk to me. Why have you done all this?"

"Because I am my mother's daughter," Jules says with a sigh. "I love you, Vic. Stay safe."

"I love you—"

But she'd already hung up.

34

FERGIE

After Claudia and Cali get off the stage, someone puts on a playlist, and Milo and Cas turn bartenders, pulling out all of Livvie's top-shelf booze to sate the appetites of our crowd. We may be holed up in this bar, and we may be walking into our doom tomorrow, but tonight we're going to party as only the Triumvirate can party.

I know it's important for the people to see me with the guys, to know that all the shit in the media about us is false. So even though it's the last thing I feel like doing, Vic's disappeared somewhere, so I drag Torsten onto the dance floor. We thrash around awkwardly until Cas comes over with drinks for us.

I take a sip of my drink and nearly spit it out. "Cas, this is practically one hundred percent vodka."

"Claudia and Cali want us to meet them on the roof," he yells over the music. "I figure we need to be fortified."

"Fortified? I'm practically mummified." I knock back the drink in one hit. The alcohol buzzes in my veins as Cas and Torsten loop my arms into theirs and lead me up several flights of stairs.

We join the Imperators and Shera Lucian on the roof, overlooking the city. Vic arrives shortly afterward, his greeting calm and collected, as he always is. I haven't had a chance to talk to him about Juliet. I hope he's dealing okay with finding out she's a two-faced traitor.

A bitter wind whips up from the street below and fans my hair around my face. I usually love being outside beneath the bright moon, but tonight I feel exposed, vulnerable. I wish I had another drink.

"Thank you for meeting us," Claudia says. "And thank you for everything you did today, especially you, Cas. I don't know what we would have done without you—"

"Don't be so fucking sentimental," Cali snaps. "This is business."

"Oh, excuse me for being happy that our children weren't eaten by a lion. And that was *my* fucking lion. Eli is very upset that Clarence was used in this way."

"Me too," Cas growls, the emotion thick in his voice.

"What's going to happen now?" Vic asks. "What are you going to do?"

"We're going to take back this city," Cali says. "This coup may have been brewing for a long time, but we can't be toppled so easily."

"We understand why this has happened," Claudia adds. "We've become victims of our own prosperity. People are sick of seeing our faces. We've given them twenty years of unprecedented wealth and peace – or as much peace as one can expect in a crime organization. So of course they want something new and exciting. I just never thought it would be my own daughter with her fucking *Gorgons*."

"You're not going to leave, are you?" Cas sounds... "They have Gaius. We need to—"

"I know exactly what we need to do," Cali snaps. "We have tomorrow well in hand. What we need to do right now is establish our legacies."

"Livvie died without officially naming her heir," Claudia says. "We can't bury her, but we need to name her successor. It will help to unite our people."

"And should something happen to us, Cali and I have made a decision about our heirs." Claudia clears her throat. "Vic, I'd like you and Fergie to be my joint heirs."

Whoa, *fuck*.

I mean, I knew she liked me and she wanted to train me, but to be named Claudia August's heir? Right now? And what will this mean for—

Cali interrupts my racing throughs. "Cassius, I'd like you and Fergie to be my joint heirs."

Um... what the fuck?

I did not *just hear this.*

"We realize this is unprecedented for us both to have our families run by two people, and for one of those people to be across two families. But we think this is the right thing to do. If we announce this now, it will help to bring unity to our people, to show that everything that's gone on between the three of you in the media is bullshit."

"What about Lucian?" I ask tentatively. "Is it a good idea to leave them without an Imperator?"

"No," Cali says simply. "Which is why we want Fergie to rule as Imperator of the Lucian family."

"I'm sorry, no," I say. "That's not happening."

"Why the fuck not?"

"Um, I can think of a few reasons. One, I'm not blood—"

"It doesn't matter if none of her children want the job. Oh, Shera here would do a fine job, of course, but she's just informed us that she won't accept the job. The Imperator is going to be on the firing line right now, and she needs to look after Isabella."

"In other words," Cali growls, "she's too chicken shit to take on the job. Not you, though."

Right, I'm the only one crazy enough to accept.

"What do you think, Torsten?" Claudia asks. "You are the eldest child, and Livvie always hoped that you would inherit. I know Fergie wouldn't take the job without your blessing."

I turn to Torsten. His fingers slide from mine as he flaps his other hand at his side. I remember the promise I made to him before his house exploded and our world fell apart. I lean in close and whisper.

"I can tell them for you, but I think it will be even more awesome coming from you."

His hand flaps harder. "I don't want to be Imperator. I'm not good at it. I don't want to lie to people and steal things and trade in drugs. I want to be an artist."

For a moment, no one speaks, and then Claudia breaks the silence. "It's fine, Torsten. We're not going to force this on you. We changed the rules exactly so that we could make sure the best people become Imperator. So, Fergie, any more objections?"

I tick off more reasons on my fingers. "I'm not even nineteen yet. None of these soldiers will listen to me—"

"Claudia was younger than you when she took over," Cali says. "Next objection."

"Um, how about that I don't know the first thing about being an Imperator? Like, you've both taught me so much, but I need years to learn this stuff. I can't just jump in and—"

"Yes, you can," Cali snaps. "It's what we all had to do."

"You have always excelled at everything you set your mind to, Fergalish," Dad adds. "If this is truly the path you want to take in life, then I believe that you'll excel as a crime lord, too."

"It's what Livvie wanted," Cassius says. "She told me as much."

"She did?" I turn to him in surprise.

"Before our fight. She came to me in the fighter's area and promised that I would have control of the Dio family if I publicly backed Fergie and Torsten's relationship as a Dio/Lucian alliance. Livvie might've been a backstabbing bitch, but she was right about two things – there would be a war for power in this city, and that you would be the source of that power."

"But..." I'm awed by it all. "I don't know the first thing about clubs and drugs and... and... whatever else Livvie traded in."

"It doesn't matter," Claudia says. "Right now, all we need is a face we can rally people behind. And after dyeing my son blue and that performance in the ring, you're it. Our people already respect you. They know who you are."

"But how can I be Imperator in three families?" My head whirls at the implications. "How can I make difficult decisions that could place one family over another?"

"We've thought about this long and hard," Claudia says. "And we've decided that the way we've been ruling – together but separate – is no longer working. Under your rule, the three families will be truly united."

35

CASSIUS

After they drop their bombshell, my mother dismisses everyone else but asks me and Fergie to stay on the roof with her.

"Your brother has been in contact with me," she says. "Your bastard of a father let him talk to me for a few minutes. He's been kept in the cages beneath Colosseum."

Gaius. My whole body burns with a need to get him back. The red mist clouds my eyes, and my rage is so intense, so heavy in my body, that I know I could walk into that place, smash through the concrete walls, and break the neck of anyone who tried to stop me.

I can get him out. I can bring him back to me.

"You're not going after him," Cali snaps. "You'll be shot full of holes like a slice of Swiss cheese before you even get near the door. They're expecting you to do something rash, so don't fucking prove them right."

"What did he say?" Fergie asks. Her fingers find mine and lace through them. I crush her hand with my grip, and she doesn't cry out.

"He says what Ares told him to say – they'll kill him if we

don't surrender the city to them. He says that we'll be allowed to leave, that all our people will be safe. I don't believe it for a second. They cannot allow us the ability to regroup and rebuild." She sniffs. "The two of you are my heirs; what do you think? What would you do if you were me?"

"We lay a trap for tomorrow," I say immediately. "They're holed up in Colosseum, right? That building has vulnerabilities. If we can—"

"Fergie?" Cali barks, interrupting me.

I turn to my girl. She fixes me with those unseeing eyes of hers, those deep emerald orbs that have the uncanny ability to draw my most intimate fears to the surface. "How do we know Gaius is even a prisoner?"

"What?" That's the absolute last thing I expect her to say.

"He could be acting. He could be in on this with Juliet and Ares."

"No, he isn't."

I'm a hundred and twenty percent sure of that.

"Think about it – we went to Colosseum because of Gaius, remember? I think he led us into a trap, Cas." She turns to Cali. "Gaius was in jail for years and you never got him out, even though we all know you had the power to. Instead, he found Ares, who has his own grudge against you. Gaius has always been clear about his goal of becoming an Imperator. Is it not possible that he's switched loyalties and is lying to us all?"

"Gaius would never do that," I shoot back. "He's family. He's loyal."

"*You're* loyal, Cas. You're the most loyal, devoted person I know. I'm not sure if Gaius is loyal to anyone but himself—"

"Enough," Cali snaps. "Thank you. That's all. I have decided what we're going to do."

"Which is?"

"On a need-to-know basis. And you do not need to know.

That's all, Cassius." Cali points to the door back into the club. "Leave us. I need to speak to the Lucian Imperator, *alone*. Tell Milo to send up some of his hot chocolate."

I shoot my mother a scathing look, but her face is completely unreadable. She turns her back on me. I long to shake her until she spills the plan, but it will take more than even the monster inside me to make Cali Dio give up her secrets.

Fergie looks miserable, but as she reaches for me, I shrug her off. "This is your duty now," I say with more venom than she deserves.

"Cas—"

I don't look back as I hurry off the roof.

The red mist cloaks my eyes and pushes into my throat, choking off the scream that longs to escape me. I know that I need to talk to Fergie about her distrust of Gaius, but I also know that even if she were here beside me, even if she weren't conspiring with my mother, I can't *talk* now. I need to get rid of this homicidal rage, or someone is getting their head put through a wall.

I stand in the doorway of the main club area, watching our soldiers talk and carouse while the red mist creeps through my veins. I don't know how much time has passed, but I see Fergie emerge onto the VIP staircase, her features grim, a cute little crease between her eyebrows.

People jump out of Fergie's way as she sweeps her cane across the floor. She heads to the kitchen to put in Cali's hot chocolate order while I go to the bar and slam back a couple of tequila shots. Vic sees me across the room and starts toward me, but one look at my face has him turning around again.

I toss the bottle in my hand. It smashes on the floor, sending glass and expensive tequila everywhere. The red mist *burns*. I follow it with more booze. I go to that dark, red place inside me where all I see and feel is the burning, seething hate.

The monster inside me takes over, and I lose myself in the rage—

"Cas?"

Her voice brings me back. I blink, and the red is gone. I'm back in the club. I'm standing by the bar, a pile of broken glass and splintered furniture all around me. Everyone has fled to the other side of the room, but not Fergie. Not my Queen. She stalks right up to me, her cane catching on the debris. "Cas, I know you're angry about what I said about Gaius—"

"I'd stay away from me if you know what's good for you." I grab another bottle. "I don't want to hurt you."

"Yes, you do." Fergie flashes me a defiant smirk that has my cock instantly standing to attention, and my fingers itch to teach her a lesson about loyalty. "You know exactly what you want to do to me, Cas."

"Yes." My voice strains. My cock is so hard it's painful.

She holds out her hand. "Then put down the bottle and teach me a lesson."

Oh, fuck yes.

I toss the bottle over my shoulder and grab her. Her cane goes flying across the room as I throw her tiny body over my shoulder. "Let's get you battle ready, my Queen."

Even though I'm positive Fergie is exactly where she wants to be, she howls in protest and pummels my back. She knows what I like and she's roleplaying the innocent victim caught by the monster for me, even though that's not even close to what she is to me. I carry her past the room we're sharing with Vic and Torsten, through Livvie's old office, to a secret panel I found in the wall. I punch a couple of buttons, and a small door opens behind the desk. I have to stoop to get us both through.

"Where are we?" Fergie asks as I put her down so I can figure out how to close the door behind me.

"I found this room while we did our security sweep earlier." I punch random buttons until I get the door to close and the low lighting to come on. "It made my dick hard, thinking of all the things I'd like to do to you in here. Shall I describe it to you?"

"Please." Her voice strains with need.

"Well, dear sister. In the corner is a St. Andrew's cross. Do you know what that is?"

She shudders. "No."

"It's a big wooden X. I tie your hands to the top and your feet to the bottom, and you're completely at my mercy. What do you think of that, my Queen?"

"I think, sign me the fuck up."

I lead her across the room and guide her hands to the wooden cross. Fergie feels it with her fingers and squeals with excitement when she touches the harsh metal restraints. My cock pulses against my jeans, desperate to get her tied up, but there's more I want to do first.

All the times we fucked before the fight, we were locked in a battle of wills. I wanted to break her, and she wanted to show me that she can never be broken. But things are different now, and I mean to honor her by showing her that when she enters a room like this with me, no matter the mask I wear, no matter what she says about my brother, I'm still her monster, and she's still my Queen.

"Hold out your hand," I command. She does so, and I place a long, wooden paddle in her hands.

"Feel that?"

"Yes." She moves it through the air. "It's heavy."

"Would you like me to use it on you?"

"Fuck yes."

"I'm going to show you all the toys in this room. You can tell me what you're most excited about."

As I place each of them in her hands, I watch her expression change. She's uninterested in the soft cat o' nine tails, but her eyes widen as she feels the weight of the steel butt plug. I love that I can read the way her body reacts, and plan exactly what I'll do to her to make her come for me.

"Okay, my Queen. Time for you to mount your throne."

Fergie lets me take her hand and lead her up to the cross. She holds her hands above her head and I pull off her black t-shirt, roll her leggings off her feet, and tear away the tiny crimson scraps of underwear so she's completely naked, except for her beautiful tattoo. I strap her into the shackles, making sure she can't slip her tiny wrists out. Both the shackles around the mid-section of the cross are padded because Livvie's guests clearly don't go in for pain quite the way I do, but I knew it would give Fergie a thrill. I kick her legs apart and secure her ankles and step back to admire her.

In the low lighting, her body appears to shimmer, her skin so smooth and vulnerable, begging for my marks. My cock twitches at the thought of how I'm going to proceed.

"What are you doing?" Her eyes widen as she hears the cap on the lube flick open.

"I'm preparing this plug for you," I tell her. I kneel between her legs, cupping her in my hand. She's wet already, so fucking wet. I can't help myself – I slide a couple of fingers inside her and pump a few times, swirling my thumb over her clit until her breath comes out in tiny gasps. When I withdraw my fingers, they're coated in her juices.

I keep swirling around her clit as I gently slide the plug into her ass. Fergie gasps and clenches, and I keep rubbing until she loosens up again and lets me in. The plug makes a sucking motion as it slides past the ring of muscle and nestles inside her. It has a little crimson jewel on the end, and it looks so pretty to me – a jewel for a Queen.

And because I'm nice, or very, very cruel, I keep rubbing her clit, faster and faster, and slamming my fingers inside her. I like the way the plug makes her tighter, more sensitive. In moments, she comes apart on my fingers, her body rocking against the restraints. I slide my fingers out and stand up.

"Taste yourself," I command her, pressing my fingers to her lips. "This is what I do to you when I touch you."

Fergie obediently opens her mouth, and I slide my fingers inside. Her eyes flutter closed as she licks my fingers clean. My dick is so fucking hard.

I pick up the next item for my toolkit – the cat o' nine tails that she rejected. I run the supple leather whip through my fingers before flicking it out expertly. She hisses as it bites her flesh. It's a different kind of pain than a flogger or the slap of a hand – more of a tickle, but the kind of tickle that can bite.

I work my way along both ass cheeks, even dragging the whip lightly over her shoulders. I avoid the parts over her back where organs are close to the surface. After a few strokes, I plunge my hand between her legs, giving her clit a little working over before I repeat the cycle again.

Fergie strains herself against the cross. She's completely in the moment. Right now, she's not thinking about Clarence or my brother or what's in store for us at Colosseum. She's not thinking about the weight of being the new Lucian Imperator or my mother's heir. She just *is*.

I drop the whip and cup her cunt. She's soaked. She trembles under my touch, and I know she's close again, so so close. I curl my fingers around, one dipping inside her as I tease her cunt and pick up the next item in my arsenal – the heavy wooden paddle.

When I hit her with that, she bellows and her body jerks, but her hips press back into me, begging for more. I fuck her fast and furious with my fingers as I bring the paddle down.

Within moments she's a trembling mess in my arms. "Cas... I don't know if I... can take another..."

"You will, and you'll love it."

I lean back from the cross and admire my work. Her lovely ass reddened by the whip and the paddle, her juices dribbling down her legs, her hair wild about her face, and that little red gem sticking out of her ass.

I can't wait a moment longer. I fling off my boxers and step up to her. "My turn," I growl in her ear as I push myself roughly inside her. She howls, and for a moment I think I might've actually hurt her and I freeze, but then she yells at me to fuck her and I obey my Queen.

I slam into her, hard and punishing, and she clenches around me. She's so fucking tight, and the butt plug inside her creates extra pressure. Not as much as if she had one of the other guy's cocks inside her, but they aren't here now and she's mine, mine, mine.

I let the red mist creep in as I fuck my Queen. I let my body take all that rage that she brought to the surface and channel it into my dick instead of my fists. I understand as I never have before that just because I am angry at her, just because she said something I don't like, it doesn't mean I still don't love her. That instead of wounding me with her words, she and I can be each other's medicine.

Her eyes are wide, her lips parted, her body so liquid I worry she might ooze from the restraints. Watching the pleasure and pain dance across her face is a sight I plan to burn into my retinas. I want to see her like this every time I close my eyes.

I fuck her against the cross until her screams become incoherent babbling. I fuck her until I don't even remember why I was so angry.

∾

"YOU'VE CHANGED A LOT, CAS." Fergie turns to face me and squeezes my hand. She's lying on her stomach on the bed, and I'm applying cream to the welts on her ass. At my request, she's still wearing the plug, and the sight of that crimson jewel between her cheeks makes me smile and my dick harden again. "You're still scary as fuck, but inside you're just a big teddy bear."

She's right. She said something unthinkable about my brother and yet all I want to do is protect her. I'm turning into a pussy like Victor. I finish with the cream and stand up. I cross the room to where a small closet stands open, revealing row after row of Livvie's cocktail dresses. I pull out a sparkling crimson gown with slits up both sides to mid-thigh, and hand it to Fergie.

"I think that you should wear this tomorrow night," I say. "And, I think you should wear your new butt plug."

"Why?" she asks as her hands roam over the fabric, taking in the sparkly beadwork and the off-the-shoulder neckline and those slits so high they should be illegal.

"Because I know shit's going to go down, and when I'm on the front lines plunging my sword into Ares' heart, I'm going to think about this little jewel—" I touch it, and she giggles. "And it will give me strength."

"Okay." Fergie rests her head against my shoulder. "I'll wear it for my monster. Cas, are you okay?"

"I've just been balls deep inside my girl, and I'm about to snap the necks of some traitors. I'm fucking fabulous. Why wouldn't I be okay?"

"Because one of those traitors is your father."

"He's no father to me," I say, and I mean it.

All my life I thought I wanted to know my father, but the moment I heard his voice on that stage, I realized that I had no loyalty to him. He tried to buy me with his brunch and his sob story about wanting to be part of my life, but he wasn't the one who raised me alone, who taught me how to ride a bike and skin a man alive. He wasn't the one who loves me with Cali's cold savagery or Milo's earnest warmth or Fergie's burning flame.

Ares only saw me as a convenient way to get what he wanted. And Gaius was so excited to find my father, to give me this gift he knew I always wanted, that he was blindsided by Ares' greed. And now he's in danger, and I need to rescue him.

I know who my true family is.

At least after tomorrow night, when I kill Ares in battle, we won't have to concern ourselves with him any longer.

It's been too long since we've had a purge. We allowed our people to become complacent, to forget that the Triumvirate can take away the riches it has given.

Whatever happens tomorrow, we're ready. We'll face it together, my red Queen and I.

We will triumph.

"How do I look?" Fergie asks as she twirls in front of me.

She's wearing the crimson dress, and it is even more sinful on her gorgeous body. The plunging neckline gives me an eyeful of her cleavage, and those slits drag my eye up her long, lean legs. The deep V of the back stops just above the curve of her ass, so that if she's not careful, you'll get a little peek of asscrack and that's the sexiest thing about it, especially when I imagine her still wearing that plug.

I glance over at Torsten, who has just come out of the bathroom. His face is open, reverent, as if he's in the presence of a goddess.

"You look like the Queen of the Triumvirate," Vic gulps out. The tie he was doing up at his neck now flaps uselessly in his hand.

"More like the princess," she corrects him. "I'm not Queen yet until Claudia and Cali step down, and they won't do that any time soon. And I won't be much of a Lucian Imperator if we can't get rid of the fucking Gorgons."

Looking at her, I'm filled with confidence that bubbles and boils beneath my skin. How can our people – for the Gorgons have once been our people – look at this magnificent creature and not want to follow her into the heart of the sun? How can they see Ares and Juliet August as superior in the face of such splendor?

Tonight, we will find out.

"Let's go," I growl, cracking my knuckles. Like Vic, I've opted for my favorite suit – a classically-tailored Armani, although I'm pairing it with my Bear mask. It'll be a shame to cover my suit in blood, but when I walk into Colosseum tonight, I need the Gorgons to fucking *tremble*.

"Cas, wait."

Vic's voice startles me. I turn around. He's sitting on the edge of the bed, pulling his jacket over his impeccable shirt. He's cut like a Greek fucking god, but his features are unusually grim. Something like unease settles in my stomach. I motion for Torsten to walk ahead with Fergie, and I step back into the room. Vic indicates the door, and I close it behind me.

"About tonight..." Vic trails off. He scratches his head.

"I've got a bunch of traitors to turn into blood eagles, and you're keeping me from them." I crack my knuckles.

"My sister," Vic says. "You can't hurt her."

Is he fucking serious?

I slide the Bear claw glove over my fingers. "She dies."

"You can't. I forbid it."

"Oh, you forbid it, do you?" I smirk as I adjust my mask, careful not to stab my own eyes with the claws. "This isn't the Poison Ivy Club. You don't tell me what to do. We're equals now, and I'm telling you as the head of the Dio family, the family tasked with the responsibility for protecting this fucking empire we've built, that I'm going to separate your sister's head from her shoulders for betraying us."

"You'll have to kill your own father, too," Vic points out.

"I know." I slice the claws through the air, testing the weight of the blades. I spent an hour sharpening them, and they feel amazing. "I have special plans for him."

Vic winces. "You're insane."

"For once, I'm the one who's talking sense here. Juliet's fucking Ares, Vic. Just like she was fucking Sommesnay. She's a whore for power, and she's been in this scheme from the beginning. She's trying to thoverow us... I mean—" the words were getting caught up on my tongue "—*overthrow* us. We can't let her live just because you shared the same womb as her."

"It's not about that," he insists, but the desperation in his voice gives him away. "She admits that she wanted to piss off Mom, but she says Ares is out of control. She's giving him to us. She's going to help us bring the Gorgons down."

I scoff. "And you believe that?"

"She's my *sister,*" Vic cries. "Of course I believe her. If Gaius was in the same position, you'd believe him."

I remain silent. I don't want to tell him about Fergie's suspicions. Tonight she'll see that my brother is loyal.

"She called me." Vic stands and straightens his cufflinks. "She'll sneak us into the Elysium, make sure Ares' guards stand down, and get us into his suite so we can get rid of him. She's serious, Cas, I *know* it. You've always trusted me before, so trust me now. Come with me, let's kill him together, and then I'll ship Juliet off to Paris and make sure you never have to see her again."

"And risk her coming back with the August blood in her veins to start another coup? Fuck off."

Vic's right. I trust him as I trust few other people. But I do not trust Juliet fucking August.

"Fine," Vic says stiffly. "Move aside. I need to join my mother."

I slam my hand onto the wall, blocking his path to the door with my body. "You're blinded by her. You always have been. You think she's a fucking saint, but she's a user."

"Fuck you, Cas." Vic shoves past me, slamming my shoulder into the wall. The red mist gathers at the corners of my eyes, and as he stalks down the hall, I grab his arm and twist, slamming him against the wall. He starts to snap at me, but I press my elbow into his throat. His eyes bug out.

Victor August is surprised. Surprised and gasping for air. It's a novel concept.

"You listen to me," I growl, digging my elbow deeper so he really gets the point. "I'll get nice and close and speak slowly, since you seem to have so much trouble understanding me. If I see your sister tonight, I will kill her, as I will kill anyone who endangers my Queen. Fergie's going to be in the spotlight tonight, and they'll come for her, and my job is to protect her and I don't need any distractions. So you get yourself in fucking line, or you go and join your sister and the fucking Gorgons. I don't care, but you will not stop me."

I drop my hold on Vic. He sinks to the ground, his hand on his throat. "Cas—" he gasps out.

But I've already turned away.

The crowd is already gathered when we arrive at Colosseum. Not a single Triumvirate soldier will risk missing what's going down tonight. Thank fuck Vic went in the car with Claudia and her husbands, because I don't think I can stand to see his fucking face right now.

This time, we don't go through the main gates. Ares instructed us to head down through the underground entrance, into the bowels of the venue, where prisoners and traitors are brought into the ring to be made examples of. I've conducted many of those executions myself, and it's strange now to walk past the cages and see them filled with our people. Men and women whose only crime is to be loyal to us await a fate worse than death.

I search every cage for my brother's face, but he's not here. Of course, they'll be keeping him somewhere more secure. They know I'll pull some outlandish rescue plan, but at least it's better than going after Ares on Juliet August's intel.

I'll make Fergie talk Vic out of it. She'll make him see that he's walking into a trap.

"This is meant to unnerve us," Claudia says as we move

through the cages. "They want us to enter that arena feeling that everything is hopeless."

"Cassius, Cali, you must help us," cries Rosalie, one of Cali's most promising young fighters. "They're going to kill us. They want to feed me to that lion tonight."

Cali keeps her eyes straight ahead. It's as if she doesn't hear them. I can't read her thoughts, and maybe she has a plan to free them, but I know that I can't walk into that arena knowing that a warrior like Rosalie is behind bars down here.

As we pass the cages, I notice some of the locks are old and flimsy. A couple of good kicks and I break a couple off. The prisoners swarm from the cages and join our ranks. Rosalie pumps my fist. She's brimming for a fight.

My veins hum with the promise of bloodshed. Tonight, I will show my father the meaning of the word 'family.' I'll carve it into his skull before I crush it under my boot.

Fergie's grip on my elbow tightens. On the other side of her, Torsten studies her with his intense expression. She's the only thing he can see, the only thing he cares about. I'm not even entirely sure he knows what's going on or what we're doing here. Vic walks behind her, and his stormy eyes meet mine. Our argument flashes between us, and he looks away.

Fuck him. I'm not going to spare his sister when she's going after my Queen.

But this is not the time to show animosity among our ranks. Vic locks his jaw and stares straight ahead, straight at Fergie. Above us, I can hear Ares ramping up the crowd. We're supposed to wait for his cue, like this is a fucking production.

Fergie squeezes my arm. It's time.

I steady her as we descend the ramp and storm into the arena. The lights burn my skin, and I experience a brief moment of blindness as I step out onto the sand before my eyes adjust and I see them – hundreds of people in the crowd, roaring and beating at the arena's cage. Only instead of calling for the Bear, these faces are hostile. And on every shoulder and at every neck is the snake, the symbol of our enemy.

The red mist circles as I survey the crowd, catching the adoring gaze of fighters I've trained with, assassins I've worked with, and girls I've tied up and whipped until they cried. People whose loyalties only extended as far as what they could get out for themselves.

I want to burn them all. But I'm here for one man and one woman only tonight. The treacherous bastard who dared call himself my father, and the two-faced bitch who has my friend Victor all twisted up inside.

Our people fan out to the sides around us, pushing Gorgons out of the front rows and surrounding the arena. Fights break out, and it takes Ares a long time to restore any kind of order. He moves around the arena, shouting into the microphone as his guards flank him. In front of the opposite entrance, Juliet reclines on a silver throne, her smile wide, her eyes sparkling as she drinks it all in.

She may have been the star of all our Stonehurst Prep productions, but she is not that good an actress.

Juliet is *loving* this.

"This is our place, our arena," Cali screams, needing no microphone. "Ares, Juliet, you and your ilk are trespassing on Triumvirate property. Our people are here to clear out the trash."

Our supporters roar their approval, stomping their feet and rattling the wire fence surrounding the arena. Someone up top overpowers the guards and throws the gates open, and more of our supporters pour in. They don't come close to outnumbering those on the Gorgons' side, but they've evened the odds so a full-on brawl no longer looks like a crapshoot.

"This isn't your city anymore." Juliet bolts from her chair and stalks across the arena. She's wearing a silver dress that's eerily similar to the style Fergie is wearing, but my girl looks a hundred times better. Juliet flips her dark hair over her shoulder and glares at Cali. "The only thing you're here to do tonight is to surrender to us, or we'll execute your son right here in front of you."

She snaps her fingers. The arena doors opposite open, and Gaius is wheeled out. My brother is slumped on his knees on the wooden platform, his arms and head in stocks, and the gleaming blade of a guillotine hanging over his head.

It takes Eli, Noah, Torsten, and three of our soldiers to hold me back.

"Cas, no," Eli cries. "If you touch him, they *will* kill him, and you, too."

Juliet tosses back her head and laughs. "Oh, Cassius, you haven't changed. Still the bear with a top hat, dancing for Fergie's amusement."

I'm going to enjoy pummeling her haughty face. I can't believe I ever allied myself with her against Fergie. I can't believe I...

Gaius raises his head. His face is bruised and streaked in sweat. I wish Fergie could see him, because if she saw the pain in his eyes, she'd know I was right about him.

"Cas..." he chokes out. "Don't worry about me. Just save them. Save as many as—"

His words cut off as one of the guards kicks him in the stomach. The crowd cheer and boo and hiss.

Ares holds up his hands for silence. "Unlike the Triumvirate, we are civilized. We will give them a chance to address you all, to answer to the charges of greed and corruption, to explain to you all why they have failed you. I must confess that I'm interested in what Dio, August, and Lucian have to say."

"It's only Dio and August," Juliet corrects him as her red lips pull back into a smug smile. "Livvie Lucian is gone, and with no heir, her family's position is forfeit."

"That's not true," Claudia steps forward. The look she shoots her daughter makes even my knees tremble as she shoves Fergie in front of her. "We have appointed a new Imperator to the Lucian family, Fergie Munroe."

A hush falls over the crowd. I feel the shift as her name registers. The curious blind girl who's been at the heart of the recent Triumvirate scandals is the new Imperator? I can see what they're thinking, and I don't blame them.

But can't they see her? Are they blind?

Look at her, resplendent in crimson, her hair a waterfall of blood down her back, her face regal, her legs fucking *electrifying*. How can anyone gaze upon her and not see a Queen?

I step up to the edge of the arena, taking my time to stare into the eyes of individual men until they turn away in fear. I grip the wire fence and shake it, rattling the entire side of the arena and knocking over several people.

"Bow to your new Imperator," I howl.

And they bow. They fucking *bow*.

Many of the Gorgons drop to their knees. They may have been won over with the promise of more money and a different future, but at the end of the day, they know that I have ripped heads off for lesser crimes than not acknowledging a ruler.

Those who remain standing, arms folded, look around at their friends on the floor, and I sense the nervous energy slipping into the room.

"Thank you." Fergie accepts the microphone from a stunned Ares. "You may rise. I was inducted in as Imperator last night, so we have not had the chance to do an official ceremony. But you can rest assured that all correct procedures were followed, and that I am now the head of the Lucian family, as well as responsible for all of Livvie's properties and projects.

"I speak to you now as your Imperator," she continues, and I'm fairly certain this is not in any script we prepared. "I make a promise that I will not begin my reign with a purge. I don't care who you were once loyal to. I know you have done rotten things, reprehensible things, evil and violent things in Livvie Lucian's name, and now you may even be against her. I was against her once myself, but that was before I understood her. I promise you that I will fight for you to have the freedom to place your loyalty where you feel it best fits. Give me that chance to prove myself and I will do it."

I move beside her and slip her hand under my armpit, and together we take a slow, silent walk around the arena – she with her head held high, listening to the whispers permeating the crowd, and me glaring at anyone who refuses to kneel. She angles her head toward the crowd so it's as if she's making eye contact with every member who still remains loyal, as if she's picking up on the subtle clues of facial expression and body language that mark out the betrayers. But, of course, she can't see their faces. She doesn't need to. She's picking up on some mojo, some sandstorm that's blown back in our faces.

Fergie steps back in line between the three of us and waves her hand. Vic practically snatches her away from me. He tosses the microphone to his mother.

"Cali and I will also take this time to announce that we have chosen our heirs. These are the people we believe will do the best for our soldiers and build a strong organization."

"For Dio, my heirs are my son, Cassius Dio," Cali states, her voice as harsh as ever. She meets my eyes across the arena, and the look she gives me is the warmest she's capable of. "And my stepdaughter, Fergie Munroe."

"And for the August family," Claudia smiles. "I have Victor August and Fergie Munroe."

With each word, the audience has grown more silent.

There's a sense of something shifting in the air, that even if the Gorgons weren't a thing, the world as we know it is toppling over.

No one has ever considered the families having the same Imperator. Vic and I step forward, holding Fergie between us. We link hands. Fergie's smile lights my heart, but I won't look at Vic.

"None of this matters," Juliet screams, shuffling across the arena in her towering heels to face us. "It's too late to hand over your empires, because they belong to us now. No one cares about Imperators or heirs, because the Triumvirate is *over*. That's why you've come here tonight, to surrender."

"It's not over," I growl, slicing my Bear claws through the air in front of her face. Juliet, to her credit, doesn't flinch.

"I'm afraid it is, son." Ares moves beside her. My so-called father folds his arms and regards me with a smug face that looks too much like the face I see in the mirror every morning.

How dare he have the same face as me?

"I'm not your son." I shift my weight, ready to jump him. Fergie tightens her grip on me, reminding me that this isn't my fight yet. As the new Imperator, she's been let in on the plan, and so I'll obey her. I know we have to let Claudia and Cali decide how tonight will go down.

"Enough posturing," Ares snaps. "Tell us your decision. Will you surrender and leave the city peacefully, with Gaius and all your other prisoners free, or will you take on the might of the Gorgons and lose?"

Claudia tosses her head back and laughs. "The two of you are pathetic. You honestly believed that we would surrender? But we respect what you've achieved here. You have alerted us to the need to evaluate our leadership, and for that, we thank you. But if you think you can stage one little flaccid coup and take the city?" To Ares, she bares her teeth. To Juliet, she says, "It takes more than promises and pantomime to run an empire, little girl."

"You can't talk to me like that," Juliet screams.

"You're my daughter and I'll talk to you how I please," Claudia shoots back. "Hell, I'll bend your ass over my knee and spank you until you behave. You know nothing about running an empire, and Ares knows even less. But out of respect to our former soldiers, we're offering you a chance to make things right."

"Oh, *you're* offering?" Juliet's lip curls. Her eyes dart to Vic, and one of those unreadable twin looks passes between them.

Hang on a sec, what do they have planned?

Nothing that Juliet talks Vic into doing will help us, of that I'm certain.

"A challenge has been made to our leadership." Cali's eyes gleam as she steps forward. "We've come to meet that challenge in the way we've always done. I will fight your leader, Ares, in the ring. A battle to the death. Whoever wins between the Triumvirate and the Gorgons, they shall walk away with the territory, assets, and power of the Triumvirate. Whoever loses, they and their people will leave this city forever."

W*hat the fuck is she doing?*
     I think back on Cali's serene expression on the roof, and a raw, primal panic seizes my body.

Juliet claps her hands together. "Oh, this is going to be delightful."

"I accept the challenge." Ares looks smug as fuck as he steps forward and shakes Cali's hand. The circumference of his arm muscles is wider than my mother's waist. He looks like a sack of potatoes with a smirk drawn on. I know the damage a body like his can do, because it's *my* body.

In her weakened state, my mother has no chance against him.

And she knows it.

And Claudia and Fergie know it, too.

I shake Fergie's arm. "Stop this."

"What? How can I—"

"You're the Imperator now," I yell over the roaring crowd. "Stop her before she kills herself."

"No."

"STOP THE FIGHT." I'm shaking now, the red mist a fire burning inside my skull.

Guards swoop around us, pushing us out of the arena to clear it for the fight. Fergie and I are swept along behind the guards, dragged through the crowd as Gorgons and Triumvirate supporters break out into fights around us.

We're led up to the VIP area set aside for our families. This time, however, there's no bottle service or platters of expensive, smelly food. The platform is ringed with guards, all wearing the snake symbol of the Gorgons. Torsten and his remaining sisters, Vic, John, and Claudia and her husbands are shoved in after us. Gorgon guards lock the mesh door over the staircase and stand guard outside, their weapons pointed straight at us.

I could tear the door off and break their necks, but I couldn't guarantee they wouldn't get a shot off that would hurt my girl.

"Cas," Fergie's voice is firm. "I'm not going to stop the fight. I made Cali a promise that I'd let it go ahead, and even if I didn't, I wouldn't interfere. Cali has to do this. Look at her. *Look.* You'll see that she's already made the decision, and nothing you or I can do will stop it."

"He'll kill her."

Fergie grips my shoulders. "She's a dead woman walking."

Her words slam into me. She's right. I've been ignoring it because my mother is the fucking toughest person in the world, but the writing's been on the wall ever since she got shot. Cali's not getting better. Galen did what he could for her, but she's not going to recover any more than she has. She's barely been able to walk since she tore apart the people we got from Sommes-nay's building, and even then I did most of the work for her.

Cali can't do the work she loves any more. It's time for her to go.

Sure, she could retire from the business of killing and become the woman behind the desk who makes the empire run. But that's never been my mother's style – it's why Dio has always been the smallest of the three families. Because we love killing too much to do it in a business-efficient way. We live to enjoy our work.

Thinking back, I don't think my mother has enjoyed the work since that night she got shot. I think she's been running on autopilot because that's what she has to do to protect her family. I think she's been trying to be brave for us, but even Cali Dio gets tired of being brave.

I look across the VIP area, and I see Fergie's father slumped on his knees, watching his wife preparing for the fight. I expect his face to be twisted with misery, but he's beaming with pride even as his eyes fill with tears. He knows exactly what she's doing.

Cali Dio is weak, and she cannot abide weakness. She can't stand the idea that she'll be picked off by some young, inexperienced assassin with an Uzi out to prove his name. But instead of going quietly in the night, she wants to wade into a spectacle of blood… against my *father*, of all fucking people.

I shake. My fists curl. I'm going to go fucking *nuclear*.

I can't lose her. I *can't*.

I'm not ready to lose her.

"I *know*," Fergie whispers. "Cas, I know what this means. I don't want her to do it, either. But we tried to save her, and we couldn't. She's given us so much, and we can give her this one gift. We let her choose her own death. This is how she wants to go – in glorious defiance."

Yes. Fergie's right.

My Queen knows best.

The red mist that clouds into my vision, that claws at my insides every waking moment – Cali gave it to me. I am her child in all the ways that matter, and if I were in the same position, I would want to walk into that ring and wet the blade of my sword with blood one final time.

As much as I hate this, as much as I'm falling to fucking pieces, I will do my mother the honor of watching every moment.

I meet Gaius' eyes, and even though he's still strapped into that guillotine, my brother and I share a silent conversation. Beside me, I notice Victor and Juliet doing the same thing. Can't he see the delight on her face? Doesn't he know that she's already twerking on my mother's grave?

Victor fucking August... all my life he's been the strongest person I know, aside from my mother and Gaius. He stands firm on his beliefs no matter the cost. When he speaks, he does so with such passion that he can make even my monstrous heart believe in angels.

But he will never, ever make me believe that Juliet means no harm to Fergie.

Cali nods at Ares. "We'll play by the old rules. But I want you to let my son go. You don't need him as a bargaining chip any longer."

Ares' lip curls back, and for one terrifying moment I think he's going to let that blade fall and sever my brother's head from his body. But he must know that his new soldiers are watching his every move – they need to see their leader act with honor. He moves behind the machine and unlocks it, lifting the stocks so Gaius can stagger out.

"Cas!" Gaius calls to me, but they drag him away backstage. Fergie's fingers squeeze mine.

Ares orders his men to clear everyone out of the ring and to bring out the racks of weapons. For a fight like this, between Imperators in a challenge for rule, we have special rules, even though they haven't been called upon since the days of Brutus.

Each opponent gets one weapon of their choice. The fight is only one round – it ends only in death.

Beside me, Victor moves in close to Fergie. "I'll narrate for her," he tells me. "You just focus on... you just try to..."

He can't find the words. Victor August, who always knows the right thing to say in every situation, is lost for words. He knows we're about to watch Cali meet her death. His face softens, and he becomes my childhood friend again, the one who always had a plan. And a flicker of hope burns inside me.

"If your sister is on our side," I whisper, "then she can stop this."

Vic glances up at the gangplank over the area, where Juliet stands alone, her glittering gown clinging to every curve of her body. "She can't do anything now, Cas. We have a plan for tonight, but she can't stop this..."

And just like that, I'm back to hating him. Fergie, thank fuck, can't see the tension between us. She grips my arm tightly as she turns to Vic and he murmurs a description of the arena in her ear.

Cali selects an evil curved sword – not a Japanese sword like I prefer, but an ancient Assyrian design that she's always loved. She gives a couple of practice slices, and the blade hums through the air. Nice and sharp. The crowd murmurs their approval.

I don't know how many people in Colosseum are actually rooting for Cali's death, but they definitely appreciate the spectacle.

Ares winks at her as he picks up a military flail – a heavy spiked ball on a chain with a shaft for a handle. I can't help but smirk at his choice. Anyone trained by Cali knows that the flail is a pointless weapon. It was likely never used on the medieval battlefield, but invented by later artists as a fantastical addition to spice up their drawings. Those who choose it in the arena are just as likely to brain themselves in the head with the sharp spikes as they are to land a hit on their opponent.

But then, my father *was* trained by Cali. Perhaps he's making a point.

Whatever that point is, I hope she slices his dick off.

They take up positions at either end of the field. The blood rushes in my ears.

I should be in there instead of her.

Juliet raises her chin, but instead of meeting her brother's watchful gaze, she only has eyes for me.

A cold, cruel smile slips across her lips – a smile that says that I'm right not to trust her, that her plan is going *exactly* as she wishes.

Ares swings the flail around his head, smiling and pumping his fist at the crowd. They roar in response, drawn in by his performance and the promise of bloodshed.

Cali does none of this. She stands still, her sword raised, the faintest smile playing on the corners of her lips.

She raises her chin and finds me in the crowd. She meets my gaze and holds it.

She inclines her head. A nod.

It's not a tearful hug, it's not a goodbye. But it's all I need to *lose my fucking shit.*

The red mist doesn't creep in at the edges of my vision. It fucking *slams* into me.

I don't remember my brain issuing the instructions for my body to move, but I'm aware in a detached sense that I've broken out of the VIP area and am barreling through the crowd toward the arena, dragging Vic, Torsten, and about five other guards behind me.

I don't hear Juliet start the fight, but I pour on speed as Ares rushes across the arena at my mother.

She doesn't move, doesn't blink, doesn't flinch.

Moonlight glints on the edge of her blade.

He swings that huge, stupid flail. The chain catches and wraps around his arm, and he gouges himself in the shoulder. His eyes widen and he tries to slow his momentum so he can untangle himself, and that's when Cali strikes.

She's on him like a bolt of lightning. Even as injured as she is, my mother is beautiful to watch. As graceful as a dancer, she slices that curved blade through the air. Ares barely gets the shaft of his flail in time to block her cut, and then he's on the defensive as she comes after him, slashing at his body, driving him back against the side of the arena.

I reach the edge and claw at the mesh. The metal digs into my fingers and I'm dimly aware that I'm tearing up my hands. The mist swells and pulses.

It should be me in there instead.

They won't let me in. The guards shove me against the mesh. It cuts into my skin, but it gives them a way to trap me. I kick and curse and scream, and I sense the dull thud of my limbs connecting, but it's all I can feel. I'm not a man any longer. I am a monster. I am inside the mist.

I *am* the mist, and it wants blood.

My mother lunges again. Ares snaps his head back in time to avoid decapitation, but he ends up with a vicious cut above his eye that pisses blood down his face.

He has to be partially blind from that – a bad move for him with my mother and that blade coming at him again. But the cut seems to give Ares a burst of strength. He swings the flail.

This time, Cali doesn't move fast enough.

The ball collides with the elbow of her sword arm. She staggers back, her face crumpling for a moment before she plasters her cold mask back on.

I know it's over.

The blow has shattered her elbow. Her arm hangs limply at her side, and the blade drops from her fingers.

My fucking heart drops with it.

Ares tries to kick the blade away, but Cali's too fast. She scoops it up with her other hand and whirls around him, going for a cut to the back of his neck. The crowd gasps. Ares ducks, but his flail is so unwieldy that he can't get his arm out of the way in time, and Cali's sword slices right through it.

His arm drops into the dirt, followed by an arc of blood from the severed artery.

Ares stares at the stump of his shoulder for a moment, as if he's not quite sure what happened. And then the pain hits.

He screams and screams and screams. I've heard many varieties of screaming over my years as Cali's student, and my father can definitely scream with the best of them.

He falls to his knees, and then topples backward, his body pissing blood as it slams into the dirt floor.

The flail rolls away from him and lands at Cali's feet. She tosses the sword away and picks it up, turning it between her fingers, savoring the weight and heft of the ridiculous weapon. She grins as she holds it aloft, and from the depths of the chaotic crowd, I hear her loyal soldiers chant her name. My black, dead heart dares to hope.

"I make this kill for the Triumvirate," she roars. "Ālea iacta est!"

Cali plants her stiletto heel in the center of Ares' chest and spins the flail expertly over her head, building momentum...

The crowd goes crazy. They know exactly what's going to happen. She's going to slam that flail down on his head, and it's going to be messy and gory and oh so good.

But my father... there is something of a monster still inside him, because as he stares up at the mythological creature bearing down on him, he pulls some strength from a dark well and reaches out with his one remaining hand for the sword she tossed aside...

He picks it up.

And as my mother leans closer to issue her death blow, Ares swings upward, and the blade's shape carries it right through Cali's chest and out the other side.

Cali's next word cuts off into a gasp.

She stares down at the blade sticking out of her stomach.

"Fuck," she growls.

Cali crumples to the ground.

She doesn't move.

"Cali!" my dad screams.

I never knew a sound like that could come out of my father. The anguish erupts inside him like a maelstrom forming where there had before been a calm sea. I know that he, like me, walked into the arena tonight knowing that Cali didn't expect to walk out, but knowing it and feeling it are two different things.

His scream becomes a wail, a keening sound without end – a sound beyond sound, beyond pain. And I know that it's over.

Cali's gone.

My heart breaks for Dad. I was too young to really under-stand what happened when my mom died, but I'm listening to my father's world shatter in real-time, and it's the worst thing I can possibly imagine.

All I want in the whole world is to protect him from that, and I can't. Cas begged me to stop this, and he was right – I had the power. But I didn't. Cali told me, Imperator to Imperator, that it's what she wanted.

But right now, I wish I could take it back. The only thing in the world I want is to take the hurt away from Dad, and from Cas.

Thousands of memories slam into me at once, all the times my dad was there for me, all the millions of ways he made my childhood fun even when I was lonely and he was lonely. He deserved to live a long, happy life with Cali. He should not have to see his wife killed and desecrated in front of him.

But that's exactly what's happening.

Vic's stopped giving me commentary, but I can hear the cutting and tearing of flesh, the sickening crows of the people as they break through the barrier around the arena and drench themselves in her blood. Ares is dead, too, so I hear. He's died of blood loss, but since he dealt the death blow, he's still the victor.

The Triumvirate has lost.

I cling to my dad. He buries his face in my shoulder, not caring that his grief is on display. No one's paying attention, anyone. The place has erupted into chaos.

Cas is gone, of course. He threw himself into the crowd. I can only imagine the damage he's doing, but I don't have the heart left to stop him. Let him tear the world apart. I feel like doing the same thing.

"We have to get out of here," Vic yells.

I'm dimly aware that the sounds around me are changing. The yelling of the crowd has become a pure, wild rage. I hear glasses and furniture being smashed, women sobbing, and people screaming – the unmistakable orchestra of violence unleashed.

"John," Victor tugs on my dad's arm. "Cas has gone to get her body. He'll bring her back to us. I know you're hurting, but we have to go."

Vic leads us to the back of the VIP section, where Cassius tore a hole in the mesh, as if it was cardboard. It seems that the guards have fled into the crowd. They don't give a fuck about us because they know we're powerless, or maybe it's their intention that the crowd will finish us off. Vic fiddles with something and then helps me down another steep set of hidden stairs. What is it with Victor August and narrow staircases? Maybe that's what I'll do for a job after I graduate Stonehurst Prep – design secret passages that are accessible to people with disabilities. I'm sure there'll be a huge market.

"Vic... slow down... I can't..." He's dragging me too fast. I don't have time to plant my feet properly. Any wrong move and I'll end up on my face.

He doesn't slow down. I don't even know if he hears me. Behind us, my dad's sobs grow weaker as he falls further behind.

"Juliet knows these tunnels exist," Torsten calls from behind us. He's with my dad. I'm so happy that he's with my dad. "The guards will be on us any second now."

"I know," Vic says tersely.

I don't have time to ask if that means he's decided his sister is no longer on our side. Cas told me that Vic keeps insisting his sister is innocent. Cas thinks that Vic might've been in contact with Juliet, and that they might have planned something foolish.

But there's no way Vic would be that stupid, would he?

We emerge into some kind of building. I can sense the echoes of our footsteps on high walls. It's probably one of the abandoned warehouses that surround Colosseum, judging by the smells and the pitter-patter of rats' feet in the rafters above our heads. Vic shoves open a door and then we're outside, our feet crunching on gravel. I hear the wheels of a car spin, and a door open.

"Get in," a voice yells. It's Seymour.

We pile into the car. Torsten's elbow's in my face. Seymour yells at us to shut the doors, but...

"Where's Cas?" Panic seizes me. I can't leave him behind, especially since he waded in to collect his mother's body.

"I'm here," Cas calls. The trunk pops open, and he drops something onto the tray. A moment later, the door opens and Cas slaps my ass as he squeezes into the vehicle, giving me even less room for myself.

"Just you settle in there, Sunflower," he tells me. "We're in for a wild ride yet."

He's not kidding.

We tear away from the carnage. Claudia screams as something pings off the side of the car. Rough fingers slide around my neck and push my head down into the footwell. "Ow, what the fuck?"

"Those are bullets."

Well, fucknuggets.

Seymour drives like a wild thing. The rest of the car ride is a blur. More bullets slam into the car. Cas's fingers trail between my legs and stroke me as Seymour tears around the corners. By the time he parks and tells us to get inside Tombs, I'm a mess of frayed nerves and horniness.

Milo has the doors thrown open. We're not the only ones arriving. The parking lot is filled with cars and people running and shouting, and I hear more bullets in the distance and... I hold Torsten's arm extra tight. Cas disappears into the fray. I worry for him, for what he might do in his grief.

Once we're inside, we're swept along with our people. I hear families checking in with each other and children crying for their parents. Torsten leads me through it all and up the stairs to the VIP floor, where our family has gathered.

"Dad..." I have no words for what he's going through. I can't even imagine if I lost one of the guys, and...

"Fergalish." He pulls me close. His arms tremble. "Go to Cas. He needs you."

"*You* need me." I think that if Cali and my dad had never met, we might not be here. My dad never would have gone through the pain of losing her, and...

"I love that you think that, but no," he sniffs. "I've lost love before, Fergalish. I know how it goes. I know that this is the end she wanted. As hard as it is for us to imagine, Cali is at peace. But Cas is new to this kind of grief. Go to him. I want you to. Please, I'll be fine."

"Fine?"

"Sad beyond comprehension, but I'll live." There's a resigned smile in his voice. "I have to be fine. I've still got a headstrong, impossible daughter to raise."

I smile back. "Okay. Does anyone know where Cas went?"

"I saw him go into Livvie's suite," Dad says.

I know the VIP floor well enough now that with my cane I can find the room on my own. It's Livvie's old office, which the Imperators have been using as their war room (when they're not on the roof). I press my head to the door, but I can't hear furniture smashing or walls being punched, so I deem it safe enough to enter.

I open the door a crack. "Cas?"

He doesn't speak, but I sense him. His bulk changes the echoes of the room. His plum and musk and carnation scent fills my nostrils. I move inside and shut the door, swinging my cane across the floor as I move around the sofa.

I bump into him at the bar. He's leaning over it. I cry out as he grabs my wrist. His thick fingers dig into my skin. He slams my hand down on something.

Cold metal objects in a leather pouch.

"These were her tools," he says. His voice is steady, eerily calm. I can *feel* the red mist surrounding him. Tendrils of it curl through the air and touch me. "Lock picks. Torture implements. With this tiny rod, she could inflict so much pain to a man's urethra that even the most hardened spy will break."

"She would want you to have them," I say.

With a howl like a wild beast, he sends the implements flying.

"Cas?" I need to be careful. The way he feels right now, he might not see me. He might simply see someone who needs to burn. "We can—"

My words turn into a squeal as he slams me into the bar. His mouth finds mine and he *tears* my pain cruelly from my body and takes it into himself. Glass shatters all around us, but we don't even care. All I know is that he needs this.

The bar taps bite into my back and I taste metal as Cas' teeth drag over my lip. His fingers circle my throat, his weight bearing down on me, and all of him trembles with pain and loss and need. I can tell the red mist is upon him – it's an inky mask surrounding him, a wall between us that I need to break through.

He's on the very edge of losing control, and as he devours my mouth with his and his fingers press deeper into my skin, the hair at the nape of my neck stands on end.

Every instinct in me burns to run, to cry out at him to stop. What we're doing is dangerous. At any moment Cas' red mist could take him over completely, and if that happens... I'm dead.

But I trust him.

I love him.

He needs me now, he needs me to be his monster in the dark.

And so, I fight against Old Fergie's terror and I go to him. I fall into the mist and let it take me over.

I wind my legs around Cas, pulling him closer, opening for him, inviting in the darkness. I press my hand to his chest, feeling the ridges of his scarification. My mark over his heart. He's like a wild animal, his hands leaving my neck to tear at the dress. In moments, it's in tatters on the floor. I manage to unbuckle his belt and shove down his pants and boxers without breaking our kiss.

Cas is the one who breaks it. He grabs me under the ass and hoists me higher. He nips at my breasts, and I gasp at the pain as his teeth clamp down on my nipple. His cock slides up my wetness – because even though he scares me, he makes my whole body sing – and hits my throbbing clit.

"Help me," he gasps. "Help me not feel dead inside."

It's the most vulnerable thing Cas has ever said to me. Tears well at the corners of my eyes. I hate that this broken boy has lost the first person he ever trusted. I hate that he's so hurt and sad, and that he doesn't know what to do with that. I wrap my arms around his neck and pull him closer.

He can pour his pain into me. I will take it from him.

"We're not dead yet," I whisper. "Our coal-hearts are still beating."

"Good. Because I'm not done with you yet, sister."

His fingers dig in deeper as he rocks his hips back and thrusts roughly inside me. It feels as though I'm taking more than just his enormous cock. I'm taking his darkness. The red mist is inside me, crawling in my veins, wrapping around my heart so it no longer feels cold and dead but warm and living and whole.

This is Cas, who woke me up when I was numb, when I didn't want to feel anything ever again. And now, I feel all of him. For the first time, I truly see him, the way he's always seen me.

And I love it.

I love him.

Cas thrusts deeper, filling me up, pouring his darkness into me. He fucks hard, fast, brutal. The bar rattles. I don't expect to come from the onslaught, but even in his pain, my stepbrother knows what I need. He presses his fingers into my throat, and the angle of his thrusts rubs his pubic bone against my clit, and he wrenches that orgasm from my body like a dentist pulling a particularly difficult tooth.

He is relentless, wild, monstrous. I hold onto him for dear life as the darkness consumes us both.

Cas cries out as he comes, the sound like thunder. I hear wood splinter as he slams into me one final time, spilling inside me. The darkness settles on our skin, not claiming us but a part of us.

My stepbrother gathers me in his huge arms and lifts me. He slumps down on the shag rug and pulls me down beside him, tucking me into his shoulder. I place my hand on his chest, feeling his heart thud its relentless rhythm. *We're not dead yet.*

"What are we going to do?" Cas swallows. "Cali's left me, and everything's a mess. I don't know what to do without her."

"I don't know, but we'll figure it out together."

"I can't do this, Sunflower. I couldn't even save my mother or get my brother back. I'm not a leader."

"You are," I say. "Cali believed in you, otherwise she wouldn't have left her empire to you. And *I* believe in you. I've seen what you can do, Cas. You are loyal and fierce. My favorite thing about Cali was when I learned that she took kids from the streets, kids who never had anyone stand up and fight for them before, and she taught them to fight for themselves. That's the gift that she gave the world, and it's the same gift you can give. No one has ever fought for you, and yet you'll put yourself on the line for others. What the soldiers of Dio respect above anything else is a leader who will wade into battle alongside them. We'll get Gaius back—"

I'm interrupted by a knock at the door. "We're busy," Cas barks.

"I'm sorry to interrupt, sir." Seymour's voice calls through the thick door. "But I have a messenger here who wants to talk to you. He's from the Gorgon Queen."

I swallow. I knew that sooner or later Juliet would come with her demands. "Let him in. I promise Cas won't hurt him."

"Don't make promises you can't keep, Sunflower," he growls.

Cas," I growl back. "You don't kill messengers, because then no one volunteers to be a messenger. It's kind of a sacred thing."

The door clicks open, and someone steps into the room. I can sense his nervous energy. He doesn't like being in Cas' presence. Honestly, I wouldn't, either, not when Cas is still dripping with his mother's blood and they're on the side that killed her.

"I've brought you a letter from the Gorgon Queen," he says.

"Is that what she's calling herself now?" Cas snorts. "Go on then, come closer and hand me the letter."

"What if I just leave it on this table?"

"That's not very polite. You're supposed to offer person-to-person service between Imperators. The table isn't a fucking person, now is it?"

Cas keeps his tone even, polite. And that's even more fucking terrifying because I can feel the red mist swirling around him. The floor creaks as the messenger moves around us.

"H-h-here you go, Imperator."

Cas takes the object from the messenger. "Thank you for your service," he says.

And then he lunges. The messenger's scream is cut off with a wet gurgle. I catch only the glint of one of Cali's tools moving in the light and the thud of the messenger's body hitting the floor.

"You're supposed to keep the messenger alive to deliver a reply!" I scold Cas.

"When I throw his body into the fucking snake queen's lair, she'll know what our reply is." He comes back to me, wrapping his arms around me and kissing my neck. The envelope crinkles in his hand.

"You don't even know what it says yet."

"I don't have to," he says simply. "My reply is only going to be, 'fuck you, bitch.'"

"Can you just read the message?"

Cas makes a big show of unfolding the sealed note and clearing his throat. "Here ye, here ye—"

"Cas," I warn.

He puts on a posh accent and reads aloud:

Dearest Cassius,

You came to me once because you had a problem, and her name was Fergie Munroe.

She was my problem, too. She still is.

This city is only big enough for one Queen. Fergie is not born for this life, for our life. She's a blind, goody-goody nerd from Nowheresville, New England. She's not one of the monsters, and I can't understand why the three of you are so blinded by her poison kiss and magical pussy that you can't see it.

I see it.

I see you, Cas.

I've always admired you. We're too alike, you and I. That's why we always butted heads. It drove Vic wild, but I know part of the reason he loves you so much is because you remind him of me.

Vic and I were planning to kill Ares, did he tell you that? But your mother did that for me. I'd thank her if she weren't worm food.

This brings me to the point of this letter. You're hitching yourself to a dying horse, Cas. You wanted to be Imperator your whole life, and you only just got Gaius out of the way and now you're going to rule a ruined empire.

Or, there is another way.

Join me.

Rule with me.

Bring my brother. And my parents.

Bring Torsten if you have to.

I have a long list of people for you to torture.

I'll give you everything you've ever wanted. You'll no longer live in the shadow of Gaius and Cali. I'll make The Bear the most feared name in all the world.

Join me.

Join me and I'll call off the violence.

Join me and I'll welcome your people into our ranks.

Join me and I'll give you back Gaius.

Join me and we can become a family again.

Join me and get rid of Fergie.

Join me, or watch everyone you love die by my hand. The great Cassius Dio will be felled by the Gorgon Queen. You'll no longer be a legend, Papa Smurf – you'll be the butt of every joke.

I learned a thing or two from Sommesnay.

Juliet August

39

FERGIE

Claudia sinks into the cushions on Livvie's plush sofa. "So... this is a clusterfuck of epic proportions."

"That's the understatement of the year," Vic says.

Me, Vic, Cas, Claudia, and Noah are sitting in Livvie's private office, reading over Juliet's note and trying to figure out what the fuck to do next. All I feel is the heaviness in my heart.

Cali's gone. Livvie's gone. The foundations of my world are crumbling away beneath me. My skin is so raw and flayed with grief that I haven't even been able to process the fact that I'm now technically the new Imperator of the Dio and Lucian families.

We haven't even done my initiation ceremony yet. It's fucking wrong to chant Latin when outside the walls of our neon Egyptian fortress, our city is burning.

Literally.

Half of Tartarus Oaks is on fire. Random acts of violence are erupting all over the city, and Gorgons are storming Triumvirate buildings, taking them over, and killing anyone who stands in their way.

I'm the Queen of a shattered empire.

Juliet has made her demands.

Claudia sighs. "I know it's fucking hard, and everything feels impossible, but we have to put their deaths aside and focus. The Gorgons may have been harboring their resentment over years, but their identity as a group is new. We've already destabilized their leadership by getting rid of Ares—" Claudia pauses for a shuddering breath. "But Juliet…"

"We have to kill her," I say.

"No," Vic snaps. "That's my sister you're talking about."

"Vic, I know what she is to you, but that woman out there is no longer your sister. Or your daughter," I say to Claudia. "She's our enemy. She let Sommesnay gas you, and she's still trying to manipulate Vic—"

"I'm not being manipulated. I know my sister. She wants to end this." Vic's voice is firm. "That's why she sent Cas that note. She's trying to find a way to stop all of this."

"Or she wants the legitimacy the two of you would give her reign," Claudia says sadly. "I see what she's doing, but she's my daughter. I know that I'm allowing my feelings to make me weak, but I… I love her. She's my own flesh and blood. I can't kill my own child. She's given us another way."

"What, join with her? Pretend none of this ever happened?" I snap. "And what do you think my role will be in her new world order? Juliet's made it clear that I'm not welcome in her Gorgon court—"

"Let me talk to her," Vic says. "I'll make her end this stupid feud with you. I'll—"

"She's not some puppy!" I cry. "She's a grown woman in complete control of her own decisions and an army of homicidal criminals, and she's not going to be dissuaded from this path that she clearly designed. Not everyone wants to be saved, Vic, and she doesn't. She has to die—"

"She's my *sister*," Vic's voice drips with danger, with finality.

"I'd rather walk away from the August family and everything we've built and start from nothing, than hurt her."

"I agree," Claudia says. "I think we go to her, as the note says. We stop the violence. We protect our people. I'll give up the Imperatorship, the Triumvirate, if it means getting my daughter back. She could be a wise leader if we give her a chance—"

"This is insane. Do you hear what you're saying?" I can't believe this is Claudia August speaking. She can't seriously believe Juliet is ready to play happy families after everything that's happened. "Juliet just got exactly what she wanted – absolute power. She's not going to share it."

"You don't know her," Vic says. "She—"

"I know her. I'm not blinded by her. You don't have to kill her, Vic. Cas will. And he'll do it fast and clean, and she won't even suffer—"

"I won't do it," Cas says.

I turn in his direction. "What?"

"I *want* to," he growls. "Fuck knows I want to wring her stupid fucking neck. But she has Gaius. And Vic doesn't want me to hurt her, so I won't hurt her."

"What about what's best for the Triumvirate?" I yell. "What about everything we just talked about, loyalty and strength and fighting for our people?"

"This *is* loyalty," he says. "I'm the Imperator of this family alongside you, and I vote with Claudia – we surrender to her. We join her under the Gorgon banner, and the violence stops. She wins. I get my brother back. I fucking hate it, Sunflower, but you taught me that I'm lost without my family. You're my family, my heart, and I won't let her hurt you. But Vic and Claudia are my family, too, and I won't hurt them when there's another way."

Another way.

My mind whirs. I'm Imperator of both Dio and Lucian, so I have two votes against Claudia and Cas' two. If I vote against them, we end up in a stalemate. Nothing will be done and Juliet will take that as permission to bring down the full weight of her power upon us.

But if I let them believe I'm happy to surrender, then I can buy myself some time.

Cali taught me that being an Imperator is about making tough decisions. And I will not let her death be in vain.

I know what I have to do.

40

FERGIE

I remain mostly silent as the others get Juliet's people on the phone and hash out the details of our surrender. It will be a public ceremony tomorrow at Colosseum, and as long as they all kneel for her, she will return Gaius to Cas and call off the war. As a show of her 'goodwill,' she declares a cease-fire over the city so that we can have a funeral for Cali and Livvie.

As for me, Juliet is resolute, as I knew she would be. I cannot be part of the Gorgons. I am not welcome. She and Vic argue back and forth, but decide that my father and I will move out of the city, and Vic will use his contacts to get me into the school of my choice. I will pick up my old life where it left off, and I can still see the guys as long as I never step foot in Emerald Beach again and I never take up with a criminal organization.

I can go to Harvard after all.

Woo-fucking-hoo.

I'm numb as Torsten leads me outside for the funeral. I can't believe that after everything we've been through together, every obstacle we've overcome, Vic and Cas are willing to accept Juliet's shitty offer. They are willing to say goodbye not just to the empire their mothers built, but to the future we had together.

I thought I was their Queen.

I don't want to be a little bit in their lives, a side-piece, an afterthought. I'm an all-or-nothing girl. And I don't believe that being Juliet's indentured servants is the only option available. Especially since I don't believe for one second that she's genuine about them being a family.

But I nod and agree and go along with the plan. I need them to believe that I've accepted it. Because I know they're doing this out of love and fear. And it's the same reason I'm going to burn it all down.

Before I destroy everything, before I betray Vic in a way he will never forgive, I want to feel their arms around me and hear the love in their voices. So I stand between the three of them, relishing the weight of their arms around me, as Dio and Lucian soldiers carry the shrouded bodies of Livvie and Cali onto the hastily prepared pyres.

Claudia says a few words as the pyre is doused with gasoline. She lights a match. A great mushroom of light bursts in front of my eyes. The flames glow orange as the cleansing fire carries their spirits to the underworld.

I snuggle into Vic's coat. I rest my head on Cas' shoulder. I squeeze Torsten's hand.

I hug my dad.

I listen to the Latin songs the soldiers sing – the funeral dirge of their fallen Queens.

Their bodies burn long into the night. I didn't know it took such a long time for a body to be consumed by flames. No wonder the Triumvirate method of body disposal has long been a hungry lion. Much faster.

All around the bonfire, people tell stories about the wild jobs they did with Cali, or the crass or violent responses she had whenever she was challenged. They talk about Livvie's generous spirit and the way she could make any event into a party, and how she made criminal enterprises fun in a way no one else does.

I get to know my stepmother more in that one night than I did while she was alive, and that alone makes me sadder than I thought possible.

I fucking hated Cali when I first met her, but now... now I admire her. I had so much to learn from her still.

When the flames die back and the drinking and toasts get too raucous, Cas, Vic and I trudge back to our room. I don't particularly want to touch either of them right now, but I let them both link arms with me and lead me. I need them to believe that I accept their decision.

Once inside our room, I make a beeline for Torsten. He's sitting with his sketchbook in the corner beside a large TV screen that's meant to stimulate a window (there are no windows in this room – Cali helped Livvie design this floor to keep her family and her top clients secure). He has it set to a spinning, sparkling solar system that I can see. Pinpricks of light unfurl, the big bang in miniature. A new beginning.

A universe born of destruction.

"What are you drawing?" I ask him, touching the edge of his sketchbook.

"New designs for my accessible art."

My chest tightens. I wish... I wish that I could be around to see his first public exhibit, to feel his whole body light up when he discovers how much his art makes a difference. "You still want to do that? Even after all your work was destroyed?"

"I wasn't happy with those ones, anyway," he says. "They were just for you. But the new designs will have to work for lots of people. I have to make the bridge at least seven times the size..."

I curl up in the chair beside Torsten, listening to his voice rise with excitement as he talks about what he's creating. He goes off on tangents about the paintings he's chosen, the artists and their lives, and the techniques they pioneered. I don't want to stop him to ask him for explanations of the complex art terminology, so I simply listen. I enjoy his passion and his thoughtfulness. I'm going to miss that about him most of all.

"Promise me something," I say. I swallow because I know what I'm asking. If Torsten makes a promise, he will keep it even if it means endangering himself.

"What?"

"Promise me that whatever happens, you will take Livvie's money and create this exhibition. Do not allow yourself to be drawn back into the criminal world. Can you promise me that?"

"Yes."

"Good."

Behind me, I can hear Vic and Cas on the other side of the room whispering frantically to each other. I'm too far away and they're speaking too quietly to pick up more than snatches of words, but I can tell that they're talking about the surrender.

Without me.

"Excuse me," I interrupt Torsten in the middle of a rant about Marcel Duchamp to escape to the bathroom. I flush the toilet and run the sink while I splash cold water on my face. I can't allow them to see that I'm crying.

I don't want to do this.

But I must.

I can see everything so clearly now. When I accepted the role of Imperator, I made a vow to put the people of this family first. That's the role of a Queen, and over the last few days, being holed up here in Tombs, I've had the chance to get to know some of them. Benni, the Argentinian street fighter who Cali helped secure a green card, Alison, a runner for Claudia August who's now Euri's number one knitting buddy. Davis, the staunch club bouncer turned head of our personal security who's so proud of his daughter getting into Brown.

I have to do this for them.

I wipe away the last of my tears, straighten my shoulders, and step into the room.

Torsten's pencil scrapes across the paper, and I can hear Cas and Vic still whispering.

I walk toward the door.

"Where are you going, Duchess?" Vic asks.

"Don't leave me alone with him," Cas growls. They're still not each other's favorite people.

"You're not alone. Torsten's here, too." (I think, he's pretty quiet sometimes.) "I'm just going down to get some of Milo's hot chocolate. I'll be right back, I promise."

"Bring me back one, too," Cas pipes up. "Torsten wants one as well, don't you?"

"Yes."

"I'll come with you," Vic offers. "You'll need help carrying them back."

"No, that's okay. Milo's got this cool tray that they clip into. I'll be fine."

"Duchess—"

"I just need a minute to myself, Vic," I growl. "Is that too much to ask?"

"No." He backs off. "I'm sorry. We'll see you in a few minutes."

"Good." I smile softly, trying to show him that we're okay. "Do you want a hot chocolate?"

"Yes, please."

I close the door behind me. My legs tremble as I descend the stairs and make my way to the kitchen behind the main bar area.

"Hey Milo, I need three of your famous chili hot chocolates."

"Anything for you, Imperator." Milo hums to himself as he works. He has Benni and another guy helping him out, making meals and snacks for our horde practically 24/7. I don't know how he does it and still remains so cheerful, but I love him for it.

I realize that in all of the chaos following Cali's death, I hadn't checked in with Milo. "How are you holding up after... everything?"

"It's... Seymour and I have been with Cali for over twenty years," Milo says. "We struggled to find domestic work – some people either don't want a gay couple living in their house or they wanted us to be a feature of their Instagram feed, and we're not into that. The day we went in for our interview, Cali looked me straight in the eye and demanded, 'Tell me what you'd do if you worked for me and I dragged a bloody corpse through the kitchen.' I said that my dear momma had a magic recipe for a cleaning solution that would lift bloodstains right out. She hired us on the spot."

I laugh. "I can just imagine it."

"She was a difficult woman, no doubt," Milo says as he stirs the chocolate. "But you couldn't help but love her. Neither of us had the best life growing up, and being gay in a criminal empire isn't exactly fashionable, especially among people our age. But Cali never let anyone say a nasty word to us. She treated us like family, and we became hers, especially while the boys were growing up. She raised the two of them all by herself, and I knew she was too proud to ask for help. How is Cas?" Milo's voice turns worried. "That poor boy. He's already suffered so much, and now..."

"He's..." He's being his infuriating, loyal, impossible self. "He's coping. I think he will do his mother proud."

"As will you." Milo slides a tray across the counter to me. "Cali was awfully impressed by you. She said that you were the only person she trusted to be ruthless enough and compassionate enough to do what needed to be done."

"Thank you, Milo." I swallow a lump in my throat. "That means the world to me."

I hope I do her proud now.

"Always, sweetie. And I know you're busy looking after everyone else, but you need your own time to grieve, don't forget that. Do you need some help with the tray?"

"I got it, thanks." It was a neat little tray with a loop underneath that I could carry in one hand while using my other to hold my cane. I gave Milo a final nod and moved as far from the kitchen as I could, into a dark, hidden corner of the bar. I hid behind a velvet curtain and listened.

Once I was certain no one was watching me, I leaned my cane between my legs and drew a tiny vial from my pocket.

The vial I nicked from Victor's toiletry bag. He'd shown me the collection of poisons and potions made from the plants in his greenhouse. He'd taken great pains to explain to me what each did and what dose was appropriate, and he'd even got Torsten to stick Braille labels on the jars so I could feel which was which.

"Just in case you need these, Duchess," Vic had said. "I know from experience that you can drop a man, but sometimes you might need something more subtle."

Three drops per drink.

I can't see what I'm doing, so I put drops on my fingers and let them roll off into the chocolate. Three drops per mug.

I had to hope like hell that was the right dose.

That done, I drop the vial into my pocket and continue up the VIP staircase, hot chocolates in hand. My heart hammers so loudly that I'm certain that everyone nearby can hear it and see through my fake smile.

"Look what Milo made," I coo as I push open the door to our suite.

"Oh, excellent." Cas grabs one of the cups. I bend down and hand one to Torsten. I hear him slurp loudly as he continues to draw.

"Where's yours, Duchess?" Vic asks as I hold out the final cup for him.

"I drank it in the kitchen with Milo. He looks so upset about Cali, and you know what he's like. I could barely get away."

I try to act normal while the guys lounge around and drink their chocolate. No way could I have one – I'm so nervous I'd throw it all up again.

About fifteen minutes later, Torsten's head thumps as it hits his desk.

Vic follows him, collapsing in a heap on top of the toilet. Cas was already lying on the bed, and his loud snores rumble the walls. Three out of three.

Time to move.

I check their pulses – all three of them are still alive. Good. I pull a blanket over Cas and wrap a jacket over Torsten's shoulders. Vic I leave on the toilet, because there are only some things I'm willing to do in the name of love.

I grab the bag I stashed in the shower and head out.

You'd think it would be tough for a blind mafia Queen to walk out of a locked-down nightclub filled with her loyal subjects, but the cool thing about being Queen is that no one questions what the fuck we're doing. "Be careful," Davis says as I walk past, but he doesn't follow me. He has his orders – I know this because I gave them to him.

I walk a couple of blocks and call a taxi. I'm not going to use Seymour for this, because he'd just as likely go back and report me to Claudia. Hopefully, no one discovers the guys until I've done what I need to do.

I wrap my arms around myself against the chill as I wait.

A few minutes later, the car pulls up. The driver comes around to my side and helps me with the door. "Where are we going tonight, ma'am?"

I flash him the grin of an Imperator. "The Elysium hotel."

41

CASSIUS

"Oh, little sis," I tsk under my breath as I watch Fergie step out of the taxi at the Elysium hotel.

I have to hand it to her – her plan was *almost* foolproof. But you can't trick an assassin, especially not one trained by Cali Dio.

Vic and Torsten don't have my training – they don't inspect their food before eating it. If they had, they'd notice the clear film on top of their hot chocolate froth as I did. While they gulped their drinks down, I pretended to sip mine and poured it into a potted plant when no one was looking.

As the two of them grew drowsy and dropped off to sleep, I pretended to join them. I watched Fergie as she held us, kissed us, and tested us to make sure we were out by feeling for our pulses and calling our names. Neither of them stirred, and so I faked some pretty impressive snores and she left me alone.

I should have been an actor, like Juliet.

I watched with my eyes wide open as Fergie took the knife from my boot and slid it into her own. She kissed me on the forehead and left, closing and locking the door behind her.

The second she was gone, I threw off the covers, loaded myself up with backup knives and my gun, pulled on my leather jacket, and went after her.

I had a feeling I knew exactly where she was going.

We're the same, after all.

The taxi driver walks her into the opulent lobby. No way can I follow her – someone will recognize me and I'll lose the element of surprise. I get out of the van and head around the back of the building, through the kitchens, and into the labyrinth of service tunnels.

"You can't be back here—" a porter yells, but I slam him into the wall as I pass him, and he doesn't yell after that.

No one stops me as I move through the hotel, hammering my fists on doorways until someone opens up. A yawning middle-aged man glares at me through the gap in the door.

"What the—"

He doesn't have a chance to say another word. I knock him out with a single blow to the head. He crumples in the doorway.

I step over his body and drag him inside the room after me. The door swings shut behind us. His wife's in bed. She starts screaming, but I growl at her. "I'm going for the balcony and I'll be gone. Your husband is out cold, but not dead. Tend to him because he's going to have a fucking headache when he wakes up, but if you call the front desk or the police and tell them about me, I'll know. And I'll come back and slit both your throats."

I wait for her to nod. I have to hope she's smart enough to obey, because I won't hesitate to make good on my threat.

I storm out of their balcony and haul myself over the edge. My foot slides between the decorative metal railings, and propel myself up onto the top of the railing and grab the edge of the next balcony for support.

I'm coming for you, little sis.
I'm coming to make sure you don't do something stupid.
I'm your monster. We're supposed to do this together.

42

FERGIE

When you're blind, people often go out of their way to make sure you're safe and secure. Usually, this is awesome, but when you've got a covert mission, it can be a real fucking hassle.

The driver insists on walking me into the hotel and waiting in line with me until we get to the front desk. I have to actually purchase a room to get him to leave. Oof, four hundred and fifty dollars for their cheapest suite. I'd feel that. I don't yet have access to the Lucian or Dio coffers.

Good thing I have that college fund gathering dust.

"Staying alone tonight, Ms. Munroe?" It's Robert, the concierge who was so kind to me and Torsten during our last stay.

"Yes," I say. The word catches in my throat. After tonight, I'll be more alone than I've ever been before. I'll lose everything that I've fought so hard for.

Robert offers to walk me up to my room. I have no intention of staying at the hotel, but having the room might give me some advantage, so I accept with a smile. I ask if he can give me a room on a higher level, with a balcony facing the street. If he wonders why a blind girl cares which way her room is facing, his training doesn't allow him to ask.

I'm a ball of nerves when I step onto the elevator with Robert. It's late at night now, and not many people are in the hotel's public spaces. But I can't risk running into Juliet. Luckily, when the doors open onto my floor – floor seven – the corridor is silent.

Robert makes sure I remember how the electronic key works, and then leaves me to it. I shut the door behind him, turn on the light (yes, even blind girls turn on the light. Sometimes it helps me make out the shapes of the furniture better), and dump my bag on the bed before flopping down beside it.

The bed is enormous and covered in expensive, silken sheets. I can tell by the echoes that I have a large, premium room, although it's nothing on the penthouse where Torsten was staying. I throw my arms wide and run my fingers over the linens, savoring the rich textures and imagining what the three of them could do to me after Cas tied me to this bed...

It's weird being here alone, without the guys. It's horrible to think about them and know that we'll never have another moment like that. I miss them already. It's going to hurt so much to be without them.

But I have to do it. I don't have a choice.

After all, there can be only one Queen in Emerald Beach.

I move to the window and cautiously slide the door open. I step out onto the balcony, breathing in the city as she unfurls beneath me in an ocean of twinkling lights.

I know my plan is crazy. It's utterly bonkers. I have no way of knowing if Juliet is even in her room tonight. But I know I have one chance to do this, and I have to take it. When the guys wake up and I'm not there, and they hear the news from the gang grapevine, they'll know what I've done.

I return to my room and unpack my bag. I knot the coil of

rope I brought with me around my waist. I slide Cas' knife into my boot, and the little device Torsten uses for hacking electronic locks goes in the zippered pocket on my skintight liquid-look leggings. Who says you can't have spice and practicality?

I go to the bathroom, eat both the pillow mints for strength, and then head back out to the balcony. I pull one of the patio chairs over to the edge, stand on it, and reach up, feeling around until I grab the bars of the balcony above. I haul myself up, swinging my leg to hook between the metal rungs and praying to any god who'll listen that no one's in the room above mine.

I have pretty decent upper-body strength, but holding a pull-up from the ground is fucking hard work, y'all. My shoulders scream with agony, but I manage to haul myself up so my head could peak through the rungs into the room beyond, if I had eyes that allowed peeking. I grasp the handrail and swing my body ungainly over the balcony to land on the tiles. I breathe hard, giving myself a few moments before I attempt the next one. I have six balconies to climb tonight. It's going to be slow going.

I do exactly the same thing I did before. This time, the backpack slides off my shoulder, throwing me off-balance just as I swing my leg, leaving me dangling over the parking lot. Panic surges inside me, but I'm not going to give Juliet August the satisfaction of looking over her balcony and seeing me splattered on the pavement, so I strain and swing and manage to hook my leg again. This time, I drop heavily onto the ninth-floor balcony and take a good ten minutes before I'm ready to try again.

I'm drenched in sweat by the time I drop onto the twelfth-floor balcony. My arms are shaking so hard I can't make them stop. Luckily, whoever's staying in this room left a jacket slung over the back of the chair, and I use that to wipe off my sweaty palms.

The final balcony is the worst. When Torsten and I stayed in the Elysium penthouse suite, I spent enough time sitting outside to know that it doesn't have the same wrought-iron railings as the floors below. Instead, it's a wall of solid concrete cast with rococo designs. I'm going to have to hope like hell I can hold on.

I swing myself up and grab a knobbly bit. It's more difficult than I ever imagine. My whole body screams in protest, but I hang on with one hand as I thrust my other hand up. I run my fingers over the design, searching for a handhold.

Fuck, fuck. My hands are so slippery.

I'm going to...

My fingers close around what feels like the upper petal of a flower. I swing to my right, then fling myself back to the left and reach with my left hand. I manage to grab the top of the balcony, and I know I'm okay. I hook my foot on a concrete vine and hoist myself up and over.

I did it.

I'm in.

Well, not yet. Let's not get ahead of ourselves. I'm sitting on Juliet's balcony, but we're separated by a thick doorway of bullet-proof glass.

Luckily, I'd managed to keep hold of my backpack during the perilous climb. I tug it off my shoulders and pull out Torsten's little box. He showed me how to use it and it's not difficult... well, it's not difficult for a sightie. But I'm going to have to do this without being able to see the screen. For a second, I squeeze my eyes shut and let the frustration of trying to do this completely blind fizz in my body.

No, I can figure this out.

I feel around the glass until I find the lock. The door locks from the inside but there's a safety panel on the outside in case someone gets locked out here – the lock opens with the room's key card or a combination. I use the screwdriver to pull off the panel and attach Torsten's box. I can't remember what I'm supposed to do next but apparently it works automatically, because in a few moments something clicks. I push the door and it slides open silently.

I leave the backpack on the balcony and slip inside. I'm in the living room. There are no lights on but I don't need them. I remember where every item of furniture is. I move to the left to get around the coffee table and—

CLONK.

My heart leaps into my throat as I hit something tall and metal, and it topples over and hits the side of the coffee table before rolling against my feet.

The fuck?

Who put a fucking *lamp* there?

That wasn't there when Torsten and I lived here.

Okay, calm down, Fergie. Maybe you're safe. Maybe she didn't hear—

I freeze as lights flick on in the bedroom. "What was that?" a sleepy voice mumbles.

Juliet?

She *is* here.

"Carlos, if that's you, you know that I don't want guards in my rooms. Get the fuck back outside the door, you lazy ass."

I feel a flash of pride that I'd climbed over those balconies instead of trying to get through her guards. But pride won't get me out of this mess, because if Juliet sees me standing here—

I know I'm too obvious, that I need to go back on the balcony, but I can't risk moving now. Besides, she'd hear the balcony door open.

Fucknuggets.

An idea occurs to me. I creep around the table and into the kitchen, as near to the front door as I dare to go. "Sorry, my Queen," I call out in my deepest voice. I open a cupboard door and slam it shut, muffling it a little with my hand so that it sounded more like the heavy suite door.

"Fucking imbeciles," Juliet mumbles from the bedroom. "Can't listen to simple instructions."

Don't come out here. Don't—

I hear a click, and a thin shaft of light flicks on. It takes me a moment to figure out that it's the light from the ensuite being projected through the open bedroom door.

Good, she hasn't seen me.

Juliet's going to the bathroom. It's a great place to ambush her. I dig the knife out of my boot and hold it up as I creep through the kitchen. I can't risk hitting anything else.

I reach the bedroom door and flatten myself against the wall. I can hear the sink running and Juliet humming under her breath.

I launch myself at the bathroom door, reaching for the handle, and—

A lot of things happen at once.

Something slams into me, knocking me to the floor.

Bright lights impale my skull.

A pair of hands go around my neck, whipping my head around and slamming me against the floorboards.

Vic's sister whispers in my ears, "You're not as clever as you think you are, bitch."

If that's Juliet, then who the fuck is in the bathroom?

But I don't have time to think about that because Juliet shoves something cold and hard into my temple. The barrel of a gun.

"Drop the knife, Fergie."

43

FERGIE

I drop the knife.

The bathroom door swings open. A male voice says something, but my head is swimming from the blows and I can't place it beyond a certain deep, familiar tone.

"On your feet, Imperator," Juliet snaps. "Or I put this bullet between your eyes."

It's hard to do when I'm so shaky, but I stagger to my feet. Juliet shoves the barrel into the back of my skull. She grabs my arm with her other hand. "Walk," she growls.

I walk.

Juliet yanks my arm to guide me. She walks me back through the living room and out onto the balcony. I stumble over the lip of the doorframe and nearly go down and bring her with me, but I'm too out of it to use the fall to my advantage. I roll onto my back. Juliet whips the pistol across my cheek, sending my head cracking against the tile.

"I could shoot you," she says. "I'd take a lot of pleasure in seeing your brains decorating the pavement, but I have an even better idea. One thing you and poor old Cassius don't understand is that whoever controls the stories controls Emerald Beach. And I get to tell your story however I like.

"Let's see," she pretends to think. "The poor little blind girl who got mixed up in something she didn't understand. Sweet, clever Fergie with her whole life ahead of her until the bad boys corrupted her. And finally, after seeing her stepmother slaughtered in front of her – or, I guess, hearing it, in your case – the dumb little bitch's brain finally snapped and she threw herself off my balcony."

"No one will believe you," I whisper.

"Won't they?" Her lip curls back. "They believed me before. They believed that I was kidnapped all those years ago, when I planned the whole thing. Stupid Hermann was a bad choice, but Sommesnay was so much more resourceful. Even now, my sweet little brother believes I'm here against my will, that all I want to do is get back into Mom's good graces. Even you believed that I wanted to be your friend. You were so fucking desperate for friends when you came to Emerald Beach that I practically had you eating out of my hand. But when my poor, gormless brother showed an interest, I saw how much of a threat you truly were. Turns out, you've been pretty disappointing, but it has been fun to dangle you on my hook and watch you squirm."

She kicks me in the ribs.

With a start, I realize what she's saying. All of this has been a game to her.

Juliet pretended to like me when I arrived in Emerald Beach.

But worse, she wasn't actually kidnapped by those guys when she was thirteen. She *orchestrated* it, in the same way that she's orchestrated... *everything*. The way she stole Vic's phone to post those videos, used Cas to hurt me, and fed Sommesnay information so he could kidnap me and hurt the others.

"Why... all this?" I gasp out.

"Isn't it obvious?" she smirks. "My mother has no ambition,

no sense of *story*. She swooped into the Triumvirate and took over, gave our family its first Queen, and then, what? She sits around having manicures with her girlfriends and messing about with crusty old scrolls. For all her feminism, she wanted a male on her throne – my brother. He was the perfect son, but I was always too much. Too loud, too demanding, too desperate for attention. Of course I was desperate. She always put Vic first."

"And that's a reason to seize power by force, to have Sommesnay gas your parents?"

She laughs cruelly. "I had to take matters into my own hands. My first attempt had elements of genius – using myself as bait to destabilize the empire she had built. Claudia August, the great family woman, could not allow her daughter to remain in the hands of kidnappers. So I struck a deal with a guy I'd been seeing at the time – he gets the word out to his followers that a coup is going down, and when my mother is off the throne I'll marry him to give his rule legitimacy. Then, after I'd taken Cali and Livvie by surprise and knocked him off, I would have ruled all three families."

"Rather ambitious for a thirteen-year-old," I can't help but blurt out.

"It would have been magnificent, but those lug-heads messed it up." Juliet grabs me under the arm and tries to hoist me to my feet. "This time, I made sure everything was perfect, right down to the deranged psychopath to distract my mother from the real mastermind behind the coup – *moi*. I don't have to hide anymore. Now everyone in the world will know my truth. They'll whisper that one word from me and Fergie Munroe killed herself. Think about how powerful that story will be. I'll be the Gorgon Queen who can turn men to stone and women into birds." Juliet chuckles at her joke. "Now, be a good little puppy dog and get on your feet. It's time to finish this."

I'm too frightened to move.

"Stand under your own weight or I'll shoot your kneecaps out. I've heard it's an excruciating way to go."

A hand presses into my lower spine, shoving me forward. I stumble over the table and push something out to halt my fall.

Juliet gets ahold of my hair, bending me down, down. I'm powerless against her. I throw out my arms, but there's nothing to grab. Any second now I'll go over—

"You stole my brother from me," she growls. "You die tonight, bitch."

Juliet shoves me against the edge of the balcony. I see that she's trying to push me over. She's stronger than I expect, and she's got me in such a tight position that I don't have room to twist and get a hold of her.

The empty expanse of space beneath me yawns open, pulling me down. In my panic, every jiujitsu move I've ever learned flies out of my head.

I'm dead.

I'm so sorry, Vic. I came here to save you. I hope you know that.

I love you, Torsten. I wish you could see how much.

Cas, thank you. Thank you for helping me find the monster inside me.

I think about Cali walking into that arena, serene in her duty.

I relax my muscles and fall forward.

It's time to go...

Something slams into Juliet from the side, tearing her away. Her weight no longer bears down on me.

I'm free.

I don't hesitate, don't stop to figure out what's going on. I grip the railing to stop myself from toppling over. I whirl around, kicking out my foot until it connects with her body. Whoever attacked her is holding her, and I don't even stop to find out who they are.

I grab her in a jiujitsu hold and hurl her with everything I have at the balcony.

Juliet hits the concrete railing with a squeal, but I'm right there on top of her. And unlike her, I know how to leverage a heavy body.

She shrieks and paws at my skin, grabbing handfuls of my clothing, but it's pointless. I give her one final shove, and she goes over.

She screams all the way down.

And then, she stops screaming.

I grip the balcony, panting. *Is she... is she really gone?*

"She's dead, Sunflower."

Cas?

I think I must be dreaming. This can't be real. I didn't just kill Vic's sister, because Cas isn't here with me.

But he is. His thick arms encircle me, his strong body drawing me back from the edge. "You didn't think you could pull the old 'drug your boyfriends so you can sneak out and kill their enemy' trick on me? Sunflower, I invented that trick."

"Oh, did you just? And here I was thinking I was original." I sink into his embrace, grateful for the weight and assurance of him. "Where are Vic and Torsten?"

"Sound asleep back in the room. I left them to come after you, and it's just as well I did. I was hiding on the balcony when you climbed over. I am so fucking impressed. You're amazing. Anyway, I heard everything. Vic can't be mad at you when he hears what that bitch did—"

Cas keeps talking, but I don't hear him. I bury my head into his shoulder. I wish with all my heart that's true, but I know Vic. He loves his sister, and I killed her. This is just like the time when Juliet and Cas shared the video and Vic went after Cas instead of me.

All he'll ever be able to see is his sister's murderer.

I don't blame him.

It's what I am. I am the monster. And how can he ever love a monster?

"All I wanted..." I sob, "...is for Vic to be free of her. As long as she was the Gorgon Queen, he'd always believe that he can change her mind, that she'd come back to him."

"You don't have to convince me. You did the right thing, Sunflower. She can't hurt him anymore. She's gone."

"She is," an amused voice says behind us. "But I'm not."

44

CASSIUS

My chest tightens as I turn my gaze toward the all-too-familiar voice, raising the gun I picked up from Juliet and pointing it at the newcomer.

My stomach sinks into my feet.

Leaning against the doorway wearing only a pair of silk boxers and the grin that always melted our mother's steel heart is Gaius.

And he's pointing a gun at Fergie's head.

"Surprise." Gaius lifts a cocky eyebrow. "I bet you didn't expect to see me here, little bro."

He's not wrong.

What is he doing here?

Why is he threatening Fergie?

I just... I don't understand. The pieces are floating in front of my face, but I can't put them together.

My brother has a towel wrapped around his narrow hips, but it's clear that he's naked underneath it. There's red lipstick staining his neck, and claw marks on his shoulders.

"You... you were fucking Juliet?" I grasp at the one conclusion that might make sense.

Honestly, I don't know why I'm surprised. Gaius will fuck anything with legs and a warm pussy.

But Juliet was gay. At least, last time I checked...

"She's bi, and she wanted to find out what Dio dick was like. Apparently, quite good." He shrugs. "You did me a favor. Juliet had her uses, but she had all kinds of crazy ideas about running a criminal empire. The Gorgon Queen? Have you ever heard of something so ridiculous?"

"But you—"

"I what?" Gaius smirks. "I'm supposed to be locked in a cage or with my head in a guillotine? Please, brother. Juliet's not the only one around here who can act. Do you think I was going to stand idly by while you took away my birthright?"

"Please..." I can't believe I'm begging. "Please, Gaius. Drop the gun."

"I'll drop mine if you drop yours."

Neither of us move.

"I thought so. Oh, Cas. You haven't figured it out?" He throws back his head and laughs. "I'm not surprised. You always were too stupid to live. Juliet and I were in this together. We've been planning it for years, ever since her kidnapping plot fizzled and died."

"You knew about that?"

"Of course. It was obvious that she'd been in on it. It was obvious to Cali, too, but Claudia wouldn't listen to her, and Cali didn't believe Juliet capable of anything more sophisticated, so the whole thing was forgotten."

Not by Vic.

How could she do that to him?

Gaius continues. "Juliet and I realized that we couldn't count on anyone else to set this up for us – we had to orchestrate the coup ourselves. Sommesnay falling into our laps and yours and Fergie's prank war were ideal timing. It's taken years of planning to get us to tonight, and so far everything's gone perfectly... for me, anyway. Juliet might disagree."

I stutter, struggling for the words. I can't take my eyes off the gun in his hands, pointing directly at Fergie. My hand on my gun trembles. *Fuck.*

Now I understand how Vic felt about Juliet. I can't hurt him, I *can't.* But Fergie...

"Poor, poor Cassius. I've rendered you speechless. Do you want another revelation?" Gaius steps toward us, that gun trained. "I set you up with the fire. Juliet and I did, actually. We've always made a good team."

"The fire?" For a moment, I wrack my damaged brain for what he's talking about. But of course he means the first at the greenhouse. "That was me. It was my crime."

"Don't you remember? I talked you into inviting Gemma's parents and Konrad to the old horticulture building. I made all the arrangements for you. Well, Juliet helped. She always was a good actress – impersonating the principal on the phone was nothing for her. And while I talked you into dousing the building in flames, she called the police. It was phase one of our plan – get rid of the golden children first, the ones our parents wanted as their heirs, and then we would take them out of the picture. That day, I was going to get you sent to jail for a long time, out of my way so I could focus on what I was born to do – run an empire. But then I got that phone call. Do you remember?"

That day is a blur to me. I don't remember. But Fergie says, "He doesn't remember. You got a phone call?"

"From Bob the Builder. He was one of my contacts, a fixer in prison. That's why they call him Bob the Builder, because he can fix anything. Bob told me that he'd finally tracked down the guy who impregnated Cali with you, Ares Valerian. The guy who'd very nearly overthrown Cali, the only man to ever come close.

Ares wasn't dead, as our dear departed mother always told me. He was in prison – the *exact same prison* they'd likely send you to after you were convicted. I couldn't risk it. If you found him first, his power would solidify your inheritance, even if Cali was gone. I'd been looking for your father for years, because I had a feeling that he'd want to finish what he started and take over the Dio family. So I did what any true leader would do. I thought on my feet."

"You went to jail in Cas' place," Fergie says.

Gaius grins. "Very good, Fergie. You're definitely the brains of this operation. Yes, I went to jail. I pitched it to Mom as a great sacrifice for our family, on the condition that she pulled her strings to get me out after three years. As soon as I got there I found Ares, and we put our plan together. I got in touch with Juliet and she fed me information about what was going on in Emerald Beach, and when Sommesnay came along with his vendetta against Claudia, it seemed like our time to strike had come. A bribe or two in the right hands and Ares and I walked right out of prison, full pardon and everything."

"I don't understand," I manage to say. "Why did you need to do all of this? You were already Cali's heir. You would have taken over Dio anyway. Why did you have to do all this?"

Why did you have to kill our mother?

Why are you pointing that gun at my Queen?

"You were Cali's favorite," Gaius says, his mouth tugging up at the side into an ugly scowl. "You were the son she birthed herself. I know nothing about my parents except that they were enemies of the Triumvirate, and Cali executed them and raised their child as her own. But I was never truly hers, she never trusted me the way she did you. I could have been the greatest asset to our family if she'd given me what was rightfully mine, but no, it didn't matter that I was the most qualified leader, or that they'd changed the rules, *blood* came first. I would have made our family the greatest, instead of the smallest and most timid. But Cali wouldn't hear of it. She wanted you to be her heir.

"But she's been blind to your faults for so long, little bro. I don't blame her; it's the way of mothers. I see myself as your kind of surrogate father, and because of that, I can appraise your skills accurately. You do not have what it takes to lead this family. You're too easily manipulated, as Juliet and I have proven countless times by manipulating you. As you're proving right now, by being manipulated by Fergie Munroe."

"Juliet's gone," Fergie points out. "Are you the Gorgon King now? Is that what you want?"

Gaius scoffs. "I *want* the Dio family to have what we deserve. I *want* everything back that was taken from us by August and Lucian. I want to give up this ridiculous fucking farce that three families can rule harmoniously like we're some fucking hippie commune. And now that I don't have to placate the fucking Gorgon Queen, I want my brother by my side."

That's when I know something is truly broken inside me, because even after everything he's just told me, at those words, my coal-heart soars. This is all I've ever wanted, to be with my brother, and to rule our empire together. We could make Cali so proud. We could—

"What about Fergie?" I ask, my chest swelling with hope.

The gun weighs heavy in my hand.

"What about her?" Gaius nods sagely. "There's no place for her in our world, Cas. She's trouble. Look at everything that's happened since she came into our life. Look at your *skin*, Papa Smurf. Can't you see that she's manipulated you worse than anyone? She's talked you into an absurd relationship with two other guys; she's made you give up half your power to her. She's the one who drove a wedge between the three Imperators in the first place. She has to go, and you're going to be the one who kills her."

"What if I refuse?" The gun wobbles. "What if I say that I'm no longer loyal to you and that I don't want to be part of this family if I can't have Fergie?"

"Then I have no choice." Gaius slides off the safety. "Either way, she dies tonight. But I want you to do it, Cas. It's the only way to be free of her."

"Cas, no," Fergie's voice trembles.

I turn to her, bringing the barrel of the gun with me until it's pointing right between her shattered emerald eyes. I study her perfect features, her wobbling lip, her heart-shaped jaw. I think back to when she first came to Emerald Beach, when I tried too hard to hate her, to break her, but instead she got under *my* skin. She dyed me blue. She made me believe that the four of us could have a life together. She made me feel things I never thought I'd be capable of feeling.

Lies. All lies.

She *is* the monster.

"It's for your own good, Cas," Gaius says. "She's made you soft, weak. Get rid of her and become my brother the monster once more."

Yes, yes. I am supposed to be the monster. I am the one who destroys.

"Cas, no," Fergie cries. "Don't listen to him. Everything out of his mouth is a lie."

"He's my brother," I say. "He doesn't lie to me."

"That's exactly what Vic said." Fergie's voice hammers inside my skull. "Cas, he's going to kill *you*. He doesn't want to share his rule with anyone."

"She's lying to you, Cas," Gaius says. "I went to jail for you, remember? And now I've come back for you. So we can rule together. But you have to get rid of her first. She's poison. She's ruining you."

"You are so much stronger than this, Cas," Fergie says. "You're so much more of a man than him. You're brave, and terrifying, and loyal. You are loved, just as you are. Just because Gaius is your brother doesn't mean he's family. We're a family, you and me and Vic and Torsten. *Please*. We'd never ask you to do this. You are loved so much. You are enough, just as you are. Cas, *please*—"

"He's *my* brother," I growl. "We're family."

"I won't hurt you, Cas." Gaius takes a step toward me. He removes one hand from the gun and stretches it out toward me. "I've missed you so much, brother. We're family. We stick together."

"Yes," I say. "We're family."

I pull the trigger.

45

FERGIE

The bullet tears through my body.

I scream, and scream and scream and scream because I'm hit, I'm hit and Cas shot me and I'm falling and I'm dead—

No.

I'm not falling.

My body isn't exploding in pain.

My life isn't ebbing away from me.

But a hand is on my arm, steadying me, pulling me in close, wrapping me in the scent of plum and musk and carnation.

"Sunflower." Cas' voice chokes with pain. "I had to do it. I had to. I couldn't live without you."

Cas falls into my arms, burying his face into my shoulder. My *wet* shoulder. Both Cas and I are soaked with something sticky.

Blood? He's hurt?

No, not blood. Tears.

And also some blood.

Cas' body shudders as he sobs. "I had to do it," he repeats, over and over.

I don't have to see to know that his brother's body lies on the floor in front of us, and his blood is splattered over my favorite black leggings.

Cas shot Gaius.

All his life, Cas has been told that he's a monster. He's been molded and shaped by his mother and his brother into the perfect weapon – a bomb they can throw into a room. A final solution to any problem they might face or any enemy that gets in their way.

But he's so much more than that. Inside his chest is a human heart that loves with a fierceness that will never be equaled.

All along it was his brother who was the monster, who's been planning his move ever since he was a teenager. And now, thanks to Cas, he's gone.

We have so much work to do to rebuild what has been broken. But with this strong, loyal, impossible man at my side, we can do it together.

"It's over." Cas sags against me.

"No." I hold his cheek and tilt his face up to kiss away the salty tears on his lips. "It's only just begun."

46

FERGIE

I don't know how long Cas and I stand on the balcony, holding each other. It could have been minutes, or hours, or days even.

But I don't think it's long before someone's banging on the suite door. The hotel staff must've heard the gunshot. Neither of us makes any move to answer it. I want to hang in this liminal space with Cas, basking in the afterglow of slaughter, for just a little bit longer before...

"What happened in here? What's—oh, my god. There's so much blood."

The door bangs against the wall. Several people storm in. Robert's the guy who spoke, and I feel bad for him. I hope it isn't his job to clean Gaius' blood from between the floor tiles.

Then I hear another voice. They don't speak so much as let out a horrid, strangled cry.

Vic.

I smell him – that dark chocolate and hazelnut scent of him floods the room. I hear a crash and Robert yells as Vic barrels onto the balcony. How is Vic even walking right now?

Not well. I can hear him stumble and crash into the furniture, but he's fighting the sedative so he can get to us. So he can—

"Jules?" he whispers. He grasps the edge of the balcony, the strangled sob rising from his throat when he realizes that whatever's in the parking lot beneath us used to be his sister.

The sound breaks my heart. Vic is hurting. His whole heart is breaking. A piece of him has been torn away and he will never, ever be whole again.

And I did that to him.

"Who killed my sister?" Vic's voice whirls around the room. "I'll kill whoever did this."

Everyone remains silent.

"You did this," he growls at Cas, getting right in close. "How could you do this? I said I would fix it. But you have to go and break everything again..."

I don't quite know what's happening, but I think Vic launches himself at Cas, but I'm in the way, so he kind of topples into me. I grab him and pull him close.

"Cas didn't do it. I did."

The world stops.

Vic's body convulses as my words register. He tries to pull away from me, but I'm the only thing holding him upright, so he crashes to the floor.

I didn't intend to tell him the truth, not ever. Because there was a moment when I was holding Cas where I actually believed that we could have had our happily ever after – all four of us. All it would take was Cas and I telling Vic that Gaius threw Jules over, and everything would go back to the way it was.

But that would be a lie.

Happily-ever-afters are for Harvard-bound nerdy girls, not stone-cold mafia Queens. It's like how everything changed after

Cas released that video of us. I can never be the woman in the video again – she was lost forever that day. I had to become the monster to survive it, and against all odds, the monster fell in love.

But Vic, Vic is righteous and good. There is no monster inside him who can love the woman who killed his sister. And I love him too much to trick him into it. Instead, I take the broken pieces of his heart and stomp them into ash.

"F-F-Fergie?" He freezes, his body stiff and unyielding.

"I had to, Vic." My words sound so feeble, so weak. But I stand by them. "She was going to destroy you."

"I can't... I don't..." he slurs. "You killed my twin?"

"I got rid of a threat. I hated doing it, but it had to be done. Your dad said something once, that we can't let sentiment make us weak. And it's good I did it, because she was shacked up in here with Gaius and he—"

"No," Vic cuts off. "Stop talking."

I snap my mouth shut. Cas moves beside me, wrapping his arms around me. He seems to sense that I need a shield. I smell Torsten nearby, too.

"Vic," Torsten says, pronouncing each word slowly, "you're yelling at Fergie."

"Of course I fucking am!" Vic screams. "She killed my sister."

"She must have had a good reason."

"Don't you understand? The reason doesn't matter. She cut my heart out of my chest and ate it in front of me."

I squeeze my eyes shut, willing my head to stop pounding, and my own heart to stop breaking. "Vic, what are you thinking?"

For several long moments, he doesn't answer.

"I'm thinking... I'm thinking that I can't do this. I can't..." he swallows again. "I can't look at you in the same way again."

"Vic—"

"Ow," Robert cries out as Vic shoves past him.

I hear his footsteps pound in the hallway. And then the elevator dings and he's gone.

47

FERGIE

We bury Juliet in the Beaumont Hills cemetery.

It's a far more lavish affair than Cali's and Livvie's funeral pyre, and much more dignified than Cas tossing his brother's body to the coyotes at Everlasting Hart ranch, but that's the August way. Always proper, always kind to those who betray them, even in death.

I cling to Cassius as we gather around the coffin. A huge crowd has turned out – practically the entire senior class is here. Dru says hello to me before the service. If she's there to gloat over Juliet's corpse, she at least has the decency to do it silently.

Members of the Gorgons and the August family are here under a special amnesty. All weapons had been handed over as they entered the cemetery. Even traitors hold death sacred.

The wind off the ocean is strong today, and it tears away the priest's words as soon as they leave his lips. I don't hear a word of the ceremony, but not even the wind can buffer Claudia's weeping. She's beside us, and her desolation is an ocean that will consume the Earth.

I wonder if she weeps for the daughter she had, or the one she's created in her head.

How can you cry so many tears for someone who hated you so much?

Speaking of tears... I know Vic's somewhere in the crowd. I can sense the weight of his sorrow in the air. He hasn't said a word or even been in the same room as me since he walked out of Elysium.

It's getting easier to pretend it doesn't hurt.

The crowd shuffles. Cas whispers to me that a basket of sand is being offered around – we can choose to ceremonially drop a pinch into the hole, a way of saying goodbye.

Cas and Torsten both refuse, but I take the basket.

Torsten leads me to the edge. I sense the earth dropping away in front of me, and the gaping darkness of Juliet's grave – the kind of darkness that has form and substance.

I dip my hand into the bowl and pull out a small handful of soil. I hold it out and let it drop through my fingers.

When I first came to Emerald Beach, Juliet had been friendly to me. We could have been sisters. Allies. I could have loved her as I love her brother and her family.

But that friendship was a lie, like so much else in her life. She chose to turn her back on everything Claudia taught her. She chose to chase power without responsibility, and she paid the price.

I don't regret what I did.

I just wish... Vic...

Torsten's fingers brush the small of my back, and the weight of that responsibility rests heavily on my shoulders. I have the job Juliet coveted – I am one of the most powerful women in this city.

I have a duty to bring together the Dio and Lucian families, to create something new with Claudia, something that will last.

The last of my sand falls through my fingers.

"Illis quos amo deserviam," I say.

For those I love, I sacrifice.

I turn.

I walk away.

Out of the darkness. Away from my past. Away from the old Fergie Macintosh.

And into the light.

"Do you see Vic?" I whisper to Cas as the funeral party starts to break up into little groups. People crowd around Claudia to offer their condolences, but I can't quite bear to face her today.

Juliet may have been our enemy, but she was also Claudia's daughter... and I killed her.

We've talked about it, and she understands. Unlike Vic, Claudia knows I did the right thing. But that doesn't mean it doesn't hurt her. And today of all days, I can't bear to hurt her more.

"He was behind the priest during the service, but..." Cas' body moves as he searches the crowd, his assassin eyes trained to spot his target. "There he is. He's slipping away down a side path. Do you want to go after him?"

My chest tightens. "Yes. Please."

Cas moves me through the crowd, tossing people out of our way. Even at a funeral, Cas is still Cas.

The voices become a din as we move away from the main space, and the ancient trees bend their branches toward us, further distorting the sound and occasionally brushing the top of my head with their soft branches.

Cas stops. "I see him. There's an overgrown path in front of us, between two lines of gravestones. Vic's at the end, looking out at the ocean. Be careful – this is an older part of the cemetery, so there's no handrail there. Don't let Vic push you over the edge."

"I won't." I place my cane in front of me and sweep it over the ground. Cas wasn't wrong about the path being overgrown. I fumble my way around twisted roots and broken pieces of stonework.

"Vic," I call out.

No answer.

"Vic? I want to talk to you."

I sense him watching me. He has always possessed the ability to see under my skin, right into my heart. I move my legs faster, I have to get to him before he changes his mind and leaves—

"Stop." His hand closes around my wrist, pulling me up short. "The edge is right in front of you. One more step and you're going for a swim."

His voice makes my throat constrict.

"Vic." I squeeze my cane to my chest. He doesn't let go of my wrist. His touch is so warm, so familiar, so unsettling.

There are so many things I want to say to him, but standing on the edge of this cliff, with the ocean roaring beneath me, all my words seem small and hollow and meaningless. "I'm so sorry."

The silence stretches between us.

How fucking small and useless those words are.

"I'm sorry," I say again. "I know that you can never forgive me. I know that there's no going back from what happened. I hate that I hurt you."

Nothing.

His fingers twitch an inch.

"But I'm not sorry I did it. We're more like each other than we know, Vic. Your whole life, you've done everything in your power to look after the people you love. Before I came to

Emerald Beach, the family I had to fight for was pretty small – just me and Dad. But then I met you and Cas and Torsten, and everything happened, and now..." I sweep my arm around in what I hope is the direction of the city, "...now my family is so much bigger."

"Fergie..." his voice strains.

"Please, don't say anything yet. I have to get this out, and then I promise that I'll leave you alone forever." I steel myself to keep talking. "I just want you to know that I respect that you can't love me now. I'm not going to ask anything of you that I know you can't give. But I am always going to be here, Vic, loving you from afar. I cannot stop loving you because it would be like asking the ocean to stop being water. You will never have to see my face again, but I will always be in the shadows, making sure that you're safe. You don't have to be the protector anymore. You don't have to be trapped. You can be whoever you want to be. You can leave Emerald Beach and go to college and be the best botanist the world has ever seen, and I will make sure that no one from your old life comes after you. It's the least I can fucking do—"

"Fergie," he snaps. "Stop."

My heart stutters.

"I've thought a lot about this. I need to say something, too." His fingers tighten around my wrist, and he sucks in a weary breath. "Torsten sent me a packet of evidence. He dug through years and years of Juliet's emails and texts. He found conversations between her and Hermann, and her and Gaius. I didn't want to believe it, but it's all been under my nose this whole time."

Oh, Torsten. My chest swells. *I can't believe he did that for me.*

Vic continues. "Last year, my life had been laid out before me with crystal clarity. I would go to Harvard. I would study botany. I would set my sister up in our Cambridge house and do everything I could to get her fashion label up and running. And then, when the time was right, I would take over the family business from our mother. I had everything I ever wanted in life, and I was bored to tears with it. I didn't realize how much that plan felt like a trap to me until you came to town and shot it to shit."

Vic's voice cracks. His pain bleeds into my skin.

"I thought I needed these things to be happy. I thought I needed my twin. But you..." he shudders again. "So much in life is fragile, Fergie. We think we live in absolutes – love, loyalty, family. But all it takes is a lightning strike, and everything is burned up and broken."

"Vic, what are you saying?"

"I'm saying... that you are it for me, and there is nothing on this earth you can do that will stop me from loving you." Vic laughs bitterly. "You've proven that by killing my sister."

"I'm sor—"

"I know, you told me." He presses his lips to my forehead. "A piece of my heart is buried in that coffin with her, but I still love you with everything I have left. Can you love a man who only has a fractured heart to give?"

"A heart can heal," I say. "Can you love a woman whose kiss is poison?"

Vic's lips meet mine, and he sweeps me into his arms, the way I always imagined heroes do in romance movies. The wind picks up my black skirt and blows it around us, so the fabric is billowing as we kiss.

And oh, how he kisses.

Like the ocean churning beneath a storm.

Like lightning burning the world down.

How I've missed him.

Vic pulls back. His hands capture mine, and he knits his fingers in mine and places them over his heart. "I'll be loyal to you for the rest of my days."

I laugh. "I don't know how many days I have left. In case you didn't know, it's a dangerous world out there for an Imperator."

"I know. This cemetery is filled with them. My mother was even buried alive here once." He pulls me to him. "It's good that you have us at your side."

"What's going on, Sunflower?" Cas calls from up the hill. "Do I need to castrate him?"

Vic shudders. I wave to Cas. "We're good. Get down here."

"Okay. I've got Torsten with me, too."

A few moments later, they join us at the cliff edge. The three of them crowd around me. The wind whips up and my chest opens to the vastness of the world out there.

We're free. And this life can be whatever we make of it.

EPILOGUE

TORSTEN (TWO YEARS LATER)

"It's your last chance to back out," Cas says as he fiddles with his cufflinks.

"Why would I want to back out?" I raise my head to face him, confused by the question. My silk tie slips through my fingers and drops to the floor.

"Relax, friend. It was a joke."

"I don't think it's funny." I glare at him.

Cas laughs. "Of course you don't. It's okay, friend. We'll make a comedian of you yet."

"I don't want to be a comedian. I want to get my tie straight."

Cas laughs harder, and I try to ignore him. Cas has been a nightmare for Fergie throughout the whole suit-buying process. We had to get his custom-made by some fancy tailor because his shoulders have gotten too broad for standard measurements to contain. Then, he tore the first suit during a brawl at Tombs, and so we had to get a second one made.

I thought he might turn up today in his boxer shorts, which honestly, I'd prefer. It would take everyone's eyes off me.

I pick up my tie and frown at it. Thankfully, it's not creased. I hold it up and replay the YouTube video I've found on tying it. Up, down, around...

Vic walks in from the bathroom, running his fingers through his dark hair to get it to sit just the way he likes it.

"Torsten, your tie is all wrong." He points to the mirror. "Stand there. I'll do it."

I obey, and Vic fixes my tie. He stands back and looks me over. "You look perfect."

I bend over to check my socks, but Vic pulls me up, wrapping his arm around my shoulders. With his other arm, he makes a gesture at Cas, who comes skipping over and throws his arms around both of us.

Over the last couple of years, I've got a bit better at letting people touch me – people I trust, anyway. And the three of us are together in bed with Fergie so much that I've had to get used to their skin and scents and sounds. But today I'm so nervous that it's all starting to feel like a bit much. My hand starts flapping against Vic's shoulder.

What am I nervous about? Not the marriage. I know that Fergie is it for me. She's all I ever wanted. But doing the ceremony in front of everyone is not my idea of a fun night, and I have a surprise planned for Fergie because she loves surprises, but now I'm regretting making it a surprise because not knowing what she thinks of it is making my stomach churn.

Vic notices my hand and drops his embrace. "Sorry, bro, I was just thinking about the day we all became friends. We were five, and Livvie and Cali came around to our house for some kind of war council, and they left the three of us alone in the ballroom. Do you remember?"

"Do I ever?" Cas grins. "Torsten unlocked all the cat cages."

"I thought they looked sad," I say.

"You did think that! But then we had twenty feral cats zooming around the house," Cas hoots.

"I still don't think Eli's found them all," Vic laughs. "And then Cas found that old knife-throwing target, and we decided that we could spin Torsten on it and throw knives at him, like that cartoon on TV."

"That's right!" Cas slaps his knee. "And Gabriel came in just as we were tying him on and—"

"—gave us an absolute bollocking," Vic laughs. 'Bollocking' is a Gabriel word – it's British for 'yelling extremely loudly about how stupid we are.' "He screamed at us until all our mothers came running—"

"—and then Cali said, 'if Cassius wants to practice throwing knives, he shouldn't be aiming to miss,'" Cas says in a perfect imitation of his mother's stern voice. "She suggested we hand over the blades so she can throw them at us for being so naughty."

"And then Cassius said, 'the only person who gets to torture my new friend Torsten is me,'" I remember. "And everyone laughed."

I didn't really get the joke, but I remember how firm Cas sounded, and how Vic moved in front of me to block me from Cali. We were friends from that moment onward. Inseparable. Bonded.

We smile at each other. It's a good memory, one of my favorites.

"I can't imagine not having the two of you in my life." Vic grins. "You're my brothers."

"Brothers who fuck the same girl!" Cas pipes up. "That's my kind of family."

"Shut up, you sicko. I'm trying to have a moment here."

Cas glances at his watch. "Moment's over. We'd better get out there or our Queen will have our heads."

Vic and Cas link arms with me, and we walk down through the VIP area of Tombs, passing the tables where we've spent so many nights together. The club has become a favored hangout of the Triumvirate, especially since Cas had us shut down Colosseum. After his mother died in the arena, he couldn't bear to set foot in the place.

The Triumvirate still exists. After Fergie and Cas killed Juliet and Gaius, nearly all the soldiers who went over to the Gorgons came back and begged to be let in again. The Imperators agreed to an amnesty, and – with the exception of a few of Gaius' closest advisors who Cas took care of – no more blood was shed over the coup. Things went back to the way they were. Sort of.

Fergie and Cas have introduced a lot of changes to the Triumvirate. They brought on a committee of thirteen top soldiers to oversee the running of the organization and make sure that everyone's voice is heard. They started a recruitment drive, bringing the best and brightest from other crime families to Emerald Beach to find new ways to compete in the black market. And they've started the process of combining the assets of all three families into one.

Juliet was right about one thing – the Triumvirate is a failing idea. The families will never truly work together if they are separate. So instead, we're going to be one family, but it will take time to make that happen.

Today is the first step.

We descend the spiral staircase into the crowd. The venue is packed with soldiers from all across the Triumvirate's empire, as well as important guests from other crime families we have close ties to. I see Fergie's friends Euri and Dru at a table near the front, with bright-colored drinks clutched in their hands. They wave at us, and I wave back. Fergie's so happy that they could come. Dru works as Fergie's secretary, and she arranged this day to fit around Euri's college schedule.

I swallow hard as the crowd closes around us. Faces swirl by like funhouse mirrors as people congratulate us. They all talk at once. The crowd makes me nervous. I wanted to do this in private, just the four of us, but nothing's private when Imperator Fergie is involved.

Nothing... except what we got up to last night.

I glance up at Vic, and he must read the distress on my face, because he nudges Cassius. Cas cracks his knuckles and makes a face, and the crowd leaps back like they've been repelled by some invisible force. I'm grateful for my friend's monstrous nature, because all these faces, all these eyes staring at me...

What if I do something bad?

What if I say the wrong thing and embarrass Fergie?

I look at my two friends, but they don't seem nervous at all. Cas storms through the crowd like he's a Visigoth descending on Rome, and Vic stops and smiles at people and shakes hands. Thankfully, most people seem to know now that I don't like small talk or being touched, so they stay away.

Finally, we climb up onto the stage. I thought this would be better up here because I don't have to be close to the people. I don't have to smell their perfumes and listen to them scratching their asses.

But up here, the prickling feeling in my skin is a hundred times worse.

I'm the center of attention, and I'm so painfully aware that I'm not like the other two. I'm not part of the organization any longer. I'm not an assassin or a leader. I'm not normal. I don't fit. They all must be wondering what I'm doing here...

In the corner of the stage, Gabriel Fallen grins at the three of us. His band is set up behind him – two violin players, a cellist who's almost as big as Cas, and the cocky piano player. Vic gives Gabriel a signal and they begin a slow, joyful tune.

The music dips and swells and fills the room. Everyone falls silent, and heads turn to the back of the room.

There she is.

Fergie.

My Fergie.

Our Fergie.

The crowd parts, leaving the red carpet free for our Queen. She wears a crimson dress decorated with sparkling silver beads. Her arm is looped in John's, and her other hand moves her cane, which is decorated with matching ribbons and beads and bright crimson flowers.

Even though she can't see us waiting for her, she smiles up at us, and it feels as though that smile is only for me.

Everyone in the room ceases to exist. I can no longer feel the prickles in my skin or smell the hundreds of mingled body odors. I no longer feel *other*.

I *belong*.

My whole world is this beautiful woman walking toward me.

Fergie reaches the steps, and John helps her onto the stage. That's my cue. I walk over and loop her arm in mine.

John rests his hand on top of mine. He peers up at me and says, "You take good care of my daughter."

"We will."

"I'm not talking about those other two," he says. "Cas will get her into all kinds of trouble, and Victor will help her make the tough decisions. You are the glue that holds this marriage together, Torsten. My first wife – Fergie's mother – once said that in a relationship one person is an ocean, and the other person is the lighthouse."

"But a person can't be a lighthouse," I point out. "They wouldn't be able to stand still with a light on their head—"

He laughs. "It's not literal. It means that one person is this wild force of nature, a tempest that cannot be contained, and the other person is the beacon that brings them home again. From the day Cali Dio rang me up at midnight and offered me a ridiculous fee if I'd do some cosmetic dental work on one of her men who needed to disappear, and I fell in love with this fierce, impossible woman, I've always been her lighthouse. I recognize the same quality in you. You are the lighthouse for all three of them, Torsten. You help them find their way home. Don't ever forget that."

"I won't. I don't forget things."

I don't entirely know what he meant, but I'd ask Fergie later, and she will explain. Now, though, I look over at her, in her red dress, with her fiery hair spilling down her back in long waves, and that sunshine smile, and I feel like the first day I met her again, when she smiled at me and it felt like I had been chosen for something truly special.

I squeeze her hand. She slips her arm through mine and lets me lead her to the center of the stage, where Vic and Cas and Eli are waiting. The three of us surround her as best we can. I face away from the audience, although I can still feel their eyes on my back.

"I'm excited to welcome you all here today," Eli says as he opens the book in his hands. "Today is a special day for all of us, but most of all for the four people standing on this stage with me. Today is the day that Fergie Munroe will marry Torsten Lucian, Victor August, and Cassius Dio."

Fergie nods to each of us in turn. When her face turns to me, my whole world lights up. She squeezes my hand.

I squeeze back.

"Since four people cannot legally wed in this country, this ceremony isn't legally-recognized. But these four wanted to make their commitment to each other in front of the people who matter most to them – their family, their friends, and those they serve. You are here today to bear witness as the three families of the Triumvirate – August, Dio, and Lucian – officially become one. The Triumvirate is no more. The Empire is born."

The shouting and cheering of the crowd drown out Eli's next

words. But I don't care. I don't need to hear them. I look into Fergie's face and she's smiling, for me, for us.

For the Empire.

The Empire is the new organization that is replacing the Triumvirate. The Imperators no longer want to be three separate families trying to work together while also advancing their own agenda. Fergie, Cas, and Claudia still rule, but Cas says it's "all for one and one for all," and everyone laughs at him, but I like the sentiment.

Everyone looks out for each other, like a family.

The idea has been in the works for a long time, but the final pieces have only just come together. Our wedding's been put off three times because Fergie didn't like any of the suggested names for the new organization. But finally, she came up with Empire, and it's perfect. I drew a *sacer* for us that combines the symbols of all three families. And just like that, three became one.

Eli says a few more words, but I'm so distracted by Fergie to hear any of them. That is, until she turns to me and clasps my hands. My heart hammers against my chest.

"Torsten, we're saying our vows now."

"Okay," I say.

"I pick you." Fergie squeezes my hands tightly. "I pick you, Torsten, and I pick us, and I pick our family, now and for the rest of our days."

I repeat the vows with tears rolling down my face. I can't believe this is real. I can't believe I get to have this woman in my life, forever.

She picked me.

"Will you kiss me?" Fergie asks, wrapping her arms around my neck.

I forget the hundreds of pairs of eyes poking at my skin.

Fergie's here, in my arms, and she wants to be kissed. And I can't deny my Queen.

I lean down and brush my lips against hers, softly, the way she likes. She tilts her head back and lets her lips fall open a little, and I truly taste her – the tangy raspberry scent of her that tastes like home and happiness.

Fergie draws back, and the corners of her mouth turn up into a smile that's just for me. "Hey, you," she says.

"Hey, you."

I lean in to kiss her again. I can't get enough of her—

"You're hogging our wife," Cas snaps. Fergie glares at him.

"Husbands, don't fight. There's plenty of me to go around," Fergie pretends to wipe sweat from her perfect forehead. "I have a feeling that this marriage will keep me busy."

"I won't," I say. "Because I'm going on tour in a few days. Don't you remember? The exhibition is opening at the Met and—"

"Torsten."

"Yes?"

"Shut up." And she kisses me again.

Her kiss obliterates the world, and I'm swept out to sea in the ocean of her love, and I'm lost.

And I'm home.

Our wedding party rages all night. I surprise myself by how long I last. Euri drags me onto the dance floor and I end up staying there for most of the night. I don't get dancing, but as Euri and I shuffle awkwardly in the corner, we can talk.

And we have a lot to talk about. Euri's finished her journalism degree and she's agreed to come on tour with me to manage the show. It turns out that running seventeen different student clubs at Blackfriars has made Euri a bit of an expert at logistics, and that's the sort of stuff that gives me a headache. So she's put her journalism aspirations on hold to work for me. We've been organizing the world tour for eighteen months, and finally, it's nearly here.

My accessible art is going public.

We open at the Met in New York City next week. We've invited blindness organizations from all over the world to join us for the opening, and Fergie's put up money so that we can sponsor kids from poorer backgrounds to attend. We're putting them up in fancy hotels and treating them like royalty for the weekend. I know what it's like to feel like a place isn't meant for you, so we've done everything we can to make them feel like the guests of honor.

After Euri and I go through all the details one final time, and she gives me a quick hug and whispers to me that my wife would probably like to see me, I go to find Fergie at the bar. She and Cas are doing shots while a bunch of their assassin buddies cheer them on.

"Torsten, I'm glad you found us. I think we should go upstairs." Fergie slams down an empty glass.

"Why?"

"Because I want to rip my husband's clothes off and suck his dick until his eyes roll in the back of his head," she purrs.

I love when she's so specific.

Vic appears at my side. "Torsten, I saw you out on the dance floor with Euri. Good stuff. You *almost* held the beat. I got you a drink."

He offers up something pink and sugary.

"No drink," I say. "I'm going to take my wife upstairs and fuck her senseless."

"Not without me, you're not."

"I also vote for the fucking," Cas adds.

"If you insist, husbands," Fergie laughs as she slips her arm into mine, and I lead the way to our honeymoon suite.

EPILOGUE
FERGIE

I hold my dress with my other hand as Torsten leads me up the winding spiral staircase. I lost my cane somewhere around the bar when Cas and I were doing shots. My mind buzzes with just enough alcohol to make my blood run hot.

I'm *married*.

I'm married to the three hottest, most loyal, most amazing guys in the world.

The club music becomes muffled as we move through the VIP suite into the labyrinthine hallways and secret rooms, following a path familiar to me from the time we hid in Tombs during the short-lived reign of the Gorgons. Torsten finds his way to the room we all know well – the throne room where we've had so much fun over the years.

"Surprise." His voice chokes with excitement.

"Oooh, did you get your dick pierced like Victor?" I grab at his crotch and nearly fall over. Yup, I've definitely had enough to drink.

"No, but I will if you want me to." Torsten leads me over to the wall. "Here's the surprise."

I can't see anything different, obviously, but Torsten flicks on the lights and holds my wrist, moving my hand so that I can 'see' his surprise.

I gasp. The wall used to be covered in rows of hieroglyphics, backlit so that they stood out from the gloomy interior. Even I could make out some of the shapes and designs.

Now, though, when the lights flicker on, they reveal the shape of something different. My fingers sweep over layers of plaster and wood that create a raised, textured design. A human figure, familiar and yet completely unique...

"It's you," Torsten says.

It *is* me. I recognize the shape of my lips, the stream of flaming hair flowing behind me, and the sparkling dress I wear. I'm reclining on a throne with Spartacus curled in my lap and bands of light and texture around me that remind me a little of the swirling sky of *The Scream*. But while that painting was all about chaos and desolation, Torsten's lines here are powerful. Hopeful. Beautiful.

Tears prick in my eyes as I see myself as he sees me – a mythological creature of beauty and power and grace. I don't know if I live up to those things, but Torsten makes me want to try.

"Which artist is this inspired by?" I ask. "I don't recognize the style."

"It's inspired by you." His voice fills with awe. "Only you."

A jolt of realization shoots through my body. Torsten has created this work without drawing on his vast, photographic knowledge of art history. For the first time since I've known him, he's created a piece that reflects only him – his thoughts, his ideas, his creativity. And it's *amazing*.

I squeeze his hand. "Thank you," I whisper, the tears flowing freely down my cheeks now. "This is the most beautiful thing anyone has ever done for me."

"Sure, it's great," Cas drawls as he comes up behind me, slipping his hands around my waist and reaching up to squeeze my tits through my dress. "Top marks to Torsten Lucian. But is this as good as the shiny new crimson butt plug I got you as a wedding gift? I don't think so."

I turn around to glare at Cas, but Torsten just laughs. In all the time we've spent together, he's grown so much more comfortable with himself, and he knows that he's always free to express himself around us.

"I don't think your butt plug compares to this amazing work of art," I declare.

"That's not a fair comparison. You haven't felt it yet. My butt plug has knobbly bits. It too is a work of art."

Before I can protest further, Cas scoops me up and carries me across the room. I struggle and kick and yell, because I know it gets him excited. Hell, heat's racing through my veins now at the thought of what my three husbands have planned.

My husbands.

It doesn't feel real. And yet, at the same time, it feels as if my whole life has been a prelude to this night, this moment, this vow between the four of us. How did I go from the nerdy blind girl who accidentally slept with my stepbrother to being the Queen of a criminal empire and marrying three guys who adore me and worship me?

All I know is that they're mine, and I'm theirs, and nothing will change that. We've fought against incredible odds to get to this day, and no doubt there will be other challenges to my power, other threats to our happiness that will need to be dealt with. But I know that no matter what happens, we will triumph.

Illis quos amo deserviam. For those I love, I will sacrifice. Livvie's favorite motto and now the motto of the Empire, although Claudia still prefers her favorite Caesar quote, *Ālea iacta est* – let the die be cast.

Both feel apt.

But I'm not thinking about Latin anymore as Cas seats me on the throne. "My Queen." His knees hit the carpet in front of me. He kneels. He kisses the toes of my favorite spike-heeled boots.

My dress rustles and my pulse quickens as he bunches up the skirts. "Fuck, I can't find you under all this," he grumbles.

"Let us help." Vic comes over. He holds up the fabric for Cas so my stepbrother can slide his hands around my thighs. My whole body is alight now, aware of the two men who hold me, and the third who watches with such intensity that I can feel his eyes on my skin like a physical touch.

Cas nips at the sensitive skin on my thighs as he inches closer, closer to the source of the ache growing inside me. His hands slide up, shoving the tulle and chiffon aside so he can find my underwear.

Only, he can't find them. Because I'm not wearing any.

Cas cracks up laughing. "Look at this, boys," he says. "When you peel off her layers, our Queen is a filthy little minx."

I grin indulgently down at them as I open my thighs wide, giving them a view of my battered old boots and the three crimson garters I'm wearing around my thigh, and my shaved, bare pussy, already wet for them.

So many things have changed over the last few years, but these boots are forever.

Underneath, I'm still the same Fergie.

"Duchess..." Vic's voice catches. I smirk. I love knowing that after all this time, I can still render Victor August speechless.

Behind him, Torsten purrs in his throat. It's the sexiest sound I've ever heard.

"These boots are amazing, but they're not going to work for what we have planned." Cas grabs my ankle and rests it on his knee. He undoes the laces and slides my boots off – first one, then the other, slowly and carefully, ignoring my protests that he pay more attention to my demanding clit.

"Patience, Sunflower. We have all night," Cas chuckles.

"We have the rest of our lives," Vic adds. His finger goes under my chin, and he tilts my head up to claim my mouth with his. His kiss too is languid, unhurried.

I want to scream at them both, but then Cas thrusts his head back under my skirts. He's like Indiana Jones, because even in the labyrinth of my skirts he manages to find my clit. He sucks it into his mouth like it's his favorite Popsicle.

I gasp at the intensity of it. Cas lets his lips fall away, but then his tongue makes little wet circles that drive me absolutely wild. Vic's tongue draws out a moan from deep inside me as his hands wander downward and slip into my dress to fondle my breasts.

And all the while Torsten watches, his eyes a caress that's every bit as real and sensual as the others' touches.

I whimper as Cas' thick finger plunges inside me.

I'm dizzy, but not from the alcohol. I'm drunk on the three of them, high on their love, blazed by the heat that blooms between us whenever we're together.

I want this night for the rest of my life.

Cas adds a second finger, pumping in and out with that infuriatingly slow pace, laughing darkly as he feathers my clit with the lightest touch. He knows he's keeping me just on the edge. Bastard.

I'll show him.

I buck my hips, forcing his fingers deeper, rubbing his tongue against my clit. I reach up and circle Vic's wrist with my hand. "Make me come," I growl into Vic's mouth. "Or I'm kicking both of you out and spending the night with Torsten."

"That works for me," Torsten says from across the room, his voice tight with need.

"As our Queen wishes." Vic pinches my nipple hard, and Cas finally gives me what I want. His fingers slam into me while he sucks my clit deep into his mouth.

And that's it, I'm gone.

The euphoria begins in my toes and climbs through my whole body, a tidal wave sweeping through my veins and swelling beneath my skin until it's too big to be contained inside me. It explodes outward, and I lose myself inside it.

When I come back, I realize that somehow – and I don't exactly know how because with Cas between my legs I'm not really paying attention – I'm no longer sitting on my throne but on Vic's lap. And his cock digging into my ass is making it very clear how our wedding night will proceed.

"I'm ready for my wedding present now," I tell Cas.

He laughs cruelly. "Oh, don't worry. You'll get to meet your new butt plug soon. But the three of us actually have another present for you."

"You do?" I perk up.

"We took the liberty of having it installed for you," Vic says as he takes my hand and helps me to my feet. My legs are a little shaky from the orgasm, but I'm too excited about my present to let that hold me back.

Vic places leather straps in my hands. I feel around them, my fingers brushing steel D-rings and rigging. My heart races. *I know what this is...*

It's a sex swing, similar to the one they had in their library. The first time the four of us were together, it was in that swing, and it was amazing, but then Cas and Juliet shared the video and I...

...I have complicated feelings about that swing.

I stroke my fingers over the leather, remembering the way it held me, remembering the groan of the restraints as they applied their weight to it, and the way I was completely at their mercy as they took all three of my holes. Fuck. *Fuck.* What a fucking ride that was.

"What do you think, Sunflower?" Cas asks. "Are you ready to try this again?"

His voice catches. This is Cas' way of writing a new story for us. And even though I've told him again and again that I forgive him, that I've made my peace with what he did and why he did it, that the brain damage I gave him in the ring more than makes up for the emotional trauma of having that video online, forever, I don't think he's ever quite forgiven himself.

This gift is so much more than a fun toy. It's my unhinged, possessive stepbrother reaching across the barriers of his own monstrous nature to seek absolution.

And if he wants to worship at the altar of my pussy while doing it, who am I to stop him?

"Fuck yes." I hold up my hands. "Strap me in. I want to ride all three of you all night long."

EPILOGUE
FERGIE (TEN YEARS LATER)

"Momma, Momma, it's time."

Helen clomps into the throne room, where I'm getting ready. In recent years, I've renovated the space, transforming this room into a closet and dressing room, because it turns out being a crime lord means a lot of fancy cocktail parties, and I'm a sucker for a Rick Owens dress. The sex swing and the other toys are cleverly hidden behind secret panels. I'm not quite ready for my nine-year-old daughter to learn about her mother's kinky side.

Helen's at the age now where she's very particular about her clothing, just like her mother. We were in New York City recently at the Met opening gala for Torsten's latest show, and I took Helen shopping on Fifth Avenue. Faced with all the designer shops in the world and a Mafia Queen's black card, all Helen wanted was a pair of New Rock boots, just like mine.

I've never been prouder than that moment.

Plus, now I can hear her coming. It's good to know from which direction the tsunami will hit. My daughter tears through the world, destroying anything and everything in her path. She's an endless source of frustration and delight, because she has all the best qualities of me and her father.

Of *course* Cas' sperm would beat out the others to take out the prize. And after a traumatic twenty-two-hour labor I declared my womb off-limits to more interlopers, so Helen is our only kid. Vic and Torsten don't mind that they didn't get to contribute any genetic material. They see Helen as their daughter.

Vic's been trying to teach her to raise flowers, but she keeps tearing off the petals because she thinks they look better that way. She loves hanging out in Torsten's workshop, helping him build new displays for his accessible art exhibitions and cutting the large slabs of marble he's using for his series of stone sculptures. Torsten's making a name for himself in the art world, not just as the creator of accessible displays of famous paintings, but as an artist in his own right.

I worry about Helen every time she trots off after him to play with his circular saws and chisels, but Torsten is so patient and attentive, I know she'll be okay.

"How do I look?" I twirl for my daughter, letting the crimson dress fan out around my hips. It makes me think of a similar dress I wore ten years earlier on my wedding day, although that dress was much more low cut. I'm in my thirties now – I'm trying to tone it down.

"You look like a queen," Helen says with a delightful smile in her voice.

"That's exactly what I was going for." I open my arms and she falls into them, wrapping her hands around my waist and squeezing tight. I kiss the top of her head, breathing in the raspberry-scented shampoo Cas loves to use on her.

"Yoohoo, Duchess?" Vic pokes his head into the room. "They're ready for you. Helen, stop bugging your mother. And put that knife away. What have I told you about knives in the club?"

"Only concealed weapons are allowed," Helen says primly. "But it won't fit in my sock!"

"That's because it's a hunting knife. It's not going to fit into anyone's sock. I'll tell you what, if you're a good girl tonight, I'll buy you a special knife that's small enough to fit in your boot. How does that sound?"

"Or a hip holster?" Her voice perks up.

"Or a hip holster," Vic says with a laugh. "Cas should have never been allowed to breed."

Vic takes my arm and leads me through the winding passageways of Tombs. We've made the club into our headquarters – unlike Claudia and Cali, I prefer not to bring my work home with me – and I've remodeled the VIP section and secret rooms into a private apartment for us. We live here when we are in Emerald Beach, but we spend a lot of time in New York City and London for Torsten's work.

As I walk, my nerves swell, and I'm struck by a memory that hasn't visited me in many years – of a time when I was ushered down a similar tunnel to fight Cas in the arena. My monster still carries the scars from that fight – the brain damage that means he occasionally mixes up words and struggles with impulse control. My own scars are on the inside.

But our scars make us who we are. They make us stronger. They are signs that we fight for what we believe in. Our own personal *sacers*.

A roar courses through the assembled crowd as I descend the new staircase I've installed onto the stage. Harsh lights burn my eyes, and if I could see I'm certain in this moment I'd have gone blind.

A familiar hand touches mine. Claudia.

My fellow Imperator. She's been a constant in my life – my mentor, my challenger, my fellow Queen. We've dealt with some bullshit over the years, but we've always been able to come back to each other and find strength in our friendship. She wraps her arms around me and embraces me, and the crowd goes nuts.

"We're going to keep this short and sweet tonight," Claudia says into the mic. "Because I know you have a raucous party to get back to. It's not every day that Broken Muse plays an exclusive Empire event, so we want them back on stage as soon as possible."

The crowd stomps their feet and roars their approval.

"I have some good news, and some bad news, to share with you tonight. First, the bad. I, Claudia August, am stepping down as Imperator."

A collective gasp sounds through the room.

Claudia tsks. "Don't be sad. My time has come. I've done all I can do to take this organization as far as it can go. Now it's time for me to retire and enjoy my life with my husbands and our children and grandchildren. But you'll still see me around Emerald Beach – after all, the rebuilt archaeological museum needs someone ruthless at the helm."

Laughter ripples through the room. I beam. I'm so happy that she's still going to be around as the museum's director. Claudia August was never going to be able to rest on her laurels.

Cassius is next to step up to the microphone. "I too will be giving up my title of Imperator. I'm not retiring – I've simply had enough of the bureau—bureau—bullshit. I'm going back to what I enjoy – torturing and killing our enemies in imaginative ways."

That gets a huge whoop of applause from the crowd.

"But I'm pleased to announce that the Empire will continue to flourish," Cas says. "We've been working for years to bring the three families of this organization together. Well, finally, that process is complete. The Empire will be ruled by one woman, a woman who over the years has proven she has what it takes to be our Queen. Fergie Munroe."

Vic guides me forward as the applause washes over me. The spotlights shine hot on my face, and my heart soars. Claudia's hand touches mine, and before I know it, she embraces me again.

"You're going to be amazing," she says, and I can tell that she means it. "Cali and Livvie would be so proud of you."

Claudia places a crown on my head. It's a bit ridiculous, but what's a Queen of crime without a little pageantry? Torsten made the crown and set the small obol Claudia gave me once as the main jewel. I touch the crown, feeling the sharp spiky bits and the glittering jewels. The weight of it bends my neck forward.

A lot of responsibility sits on my shoulders now, but I've spent the last twelve years training for this.

I'm ready.

As the crowd explodes with mirth, I hold out my hands, and in moments, warm fingers slide into mine. Torsten. He's right there beside me. He may not be part of the Empire, but he's in this family.

He's joined a few moments later by Vic and Cas. My stepbrother wraps his huge arm around my waist and pulls me against him. "You're so fucking beautiful, my Queen. Now, let me take you back to our suite and fuck you senseless."

"Cas," Vic laughs. "Show a little restraint. We have a coronation party to attend."

"I am showing restraint. Have you seen this dress she's wearing? I've had to hold myself back from bending her over and slipping it in during Claudia's speech…"

As we descend the steps of the stage and are swallowed by the crowd, I feel all three of them around me – touching me, holding me, keeping me safe.

I don't know what the future holds. Everything in our world balances on the edge of a blade. What we've created here tonight could be torn away in a heartbeat. But as long as we hold on to love, and to family, we will be just fine.

Illis quos amo deserviam. For those I love, I will sacrifice.

That sacrifice is always worth it.

THE END

"I was baptized in bloodshed. To the bloodshed, I return."

Discover how the three women of the Triumvirate became who they are in the complete Stonehurst Prep dark contemporary reverse harem series. Start with book 1, *My Stolen Life*: http://books2read.com/mystolenlife

Turn the page for a sizzling excerpt.

Victor, Cas, and Torsten think they know everything that goes on in Emerald Beach, but do they? Find out when you sign up to Steffanie Holmes' newsletter and get a bonus scene from *Poison Ivy*, along with a collection of other bonus material from Steffanie's worlds.

Sign up here: https://www.steffanieholmes.com/newsletter

FROM THE AUTHOR

Whew! Hello.

I hope you enjoyed this thrilling end to Fergie's story!

It's been so much fun to return to Stonehurst Prep with a new leading lady. Fergie is one of my favourite heroines that I've ever written. She's bold and sassy and she acts before she thinks and she's not defined by what she can't see.

Too often in books, blindness is conflated with weakness. As a blind reader myself, I'm always desperate to see more women like me in books, having adventures and doing normal things and getting our happily ever afters. I wrote Fergie for a teenage Steff who desperately needed a heroine and to believe that life gets better.

But Fergie's also not superhuman. Everything she does – the echolocation, her martial arts skills – is a normal part of the lives of many blind people, including me. (I have a brown belt in Gojo Ryu karate and I've done a bit of Jiujitsu, but now I pole dance instead). She's fallible and way too headstrong and stubborn for her own good. In short, she's a person, with all the traits and foibles and hopes and dreams that we all experience. I wanted you to see her, because too often, women like her are never seen.

Also, my health & safety conscious husband wants to warn everyone that Methylene blue is toxic and getting it on your skin or in your eyes or mouth could make you seriously sick...or worse. Artie carefully gives Fergie only enough to dye Cassius blue without seriously hurting him, but this is NOT a trick to try at home.

Thanks as always to my husband James, and to Meg for the epically helpful editing job, and to Acacia and CJ for the stunning covers. To my crew of Badass Author friends – Bea, Danielle, Kim, Erin, Selena, Victoria, Angel, and Rachel, who have cheered me on while I've torn my hair out writing this doorstopper of a book.

And to you, the reader, for going on this journey with me, even though it's led to some dark places. If you're curious about Claudia, Cali, and Livvie and how they became who they are, then you *need* the complete Stonehurst Prep dark contemporary reverse harem series. Start with book 1, *My Stolen Life*: http://books2read.com/mystolenlife

If you want to keep up with my bookish news and get weekly stories about the real life true crimes and ghost stories that inspire my books, you can join my newsletter at https://www.stef fanieholmes.com/newsletter. When you join you'll get a free copy of *Cabinet of Curiosities*, a compendium of bonus and deleted scenes and stories. It includes a fun bonus scene from *Poison Ivy* where you'll learn a little more about the Triumvirate.

I'm so happy you enjoyed Fergie's story! I'd love it if you wanted to leave a review on Amazon or Goodreads. It will help other readers to find their next read.

Thank you, thank you! I love you heaps! Until next time.

Steff

ENJOY THIS EXCERPT FROM MY STOLEN LIFE
PROLOGUE: MACKENZIE

I roll over in bed and slam against a wall.

Huh? Odd.

My bed isn't pushed against a wall. I must've twisted around in my sleep and hit the headboard. I do thrash around a lot, especially when I have bad dreams, and tonights was particularly gruesome. My mind stretches into the silence, searching for the tendrils of my nightmare. *I'm lying in bed and some dark shadow comes and lifts me up, pinning my arms so they hurt. He drags me downstairs to my mother, slumped in her favorite chair. At first, I think she passed out drunk after a night at the club, but then I see the dark pool expanding around her feet, staining the designer rug.*

I see the knife handle sticking out of her neck.

I see her glassy eyes rolled toward the ceiling.

I see the window behind her head, and my own reflection in the glass, my face streaked with blood, my eyes dark voids of pain and hatred.

But it's okay now. It was just a dream. It's—

OW.

I hit the headboard again. I reach down to rub my elbow, and my hand grazes a solid wall of satin. On my other side.

What the hell?

I open my eyes into a darkness that is oppressive and complete, the kind of darkness I'd never see inside my princess bedroom with its flimsy purple curtains letting in the glittering skyline of the city. The kind of darkness that folds in on me, pressing me against the hard, un-bedlike surface I lie on.

Now the panic hits.

I throw out my arms, kick with my legs. I hit walls. Walls all around me, lined with satin, dense with an immense weight pressing from all sides. Walls so close I can't sit up or bend my knees. I scream, and my scream bounces back at me, hollow and weak.

I'm in a coffin. I'm in a motherfucking coffin, and I'm *still alive.*

I scream and scream and scream. The sound fills my head and stabs at my brain. I know all I'm doing is using up my precious oxygen, but I can't make myself stop. In that scream I lose myself, and every memory of who I am dissolves into a puddle of terror.

When I do stop, finally, I gasp and pant, and I taste blood and stale air on my tongue. A cold fear seeps into my bones. Am I dying? My throat crawls with invisible bugs. Is this what it feels like to die?

I hunt around in my pockets, but I'm wearing purple pajamas, and the only thing inside is a bookmark Daddy gave me. I can't see it of course, but I know it has a quote from Julius Caesar on it. *Alea iacta est. The die is cast.*

Like fuck it is.

I think of Daddy, of everything he taught me – memories too dark to be obliterated by fear. Bile rises in my throat. I swallow, choke it back. Daddy always told me our world is forged in blood. I might be only thirteen, but I know who he is, what he's capable of. I've heard the whispers. I've seen the way people hurry to appease him whenever he enters a room. I've had the lessons from Antony in what to do if I find myself alone with one of Daddy's enemies.

Of course, they never taught me what to do if one of those enemies *buries me alive.*

I can't give up.

I claw at the satin on the lid. It tears under my fingers, and I pull out puffs of stuffing to reach the wood beneath. I claw at the surface, digging splinters under my nails. Cramps arc along my arm from the awkward angle. I know it's hopeless; I know I'll never be able to scratch my way through the wood. Even if I can, I *feel* the weight of several feet of dirt above me. I'd be crushed in moments. But I have to try.

I'm my father's daughter, and this is not how I die.

I claw and scratch and tear. I lose track of how much time passes in the tiny space. My ears buzz. My skin weeps with cold sweat.

A noise reaches my ears. A faint shifting. A scuffle. A scrape and thud above my head. Muffled and far away.

Someone piling the dirt in my grave.

Or maybe...

...maybe someone digging it out again.

Fuck, fuck, please.

"Help." My throat is hoarse from screaming. I bang the lid with my fists, not even feeling the splinters piercing my skin. "Help me!"

THUD. Something hits the lid. The coffin groans. My veins burn with fear and hope and terror.

The wood cracks. The lid is flung away. Dirt rains down on me, but I don't care. I suck in lungfuls of fresh, crisp air. A circle of light blinds me. I fling my body up, up into the unknown. Warm arms catch me, hold me close.

"I found you, Claws." Only Antony calls me by that nickname. Of course, it would be my cousin who saves me. Antony drags me over the lip of the grave, *my* grave, and we fall into crackling leaves and damp grass.

I sob into his shoulder. Antony rolls me over, his fingers pressing all over my body, checking if I'm hurt. He rests my back against cold stone. "I have to take care of this," he says. I watch through tear-filled eyes as he pushes the dirt back into the hole – into what was supposed to be my grave – and brushes dead leaves on top. When he's done, it's impossible to tell the ground's been disturbed at all.

I tremble all over. I can't make myself stop shaking. Antony comes back to me and wraps me in his arms. He staggers to his feet, holding me like I'm weightless. He's only just turned eighteen, but already he's built like a tank.

I let out a terrified sob. Antony glances over his shoulder, and there's panic in his eyes. "You've got to be quiet, Claws," he whispers. "They might be nearby. I'm going to get you out of here."

I can't speak. My voice is gone, left in the coffin with my screams. Antony hoists me up and darts into the shadows. He runs with ease, ducking between rows of crumbling gravestones and beneath bent and gnarled trees. Dimly, I recognize this place – the old Emerald Beach cemetery, on the edge of Beaumont Hills overlooking the bay, where the original families of Emerald Beach buried their dead.

Where someone tried to bury me.

Antony bursts from the trees onto a narrow road. His car is parked in the shadows. He opens the passenger door and settles me inside before diving behind the wheel and gunning the engine.

We tear off down the road. Antony rips around the deadly corners like he's on a racetrack. Steep cliffs and crumbling old mansions pass by in a blur.

"My parents…" I gasp out. "Where are my parents?"

"I'm sorry, Claws. I didn't get to them in time. I only found you."

I wait for this to sink in, for the fact I'm now an orphan to hit me in a rush of grief. But I'm numb. My body won't stop shaking, and I left my brain and my heart buried in the silence of that coffin.

"Who?" I ask, and I fancy I catch a hint of my dad's cold savagery in my voice. "Who did this?"

"I don't know yet, but if I had to guess, it was Brutus. I warned your dad that he was making alliances and building up to a challenge. I think he's just made his move."

I try to digest this information. Brutus – who was once my father's trusted friend, who'd eaten dinner at our house and played Chutes and Ladders with me – killed my parents and buried me alive. But it bounces off the edge of my skull and doesn't stick. The life I had before, my old life, it's gone, and as I twist and grasp for memories, all I grab is stale coffin air.

"What now?" I ask.

Antony tosses his phone into my lap. "Look at the headlines."

I read the news app he's got open, but the words and images blur together. "This… this doesn't make any sense…"

"They think you're dead, Claws," Antony says. "That means you have to *stay* dead until we're strong enough to move against him. Until then, you have to be a ghost. But don't worry, I'll protect you. I've got a plan. We'll hide you where they'll never think to look."

Start reading:
http://books2read.com/mystolenlife

MORE FROM THE AUTHOR

From the author of *Poison Ivy* and *Shunned* comes this dark contemporary high school reverse harem romance.

Psst. I have a secret.

Are you ready?

I'm Mackenzie Malloy, and everyone thinks they know who
I am.

Five years ago, I disappeared.

No one has seen me or my family outside the walls of Malloy
Manor since.
But now I'm coming to reclaim my throne:
The Ice Queen of Stonehurst Prep is back.

Standing between me and my everything?
Three things can bring me down:
The sweet guy who wants answers from his former friend.
The rock god who wants to f*ck me.
The king who'll crush me before giving up his crown.

They think they can ruin me, wreck it all, but I won't let them.
I'm not the Mackenzie Eli used to know.
Hot boys and rock gods like Gabriel won't win me over.
And just like Noah, I'll kill to keep my crown.

I'm just a poor little rich girl with the stolen life.
I'm here to tear down three princes,
before they destroy me.

Read now:
http://books2read.com/mystolenlife

OTHER BOOKS BY STEFFANIE HOLMES

Stonehurst Prep

My Stolen Life

My Secret Heart

My Broken Crown

My Savage Kingdom

Stonehurst Prep: Elite

Poison Ivy

Poison Flower

Poison Kiss

Dark Academia

Pretty Girls Make Graves

Brutal Boys Cry Blood

Manderley Academy

Ghosted

Haunted

Spirited

Briarwood Witches

Earth and Embers

Fire and Fable

Water and Woe

Wind and Whispers

Spirit and Sorrow

Crookshollow Gothic Romance

Art of Cunning (Alex & Ryan)

Wolves of Crookshollow

Want to be informed when the next Steffanie Holmes paranormal romance story goes live? Sign up for the newsletter at www.steffanieholmes.com/ newsletter to get the scoop, and score a free collection of bonus scenes and stories to enjoy!

ABOUT THE AUTHOR

Steffanie Holmes is the *USA Today* bestselling author of the paranormal, gothic, dark, and fantastical. Her books feature clever, witty heroines, secret societies, creepy old mansions and alpha males who *always* get what they want.

Legally-blind since birth, Steffanie received the 2017 Attitude Award for Artistic Achievement. She was also a finalist for a 2018 Women of Influence award.

Steff is the creator of *Rage Against the Manuscript* – a resource of free content, books, and courses to help writers tell their story, find their readers, and build a badass writing career.

Steffanie lives in New Zealand with her husband, a horde of cantankerous cats, and their medieval sword collection.

Steffanie Holmes newsletter

Grab a free copy of *Cabinet of Curiosities* – a compendium of short stories and bonus scenes, including a bonus scene from *Poison Ivy* – when you sign up for updates with the Steffanie Holmes newsletter.

http://www.steffanieholmes.com/newsletter

Come hang with Steffanie
www.steffanieholmes.com
hello@steffanieholmes.com

Made in United States
Troutdale, OR
03/18/2024

18547064R00260